Steps to Salvation

Steps to Salvation

by

Shlomo Attia

ISBN: 978-0-578-13568-7

Library of Congress Control Number:
To be determined

Dedication

To my family—my late father Daniel, my mother Mazal, my sisters Yudit and Ariela, and my brother David. Thank you for your love and support. Thank you to Katie Kato for her constant trust, support and help in the accomplishment of this book. Thank you to Daria DiGiovanni for the technical support, creativity and patience in working with me. To good friends Alan Danver, Elango Ellapen, Eyal Grad, and Nisim Zabory, thank you for being there when I needed you and for your constant encouragement and belief in this project. And to 'The Council,' thank you for sending me back to finish my work once I finally figured it out.

Contents

Forward

It took me more than ten years to figure out the system and finally complete this book. Since 2010 *Steps to Salvation* has dominated my thoughts and provided the motivation behind everything I do, including my day job.

I am not a writer by profession. I'm an engineer who builds prototypes for small businesses. I also own and manage a commercial appliance installation and service company in South Florida. Born with a natural curiosity, a passion for learning and a desire to contribute to the betterment of the world, I've always been an avid student. Sometimes that involves taking classes and attending seminars; other times, watching documentaries. But no matter the method, whenever I discover something useful, uplifting and good my first impulse is to share it with others.

During my childhood, my insatiable thirst for knowledge and truth often landed me in trouble. I was raised in Tel Aviv, Israel in a traditional Jewish home, where my constant questions about the nature of God and challenges to my faith were not always well received. Infused with an entrepreneurial spirit and a drive to succeed, I was earning more money than my father by the time I was 13 years old. Only problem was, I was doing so by retooling and selling "hot" bikes in my neighborhood. Once caught, I was not only severely beaten by my mother in front of my friends, I was also sent to a judge who gave me a choice of punishments: attend a religious school or go to a kibbutz.

At first I selected the religious school. But since the Rabbis didn't appreciate my relentless questions about God and the traditional Jewish religion, they threw me out after four days. That's when the very best thing that could have ever happened to me took place: I went to live on a kibbutz.

This kibbutz literally saved my life by giving me the opportunity to channel my restless energy into productive endeavors like learning how to become an electrician and a mechanic. The discipline and skills I developed set me up for success. I was further influenced by my service in the Israeli Defense Forces, which I joined in 1981 at the age of eighteen. Among other duties as a volunteer paratrooper, I served in Beirut in 1982.

Following my honorable discharge, I spent time in Germany and France before relocating to the United States in 1990 and setting up my Hollywood, Florida-based business. In spite of my success, I'd always felt I'd been called to a higher purpose, though I didn't quite know what it was until August of 2003. That's when a horrific motorcycle accident nearly ended my life.

Upon arrival at Memorial Hospital, I was pronounced clinically dead—a diagnosis that the medical team would proclaim a second time after I spent 4 ½ weeks in a coma. I was on my way to the morgue with the nurses removing me from all life support. But before they took off the last EKG probe, they saw a pulse and immediately hooked me up again, realizing I was still (barely) alive. It was during this period that my soul traveled to the other side.

Thanks to a caring, interested nurse my memories of this experience were well-preserved. After I finally woke up, she asked me questions like 'What did you see?' and 'Who did you talk to?'

As I answered her in detail, it occurred to me just how important it was to remember and retain as much of this information as humanly possible. While in heaven, I'd been told by three angels I call 'The Council' that I still had work to do on earth. They highly recommended that I go back even though I really wanted to stay. With my God-given free will the choice was mine to make and I ultimately returned to my body with the promise I'd be 95 percent "normal." They did not give me details about the work they wanted me to finish, but I firmly believe this book is an essential part of it.

Ironically it wasn't until 2009 that I realized what was going on between this world and the other world, and I felt an urgent need to let people know about it. That's when I knew for sure that this book was a big part of the work The Council asked me to complete when I was in heaven.

The flip side of my quest for knowledge is an equally powerful drive to fight ignorance. Our lives on earth are miserable as a direct result of unawareness but this can be remedied in many ways. There is another dimension to life and I was fortunate enough to experience it after a seemingly tragic event. But suffering through the pain of that brutal accident enabled me to visit heaven, where my beliefs were validated.

Our life, in essence, is spiritual. Everything that exists in the material world—whether a chair, a computer or a smartphone—first existed in the non-material world. I've also come to understand a truth that will most likely shock the traditionally religious faithful who hold the concept of hell as a fiery punishment reserved for bad souls after the death of the body: this earthly existence *is* hell. We're not potentially on our way to hell as a result of the evil actions we commit, we're *already* in it. That's the bad news.

The good news is that God has equipped us with the ability to transform this imperfect, physical life into something much closer to heaven. No, it will never attain heavenly perfection because while our souls inhabit human bodies, we will all have human failings. But by overcoming ignorance and employing common sense we can solve a multitude of earthly problems. We no longer have to be slaves to our need for food, money, medicine, energy and education. As it stands right now, we're wasting a tremendous amount of resources on these basic survival necessities—the very things that should be inexpensive.

What ought to be expensive are the ideas conceived by and brought into material existence by entrepreneurs, artists and producers. Of course we will always have challenges on earth; it's the way God, as our software writer, set it up. We are programmed to learn, contribute, move to the next level in our soul development, return to heaven, and then come back again in a new body under different circumstances. So there really is no such thing as death.

Our eternal souls come to earth in human form over and over again to raise our moral consciousness—which is the only thing we take back with us. It's also for this purpose that God allows about ten percent of the earthly population to be messed up that the rest of us might learn to confront evil and use logic in resolving our problems.

One of the major obstacles to living an abundant, peaceful and joyful life is a lack of money. Money, after all, is freedom. When human beings have money in their pockets, they can relax knowing they have the ability to care for themselves and their families. With an abundant flow of money life becomes easier for everyone: crime is reduced, the divorce rate goes down and society begins to stabilize. *Steps to Salvation* offers a blueprint for giving individuals more freedom and control over their own lives enabling them to be self-reliant, productive and happy.

But first we must learn from history which is why Step One, the first section of the book, identifies many of the world's evildoers and expounds upon their crimes against humanity. It takes place in 2412 in a history class at the Race Unity Regional High School, taught by a wise teacher named Mr. Bauer. Just like the students in Mr. Bauer's history class, we must fully absorb and comprehend the lessons of history if we're to put an end to the vicious cycle of war, poverty and enslavement to central authorities.

I've also discovered that a true hero is a person who knows how to control himself. That's why the students at the Race Unity Regional High School are also required to pass a morality test prior to graduation. We as individuals must hold ourselves to a higher standard even as we inevitably fall short as a result of our flawed humanity. Life is an eternal opportunity to learn, grow, fail, endure and overcome.

It's my fervent hope that by reading and understanding *Steps to Salvation*, all people will be motivated to incorporate its practical ideas and principles worldwide so that together we can finally bring Salvation to earth.

God bless you,
Shlomo Attia

∞ Step One ∞

The End Days

Arusha Tanzania, Africa – 2412 A.D.

The glorious sun rose high above Mount Meru, casting a golden glow upon the Great Rift Valley which was slowly awakening to another magnificent morning. Nestled on the valley's eastern edge, surrounded by some of Africa's most renowned landscapes and national parks, the distinguished city of Arusha stood as a remarkable testament to human progress and ingenuity.

A bustling international hub that was home to a million residents the proud, multicultural metropolis had once played host to a myriad of important national and international events, including the annual Mount Maru Marathon and the International Crime Tribunal for Rwanda back in the 1990's and into the early years of the new millennium. And as Arusha continued to attract more high-profile visitors and gatherings, the world began to regard this jewel of a city as the essential capital of the East African community—to the delight of the merchants of The Central Business Area, the large vegetable and flower producers in the surrounding region, and the local miners who produced a gem-quality mineral known as tanzanite, exclusively found in the Arusha region.

A few miles from the flourishing downtown area, sequestered among the verdant hills and lush foliage of East Africa stood the neighborhood of the Race Unity Region, a walled city within the city that was home to 575,000 people. Though barred from interaction with the city dwellers of Arusha by 10,000 square miles of concrete wall 25 feet high and one-and-one-half feet thick, residents of the Race Unity Region enjoyed the same modern-day conveniences and participated in the same daily rituals as the world beyond their imposing gates.

Together, Arusha City and the Arusha Race Region comprised the new homeland for 500 family lineages immediately following the War of Armageddon. Out of these 500 families, 100 voluntarily moved to this magnificent landscape, eager to embark upon a new and improved way of life they had not yet experienced in the earthly realm. The remaining 400 however, had been physically forced to relocate to the region after the Armageddon Commission had pronounced them guilty of the most egregious crimes against humanity.

Boasting a "royal" pedigree birthed in the centuries prior to the war, these families had reveled in the unparalleled privileges of an elitist existence—whether direct descendants of European royalty, international bankers, political dynasties or religious hierarchies. As such, their resistance to moving to the Race Unity Region for the purpose of ushering in Salvation Time on earth was quite formidable. Refusing to accept the terms set forth by the Commission and make the peaceful transition to Arusha willingly, 400 of these previously privileged families had put up such fierce resistance that it was only by the barrel of a gun and the serious threat of bodily harm that they found the motivation to cooperate.

All of this was quite expected and understandable given the excessive power, wealth and status to which they'd grown accustomed over hundreds and hundreds of years. During the End Days, these dynasties had established themselves as the enemies of spiritual growth, individual achievement, financial opportunity and societal advancement. They forcefully opposed the idea of human progress, preferring instead a system in which all power, prestige and wealth was concentrated into the hands of a select few—an exclusive club of credentialed families with names like Rothschild, Rockefeller, Biddle and Bilderberg.

These families were so threatened by the concept of a world where individuals had the freedom to control their own destinies, develop their God-given talents and skills, design and create the lifestyle of their choosing, and ultimately thrive professionally, personally and spiritually that they actually sponsored and financed military armies worldwide for the sole purpose of promoting war and chaos. They also controlled every aspect of a human being's life by monopolizing vital industries and professions including food, medicine, energy, education, banking, media, industrial and weapons production, real estate, politics and the justice system.

Why?

Because they operated out of pure self-centeredness driven by ego, these elites satisfied their unquenchable thirst for power and riches at the expense of everyday people. By controlling others in order to indulge their own selfishness they perpetuated *hell on earth* for the common man while they delighted in the material extravagance characterized by their opulent mansions, jet-set lifestyles, designer wardrobes, exquisite and rare jewelry and art collections, status-symbol cars and essentially all of the hedonistic trappings that define a life of limitless wealth, power and prestige.

That was then. This was now.

On this dawning Sunday morning in Arusha the chimes of the Central Business Area's Clock Tower rang out, igniting a flurry of activity as shop-owners prepared to open their doors—quite possibly for another record-breaking week of business, thanks to the influx of prosperity and commerce ushered in by Salvation Days.

Of course, business wasn't the only activity taking place on this brand-new day. In the Race Unity Region, one of the most revered rituals was education. Therefore, when the clanging of bells alerted the students of the Race Unity Regional High School to move into their first period classrooms to begin another day of intensive learning, they eagerly obeyed.

Characterized by thoughtful question and answer sessions in which students discovered how to draw conclusions based on solid reasoning, classes at the Race Unity Regional High School were designed to stimulate every youth's intellectual, spiritual and emotional maturity, in addition to facilitating the development of each one's unique talents and skills.

The fast-paced footsteps and exuberant voices of teenagers resonated throughout the hallways as they hurried to their respective classes eager to learn yet distracted by the relentless buzz on the internet, throughout the streets, and within the private homes of the Race Unity Region over one special graduating class' forthcoming trip, signifying the end of the 400 year-old punishment known as the Race Unity Experiment.

During this long period, students and their families who'd relocated to the Race Unity Region had been separated from extended family members—who'd remained in parts of the world far-removed from their neighborhood, with the only means of communication being computers with internet access and web cams.

Through the power of advanced technology, relatives within and without the Race Unity Region could at least see and talk to each other on a computer screen, a commonplace activity that had become the norm in the days following the end of Armageddon and the beginning of Salvation Time. So it was hardly any wonder that on this glorious dawn, a mere six days away from the Race Unity Regional High School Class of 2412's much-anticipated trip around the globe, these young people would be especially hyperactive.

Even among the typically well-behaved 16- to- 18 year-old participants in Mr. Helmut Bauer's first period history class a noticeable restlessness punctured the atmosphere as distracted students awaited the arrival of their teacher. Dressed in their crisp school uniforms—the boys' featuring powder blue, short-sleeved buttoned-down shirts embroidered with the symbol of The One God Religion and khaki pants; the girls' short-sleeved powder blue blouses embroidered with the symbol of The One God Religion and demure, knee-length khaki skirts—they talked excitedly about the end of the Race Unity Experiment and their forthcoming travels, even as they played with various electronic gadgets and leaned over each other's desks to test their readiness for a very important exam they were about to take.

In between quizzing each other about the exam material, the students excitedly spoke of their impending reunions with faraway family and explorations of historical and intriguing places like the Temple Mount of The One God Religion in Jerusalem, the Dachau Concentration Camp in Germany, the Eiffel Tower in France and the Freedom Tower in New York in the United States. The entire classroom reverberated with the sounds of youthful energy, excitement and anxiety on this monumental day.

A few feet away Mr. Bauer walked down the hallway in the direction of his classroom, eager to begin the day's curriculum. A tall, dignified man of 90, he commanded the respect of parents and colleagues alike for his ability to instill cognitive thinking skills and awaken the natural curiosity that existed within the minds of his adolescent charges. Revered for his wisdom and knowledge of history, Mr. Bauer had been a distinguished faculty member at the Race Unity Regional High School his entire career, focused on the subject of history with an emphasis on the *Steps to Salvation*. Although he clearly loved his work he also looked forward to retiring once he reached his 120th birthday.

Today he looked forward to administering the crucial test that would determine his students' knowledge of Salvation Time, which Mr. Bauer had methodically imparted through an interactive approach that combined lecture and reading with question and answer sessions designed to stimulate critical analysis. Because he'd devoted so many hours educating his students on this vital topic he was looking for detailed answers from each one of them. Learning and understanding the significance of historical events and people was not simply a superficial matter of memorizing dates and events; it was something to be fully grasped in the context of the past, present, and future. On a personal level, every student had to demonstrate their knowledge of their ancestry—no matter how painful and shameful—and why the actions of their family members during the End Days necessitated punishment by the Armageddon Commission in the form of a forced relocation to Arusha.

In short, today's test would summarize everything they'd learned about the *Steps to Salvation*, a remarkable story of human achievement made all the more exciting due to the culmination of the final phase soon to take place with the end of the 400-year segregation between the Race Unity Region and the rest of the world. Upon entering the noisy classroom Mr. Bauer loudly cleared his throat, prompting his students to immediately stop what they were doing, stand at attention and welcome their teacher with a respectful, "Good morning, Mr. Bauer."

A slow smile formed on his face. He was pleased with their dignified response to his presence.

"Good morning, students. I trust you all had a pleasant weekend. Please take your seats so we can get started on this last, critically important exam on the *Steps to Salvation*. I wish each and every one of you the best of luck," he announced in a deep, baritone voice that perfectly complemented his radiant, dark skin.

In the very next moment he sensed an electrically charged current coursing through the room as before his very eyes, his students abruptly transitioned from alert and respectful to flushed and tense. Immediately recognizing the cause of their sudden discomfort, Mr. Bauer picked up the remote on his desk, pointed it at the thermostat on the wall beside the classroom door and adjusted the air conditioning. The students breathed a collective sigh of relief; Mr. Bauer not only demanded respect, he offered it in return. It was hard to think of a more engaged, caring educator even in a school populated by numerous excellent faculty members.

But just as the teacher scrolled down to the list of questions on his handheld computer screen a familiar face in the crowd raised his hand from his front-row desk by the door. Removing his reading glasses he turned his gaze to the teenaged boy with the penetrating brown eyes, dark black skin, and short kinky hair.

"Yes, Mr. Hitler?" The teacher's tone was laced with a hint of exasperation, anticipating what was coming next.

"Can I go to the bathroom?" the boy inquired almost apologetically though this little exchange had long been a daily ritual in Mr. Bauer's class. And after the traumatic events of the previous night—coupled with his nerves over today's test—Hitler was experiencing more difficulty than usual with his bladder.

"You may sir, but make it prompt. We have the all-important verbal exam and much to cover today."

The rest of the students stifled their giggles as their classmate Adolf rushed out of the room, presumably in the nick of time.

"Alright, that's enough," Mr. Bauer admonished. "We have a busy agenda this morning, so let's get to work."

The teacher well understood the deep shame and self-consciousness many of his students who bore the full name of their evil ancestors harbored. He fully agreed with the Armageddon Commission rules that each family whose history included a maniacal dictator or ruthless international banker or suicide-bombing religious zealot or any number of evildoers who created "hell on earth" had to bestow the name of that person on at least *one* of their children. Yet he also sympathized with these families and their offspring. Although the goal was to restore the name to goodness, it still posed a difficult challenge to his students who felt nothing but remorse and embarrassment for the atrocities committed by their ancestors.

This was one reason why Mr. Bauer demonstrated so much compassion and patience toward Adolf Hitler and many others in the class. Of course, poor Hitler also had the additional, humiliating problem of incontinence in spite of his young age. Mr. Bauer had engaged in several previous conferences with Hitler's concerned parents and the school nurse—who'd summoned them all to her office to discuss the matter, concerned for the boy's emotional and physical welfare. Consequently, the history teacher had promised to accommodate Hitler's need for frequent restroom breaks.

And with so much riding on the outcome of this exam including losing the privilege of going on the trip should they fail to pass it with an adequate grade, Mr. Bauer was feeling especially generous. No doubt Hitler's urgent need to pee this morning had been instigated by a bad case of nerves. Coming from a place of shame for the many sins of his ancestor Adolf, Hitler felt a relentless drive to make his parents proud by always doing his very best in class. For all of the students, knowing that their spoken answers to Bauer's exam questions would be videotaped and their grades electronically transmitted via email to their parents was a source of anxiety. But for Hitler and some others in the class these stakes were dramatically higher, given their especially egregious ancestry.

Furthermore, at his advanced age Mr. Bauer's own bladder responded to excitement much in the same way young Hitler's did. Since he was a teacher he didn't share the same luxury of having permission to relieve his natural urges by running off to the bathroom whenever nature called. For a brief moment the history teacher actually felt a twinge of envy for the boy as he sought to distract himself from his own incontinence problem. He quickly found one.

Noticing that the white plantation shutters had not been sufficiently opened, he picked up another remote control on his desk and pressed a button. In response, the window flaps closed before sliding along the grooves to the left and right of the massive picture window, allowing a flood of brilliant sunshine to illuminate the room while the palm fronds outside swayed gracefully in the gentle breeze. Turning back to the class he directed his students to shut off all electronic devices, pausing long enough to ensure his directive had been followed. Then he strode back to his desk, picked up his palm computer again from its electronic platform and pulled up the exam questions.

"Alright," he asked, having decided to begin the dialogue with an open-ended query, "which one of you can tell me how we arrived at Salvation Time? What was the specific event that started the process?"

His deep, intense eyes scanned the room as young, inquisitive faces pondered the issue. Mr. Bauer never tired of teaching this lesson, notwithstanding his many years in education. To him, each student was a unique canvas, a beautiful mind-being that simply needed the knowledge of the past in order to thrive in the present and contribute to the future.

Moreover, the continued success of Salvation Days hinged upon the youth fully grasping and learning from history to avoid repeating its mistakes as had been the case over and over again in the centuries leading up to the End Days. Refusing to learn from the past had eventually culminated in the bloody, brutal but necessary Armageddon War which had ushered in the period of peace and prosperity everyone was now enjoying.

Reflective of the residents of the Race Unity Region, Mr. Bauer's students were diverse in a multitude of ways—from their physical looks to their emotional maturity, from their personality traits to their individual spiritual development.

Yet they shared one obvious characteristic: dark, black complexions combined with Caucasian features. The 400 years spent in Arusha after migrating there from places like Europe, the Middle East and the United States had resulted in a gradual change in skin pigmentation over the generations. But in spite of the equator's dramatic effect on skin tone, not nearly enough time had passed in Arusha to transform their Caucasian bone structure and other features into those typically seen in the African culture prior to Salvation Time.

Now as Mr. Bauer stared at the sea of dark faces, he took pride in their shared curiosity and attentiveness. After a moment an impulsive boy with raven-colored curly hair, penetrating black eyes and an impressive intellect that far surpassed most of his peers raised his hand.

"We got to Salvation Time because of our multiple incarnations, designed to help our souls reach new levels of development?" he inquired.

"You are definitely on the right track, Mr. Goebbels," the teacher affirmed. "Individual soul advancement through physical reincarnation is an essential part of the Steps to Salvation. But before we discuss the role of individual soul advancement, we must look at things from a broader perspective. Does anyone know the significance of the year 2012 in world history?"

When no one responded, the teacher pointed his finger at the student sitting to his left in the third row, then inquired, "Mr. Chamberlain, can you tell us the exact event that spurred the creation of what we now know as Salvation Time?" Mr. Bauer gestured for the boy to stand at attention by lifting his hand in the air.

Rising nervously from his chair, George Chamberlain stood up straight with his hands at his sides. "The explosion at the Willis Tower in 2012, at the G20 meeting," the boy answered somewhat tentatively.

"You are correct, Mr. Chamberlain," the teacher affirmed. "Now can you tell me in very descriptive detail what this G20 meeting was all about?"

Before he could answer, the classroom door swung open, heralding the return of their incontinent classmate.

"Ah Mr. Hitler, so glad you're back," Mr. Bauer noted with a grin, much to the delight of the boy's fellow students who let out a collective, muted laugh. The teacher cleared his throat, signaling the end of the brief levity, and continued.

Chamberlain took a deep breath to regain his composure before replying. "France started the annual G20 Summit in the year 1975. Back then they called it the G6 because it only had six world governments. By the year 2012, it had 20 member countries."

"Indeed, Mr. Chamberlain. Now can you tell us the purpose of this G20 Summit?"

"Yes sir, the G20 was a meeting of the head of the financial ministers and bank heads of countries with the highest Gross Domestic Product. These countries controlled 80- to - 90 percent of the money transactions all over the world. They told everyone they were meeting because they wanted to help the world economy and help all people get the healthcare and energy they needed to live comfortable lives. But all they really did was talk to each other over breakfast, lunch and dinner; stay in fancy hotels; eat in expensive restaurants; and make private deals with each other for more money and power."

"I see you've been paying attention Mr. Chamberlain," Mr. Bauer noted with a satisfied smile. "Tell me, how many people died in the explosion—and what about that outwardly tragic and gruesome event was actually *good*?"

"Well sir, 680 people were hurt and 330 people were killed, including eight official representatives. Out of the representatives that got hurt, 12 ended up in a coma. The good thing that came out of it was that the 12 representatives from different countries who 'died' at first from their injuries came out of their eight-week comas after their doctors had given up hope. Once they came back to life they had a whole new way of thinking, thanks to their time on *The Other Side*. These leaders brought the world into Salvation Days. Up 'til then orthodox Jews, conservative Christians, devout Muslims and ancient Mayans had called it the End Days."

"Excellent, Mr. Chamberlain! Now, for your bonus question, did anyone in your family participate in these events either for or against Salvation Days?"

The boy paused for a moment, remembering the importance of the exam. Reluctantly, he answered Mr. Bauer's question.

"Yes sir, my grandfather eight generations ago was the head of the security council to the English monarch. Along with the Royal Family he sponsored the armies of the End Days to fight against the armies of the Salvation Days."

"Thank you, Mr. Chamberlain."

With that, Mr. Bauer looked at his computer to determine its grade suggestion for George's answers. Since the student's responses were nearly identical to the textbook, the computer suggested a '9' out of a possible '10', with which Mr. Bauer agreed. He made the notation in the screen next to George Chamberlain's name. Then he advised the student to retake his seat. George breathed a sigh of relief as he sat down, thankful it was over.

The history teacher scanned his handheld computer for the next question as he made his way to the other side of the classroom where a kinky-haired young girl wearing a necklace comprised of large, white beads struggled to hide her restlessness. Her dark skin displayed a visible trace of moisture brought on by agitated nerves.

"Ah, Miss Braun!" Mr. Bauer exclaimed, causing the poor girl's heart to lurch in her chest. She leapt to her feet with her hands at her sides, trying hard to conceal her nervousness.

"Yes, sir," she meekly replied.

"Tell me, who was responsible for this horrible explosion at the G20 Summit in the year 2012? What was their ideology and background?"

"Well," she began with an audible tremor in her voice, "the people who caused the explosion were the Jihad al Islam, the Islamic Peace Army, the Army of Allah and the Sweden World Socialist Organization. The first three groups believed that the whole world should be under Muslim control and ruled by Sharia Law. To them, no matter how evil the act, if it helped move the world closer to a Muslim Caliphate it was good.

"During the End Days Muslims believed they'd be rewarded in the earthly life and in the afterlife. That's because of the Arab League of Nations and Saudi Arabia. They offered cash rewards of 10,000 American dollars for every dead Infidel and 15,000 American dollars for every dead *important* Infidel.

"And what about the Sweden World Socialist Organization?"

"Sir, the Sweden World Socialist Organization was motivated by the poverty and manipulation the World Bank deliberately created—even though all members of this group came from the richest families in Sweden or the Swedish Royal Family itself," she responded somewhat haltingly.

Eva inhaled deeply and braced herself for Mr. Bauer's reaction. During her response she tried as hard as she could to match her oral answer to the one the class had studied in the workbook. She found herself regretting all the drinking she'd done at a party the previous night, still reeling from the dizzying effects of the alcohol.

It felt like hours had passed as she stood there waiting for Mr. Bauer's reaction. Adding to her anxiety was the fact that he was also her Telepathic Communications teacher and thus very much attuned to her hidden language and inner thoughts. Already this year, he'd spoken with her parents several times about her obvious love of alcohol and partying.

Wordlessly Mr. Bauer continued to gaze at Eva, suspecting she'd either consumed too much alcohol or ingested too many drugs the night before. He knew she would not have been able to resist in spite of his numerous warnings to study hard in preparation for their pivotal Sunday exam. After what felt like an eternity to the student he finally responded.

"You are correct, Miss Braun." Then, glancing back at his handheld computer before returning his attention back to her, he advised, "This is your bonus question. You do not have to answer if you don't want to, ok?"

Summoning her famous look of *innocence*, the young girl assertively declared, "It's fine by me. I have nothing to hide since everyone in this room already knows what happened. Go ahead and ask me; I am not afraid. I don't want to flunk this exam—I'd do *anything* to pass it!"

Impressed by her resolve Mr. Bauer resumed, "Does your family have any historical connection in either resisting or supporting the movement to Salvation Days?"

Eva looked at him for a moment before quickly turning her head in the direction of Adolf Hitler, who sat at his assigned seat at the head of the class, his dark eyes cast downward.

"My family volunteered to come to the Race Region because after the Armageddon War they were broke. Next to being poor, the guilt of being connected with the Hitler family was too much to bear."

"Thank you, Miss Braun," the teacher replied. As she stood there nervously, she began shifting her weight from one foot to the other, while her right hand fidgeted with the big beads around her neck. Intently, she watched while Mr. Bauer scrolled through his handheld computer screen, waiting for it to calculate a suggested grade for her responses.

"Alright Miss Braun," he finally noted. "You have earned an '8' on the exam, even though your answers were 100 percent correct. Do you understand why you haven't been given a '10'?"

Thoroughly relieved to have passed with an acceptable grade Eva relaxed a little, releasing her hold on her necklace and distributing her weight evenly in an effort to stand perfectly still. She had a feeling she already knew the answer to the teacher's question, which she hoped would turn out to be rhetorical in order to spare her any embarrassment in front of her classmates. Alas, it was not to be.

"Miss Braun?"

"Because I partied too hard last night instead of studying and getting a good night's rest as you told us?" she softly responded, eyes fixed on Mr. Bauer.

"Yes, that is correct Miss Braun. As you know, learning to develop a strong moral character and demonstrate personal responsibility is not only a mandatory part of this institution's curriculum, it's required to graduate. You could be a straight-10 student and yet if you fail to pass our basic morality standards, your grade point average could be severely affected. Instead of graduating with all 10s you'd run the risk of graduating with a lowly 6.5, which could pose a problem for your future. Here in Salvation Time, the truest mark of wealth is not in money or prestige, but in reputation.

Future employers might not be very interested in hiring a graduate whose entire grade point average was diminished by over four points because they failed morality."

Here he paused for effect as his eyes scanned the room. Every student looked back at him with a mixture of fear and acknowledgment. They knew very well from their own siblings and friends who'd gone before them that Mr. Bauer's words rang true. Eva began playing with the white beads around her neck again as moisture glistened on her dark skin. She was really beginning to regret her few hours of pleasure the previous night which not only involved alcohol but also behavior unbecoming a young lady—at least a young lady with respect for herself and her body. She prayed Mr. Bauer would have the decency not to bring it up in front of the class, if in fact he was able to discern telepathically that she had also "gone all the way" *again* with a guy at the party. And not just *any* guy but one sitting in the same history class right now, prodded on by sweet, if meaningless words, and an alcoholic buzz.

Of course big, burly class bully Joseph Stalin had a reputation for being a ladies' man. As he witnessed the exchange with smug interest, his mind along with Eva's, wandered back to his conquest the night before. When plied with wine she was no match for any boy's hormonally-charged advances. Stalin smirked in his seat remembering how easy it had been to lure her upstairs to an unoccupied bedroom where he smothered her with kisses before locking the door, peeling off her dress, discarding his own clothes, lying her on the bed, and having his way with her.

Within minutes though, it was over. That's when Eva had suddenly realized how much she stood to lose for giving in to temptation. *What was she thinking? How mortified would she have been if anyone had caught them?*

But just when she thought she couldn't possibly feel any worse there was an urgent knock on the door. She'd frantically scrambled to throw on her clothes before the knocking resumed with more intensity and a faster cadence, this time accompanied by the voice of one of their classmates.

"Eva! You in there? It's Adolf. I've been looking all over for you!" the boy exclaimed. It was well known in their teenaged social circle that Adolf Hitler carried a torch for Eva Braun, one that he couldn't easily put down—one that dated back to centuries before and a family history of shame.

Mortified, she gestured wildly at Stalin to get up and hide in the bathroom. When he refused to obey, she scooped up his clothes from the floor and threw them on top of him, prompting him to let out a sinister chuckle. Eva pulled at his arm until he finally got off the bed, encircled his clothes in a tight embrace and headed to the bathroom in tortuous slow motion. Hot on his heels, she quietly pulled the door shut behind him. Then she ran across the ivory Berber carpet to open the one leading into the bedroom. In her haste she hadn't noticed the white, cotton underpants peeking out from under the bed.

"Adolf!" she giggled. "You caught me napping. I was so tired I came up her to lay down for a few minutes. You know all the studying we've been doing for the exam and getting ready for our trip has really worn me out. I— "

Hitler eyed her suspiciously and abruptly interrupted, "You alone?" He looked past her at the tangled mess of sheets sprawled across the bed.

"Of course I'm alone silly!" she nervously giggled again, taking his hands in hers. "When did *you* get here? I thought your parents had forbidden you to come, being it's the night before our big test and everything."

"Oh just a few minutes ago," he replied distractedly, his gaze falling upon something sticking out from under the bed. Before she could utter another word, Hitler strode over to the object and bent down to pick it up while the girl panicked on the inside. In spite of his stern outward appearance he suddenly felt an urgent need to relieve himself. He ignored it and continued.

"This yours?" he demanded, holding up the underpants. Eva's dark complexion had nearly turned crimson as she stood there consumed with embarrassment, struggling for something to say. The awkward silence between them was broken by a deep voice behind Hitler.

"Actually, they belong to me," Stalin bragged, his naked sinewy muscles and private parts still out in the open. Hitler felt a twinge of envy and an increasingly critical need to pee as he looked at Stalin.

"Thanks for picking them up for me," Stalin added. Then he clapped Hitler on the shoulder, nearly causing him to have an accident right there on the carpet. Eva just looked on in horror and shame, her cheeks burning hot. She wished a giant sinkhole would open up and swallow her whole, right then and there.

Why oh why did she ever sneak out of the house tonight, against her parents' orders?

A devastated Hitler had just stood there frozen in place before his weak bladder forced him to make a run for the bathroom, lest he saturate his own underpants and potentially the carpet. In response, Stalin burst out in uproarious laughter, doubling over from the exertion.

"Knock it off!" Eva had scolded him. "I don't know why I ever came up here with you. You are nothing but a big bully!" With that she quickly turned and ran out, leaving poor Hitler to deal with his adversary alone.

"*Miss Braun*! Do you *hear* me?"

Mr. Bauer's booming baritone voice abruptly transported her back to the present and caused her heart to jump again in her chest as it had at the beginning of their question-and-answer session.

"Yes sir," she responded sheepishly. She drew her shoulders back, adjusting her posture and signaling attention. The teacher continued.

"Furthermore Miss Braun, depending on the offenses, failing our morality standards could prevent a student from graduating altogether. You are aware of this, I trust?"

Here he raised his eyebrows and paused for dramatic effect. Although he recognized that Eva's offenses—assuming she demonstrated good behavior for the rest of the week—did not rise to the level of denying her a High School Diploma, he wanted to instill genuine remorse for her actions.

"Yes, sir. I understand," she humbly replied. "I promise, I will never disrespect myself or ignore a teacher's instruction again."

Mr. Bauer could tell her words were genuine. Satisfied with Eva's ability to admit to her wrongdoing and vow to hold herself to a higher standard in front of her peers, the teacher excused his student, smiling at her as he did so. She offered a shaky smile in return before thanking him and taking her seat.

"Alright then, who's next," Mr. Bauer mused aloud as he scrolled down the handheld computer screen while the untested students fought to control their apprehension.

"Ah, Mr. Kissinger!" the teacher finally exclaimed. "Please, stand up and impress us with your knowledge."

A tall, stocky and broad-shouldered boy with thick, black-rimmed glasses awkwardly arose from his chair, his tousled Afro giving him a slightly disheveled look although his shirt was neatly tucked into perfectly ironed pants. He struggled to keep his sweaty palms out of his pockets, as was his habit when under stress. His dark eyes tentatively met his teacher's.

"Yes, sir," he mumbled.

"Mr. Kissinger, please try to enunciate your words more clearly son. You don't want to sound like you have a mouthful of marbles and although I may look youthful, at my advanced age the more you project your voice, the better able I'll be to understand your answers."

Kissinger's classmates snickered at Mr. Bauer's accurate description of his speaking style. It was often a source of ridicule among his peers who much like their teacher had difficulty understanding his words. Bauer was just trying to be nice by blaming his old age for his inability to comprehend Kissinger; it was his practice to soften the blow as much as possible when correcting a student.

"Yes, sir!" the boy repeated as clearly as he possibly could. The teacher couldn't help but grin at his clumsy yet brilliant prodigy.

"Contrast the role of politicians during the End Times with their role in Salvation Time."

A self-conscious Kissinger unintentionally slumped forward as he began to answer.

"Well—" he noted in a deep, throaty voice before Mr. Bauer interrupted.

"Please stand up straight Mr. Kissinger."

The boy rolled his big shoulders back and slightly puffed up his chest in obedience. Satisfied, the teacher declared, "That's better. You may proceed."

The student took a cleansing breath. He could feel the sweat trickling over the palms of his hands.

"In the End Days, being a politician meant having lots of power and privilege, just like being a Hollywood celebrity in the United States. During the End Days you couldn't tell the difference between a politician and a celebrity because they were always hanging out with each other on TV and at the White House. These selfish, pampered elites pretended that they cared about the middle class but loved to party on their dime. And they supported a big government that made life hard for working men and women. Lots of filthy rich celebrities back then used to complain that their taxes weren't high enough. But none of them ever wrote a personal check to the government outside of whatever they had to pay in taxes. Actually because they made so much money they could hire smart accountants to find loopholes in the law to save them as much tax money as possible. Kind of ironic, huh?

"In the End Days there were also great men and women who really did try to limit political power so that people could have more control over their lives. Even though they did make progress, their success never lasted for very long."

"Can you name some of these great men and women, Mr. Kissinger?"

"Yes, sir. We had leaders like Oliver Cromwell, General George Washington, Margaret Thatcher and Ronald Reagan. They worked hard to limit the size of government. There were important milestones like the Magna Charta, The Declaration of Independence and the Constitution of the United States. These documents upheld individual liberty but over time people and politicians would always stray far from them. They'd keep repeating the same mistakes that led back to centralized control. Sometimes back to socialism; other times, totalitarianism.

"In Salvation Days, politicians are just pencil-pushers who live modest lives and drive themselves to a humble office every day. They know that the only reason they hold an elected office is to serve the people of their nations—not line their own pockets by making deals with lobbyists and special interest groups. In the End Days, corrupt politicians only cared about themselves; their self-centeredness made it impossible for everyday people to get ahead.

"But now since politicians don't have great power, there are no more lobbyists or special interest groups. In fact, they are forbidden in Salvation Time. And all requests for elected representatives must be put online, on a special website for all citizens to see, to make sure everything is transparent. No one is allowed to speak with any office-holder in person. That is to prevent the same kind of political corruption we had during the End Times."

After a brief pause the teacher complimented, "I see you've been paying attention Mr. Kissinger. Now, for your bonus question: "What historical connection does your family have with the End Days just prior to the advent of Salvation Time?"

Listening to this exchange, two of Kissinger's classmates, Golda Meir and Anwar Sadat, braced themselves for the inevitable answer.

"Well sir," he began, somewhat embarrassed, "in the year 2012 evidence came out that my ancestor Henry Kissinger, a former US Secretary of State once worked with Nazis to overthrow the West German government in the 1970s. Not only that, but he became an informant for a secret spy network made up of former Nazis and elitist aristocrats who wanted to destroy West German Chancellor Willy Brandt."

"For what purpose?" the teacher challenged. Kissinger forced himself to keep his sweaty hands out of his pockets before continuing.

"Chancellor Brandt engaged with East Germany, even though it was controlled by the Soviets. The Soviets were communists who denied basic human rights to the people they ruled over—just like the Nazis. But Chancellor Brandt believed it was better to get along with the East Germans as best he could instead of always fighting. You could make a good case against the Chancellor's policy, but for Kissinger to side with former Nazis and the aristocracy was just trading one evil for another. By trying to overthrow the West German government for another evil regime, Kissinger was enabling a different form of control. Both communism and Nazism had caused massive genocide; *both* were evil."

"Is there anything else you would like to add Mr. Kissinger?" the teacher asked, knowing that the student hadn't yet shared the entire story.

He paused to collect his thoughts before resuming.

"Yes, sir—the October War of 1973, the Yom Kippur War. This also happened during my ancestor Henry Kissinger's time as US Secretary of State. In the year 2011, declassified documents proved that in the year 1973, he purposely caused a war that forced Israel to make concessions while it brought the United States and Egypt together. But he did not work alone. This was in agreement with the Prime Minister of Israel, Golda Meir, and the President of Egypt, Anwar Sadat.

"My ancestor admitted, 'We had two objectives in the war: to maintain contact with both sides. For this the best outcome would be an Israeli victory but it would come at a high price, so we could insist they ensure their security through negotiations, not military power. Second, we attempted to produce a situation where the Arabs would conclude the only way to peace was through us. But during the war we had to show the Israelis they had to depend on us to win and couldn't win if we were recalcitrant.'"

The student struggled to correctly pronounce that last word. After he finally blurted it out he paused for a moment, tiny beads of water forming on his forehead to match his clammy palms.

"Is there more you want to tell us Mr. Kissinger?" the teacher pressed on, ignoring the student's obvious discomfort in an attempt to keep him focused.

"Yes sir," he replied. The moisture on his palms was beginning to grate on him but he could not shut off the spigot of sweat produced by his nerves.

"At the end of World War II, Henry Kissinger helped bring the Nazi War Machine to the United States in *Operation Paper Clip.* He was the bureaucrat in charge and he brought German scientists known to be Nazis to the US and other countries like Argentina."

"Can you tell us about some of these Nazi scientists? Who were some of the worst of the worst, Mr. Kissinger?"

"Yes, sir," he complied. "One was Arthur Rudolph, an operations director of the Mittelwork factory at the Dora-Nordhausen concentration camps. That's where 20,000 workers died from beatings, hangings and starvation. Rudolph had been a member of the Nazi Party since 1931. A 1945 military file referred to him as '100% Nazi, dangerous type, and security threat! Suggest internment.'

"But the War Department's Joint Intelligence Objectives Agency allowed it. This agency did background investigations of all the scientists. It wrote in Rudolph's file that nothing in his records proved he was a war criminal or a devout Nazi, even though he was. Rudolph became an American citizen. He designed the Saturn 5 rocket used in the Apollo moon landings. In 1984, he escaped to Germany when his war record was finally investigated and exposed.

"There was also Wernher Von Braun. He was the technical director of the Peenemunde rocket research center, where the V-2 rocket was developed. This was the same rocket that ruined England during the war. Wernher Von Braun's resume had been rewritten so he wouldn't look like a Nazi. He went on to great success in the US. First, he worked on guided missiles for the US Army. Then he became the director of NASA's Marshall Space Flight Center. He even had the chance to work with the famous American Walt Disney on the "World of Tomorrow"—an attraction at the popular theme park, Disneyland.

"Kurt Blome was a high-ranking Nazi scientist. He admitted that he'd been ordered to experiment with plague vaccines on concentration camp prisoners. At Nuremberg he was tried on euthanasia charges—the extermination of sick prisoners—and conducting experiments on humans. Even though he was acquitted people knew he was guilty of the most horrible crimes against humanity.

"But even though people knew about his crimes, two months after he was acquitted, Blome had an interview about biological warfare at Camp David Maryland in the United States. In 1951, the US Army hired him to work on chemical warfare. His file didn't even *mention* the Nuremberg trial.

"So sir, my ancestor Henry Kissinger enabled Nazi evil. Even though US law banned Nazis from immigrating to their country, he helped the United States military round up these German scientists."

"And *why* did he do that, Mr. Kissinger?"

"To tap into their knowledge of foo fighters and particle/laser beam weapons, which the American government wanted the CIA and NASA to control."

The student looked at his teacher as if to say, "I'm all done."

"Mr. Kissinger, you have studied well, I see." With that, Mr. Bauer scanned his handheld device, tapping on it a few times to initiate the process of grade calculation. As the unnerved teenager watched in breathless anticipation, the teacher frowned intently at his computer screen. To the students, it looked as if he was having a silent, inner dialogue with himself over Kissinger's grade.

Meanwhile, young Henry Kissinger stood as tall and straight as he possibly could. Finally, the teacher spoke up.

"Excellent job, Mr. Kissinger," he complimented. "You have earned a '9' out of a possible '10'. You may sit down now, sir."

"Thank you, Mr. Bauer." Relief washed over the boy as he clumsily took his seat. The teacher promptly turned to another student seated in the back.

"Miss Meir." He addressed a young girl whose black, wiry hair was pulled back into a knot near the nape of her neck which was adorned with a long strand of feminine pearls. In a dignified fashion far beyond her 17 years on the planet, she moved gracefully to her feet, placing her arms and hands at the required position at her sides.

"Yes, sir," she replied assertively. Hours of independent study had prepared her well and that was evident in her entire demeanor. The teacher noted her look of confidence as he proceeded to test her.

"Tell me, what was the role of gold during the End Times and how does it compare with the function of gold in Salvation Time?"

"Sir, during the End Times gold used to be very important. It was a precious metal controlled by powerful elites like royal families and money traders. They made sure it was kept very scarce so they could expand their own power over the people. But today in Salvation Time we make our own gold. It is very cheap to produce and buy, and it is used for aesthetic and industrial reasons."

"You are correct, Miss Meir," the teacher noted proudly. "Now tell me, who pioneered the manufacture of synthetic gold?"

"Israeli Prime Minister Eyal Grad, sir," the student replied assertively. "During the time of Israel's isolation from the world, the manufacture of synthetic gold was one of many achievements under his leadership."

Mr. Bauer nodded before posing another question. "Speaking of Mr. Grad, he inspired the rest of the world to adopt his country's food standards. Can you tell us a little bit about that?"

"Oh yes, sir. Thanks to the Prime Minister, 'kosher' food became the norm everywhere."

"And what exactly *is* kosher?"

"Sir, kosher food is food that conforms to *kashrut*, Jewish dietary law. It means food that is fit for consumption because it has been thoroughly inspected by people specially trained to observe its production."

"Can you give us an example, Miss Meir?"

"Yes, sir. Let's say a vegetable farm is preparing lettuce for sale and shipment. They hire these overseers to ensure that every leaf is fresh and has no bugs or pesticides on it. If it does, it's tossed out. The same high standards apply to meat and dairy."

"Correct, Miss Meir. Now can you tell us a bit about kosher ritual slaughter for meat?"

"Sir, all meat must come from animals that have been slaughtered according to Jewish law. These guidelines are very strict and precise. The animal must be killed by a single cut across the throat to a precise depth so that it severs both carotid arteries, both jugular veins, both vagus nerves, the trachea and the esophagus. The cut must not be higher than the epiglottis and no lower than where cilia begin inside the trachea. The animal bleeds to death."

Some of the students shuddered at her explicit description even though they all enjoyed things like thick, juicy burgers and sizzling steaks on the grill. Given his family history, one especially felt a bit queasy and hoped it would be a while before Mr. Bauer called upon him to answer.

"Excellent, Miss Meir! In Salvation Time, all countries and citizens have adopted kosher because it really is best for all human beings. You've explained it well."

Golda smiled, though she knew what was coming next.

"And now for your bonus question," Mr. Bauer continued, "What role did your family member play in the final decades of the End Times in opposition to the system we enjoy today in Salvation Time?"

She answered, "My great-great grandma was found guilty by the Armageddon Commission of working with Henry Kissinger and Anwar Sadat to create the October War of 1973. This war killed 1,200 Israeli soldiers. As part of the Jewish Agency she and her colleagues were also found guilty of denying Hungarian Jews the right to their freedom because they preferred to let them die in Auschwitz. They looked down on these people as *Ostjuden*, lowly Jews from Eastern Europe. Golda was a member of the Jewish Agency that denied the ransom money the Nazis and Adolf Eichmann demanded in return for their freedom. The Nazis would have released these innocent people in return for 10,000 trucks and industrial goods in a sick program they called 'blood for goods.' But Golda, along with the rest of the agency, denied it. Because they refused to pay this ransom several hundred thousand Hungarian Jews were exterminated. Even worse, Golda Meir and the agency tried to blame it all on a guy named Kasztner.

Because of her snobbery and inhumanity, she received a guilty verdict at her trial. The Armageddon Commission decreed that all statues, monuments and other tributes to Golda Meir must be removed from the public square. And when Salvation Time finally got here, her descendants were forced to relocate to Arusha City to restore her name, atone for her sins and understand the way this world is truly supposed to work."

"Nicely done Miss Meir," the teacher replied brightly. As with all of the others he'd previously examined, his eyes moved from the student to the computer screen as he consulted the tech tool in determining her grade.

Within moments he announced, "You have achieved a '9' today. You may sit down now."

"Thank you, sir," she replied courteously, taking her seat once more next to her classmate Debbie Wasserman-Schultz—a ditzy, unserious student who was the complete opposite.

Debbie's frizzy hair, plain face and frumpy physical appearance did little to offset the poor girl's lack of intellectual curiosity and accomplishment. Glancing over at her scholarly classmate Golda, Debbie felt more than a little inadequate. She prayed Mr. Bauer would select someone else to follow Golda's act and nearly fell out of her chair when the teacher called upon his next student—which thankfully turned out *not* to be her, though she recognized the inevitability of having to deal with his questions sooner, rather than later.

"Mr. Duke," the teacher greeted a nerdy-looking kid seated diagonally across from Wasserman-Shultz. "Please stand up to answer your questions."

"Yes sir," the boy replied softly. Forgetting the prescribed posture he at first stood with hands clasped, arms falling loosely in front of him until Mr. Bauer gestured the proper etiquette. Duke immediately released his hands and placed his arms at his sides, making his lanky body appear even more feminine and willowy. It was a source of mockery among his classmates that David Duke seemed a little *light in the loafers* though he'd angrily deny such a thing whenever accused. Despite a slight trace of a developing mustache, his fine lips and perfect little nose only enhanced his effeminate looks although his dark black complexion matched that of his classmates.

"Mr. Duke, please explain how the outlook on race and race relations during the End Days differs from Salvation Time."

"Well sir, during the End Days especially in the 20th century, the Aryan race was considered superior. Many believed that people with blonde hair, blue eyes and fair skin were better than everyone else. Even if a person had no moral character, brains or heart for service as long as they had blue eyes and blonde hair they were thought of as superior. It was a false belief based only on physical looks; a really superficial way of thinking."

"Tell me, Mr. Duke, did *everyone* subscribe to Aryan race superiority during the End Days?"

"No, sir, not everyone did back then. It's just that the people who *did* used it to justify evil. This created a lot of misery for other human beings. We don't have this problem anymore in Salvation Time because we understand that all humans are made in the image and likeness of the One Creator. We can all trace our origins back here to Africa—back to Scientific Adam and Eve. In Salvation Time, we know that there really is no such thing as 'race' for human beings because depending on where they live, their features can change due to environment and geography. Everyone in this room is a living example of that."

"Very good, Mr. Duke," Mr. Bauer declared. "Now for your bonus question, please tell me how your great-great grandfather was involved in the conflict of Armageddon preceding Salvation Time."

Duke cast his eyes downward, ashamed of what he knew he had to admit. He stood there in silence for a moment until Mr. Bauer gently prodded him to continue.

"My great-great grandfather David Duke financially supported the End Times Army in their battle against the Salvation Time Army. He refused to accept the truth that we all come from the same God and that holding onto bigotry and hatred is against the laws of the Creator. He even went on television to show his support for the status quo while he was wearing his Klansman uniform—one of the most famous symbols of pure hatred during the End Days. David Duke flaunted his racism like it was something to be proud of, when he should have been very ashamed of himself.

"That's why the Armageddon Commission forced my family to come to Arusha where we could learn how to be decent human beings and repair our name and heritage."

"Thank you, Mr. Duke, you've handled yourself admirably," Mr. Bauer assured his visibly uncomfortable student who nevertheless managed to continue standing at attention. With that, the teacher began his computerized search for a grade, tapping the screen and frowning in response to whatever it was displaying. Finally, he raised his head to look at David Duke.

"Congratulations, you have earned a '9' on today's exam," he informed him. "You may sit down."

"Oh thank you Mr. Bauer!" Duke exclaimed giddily before sliding back into his seat. His amused classmates stifled their laughter as he waved his long fingers through his curly hair, possibly enjoying the activity a bit too much. The distraction didn't last for long because Mr. Bauer immediately turned his attention to another untested student.

"Mr. Sadat, there you are," he noted with a grin. "Please sir, arise from your seat that you might also share your knowledge with us."

A teenaged boy with a long, pointy nose immediately obeyed his teacher's order, hands displayed at his sides as he calmly waited for his question.

"Alright Mr. Sadat, tell us about one of the most well-known conflicts during the End Times involving three Middle Eastern countries and your ancestor's role in it."

Detracting from precedent, the teacher's testing of Sadat had purposely combined an actual event with the student's family history into one very important question. And although the conflict had already been discussed by Kissinger and Meir, it was important for Sadat to offer his own explanation.

"That would be the Arab-Israeli War of 1973 sir, when my ancestor Anwar Sadat, the President of Egypt, made a secret deal with Henry Kissinger, US Secretary of State, and Golda Meir, the Prime Minister of Israel."

Here he paused to take a brief, sidelong glance at his classmate Golda, who sat rigidly at her desk, eyes affixed to the front of the room.

"These leaders agreed to start a war that was also called The Yom Kippur War of 1973 because it began on the Day of Atonement, the holiest day of prayer and fasting in the Jewish calendar. It started with a surprise Arab attack on Israel when Egyptian and Syrian military forces knew that the Israeli military would be distracted because of their religious holiday.

"The combined forces of the Egyptians and Syrians outnumbered the Israelis. On the Golan Heights, 150 Israeli tanks were forced to face 1,500 Syrian tanks. In the Suez region, just 500 Israeli soldiers were made to fight 80,000 Egyptian soldiers. In the end 1,200 Israeli soldiers died to create peace with Egypt. So even though Meir and Sadat had agreed before the war that only 500 Israeli soldiers would die, many more than that got killed. Their agreement was corrupt from the start because turning soldiers into pawns in a political game was inhumane and evil. And once a war starts, no one knows how many casualties there will be."

"I see you've been paying attention in class Mr. Sadat," his teacher complimented. From her seat Golda snuck a furtive glance in Anwar's direction but he was too busy watching the teacher conduct his grade calculations to even notice.

"You have earned a '9' Mr. Sadat," he finally announced to his grateful student, who offered a polite "thank you, sir" before sitting down. By that time Golda had averted her eyes back to the front of the classroom, eagerly awaiting the next student-teacher interaction.

"Miss Wasserman-Schultz!" Mr. Bauer called out, causing the girl to nearly topple over as she began to rise out of her chair, smoothing her frizzy shoulder-length hair as she did so.

"Yes sir," she replied in her deep, masculine-like voice.

"Please describe the healthcare industry during the End Days and how it differs from the one we have in Salvation Days."

"Yes, sir. During the End Days the medical profession and healthcare industry had become very corrupt—driven by profit and greed. Thanks to selfish trial lawyers, doctors had been practicing defensive medicine by ordering lots of unneeded tests and surgeries. Lawyers, hospitals, insurance and pharmaceutical companies were all for-profit, so they mostly wanted to make money for themselves. Depending on whether or not it served their own greed, they'd either refuse to treat patients to save money, or they'd create more physical problems to keep the patients coming back so they could profit from repeat doctor visits.

"People liked to sue over everything back then. That's why a lot of doctors and hospitals ordered too many tests and surgeries.

They were afraid of being sued for negligence. We know God gave the human body the power to heal on its own. So doctors are supposed to guide the body to heal itself. But in the End Days, they didn't do that. The medical profession put profit first out of fear and selfishness. Because of trial lawyers, malpractice insurance was so expensive that many doctors, especially surgeons and gynecologists, were forced to retire way too early. There were also plenty of bad doctors who didn't care about helping patients and just played the game to get rich.

"In countries where medicine was under full control of corrupt, oversized governments bureaucrats without medical degrees had the power to decide whether or not a patient was 'worthy' of care. The elderly and the handicapped were often at risk because government fat cats thought they were disposable.

"By the time the Armageddon War started, even the United States had nationalized medicine. At one time during the End Days, the US had been the envy of the world because of its healthcare system. That country had created many innovations in medicine that had made life better for people everywhere. But in the final years leading up to the Armageddon War its corrupt government had rammed socialized medicine down the throats of its citizens. Most of them had been happy with their care and coverage. They wanted their government to focus on the economy and leave their health care alone. Most Americans opposed the government takeover of health care from the start. Other gullible Americans believed their administration's lies that 'If you like your doctor, you can keep your doctor' and 'If you like your plan, you can keep your plan' and that healthcare would be *free* and that everyone would be covered.

"These people were shocked and angry when their insurance premiums and deductibles went through the roof. Even worse, Americans with serious diseases like cancer who had been happy with their coverage lost their insurance and their doctors. And the middle class, the people this scheme was supposedly created to help, was hurt the most.

"Groups like AARP and pharmaceutical companies that pretended to care about the elderly went in on this health care scam just to line their pockets. Ordinary citizens were angry when they realized they'd been fooled. By then it was too late. And all of this happened under politicians who took bribes from the healthcare industry, lawyers, insurance companies and hospitals. These politicians let their own greed make health care expensive for other people while exempting themselves from the same law they forced upon their citizens. Instead of doing right by the people who elected them, most members of the US Congress put their self-interest first.

"Now in Salvation Time our medical system benefits everyone. It treats the whole person—physically, mentally and spiritually. It includes past life regression therapy, hypnosis, telepathy, relaxation, and meditation because all of these give people a better quality of life. Education for doctors is very cheap now, but in the End Days it cost a lot of money. When they'd get out of medical school, new doctors would have to start a practice with thousands of dollars in debt hanging over them. No wonder so many of them became corrupt and profit-driven—they were completely stressed out over paying their debt on time *and* having to pay high malpractice premiums.

"Another great thing about Salvation Time is there are plenty of doctors, one for every 20 patients. The better the doctors do their jobs, the better they get paid so they want to heal a patient as fast as they can. The last thing a doctor wants is for a patient to keep coming back because that would ruin their reputation and income.

"Our Salvation Time medical system is about making people well so they don't need to keep going back to the doctor. Our doctors make good money and now they don't need malpractice insurance or lawyers to defend them. There are no more trial lawyers in Salvation Time—and everyone is healthier and happier."

"Well I must say, I am pleasantly surprised by your response Miss Wasserman-Schultz," Mr. Bauer noted. "It's obvious you've done your homework."

Once again, the class collectively stifled their giggles at the teacher's justifiable surprise. Most days their flaky classmate couldn't answer any kind of question intelligently. Yet somehow she'd managed to prepare and perform well for this very important exam. Unknown to her peers Debbie's intense desire to go on their class trip had motivated her to crack open the books and practice her answers in front of a full-length mirror at home.

Still, she braced herself for the inevitable follow-up, which came a moment later.

"Now for your bonus question," Mr. Bauer continued, "what role did your family member play in all of this during the End Days?"

Wasserman-Schultz fought the urge to twist one of her kinky curls around her finger as was her habit when under duress. A moment later she replied.

"Well sir, my great-great grandmother Debbie was very selfish. She accepted huge bribes from pharmaceutical companies and hospitals to finance her campaigns. She was very hypocritical because she would go on TV and criticize them for their greed while taking their money. In public she created an image as a fighter for the 'little guy,' yet she would make shady deals with *Big Pharma* and certain hospitals that she would pay them off once she got re-elected. *That's* how she served many terms in the United States Congress. And even though she was a terrible speaker she was also the leader of the Democrat National Committee for years. She was so awful she was constantly mocked by her political opponents. And yet, the fools who lived in her district kept sending her back to Washington D.C.

"This happened a lot during the End Days—politicians taking bribes from the healthcare industry. That's why my ancestor Debbie was so angry at her Armageddon Trial. She couldn't understand why she was the only one being punished since she hadn't been the only one guilty of this crime. While she was on the stand she named names of other members of the US Congress who'd also done the same thing. She ratted them out to avoid her own punishment. From then on, people called her 'Debbie the Rat'.

"Anyway, that's why my family was forced to move to Arusha all those years ago and why I'm stuck with her name."

"Alright Miss Wasserman-Schultz, let's see what the computer suggests for your grade," the teacher replied, tapping and scanning the screen as he'd done all morning since the exam began. The student nervously licked her lips and rubbed them together as she waited for the results.

"I see the computer suggests a '7' for your efforts today," Mr. Bauer at last declared. "I'm going to agree with that even though your answers were correct. Do you know why?"

"No sir," the student honestly stated.

"It is because of your attitude," he explained patiently, without a trace of malice in his voice. "I understand the difficulty in having to bear the name of an ancestor who'd done reprehensible things during the End Days. And in your case, your great-great grandmother did much damage and employed unsavory tactics just to stay in power.

"But to refer to the people she lied to as 'fools' is wrong because they were also victimized by a complicit media, pop culture and educational system designed to keep them in ignorance. Manipulating good people's emotions was a tactic many in power, like your ancestor Debbie Wasserman-Schultz, routinely engaged in. With such a concerted effort to make them believe they were helpless without the assistance of a massive, overreaching centralized government, it's no wonder her constituents kept voting for her. And their dependency—along with the dependency mindset of individuals across the United States and the globe, solidified the entrenched power of the political class in general. Thus they continued to exploit human emotion and frailty for their own self-serving ends."

Mr. Bauer paused to let his student take it all in. God love her, she was a complete airhead but he was doing his best to educate her. And he had to admit, she had far surpassed his expectations with her responses to his questions this morning. Still, the morality component was not to be overlooked.

"Miss Wasserman-Schultz, do you understand what I am trying to tell you?"

"Yes, sir," she answered. "*Please, let him accept that I am sincere,*" she thought to herself. To her astonishment the teacher excused her and advised her to sit down. Debbie stole a quick glance at Golda as she did so, noticing the slight smirk on her classmate's face but she didn't care. All that mattered was that she passed—and would be taking the trip with the rest of the successful graduates at the end of the week.

Mr. Bauer surveyed the classroom again. His eyes soon fell upon a pleasant enough looking fellow with slightly bulging ears and a tendency to swagger when he walked. Knowing that the boy's propensity to stammer and stutter was often mocked by his classmates, the teacher hoped they'd show him a little respect and courtesy during this next exchange. As always, he was fully prepared to deal with it, if need be.

"Ah Mr. Bush! Please rise to answer your questions, sir."

The student stood up straight, his tall athletic body a testament to his daily habit of running and weight-training. His dark, close-set eyes met his teacher's gaze as he nodded slightly before replying,

"Yes *sir*, Mr. Bauer," in a slight Texas drawl carried over several generations in spite of all the years spent in Arusha.

"Tell us about the role of hydrocarbon and the petroleum industry in the End Days, versus their role in Salvation Days."

"Ahh, well in the...ahh...*End Days*, there was....uh...*major propaganda* put out by the oil industry. Mainly that oil comes from fossil fuels, which was a total lie. Uh...the myth of...uh...fossil fuels said that these were fuels formed by...ah...*natural processes* like the uh....decomposition of...uh....dead organisms. The age of these....uh...organisms and their...ah...resulting fossil fuels was usually...uh...*millions   of   years*. These   fossil fuels...uh...contained...high percentages of carbon, and...uh... included coal, petroleum and natural gas. People always feared it would run out, an emotion the oil companies exploited for their own gain to...ah...maintain their...uh...monopoly. They liked controlling the....uh...oil supply.

"But now in Salvation Time sir, we...uh...know that oil is...uh...produced as a byproduct of the earth. Every citizen understands that...uh...earth material combined with sea water is...uh...infused in the earth's mantle. Then it's pushed out as...uh...hot gas before it cools and condenses to form...uh...crude oil. We make our own...uh...oil in the classrooms because there's...uh...no   need   for   drilling.   Here   the...uh...oil industry...uh...makes its own oil with special equipment. But in Salvation Time we've...uh...also moved to...uh...electric, with vehicles that use both electric and gas. These cars...uh...have...uh... internal combustion engines....and an...uh...electric motor so they run...uh...cheaply   and   efficiently.   Our   highways   here have...uh....power strips running alongside designated right lanes so if your car is...uh...running low on power, you can...uh...just move into the right lane, reduce your speed to...uh...30 or 40 miles per hour and drive over these...uh...power strips to recharge your car, while drivers in the other lanes move at regular speeds. So no more...uh...oil monopoly in Salvation Time."

Mr. Bauer had kept close watch over the entire class as George W. Bush spoke, gratified that the students had abstained from snickering. He knew the boy had been working hard in speech class and made tremendous progress. But while under the stress of taking the final exam, it was understandable that old habits would rear their ugly heads. Although he wanted his student to overcome his oral communication problems, Mr. Bauer's first priority was that he demonstrated a sufficient mastery of the Salvation Time material—and it was obvious George W. Bush had been listening in class and studying at home.

"Excellent, Mr. Bush," he complimented. "Now, for your bonus question; what was your family's role in all of this during the End Days?"

Bush cleared his throat before replying.

"Sir, my uh....*great-great-great grandfather* Prescott Bush...a former United States Senator...uh...was a director and shareholder of companies that uh...*profited* from their...uhhh...ahhh...involvement with the....uh...*financial backers* of...ahhh....*Nazi Germany.* These...uh....business dealings...continued until his....uh...company assets were seized...uh...under the Trading with the Enemy Act...in the 20th century in the year 1942.

"But...uh...that's not all. Prescott's grandson...uh...George W. Bush...son of...uh....H.W. Bush...who broke his word not to raise taxes...as...uh...41st President of the...uh...United States of America...uh....did wrong by his country after the Islamic terrorist attacks on...ahhh... September 11, 2001. Uh...after the attack against the United States its 43rd President...uh...George W. Bush allowed the...uh...Saudi Royal family to leave the country by plane that same day, even though all commercial and private flights had been grounded.

"In the...uh...weeks after 9/11....an American ....uh...named...ah...Grover Norquist, a man very sympathetic to Muslims because he was married to a...uh...*Palestinian* woman...met with...uh...*George W. Bush*...and convinced him that Islam was....uh...a religion of peace....not a political system...uh...seeking to control the world. Bush then went soft on the...ah...real enemy, *militant Islam*...relaxing immigration standards even more to...ah....allow a steady flow of Muslim immigration into the Unites States, especially from Saudi Arabia. He uh...also...uh...refused to secure the country's borders. Islamist suicide bombers seeking to...uh...terrorize the country liked that.

"Because of greed, ego, selfishness and his lack of concern for American citizens he...uh...let the...ahh... *American madrassas* keep preaching...uh...hate and intolerance for *infidels.* G.W. Bush also....uh...accused his fellow Americans of being racists for....uh... wanting their government to secure the borders and...uh...enforce the country's immigration laws.

"The Bush family was also...uh...*guilty* of creating a market monopoly...and...uh...controlling the oil supply and the energy and technology markets, enslaving the United States and the world to energy companies and radical Islam."

The boy stopped there, his dark skin glistening as a result of his jittery nerves and self-consciousness. He chided himself for stammering and stuttering through his words, not simply embarrassed but also convinced that it would adversely affect his grade. He needn't have worried, though.

"Excellent job, Mr. Bush," the teacher enthused. "Before I begin your grade calculation, can you tell us of another lesson learned because of your ancestors, the Bush family?"

"Yes, sir....uh....thanks to my family, citizens in the....uh...*United States* finally rejected...uh....*political dynasties*, the...uh....idea that the same family had the right to produce....ah... one politician after another. The United States itself....uh...came to be in the first place....uh....because people were...uh...*tired* of elites running their...uh...lives. So...in Salvation Time....uh....political dynasties are....uh....*forbidden*. Not just in the...ah...*United States*...but....ah...every country in the world."

A beaming Mr. Bauer advised him a moment later after conducting his usual calculations, "Congratulations Mr. Bush, you have earned a '9' on today's exam. You may now take your seat."

"Uh, thank ya sir!" the student replied excitedly as he moved to sit down, sporting a big smirk on his face.

Next Mr. Bauer directed his attention to the scrawny student seated across from George W. Bush. The boy's beady dark eyes looked nervously at his teacher as he quickly yanked his finger out of his nose where he'd been picking at boogers all morning, not expecting to be caught. In his haste to get up out of his seat and answer the questions, the student neglected to realize he'd left an obvious piece of evidence now dangling from his left nostril.

"Mr. Ahmadinejad!" the teacher addressed him sternly. "Please remove the snot from your nose immediately so we can continue with your exam!"

Trying hard not to snicker, Ahmadinejad searched his pockets in vain for a tissue while his classmates muffled their laughter. In the next instant, he removed the dangler from his nose and popped it into his mouth, inciting a collective groan from the grossed-out class. A visibly disgusted Mr. Bauer fought to remove the unsettling mental image by refocusing his attention on the questions he was about to pose to the student.

Unfazed, a snide Mahmoud Ahmadinejad stood at attention, puffing up his slight, five-foot, two-inch frame as much as humanly possible. In the shadow of his statuesque history instructor, he still appeared very small indeed. Even most of the girls in the class towered over him which for some reason bothered him more than being shorter than the boys—except for one who had not yet been called upon to answer.

"Tell us about the role of religion during the End Days and its role now in Salvation Days," Mr. Bauer ordered. The student pondered the topic for a moment before answering.

"In the End Days, traditional religions battled with each other for converts to gain power. Islam was especially guilty because it used violence to conquer other people ever since it was founded by the Prophet Mohammad. The goal of Islam was a worldwide Muslim Caliphate, where all people would be forced to submit to Islam or die. Even the word 'Islam' means 'submission'.

"So Mr. Ahmadinejad, are you telling us that *only* Islam was violent?"

"No, sir. Other religions like Christianity had also been violent. During the Dark Ages, Pope Innocent III started the Spanish Inquisition, a Roman Catholic tribunal that punished people for the sin of heresy. At first the Inquisition only went after Christians but later it also went after Jews. If you were sentenced as a 'heretic' by the clergymen at an *auto de fe* or Act of Faith, you were severely punished. You'd be thrown into a dungeon, physically abused, tortured or burned at the stake. By the second half of the 18th century, the Inquisition ended with the Age of the Enlightenment.

"But Islam stayed violent all the way to the 21st century. It organized and carried out acts of terrorism against nations and individuals it believed to be *infidels*. An infidel was a non-Muslim. Even though Islam pretended to be a religion, it was really just another controlling political system. The Koran and Sharia Law were its foundation. Muslims believed that women and non-Muslims were slaves. They called Israel and the United States the 'Small Satan' and 'Big Satan.'

"Muslim women had it *really* bad. They were denied justice and basic human rights. They were forced to submit to barbaric acts like genital mutilation. Many Muslim women were 'honor killed' for dumb reasons, like going out of the house alone, driving a car, or refusing to wear a burqa. Muslims believed that killing non-Muslims like Jews and Christians was the way to find happiness in the afterlife. Muslim suicide bombers and terrorists believed they would be greeted by 72 virgins when they died."

Suddenly, the student burst out into unbridled laughter, powerless to stifle the urge.

"You find this amusing, Mr. Ahmadinejad?" the teacher sternly rebuked him.

The rest of the class sat with hands tightly clasped over their mouths as they attempted to silence their own giggles. Ahmadinejad was practically doubled-over. He fought valiantly to catch his breath, knowing this little episode could result in a failing grade and a severe punishment at home. His ribs actually ached from laughing so hard but he couldn't help himself. Mr. Bauer then took decisive action. He rapped his desk forcefully several times, bringing an abrupt end to the levity as the students quickly adjusted their behavior. Ahmadinejad stood at attention once more while everyone else folded their hands on their desks and focused their gaze on their teacher.

"That's better," Mr. Bauer declared. "One more outbreak like that Mr. Ahmadinejad and you will fail the history exam!"

"Yes, sir. I apologize to you and the class. It will not happen again," he humbly replied.

"Perhaps my next question will help you maintain a somber tone," the teacher continued. "Please tell us what happened on September 11, 2001."

"Sir, on September 11, 2001 Muslims attacked the United States. They hijacked passenger planes and used them to kill thousands of innocent people. Muslims wanted to wipe out New York City and the Pentagon because they symbolized American financial and military power. And if not for some very brave passengers on United Flight 93, they probably would have destroyed the White

House too, in Washington D.C., the nation's capital. Fifteen of these Muslim hijackers came from Saudi Arabia."

"And how did western leaders react to this event?"

"Sir, western civilization was controlled by political leaders driven by greed, selfishness, fear, ego and moral relativism. That's why the west refused to name Islam as the enemy; instead they called it a 'War on Terror.' Sharia Law slowly crept into American life in the name of 'tolerance.' Anyone who spoke out against it was called an 'intolerant bigot.' Ten years after September 11, students in the American public school system were being indoctrinated to believe Islam was a 'religion of peace.' Schools mandated the teaching of Islam and its customs yet they would not allow the Bible and Judeo-Christian prayer."

"Can you give us a specific example Mr. Ahmadinejad?"

"Yes, sir. In George W. Bush's home state of Texas under Governor Rick Perry, an online public school curriculum called CSCOPE was mandated. That meant the Texas state government demanded it be taught in their public schools. Parents and some politicians were mad about this because CSCOPE had an anti-American, pro-Islam bias. In Lumberton Texas, high school girls were forced to wear burqas as part of their study of Islam. But the burqa lesson did not teach the students about the brutality of real life for most women under Islam. They were beaten, thrown in prison or murdered by family members, vigilante groups, or the government if they went out in public in anything *but* a burqa."

"And what was a burqa, Mr. Ahmadinejad?"

"A burqa, sir, was a tent-like, long dress that hung like a curtain to cover up the female body. Even though we know God is the creator of all things including the female body, Islam believed it must be covered up for modesty. But really Islam looked upon females as whores, not children of God. Most everyday people who lived in the west knew that Islam was anti-woman."

Here Mr. Bauer interrupted again. "Tell me Mr. Ahmadinejad, what is the term we use to describe this anti-woman attitude?"

The student didn't miss a beat. "Sir, the term is misogyny. And most people in the west knew it was wrong. Muslim women had no choice. They had to wear a burqa in most Muslim societies unless they wanted to suffer horrible punishment. Yet public schools *in the US* were telling students that they were liberated and happy.

"This school teaching also praised Muslim terrorists as 'freedom fighters' and taught that the vicious Muslim Brotherhood in Egypt was all about peaceful democracy. But the MB was not about genuine brotherhood; it was really about Sharia Law and denying human rights to infidels and women. One of the Texas school teachers confessed to her class that even though she disagreed terrorists were 'freedom fighters,' the curriculum forced her to teach that. This happened in Texas but many other states in the US were telling the same lies about Islam to school kids. It is one thing for a Muslim country to use this kind of propaganda but for political leaders in free countries to mandate it in their schools proves they were corrupt. They were also cowards."

"Mr. Ahmadinejad, how did these corrupt and cowardly politicians deal with air travel after September 11?"

"Sir, under George W. Bush the American government failed its citizens. Instead of setting up a commonsense airport screening system he created another useless, big-government agency. It did nothing to keep passengers safe from another Islamic terrorist attack and it also cost American taxpayers a fortune."

"And what was the name of this wasteful, inefficient agency?"

"The Transportation Security Administration, sir."

The student George W. Bush turned to look at his classmate, a combination of resentment and embarrassment smoldering within. Part of it had to do with his competition with Ahmadinejad for another girl in the class named Hillary Rodham who had not yet been called upon to take her part of the exam. Both Bush and Ahmadinejad had spent the better part of the year trying to impress the hard-to-get Hillary who was fixated on her studies and in particular, one of her female classmates. Neither George W. Bush nor Mahmoud Ahmadinejad seemed to turn her on, but that didn't stop them from competing for her unattainable affections. Of course, they were still blissfully unaware that Hillary really didn't feel much for men in general, which was why pursuing her was a lost cause for any heterosexual male.

On honest introspection, the student George W. Bush had to admit that Ahmadinejad was right—his ancestor, as well-intentioned as he might have been at least in his *own* mind—had actually taken a bad situation and made it much worse with his *compassionate conservatism.* This was nothing more than *his* version of controlling centralized government.

Mr. Bauer listened intently before asking yet another question. "Can you tell us what agency the TSA was part of, Mr. Ahmadinejad?" The student knew he had this one nailed, too.

"Yes, the Department of Homeland Security, another stupid creation of President George W. Bush!" he exclaimed sarcastically.

"And why exactly was it 'stupid'?" the teacher inquired.

"Sir, the TSA, like the Department of Homeland Security, was run by bureaucrats. So of course it employed government workers to do a job that a private company could have done much better. If only George W. Bush had hired private contractors, he would have spared travelers lots of delays. He could have also spared them from having their private parts groped by government workers. If only the TSA had used smart profiling and behavioral strategies like the Israelis did, they could have respected individual liberty *and* helped keep air travel safe. But common sense wasn't so common during the End Days."

"Very good, Mr. Ahmadinejad. Now, can you tell us about some of George W. Bush's policies before these attacks? Had his administration actually helped the Islamists unintentionally?"

The student nodded. He'd definitely done his homework on this topic and felt confident that he could answer the question satisfactorily.

"Yes sir," he began. "Even before September 11, George W. Bush and his staff had been very lax about immigration. Saudi Arabians got off especially easy. With W's ok, a *fast-pass* system for Saudi elites called *Visa Express* was started. Because of this program, three of the 9/11 hijackers had been able to skip the normal consular interview process. If you were an elite Saudi Arabian, you could also avoid standing in long lines because this stupid system let you file your visa paperwork through travel agencies for a small fee—without ever having to appear in person or undergo background checks.

"Tell me, Mr. Ahmadinejad, how did the United States Embassy in Saudi Arabia feel about all of this? Were they angry?"

"No, sir. They were happy about it. They thought this dumb policy was a great diplomatic development. They bragged about how much easier it was for Saudi Arabians to get into the United States. These Americans were so naïve and short-sighted they hadn't bothered to ask any tough questions when they reviewed the applications filed by the 9/11 Saudi hijackers. If they'd done their job, they would have questioned the things that were left out—like how long these Saudi applicants planned to stay in the country, where they were going and why they wanted to travel to the US in the first place.

"Most of the 9/11 jihadists had been from Saudi Arabia. But even after they'd murdered 3,000 people, President George W. Bush bent over backward to appease sensitive Saudis. He promised them that no changes would be made in visa eligibility."

"So what happened to this program, Mr. Ahmadinejad?"

"Sir, the Visa Express was *expanded.* Common sense tells us it should have been canceled. But D.C. elites knew better. The Bush State Department official who'd started the Visa Express program—a woman named Mary Ryan—received *cash prizes* for 'outstanding performance' from April 16, 2001 through April 15, 2002. During this period, at least five of the 9/11 terrorists received visas that should have been legally denied. Within this time-frame, the jihadists attacked."

For a few moments the room fell silent as the students and teacher contemplated Ahmadinejad's answer. When considering the many failings of the Bush administration, everyone was shocked at how idiotic his post-911 policies really were.

Sensing eyes upon him and telepathically picking up his troubled thoughts about his ancestor the 43rd President of the United States, Ahmadinejad glanced quickly in the direction of the student George W. Bush who promptly shifted back to attention in his seat. Ahmadinejad then looked back at Mr. Bauer.

"So what's different now in Salvation Time?" the teacher asked.

"Thankfully sir, in Salvation Time most people get that we all come from the same Creator; that there is one God for all human souls—the same God known as God, Yahweh, Christ and Allah during the End Times, depending on a person's religious beliefs. Because we now understand that the same God created us all, there is no more religious separation and fighting over which religion is the 'true' religion—even though there are still some people who belong to the same religious denominations from the End Times."

"What was carried over from the End Days' religions if anything, Mr. Ahmadinejad?"

"Well sir, we took some of the best holidays from the End Times' religions and combined them into The One God Religion. Now we have more Holy Days, a total of 12 Holy Days each year. What we used to call the Ten Commandments is now the Twelve Commandments. People are free to worship at The One God Religion temples, or in the churches they attended in the End Days. Or they don't have to worship at all. But now that most people understand that there is one God for everyone, the religious tensions that created so many problems during the End Times are gone. Everyone is happy."

Here the student paused, confident he'd answered the question fully; he was ready to tackle what he knew would be the bonus portion of his exam.

"What, if any role did your ancestor have in all of this *religious tension and chaos*, Mr. Ahmadinejad?" Mr. Bauer asked pointedly.

"Well sir, my great-great grandfather Mahmoud Ahmadinejad ruled his country Iran by force, fear and violence because the mullahs demanded it. His government would hunt down gay citizens then brutally torture and kill them. Iranian women who'd been raped or assaulted by immoral men would suffer even more after reporting these crimes. They'd be beaten to death as if *they* were the guilty ones.

"My great-great grandfather allowed genital mutilation because Muslims wanted to deny women any pleasure from having sex with their husbands. They only existed to give birth to babies—preferably males—and to obey their husbands, no matter how bad they were. The Koran encouraged husbands to beat their wives for any reason. Mahmoud Ahmadinejad wanted to impose Sharia Law on the non-Muslim world, especially his arch-enemies Israel and the United States. As a famous Jew-hater, he called them apes and pigs.

"Thanks to him, peace in the Middle East was impossible. He lived to create problems and make life on earth hell in the name of Allah."

Here the student paused, signaling to his teacher that he'd concluded his answers. Mr. Bauer tapped at his screen and announced a moment later that Ahmadinejad had earned an '8' on the exam. "I would have given you a '9' but your little outburst disrupted the class and violated the rules of proper etiquette. Still, I can see that you have a full grasp of the material. Overall, I am very impressed," the teacher noted.

"Thank you, sir," Mahmoud sincerely replied. "I apologize for my actions as I did not mean to interfere with the test." He was about to take his seat when he felt compelled to speak up again in spite of the reprimand.

"Before I sit down sir, I just want everyone know that I am working hard to restore the name of Mahmoud Ahmadinejad to goodness. Thanks to my ancestor my work is cut out for me, but I am determined to do it."

"And you are off to a great start Mr. Ahmadinejad," his teacher assured him.

George W. Bush watched with a certain amount of amusement and relief. If his classmate could overcome those odds, surely he could restore his own severely misguided but basically decent great-great grandfather's name too. There was definitely hope for all of them.

"Do you have anything else to add before we absolutely must move on?" the teacher asked.

"No, I'm finished, sir, thank you," he replied before sitting down. Mr. Bauer entered his grade into the computer and raised his head to seek out another student.

"Alright then, who's next? Oh yes, our very own Charles Tudor. Please stand up sir, so we might learn from your knowledge of Salvation Time."

A young man with shoulder-length, kinky black hair slowly rose from his seat. Like his ancestor centuries before him, Charles had been sickly and weak as a baby, though he'd made tremendous progress thanks mostly to his mother. She'd devoted herself to helping him learn to walk and strengthening his ankles with leg braces. Still, at five-feet, four-inches tall he barely surpassed his classmate Ahmadinejad who, along with classmate Charles Manson, retained the honor of shortest boy in the class.

"Yes sir, Mr. Bauer," the boy addressed his teacher, having taken the required stance with arms at his sides.

"Tell me, Charles, during the End Days what was the role of a monarchy? Do we still have them in Salvation Days? Why or why not?"

Charles drew a deep breath before replying. "For many centuries of the End Days sir, monarchies ruled lots of nations because of the *Divine Right of Kings*. This theory came about in Europe during the Middle Ages. It said that kings were only accountable to God, so their subjects had no choice but to obey them. The Divine Right of Kings also decreed that God personally appointed monarchs to sit on their earthly thrones and rule over their people. Subjects who disagreed with their king were considered 'bad' Christians.

"Most End Days governments had centralized control over people. They were mostly monarchies, oligarchies, or dictatorships. But there was a famous and important break from this with the founding of the United States in 1776 when Thomas Jefferson wrote the Declaration of Independence. After a long, bloody revolution the Founding Fathers created a constitutional republic."

"Mr. Tudor, can you tell us what Benjamin Franklin told a woman who inquired about the new form of government the Founding Fathers created?"

"Yes, sir," the student answered. "Benjamin Franklin was very wise. He understood human nature very well. So when a colonial woman asked him, 'Sir, what have you given us?' he answered, 'A republic ma'am, if you can keep it.' Franklin knew that a system that respected individual liberty would be hard to keep because of human character failings. And he was right. By the late 20th century the United States had gone from a constitutional republic based on the rule of law to a democratic 'mob rule' system.

"After the Armageddon War, every country on earth set up a constitutional republic like the one America's Founders created. These governments matched the unique culture of their citizens, but the basic ideals of individual liberty and God-given rights are exactly the same. People are happy because they are free. They can work toward their goals, raise their kids, belong to The One God Religion or whatever religion they want, and live in an almost crime-free society. There's no more need for war or for sneaking into the United States illegally because no one *wants* to leave their own country."

"Charles, are you saying there's no longer a need for a police force or a criminal justice system in Salvation Time?" Mr. Bauer prodded.

"Oh, no sir! Because human nature is flawed we still need a police force and a criminal justice system. It's just that violent crime is not as bad as it was in the End Days. That's because people have money in their pockets. Life is much more stable and relaxed."

Here Charles paused. His nerves were a little frazzled anticipating the next question but he was ready to dive in and get it over with.

"Nicely done, Charles. Now for your bonus question, what was your ancestor's role in resisting Salvation Days? How did he help perpetuate this kind of slavery during the years he lived on earth?"

"Well sir, in the 17th century a common man named Oliver Cromwell challenged the Divine Right of Kings and my ancestor King Charles I. He was a devout Puritan and he hated the showy rituals of the Catholic and Anglican churches. He studied the Bible and believed that salvation was a private thing between God and the individual.

"My ancestor King Charles fought hard to keep his throne. He wasn't about to let England have a system of representative government because he loved being in control of his subjects. The tension between Cromwell and King Charles I led to the English Civil War. It was really a bunch of different conflicts between Royalists and Parliamentarians. The second civil war broke out because Parliament and Cromwell couldn't agree on how the country should be governed at the end of the first one. Parliament wanted to restore King Charles to the throne in return for a Presbyterian settlement of the church. Cromwell hated this idea because he saw it as trading one form of religious hierarchy with another.

"At first, King Charles seemed willing to compromise. He spent hours talking with Cromwell on the conditions of restoring his power. They came up with a system that would limit the King's powers and allow for elected parliaments. But Cromwell's army didn't believe this compromise was enough. Then they had the Putney Debates but they still couldn't come up with a solution everyone could agree on. Around the same time, King Charles escaped from custody and tried to regain power with force.

"In the end, Charles was tried for treason and beheaded.

"Cromwell was installed as Lord Protector and later succeeded by his son but without the support of Parliament and the army, Cromwell's son was forced to resign. And that was the end of The

Protectorate in England. They reinstalled the monarchy in 1660 when Charles II was invited back from exile to take his rightful place as the next king.

"From then on until the Armageddon War, England kept its monarchy and enslaved the English people to the Crown."

With that Charles paused and signaled the end of his answer. Mr. Bauer moved his eyes from the student, to whom he'd been listening intently, back to his computer screen, scrolling down and tapping on it. The boy stood very still, silently hoping he'd done well enough to pass with at least an '8.' He was very grateful to his parents—his mother especially—for always supporting him and assisting him in overcoming his physical problems, fully aware that his ancestor Charles had not been as fortunate as he.

"Thank you, Mr. Tudor," the teacher announced, "you have earned a '9' on your exam today.

"Thank you sir," he gratefully replied as he took his seat.

Mr. Bauer then directed his attention to the back of the room where an oval-faced, droopy-cheeked boy with noticeable body odor sat all alone. After repeated complaints from students that sitting near their classmate Mao Tse Tung adversely affected their ability to concentrate, Mr. Bauer had agreed to move the student to an isolated, far-left corner of the classroom. Since Mao had resisted orders to clean up his act, so to speak, it was the only way the teacher knew to make everyone happy. Still, getting him to develop better personal hygiene remained one of Mr. Bauer's goals although they were clearly running out of time.

"Mr. Tung, please stand up sir, to take your portion of the exam," the teacher instructed.

As the student obeyed his order, the foul stench of underarm perspiration permeated the room. The rest of the class fought to hide their disgust so as not to provoke Mr. Bauer. Yet even the dignified history teacher had difficulty maintaining his composure.

"Tell us about the role of totalitarianism during the End Days. Does it exist in Salvation Time?"

Tung answered his teacher in his forceful, robotic voice. Mr. Bauer tried not to cringe; he'd been on Mao's case daily about his personal hygiene—rightfully so, but if he could give George W. Bush a pass on his speaking deficiencies, surely he had to extend the same consideration to this student. Consistency was very important to Mr.

Bauer and as with George W. Bush his main concern was the student's demonstrated mastery of the material and the understanding as to why it was necessary to restore the family name.

"Well sir, during the End Days, central authorities gained control over people with propaganda. They used false concern for 'the poor' as an excuse. But they didn't care about poverty; poor people were just pawns in their power game.

"In the End Days, tyranny always started with a group philosophy or 'herd mentality.' Socialism was promoted under a nice, innocent-sounding name. In the United States, sneaky politicians who wanted a socialist system knew that they had to lie about their real motives. Otherwise, Americans would never willingly accept it."

Here Mr. Bauer sought clarification.

"And what exactly is socialism and how did these politicians misrepresent it, Mr. Tung?"

"Well sir, socialism takes money earned by people who work very hard and long hours—citizens like small business owners and employees—and gives this money to people who don't work in the name of 'fairness.' Politicians pretended this money was helping people couldn't work because of physical handicaps and illnesses."

"Was this not the case?"

"Well sir, we've studied in class that a compassionate society supports the truly disabled who cannot work. It provides safety nets for people who really need them. But in the End Days, because of human character failings, able-bodied citizens who just wanted to be lazy figured out how to game the system. They lived off of the fruits of other peoples' labor. So-called 'entitlement' programs were funded by taxpayers who did get up and work every day. So even though socialism was supposed to be all about 'fairness' there was nothing fair about it."

"Tell me Mr. Tung, how did socialism benefit the politicians who promoted it?"

"It gave them power and a permanent voting bloc of people who believed it was the government's job to take care of them from cradle to grave. But the money did NOT come from government. It came from productive people who *did* get up and work. That's why in the United States in the End Days entrepreneurs who created jobs were demonized as 'mean, uncaring rich people' by politicians. It didn't matter that the government taxed and regulated them to death, or that these entrepreneurs created good jobs, products and services. Most business owners often went home without pay so they could pay their employees and stay in business. Yet millionaire American politicians called *them* greedy because they loved to exploit human weakness."

"What do you mean by that, Mr. Tung?"

"Sir, politicians preyed on human character failings like envy to expand their own power. That's why they would point to successful job-creators as 'greedy' and play the 'class-warfare' game. Most entrepreneurs were decent people who contributed to the good of society. What did filthy rich senators and representatives in Washington D.C. produce? More laws and regulations to make it even harder for society's producers to get ahead."

"So Mr. Tung," Mr. Bauer interjected again, "human nature aside, why do you think these corrupt politicians had been so successful in pitting one group of Americans against the other? If entrepreneurs were creating jobs and opportunities, why wouldn't most people admire them in spite of the political propaganda coming out of Washington D.C.?"

"Sir, when no strong, brave leaders step up to help create a better way of life for everybody, people return to 'group mode.' When individuals lose power over their own lives they fall into group attitudes. This makes it very easy for a centralized government, a dictator, a king or any cult of personality to gain control over them."

The student took a breath and was about to resume his answer when Mr. Bauer stopped him once more. "Can you explain the political spectrum Mr. Tung?" The student nodded in agreement; he'd been studying this one diligently.

"Yes, sir. In the End Days most people were confused about the real political spectrum. That's because in Europe it only included the far-left systems of communism and fascism."

Here Mr. Bauer jumped in. "What do you mean far-left systems, Mr. Tung?"

"Sir, I mean centralized systems that control people's lives. Think of the political spectrum as a horizontal line with a dot in the center. Moving from this dot in the center toward the left side of the line there are powerful governments that impose more control the further to the left you go.

"The European understanding of the political spectrum only included communism and fascism. That's why people saw fascism as being to the right of the *entire* political spectrum because it was to the *right* of communism. Communism is as far to the left side of the spectrum as you can get. But fascism was also on the left side of the spectrum—just not as *far* to the left as communism."

"And why wasn't fascism considered as far to the left as communism, Mr. Tung?"

"Because sir, fascism gave people a little more freedom than communism did. But communism and fascism were still on the left side of the *overall* political spectrum."

"You are correct, Mr. Tung," the teacher affirmed, obviously pleased with his student. "Tell us then, what was all the way to the far *right* of this political spectrum?"

"Sir to the far right, there's no government at all—just anarchy and chaos, also very bad."

"So where do Salvation Time governments fit into this spectrum, Mr. Tung?"

"Sir, moving from the far-right just a little bit toward the center of the spectrum, we have a constitutional republic. This is the kind of system all countries have now in Salvation Time. This political system gives individuals as much freedom as possible. It also has a reformed foundation of law and criminal justice so everyone can live in a civilized society. This was the system created by the United States Constitution but by the last years of the End Days, the country wasn't functioning as a constitutional republic."

"True enough Mr. Tung. Now please tell us how the political systems on the left side of the spectrum operated in the 20th century specifically," the teacher ordered.

"The 20th century was the bloodiest and most barbaric century in the history of the world. That's because of leftist political systems like communism, fascism and Nazism. In that century, 250 million people died in wars, mass slaughter and political murders. Out of these three systems, communism was the worst; it killed more than 120 million people. Communism *promised* equality and justice, but really it was all about control. People living under it were ruled by fear of torture and death.

"Hitler and the Nazis killed 11 million people and 6 million of them were Jews. Mussolini killed about a million Italians, and my ancestor Mao killed 45 million Chinese."

Tung stopped there and took a few breaths. Mr. Bauer let him gain his composure then asked, "What were the two things all of these leftist political systems had in common, aside from mass murder? What were the two main tactics they all employed in order to turn everyday citizens into slaves of the authoritarian state?"

The student confidently replied, "Sir, every single one of them removed God and denied freedom of religion to their people. No one was allowed to worship in churches, synagogues or temples. God was seen as competition by the authoritarians. Government wanted people completely dependent on them so that they could control them. If people believed God had created them and given them a unique purpose they would put less trust in government and answer to a much higher power. This doesn't mean that citizens would deliberately break laws, but that they would understand that rights come from God, not government. Rights like life, liberty and the pursuit of happiness are 'inalienable.' Thomas Jefferson wrote that in the Declaration of Independence.

"The second thing these totalitarian systems took away was the right to bear arms so that everyday people would be defenseless. Living in a world where all governments were to the left of the political spectrum, the Founders knew they needed the Second Amendment in the US Constitution—the right of American citizens to bear arms to protect themselves against government. They understood that absolute power corrupts absolutely. They believed armed citizens would help preserve individual liberty. During the last centuries of the End Times many Americans thought the Second Amendment was all about hunting, but it was really about citizens being able to protect themselves from a controlling government.

"In Salvation Time we recognize that God directs the inner soul and a properly defined and limited government directs the physical body."

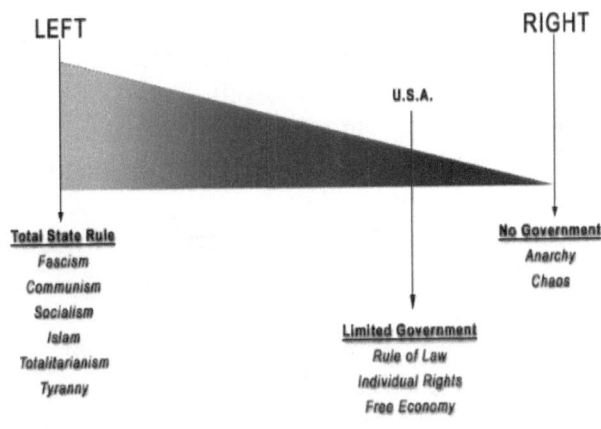

The True Political Spectrum

LEFT   RIGHT

U.S.A.

Total State Rule
Fascism
Communism
Socialism
Islam
Totalitarianism
Tyranny

Limited Government
Rule of Law
Individual Rights
Free Economy

No Government
Anarchy
Chaos

http://therightplanet.com

Mao Tse Tung stood as straight and stiff as a board, awaiting his teacher's next move. It had been a challenging yet enlightening exchange so far but he knew what was coming next.

"Alright Mr. Tung, for your bonus question, tell us about your ancestor and why it is necessary to restore his name."

"Sir, my ancestor Mao Tse Tung was a brutal dictator. Because of him, 45 million Chinese people were murdered. He was called the 'Founding Father of Modern China' because he changed the country from a backward land into a modern power but Chinese citizens paid a high price for it. When he was young, he worked as a library assistant in Beijing. That's where he found out about the communist revolution in Russia. He wanted to model the same thing in China. He became a Revolutionary Marxist and a founding member of the Chinese Communist Party.

"While moving China out of an outdated government system was a nice goal, Mao created something worse because all he cared about was power. He was also a womanizer his whole life. He couldn't stay faithful to marriage vows and cheated on all four of his wives."

Here the student paused, thinking he'd remembered everything but Mr. Bauer was quick to remind him.

63

"What else about Mao Tse Tung from the 20th century is important to remember?"

A mournful look washed over student Mao's face as he resigned himself to answering the question. "Sir, my ancestor Mao Tse Tung was known for his poor personal hygiene. He never brushed his teeth and he refused to bathe. The only thing he would agree to once a day was a rubdown with wet towels."

While he spoke, Mr. Bauer scanned the room with stern eyes in a non-verbal cue to his students to refrain from laughter or else face the consequences.

"You are correct sir," the history teacher advised his student. "And what is it that we always say in Salvation Time, an adage that originated in the End Days that we've carried over?"

"That cleanliness is next to godliness sir," the student answered sheepishly as Mr. Bauer smiled.

"You are quite right, sir," he responded, once more tapping on his computer screen to calculate a grade for Mao. "Congratulations, you have earned an '8'," he announced a minute later. "Do you know why the grade is not higher in spite of your intelligent, well-rounded answers?"

Mao hung his head in shame. He knew what was coming.

"Mr. Tung?"

The student looked up at his teacher and replied, "Because my hygiene is just as bad as my ancestor's?"

"That is correct. We've discussed this before so I won't belabor the point but please clean up before we leave on our trip. That's not a request but a requirement. I can separate you from the other students in the classroom, but on the trip you'll be sharing hotel rooms and sitting closely next to each other on the train and other forms of transportation. Do you understand that given such close proximity to other students if you refuse to start bathing and brushing your teeth you will not be permitted to go?" Mr. Bauer's words were firm but kind.

"Yes, sir," the student promised.

"Alright Mr. Tung, you may sit down."

There was a slightly audible gasp as students fought to repress their visceral reaction to their classmate's overwhelming body odor. They were grateful he was finally finished and hoped he'd take Mr. Bauer's reprimand about cleanliness to heart. While he seemed genuinely sorry about his ancestor's crimes and demonstrated remarkable intelligence, his refusal to bathe created an insurmountable barrier between him and his peers.

Poor Mao was rarely, if ever, invited to a birthday party or other social occasion. Hopefully he'd start practicing better hygiene immediately so he could go on the trip and at last get to know his classmates before they   scattered out into the big world awaiting them with new jobs and responsibilities.

Next Mr. Bauer turned to *Big Bully* Joseph Stalin. He'd been smirking during Mao's entire speech, which did not escape the teacher's notice. In Stalin's case, the smugness was not simply due to Mao's aversion to cleanliness but to an old grudge rooted in the 20th century between their ancestors.

"Mr. Stalin! Please stand for your portion of the exam."

The soccer star stood at attention while Eva Braun looked on nervously. Though she'd passed her part of the exam with flying colors, she still feared that Mr. Bauer would telepathically discern that Stalin and she had been together in the Biblical sense the night before. And it would be just like Joseph to brag about it in front of the class.

"Yes sir," Stalin addressed his teacher with a slight trace of arrogance in his voice. Mr. Bauer dramatically raised his eyebrow at the student, who quickly realized he needed to lose the attitude.

"Yes, sir," he repeated, this time in a more respectful tone.

"Tell me, since we've spoken about the political spectrum at length with Mr. Tung, what was your ancestor's role in the imposition of communism during the End Days?"

"Sir, my ancestor Joseph Stalin believed that 'one death is a tragedy; one million is a statistic'. He was involved in the evil of communism. Communism believed that endless conflict was a law of nature."

"Very interesting Mr. Stalin," the teacher replied. "But why would anyone think such a thing to be a law of nature?"

"Sir, the 'scientific' excuse for communism came from Charles Darwin's *Theory of Evolution*. Darwin believed that the differences between people *necessarily* lead to them to never-ending war, fighting and conflict."

"Tell me, Mr. Stalin, why did Darwin write this book?"

Sir, the British monarchy sponsored Darwin's book because they loved to start wars then send other people's kids off to fight them."

"I see," Mr. Bauer replied. Can you explain Darwin's belief system, Mr. Stalin?"

Yes, sir. It was called *dialectics*. It taught that every class, every nation and every society is naturally inclined to fight the other one. This was the 20th century belief that inspired communism, fascism and Nazism, and the enslavement of people by monarchy."

The student paused for a cue from his history instructor. Mr. Bauer nodded his head to continue while the rest of the class intently watched the famed school jock undergo his part of the important oral exam. As she looked on, Eva Braun hoped he'd screw up in some way. It would serve him right for being such a jerk.

"Joseph Stalin took over after Vladimir Lenin died," the boy continued. "He ruled the Soviet Union by fear and torture for almost 30 years. During that time, 45 million people were murdered—or as he would call them, *statistics*. In the year 1929, he created a policy called 'collectivization' because he was mad that there were still too many Russian peasants who owned their own land, worked their own farms, and sold their own produce in the market.

"Stalin wanted to take away all the peasants' land and produce in his quest for power. He wanted to finish what Lenin had started. That's why collectivization was promoted through propaganda films where my ancestor Joseph Stalin would pose on tractors, acting like he was a good leader who would take his people into a new dawn of prosperity."

"Was this not so, Mr. Stalin?"

"Oh not at all, sir! In 1930, my ancestor ordered the Red Army to confiscate the peasants' produce. His army seized produce from every single field. And even though some peasants hid their food, the army broke into their private homes and stole everything. They also stole the peasants' farm equipment because they wanted to them to starve to death. If they had the tools to grow more food, they would be able to survive. The Red Army's seizure of the peasants' farm equipment caused another famine like the first one Lenin created when he was in power. And in the Ukraine, six million people died of starvation.

"Even worse, the peasants turned into cannibals because extreme hunger does that to the best of people. To stay alive, they ate the corpses of their dead countrymen. Stalin's regime had turned human beings into savages, just as communism had wanted all along. And everyone who opposed Stalin and his mandated collectivism policy was murdered." Here the student paused and awaited his teacher's reaction.

"Excellent, Mr. Stalin; I see you've also been paying attention in class. Now for your bonus question since you have already made it clear why it is necessary to restore your ancestor's name to honor, what is the system we employ in Salvation Time?"

"Sir, in Salvation Time bullies like my ancestor Joseph Stalin are not allowed to create misery, suffering and death while they pretend they are helping the poor. In Salvation Time we have *positive capitalism* where people are free to pursue their goals—like owning their own business and making money. This money flows throughout society in a never-ending cycle. People make money, spread money and spend money freely in a helpful way. That is good for *everyone*. Politicians are just administrators. They don't have the power they had during the End Days, so now they work on *behalf* of individuals. Politicians only exist to make sure citizens have plenty of money to take care of themselves. They do this partly by creating programs that make it possible to earn a good living but mainly by getting out of the way."

"Mr. Stalin, where do poverty and prosperity *really* begin?"

"Both are states of mind, sir," the student answered. "In Salvation Time, everyone has a mindset of prosperity because we understand that when you're poor in your head, you're poor in your pocket. Poverty is a mental state that no longer exists. Neither does the 'slave' mentality. We also understand now that bullies like my ancestor Stalin deserve to be mocked because a soul's value is measured by the service human beings give to each other."

"Excellent, Mr. Stalin," the teacher complimented before initiating his grade calculation ritual.

From his remote desk, Mao Tse Tung watched with a mixture of anger, resentment and envy that had reincarnated through several generations. The intensity of the negative emotion his ancestor Mao Tse Tung had felt back in the 20th century for his former hero Joseph Stalin was not easily dissipated. Back in the End Days, Mao had traveled from China to Moscow to meet with Stalin, who'd kept him futilely waiting for weeks. Even all of these years later in Salvation Time, members of Mao's family tree felt the same overwhelming disillusionment at the mere mention of Stalin's name.

Coupled with the fact that the student Stalin was a star athlete and "chick magnet," it was understandable that the student Mao would feel a certain amount of envy toward his classmate. As he sat there isolated, he took Mr. Bauer's words about cleanliness to heart.

"Congratulations Mr. Stalin, you have earned a '9' on today's exam," the teacher announced. "You may take your seat." The proud jock thanked Mr. Bauer and sat down again, his mind immediately wandering back to his conquest the night before as his eyes fell upon Eva Braun. She however, remained seated quietly at her desk, eyes averted downward in an attempt to look inconspicuous. Meanwhile, Mr. Bauer called upon his next student, Nathan Rothschild. A short, rotund, prematurely balding teenaged boy stood up straight, hands at his sides.

"I am ready sir," the student announced.

"Mr. Rothschild, please talk to us about the role of the banking industry during the End Times versus its role in Salvation Time."

"Yes sir," the student began. "Back in the centuries leading up to the Armageddon War, the money supply was controlled by elite bankers. These bankers had a lot of power. They could manipulate currency at will and impact national economies for better or worse. They were driven by profit, greed and selfishness—the opposite of positive capitalism, which helps citizens become financially independent."

"Mr. Rothschild, when did this money-manipulation begin?" Mr. Bauer followed up.

"Sir, this practice goes all the way back to Biblical times and the famous story of Jesus chasing the money traders out of the temple. Back then money traders controlled the money supply. They made it impossible for practicing Jews to pay their temple tax when they came to Jerusalem because devout Jews could only pay the tax with a coin called the half-shekel of the sanctuary. This shekel was a special coin—an ounce of pure silver *without* an image of a pagan emperor. That's why the Jews believed it was the only coin God would accept. But thanks to the money traders it was also really hard to find.

"These money traders also included the *Jewish* elite and the *Jewish* leadership. Because they had a money monopoly, ordinary Jews were forced to pay whatever high price they demanded to get the shekels they needed to pay the temple tax. To Jesus, this was completely immoral and unacceptable. It also violated the sanctity of God's house. *That's* why he threw the money traders out of the temple. This was the only time he ever became violent during his ministry, at least that we know of."

"So Mr. Rothschild, are you telling us that the problem with money traders began during the time of Jesus?"

"No sir, the problem with money traders started long before him," the student answered confidently. "Two-hundred years before Jesus was born, Rome fought with money traders. Two early Roman emperors tried to rein them in. They reformed usury laws and limited land ownership to 500 acres. Both of those emperors were assassinated. Then in 48 B.C. Julius Caesar took back the power to coin money from the money traders and minted coins for all Roman citizens.

"With a positive money flow, Caesar built great public works projects and earned the love of the common people. But this also made him a target of the money traders. Some historians believe Caesar was assassinated because he took back the power to coin money. No one knows for sure if that's true. But one thing is true: Caesar's death meant the end of abundant money in Rome. Taxes and corruption went up and the Roman money supply went down by 90 percent. Regular Roman citizens lost their land and their homes. Because the Roman people lost confidence in their government they refused to support it. This plunged Rome and Europe into the Dark Ages."

Rothschild paused. He was well aware that his answer might possibly be the longest one today but that was fine with him. Accepting total responsibility for the crimes of his corrupt ancestor required him to demonstrate a thorough understanding of this topic to his history teacher and his peers. It was an obligation the student was eager to fulfill. So when Mr. Bauer asked him about money during the Middle Ages he enthusiastically resumed his narrative.

"During the Middle Ages in England, the goldsmiths started fractional reserve banking," he began.

"If I may, Mr. Rothschild, what is fractional reserve banking?"

"Sir, the term means lending out more money than you have in reserves. It started with customers depositing gold with the goldsmiths. Paper money started out as receipts the goldsmiths would give to people who'd deposited gold with them. Soon after, these greedy goldsmiths figured out that only a few customers ever came back to demand all of their gold at once. That's when their greed for even more money and power led to fractional reserve banking—the discovery that they could print more money than they had gold. They got away with it because most people had no clue about what they were actually doing.

"Then in the 15th century two powerful families in Italy linked the Vatican and the global banking system. The Borgia family took political power at the Vatican and the Medici family created the modern banking system."

Before the student could continue, Mr. Bauer jumped in again.

"Tell us Mr. Rothschild, where does the word 'bank' come from?"

"Yes sir," the student responded, "the word 'bank' is derived from the Italian word 'banco' which means 'bench'. During that period of the End Days, only Jews were allowed to trade with money. So you'd have a Jewish guy sitting on a bench in the marketplace for the exchange of money and bills."

"Very good, Mr. Rothschild, you may proceed." The student drew another deep breath before answering.

"The main practice of the Medici Bank was the secret movement of money. Even though it went through cycles of prosperity and hard times, the Medici Bank built a political power base that put the Medici family on the Papal throne 10 years after the Borgia's reign ended."

Here Mr. Bauer interrupted again. "So are you telling us Mr. Rothschild, that there was collusion between the financial industry and the Catholic religious hierarchy known as the Vatican?"

"Yes sir," Rothschild replied. "And Rodrigo Borgia had a reputation for being *the* worst pope of all. When he was elected in 1492 he took the name of Pope Alexander VI. He had already fathered four illegitimate kids, and the rumor was that he fathered at least three other kids while serving as Pope. But the Vatican was famous for its immorality and corruption during this time period, going back to Pope Sixtus IV in 1471.

"Even though he was the head of the Catholic Church and supposedly God's earthly representative, Sixtus had been anything *but* godly. He took the papal practice of nepotism to a whole new level by rewarding his nephews with money and power. He also used them as agents in the power politics of competing Italian states. At this time in history, Italy was not a unified country. It was made up of independent city-states that had their own governments.

"These nephews thought up diabolical plots for their own selfish reasons. One of these plots even ended with murder–the murder of one of the Medici's in the Florence cathedral during High Mass. One of Sixtus' nephews learned his lessons so well that he achieved even more politically when he was elected to the papacy as Julius II. Pope Julius II actually *directed* military campaigns. He also commissioned artwork from Raphael and Michelangelo. That's why we have the beautiful frescoes of the Vatican and the Sistine Chapel—and that's also why we had the Protestant Reformation."

"I see Mr. Rothschild," Mr. Bauer declared, pleased thus far with the student's lengthy and detailed response to this crucial question. Since the tentacles of the money traders and centralized banks ran far and deep during the End Days, intertwined with governments and religious hierarchies, the teacher acknowledged that the topic demanded more from this particular student than any other in the class. And so far, Rothschild was delivering admirably.

"So you're telling us that the Protestant Reformation was a reaction to commissioned artwork?"

"No sir, the Protestant Reformation was a natural reaction to the outrageous materialism of the Catholic Church. The Church's love of money, power and earthly possessions had been really bad in Germany. In that country, greedy prelates lived like Renaissance princes, not humble men of God. One of them was Albert, Archbishop of Mainz. By the time Albert was 24 years-old he held another bishopric and archbishopric, on top of the one he already held in Mainz. This was against Canon Law, the law of the Catholic Church, but Pope Leo X agreed to let it go in exchange for a big donation to help cover the construction costs of the new St. Peter's.

"Pope Leo X was a Medici—and he was just as greedy as the rest of the family. So he and the Archbishop made a corrupt deal where the Pope let the archbishop sell indulgences. Half of each sale would go to Rome, the other half toward helping Albert pay off his debts. This secret deal would have made faithful, everyday Catholics very angry if they had known about it. But when Albert hired Friar Johann Tetzel to sell these indulgences, everything really hit the fan.

"If I may, Mr. Rothschild, what are indulgences?"

"Indulgences were promises sold by the Catholic Church to its members in exchange for money. They promised the buyer that in return for their money, the soul of their deceased loved one would be freed from purgatory right away. The church taught that purgatory was sort of a 'waiting room' for souls who weren't quite good enough to get into heaven yet not bad enough to go to hell."

"And what do we now know in Salvation Time concerning hell and purgatory, Mr. Rothschild?"

"That neither one exists, sir. There is no hell. Hell is life on earth when we live in a physical body and have to go through all kinds of tests and hard times for our soul's growth and advancement. In Salvation Time we understand that a soul reincarnates over and over again in different bodies and earthly situations so it can draw closer to God. During the End Times, the whole idea of hell and purgatory was just another way for powerful organizations like the Catholic Church to control people."

"Excellent Mr. Rothschild, you may continue your answer. Please finish telling us about how the Protestant Reformation came about."

"Thank you, sir," the student continued. "Because people believed so strongly in hell and purgatory at the time, they were easy dupes for a liar like Tetzel. He even wrote a catchy jingle: 'As soon as the coin in the coffer rings; the soul from purgatory springs.' And they believed him!"

The student danced around, waving his arms and hands dramatically as he gave his own rendition of the jingle in a sing-song.

The entire class burst out laughing. Mr. Bauer tried to hide his own amusement; he also enjoyed Rothschild's entertaining answer but knew he had to maintain decorum in the class to keep them on schedule. With one stern glance from their teacher, the students—including Rothschild—immediately regained their composure.

"You may continue," Mr. Bauer informed him.

"Yes, sir," he humbly replied. "In 1517 some parishioners returned to the town of Wittenberg with indulgences they'd bought from Tetzel. They announced that Tetzel had told them these indulgences were so powerful that they could even pardon a man who'd raped the Virgin Mary. Martin Luther was an Augustinian friar who taught theology in a Wittenberg university. When he heard about this he was angry.

"Luther always argued against indulgences in his sermons because he believed they were immoral and against God's teachings. But when he heard about Tetzel he went even further by writing out 95 propositions about the nature of faith and contemporary church practice.

"When he nailed the 95 theses to the door of the All Saints Church in Wittenberg, he wanted to reform the church from within but he ended up starting the Protestant Reformation. This created chaos and conflict within the Christian faith for over a century. It was bitter and destructive. But Luther had been right about the corruption in the Catholic Church. In later centuries this kind of fraud would come to be known as a 'Ponzi Scheme'.

Here the student stopped to catch his breath and ask for his teacher's permission to continue on this very important topic. Mr. Bauer nodded his approval, fully aware of the need for the class to completely comprehend these historical events and absorb their lessons. They'd soon be leaving the sanctuary of the classroom to interact in the world and it was critical that they understood the role of centralized bankers in the End Days and why money operated quite differently now in Salvation Days.

"In the 18th century," Rothschild continued, "the American Revolution led to the world's first constitutional republic, the United States of America. It is true that the American colonies revolted against Mother England because of taxation without representation and other British abuses. But the real reason for the Revolution was the Bank of England, even though this was hardly ever taught in school during the End Days.

"When one of America's most famous founders Benjamin Franklin went to London in the year 1764, he couldn't believe all of the poverty and unemployment among the British working classes. It shocked him. Someone asked Franklin how the American colonies supported their own poor houses and he said, 'We have no poor houses in the Colonies, and if we had some, there would be nobody to put in them, since there is in the Colonies, not a single unemployed person, neither beggars nor tramps.'

"When the Bank of England heard about this, they were not happy. So the greedy bank pressured Parliament to pass a Currency Act. This made it illegal for the colonies to print their own money. The colonists were forced to pay all future taxes to Britain in silver or gold. Anyone who didn't have these precious metals had to borrow them at interest from the banks.

"Just a year later Franklin noted that the streets of the colonies had filled up with unemployed beggars, just like in England. The money supply had been reduced by half, wiping out funds that could have been used to pay for goods and services these unemployed workers could have provided. Franklin said, 'the poverty caused by the bad influence of the English bankers on the Parliament which has caused in the colonies hatred of the English and…the Revolutionary War. The colonies would have gladly borne a little tax on tea and other matters had it not been that England took away from the colonies their money, which created unemployment and dissatisfaction.'

"During the End Days in the 20th century, every bank in the United States was allowed to loan out at least *ten* times more money than it had in reserves and charge their customers interest, just like fractional reserve banking in the Middle Ages. In the year 1913, the country changed forever when the Federal Reserve Act was passed. This name was misleading because the Federal Reserve was a private corporation with no reserves. It operated independently of Congress— a violation of the United States Constitution. James Madison, who wrote the US Constitution, took a strong stand against centralized banks. So did Thomas Jefferson and many other Founding Fathers. That's because they knew how dangerous it was for an unchecked, unelected bank to control the money supply.

"In the 19th century two American presidents, Andrew Jackson and Abraham Lincoln fought back and won against the centralized banking system of their time, The Bank of the United States. Jackson was a war hero. He defeated the British Army in the Battle of New Orleans during the War of 1812. The troops under his command nicknamed him 'Old Hickory' because he was 'as tough as hickory.' He respected the people's will because of his own humble start in life. When he was a boy, he'd been a prisoner of war during the American Revolution until his widowed mother rescued him. Then she died and left him an orphan.

"Jackson always stood up for the rights of everyday working people. This helped him win the popular vote and an electoral majority during the Election of 1828. He believed the Bank of the United States gave too much power over the American economy to private bankers. That became the main issue of the 1832 Election. Jackson won re-election while he fought with Nicholas Biddle, the country's first central banker. People called him 'Czar Nicholas.' Biddle made life very hard for small businesses and individuals by raising interest rates and controlling the money supply.

"But President Andrew Jackson won. He destroyed the US Bank and paid off the national debt. It's part of his unique legacy because he's the only president in the history of the United States to do it. It is kind of funny that even though Jackson always liked gold and *not* paper money, he still ended up on the American twenty-dollar bill.

"President Abraham Lincoln is famous for freeing the slaves during the End Days but he also fought back against powerful centralized banks. When international bankers wanted to give him loans at 24-36 percent interest to finance the American Civil War, Lincoln turned them down because he did not want to plunge his country into huge debt.

"Then he went straight to Congress about passing a law to authorize the printing of US Treasury Notes. After the law was passed Lincoln said, 'We gave the people of this Republic the greatest gift they ever had—their own paper money to pay their debts.' During his term, over 400 hundred million debt and interest-free 'Greenbacks' were printed. They were used to pay the soldiers and US government employees, and to purchase war supplies.

"But the international bankers hated this because they were very threatened by the United States staying a unified, free and prosperous country. If that happened it would stop their monopoly on money. The bankers wanted the American people to be indebted to them but thanks to Lincoln that didn't happen. No wonder Abraham Lincoln and Andrew Jackson were both marked men for assassins, just like the early Roman emperors. Jackson was lucky because his assassin failed. But Abraham Lincoln was killed. So were the Roman emperors who'd made money plentiful to their people. After Lincoln died, a new national banking law was passed and all currency became interest-bearing, debt instruments again."

Here the student finally paused for air, his gaze never leaving his teacher. "Sorry sir, I know I rambled on," he apologized.

"On the contrary Mr. Rothschild, you managed to condense a large period of history into an intelligent exam answer," Mr. Bauer assured him. Now, tell us about the role of these central bankers or *money controllers* in Salvation Time."

"Well sir, in Salvation Time the role of the banks is very limited. We still have banks but they are only allowed to operate as enterprises that help individuals get the capital they need to start their own businesses and prosper. And the Israelis under Prime Minister Eyal Grad's smart leadership created the successful Citizens Lottery System a few years before the Armageddon War in 2012. The CLS became the envy of the world and a prototype for other countries."

"Nicely done, Mr. Rothschild," the history instructor beamed. "Now for your bonus question, why is it necessary for you to restore an ancestor's name to honor? What role did he play in the End Days to force your family to relocate to Arusha?"

Like so many others before him, Rothschild hated having to field this family heritage question because he felt so much shame for what his ancestor had done. But graduation and a much-anticipated trip hinged upon passing the exam, so he took a deep breath and dove in.

"Sir, Nathan Rothschild was a German banker and financier in the 18th and 19th centuries. He was one of five sons of the second generation of the Rothschild banking dynasty. Like the money traders from Roman and Biblical times, The Bank of England, and The Bank of the United States, this family also controlled the money supply for their own power, ambition and greed. Rothschild first operated as a textile merchant in Manchester, England. In the year 1804 he began to deal financial instruments on the London stock exchange like foreign bills and government securities. In the year 1809, Rothschild began to deal in gold bullion and developed it as a cornerstone of his business. From 1811 on, in negotiations with Commissary-General John Charles Herries, he took on the job of transferring money to pay for Wellington's troops on campaign in Portugal and Spain against Napoleon.

"Nathan and his four brothers made money off of the war by funding Wellington's troops against Napoleon and after the war ended, to make subsidy payments to British allies. The family developed a network of agents, shippers and couriers to transport gold and information across Europe. This private intelligence allowed Nathan to receive in London news of Wellington's victory at the Battle of Waterloo a full day ahead of the government's official messengers.

"By the time he died in 1836, Nathan Rothschild had a net worth of 0.62% of the British national income. He'd also secured a Rothschild family dynasty as the most powerful investment bankers in Britain and Europe. But the family was very sneaky in the way they hid their power and influence. They only used the 'Rothschild' name on a few of their many businesses. They didn't want anyone to know how guilty they were of manipulating money, but they were just as guilty as the money traders that had gone before them centuries before. Nathan was the hot shot in the expansion of the Rothschild Empire. He ran the show and he didn't care about the damage it did to whole national economies or how much it hurt the everyday working man and woman. He saw nothing wrong with controlling the money supply and enslaving individuals financially."

Here the student stopped, awaiting his teacher's reaction.

"Thank you Mr. Rothschild, you've done extremely well," he announced as he began his calculations. Nathan watched as Mr. Bauer tapped and scrolled, hoping he'd achieved at least an '8' for his effort. His 19th century ancestor had caused his family enough shame and guilt; it was time to restore the name Rothschild to decency and honor.

"Congratulations sir, you have earned a '9' today. You make retake your seat."

"Thank you sir!" Rothschild exclaimed, overwhelmed by the satisfaction of knowing he'd taken a huge step today toward his goal.

"Alright class, we're down to only six more students," the history teacher noted. "Let's see, who should we hear from next?" His dark eyes took inventory of the classroom until they fell upon what could only be described as his most unique student, a transvestite cross-dresser when not required to wear the school uniform. Wearing round, wire-rimmed glasses held up by a long, pointed nose, the student met his teacher's gaze with a trace of dread though eager to get his testing over with. He scratched his barely protruding whiskers as he smiled at Mr. Bauer.

"Ah Mr. Spielberg! At last it's your turn to share your knowledge with class. Please stand to take your exam."

Spielberg lifted his five-foot, eight-inch frame out of his seat and stood at attention, a silly grin displayed on his face mainly due to nerves. The teacher understood, having known this student long enough to comprehend that what many adults viewed as surliness was actually self-consciousness mixed with embarrassment carried over several familial generations.

"Yes, sir," the student replied respectfully.

"I have a total of three questions for you today in addition to your bonus question Mr. Spielberg, the answers to which will show up on the electronic board here at the front of the classroom."

Mr. Bauer gestured toward the large LCD screen mounted on the wall, directing the entire class to place their focus upon it while listening to his responses.

"First, tell us Mr. Spielberg, what was the role of the filmmaking industry as controlled by Hollywood in the United States during the End Days, compared to its current role now in Salvation Days?"

"Well sir, like Henry Kissinger said, during the End Days there was really no difference between Hollywood celebrities and politicians. Both groups were ruled by the self-directed big ego. They piled up obscene amounts of money while they kept people in the dark about what was really going on in the world. Joseph Stalin told us about his ancestor who made propaganda films to trick Russian peasants into believing he was leading them into a new dawn of prosperity when it was really the opposite. He was using cinema like a weapon against them in his quest for domination.

"During the 20th century Joseph Stalin said, 'America is like a healthy body and its resistance is threefold: its patriotism, its morality, and its spiritual life. If we can undermine these three areas, America will collapse from within.' Making movies was one of the best ways to do it because you could embed the indoctrination in entertainment. And people wouldn't even know what was happening. Back in the 1930s when Ronald Reagan was an actor he saw what was going on and he started to fight back against the communist takeover of Hollywood. In the 1950s Senator Joseph McCarthy investigated and found evidence of communist infiltration within the United States government. Some saw Reagan and McCarthy as patriots but many saw them as crazy conspiracy nuts."

The student paused for a moment before picking up on his teacher's nonverbal cue to continue.

"But now in Salvation Time the filmmaking industry promotes our worldwide system of positive capitalism. Instead of turning people who do bad things into 'anti-heroes' or victims of an 'unfair' system, it tells stories of everyday people who do good things for others through their service. It produces films that inspire, educate and uplift because Salvation Time cinema wants audiences to be inspired to do these things in the real world. The goal is to encourage them to imitate the examples of ordinary heroism and honor they see on the big screen.

"Instead of covering up truth and promoting excessive immorality, those who work in the film industry now make a good living by producing virtuous movies that people really want to see. And it's ok to make films that portray a positive image of God and those who worship him. During the End Days, most believers were portrayed as crazy.

"So in Salvation Time, creating cinema is all about doing the right thing even though it's tough. It's courage over fear, service over self-centeredness."

The student again paused for a reaction from his satisfied teacher who complimented, "Very well put Mr. Spielberg. Now for the next question, what human characteristics inspired movie production during the End Days?"

"Sir, during the End Days film production glorified the worst characteristics and behaviors of human beings. In order they were: fear, hate, ignorance, backstabbing, jealousy, lying, greed, violence, laziness, stinginess, hypocrisy, vulgarity, cowardice and whining. So the plots, themes and characters in films made during the End Days focused on all of these negative emotions and traits."

As the student articulated his answers, each one appeared in a column on the electronic board, under the heading *End Days*, in order to emphasize the importance of this lesson for the entire class.

"I see, Mr. Spielberg," the teacher agreed. "Now, tell us what human characteristics inspire movie production in Salvation Days."

Spielberg smiled as he began his answer, noting the column on the right side of the electronic board where each of his answers to this question would appear as he spoke them aloud, this time under the heading of *Salvation Days*.

"In Salvation Days film production is driven by good human characteristics and behaviors in this specific order: generosity, loyalty, peacefulness, positive courage, positive ambition, approachability, awareness and sensitivity for others, lifestyle balance, bravery, calculated and intelligent risk-taking, compassion, simplicity, honesty, honor, good work ethic and love for all."

"What else is different about films today, Mr. Spielberg?"

"Sir, one thing I love the most about living in Salvation Time is that we reward the people who do the hard work. When we're talking about films, the people who work the hardest and take the most risk are the crew members and investors who finance the entire production. Really, it's thanks to the investors that film crews even have a job. So in Salvation Time when movie credits roll, the first names you see belong to the investors who put millions of their own money into the project.

"Next you see the names of the film crew—people like casting directors, make-up artists, stunt doubles, boom operators, camera operators, script writers, electricians, carpenters and so on. These are the real creators. And their names and pictures stay on the screen for a minimum of two minutes so that everyone knows who they are.

"Yes, it takes actors to complete a film but they owe their success to everyone else involved in the technical and financial side of things. During the End Days, the actors alone got all the glory and money. At the Oscars, the awards would start with the production people and lead up to the grand finale of honoring the best actors and actresses as if they were the most important. All of the anticipation used to lead up to which actors would win the Oscar. In Salvation Time, awards ceremonies begin with the actors and lead up to the production crew and financers. It's very different now because of all the individuals involved in film production, actors now make the *least* amount of money and get the *least* amount of credit. What a change-up; I love it!"

"Excellent, Mr. Spielberg, I am so glad you feel that way!" Mr. Bauer chuckled. He loved Spielberg's enthusiasm and energy. "Now for your bonus question, what was your ancestor's role in all of the Hollywood propaganda during the End Days?"

Spielberg transitioned from euphoria to disappointment because he knew his grade hinged upon total honesty in telling the story of his shameful ancestor. This guy had been one of the most fêted men in Hollywood who'd amassed a fortune by promoting lies and hiding the truth in his well-received films. Still, the student was aware that coming clean was the best way to aid in the process of restoring the Spielberg family name so he set about making his confession in front of his teachers and classmates.

"Sir, my ancestor Steven Spielberg was one of the most successful, adored and wealthiest filmmakers in Hollywood during the End Days, even though his movies were filled with propaganda and lies. Take his popular film *Schindler's List*. Spielberg insisted that the movie be filmed in black and white so he could whitewash evil. He didn't want to 'offend' anyone by accurately portraying Nazi crimes against the innocent. Considering that Spielberg was also a Jew, this was even more disgusting. But his main motivation was money. He didn't want to risk losing a fat paycheck for honestly telling the story of Jewish oppression by socialist Nazis who blindly obeyed a madman.

"So that's why my family was expedited to Arusha after the Armageddon Commission—to begin to make up for the sins of our ancestor Steven Spielberg, a man who valued money and fame over truth. He makes me very ashamed."

Mr. Bauer looked at his student with respect and pride. He knew this boy had all sorts of challenges in this life not simply because of his family ancestry but also because of his uncontrollable desire to cross-dress. Naturally, the other students teased him unmercifully for his weakness when they were outside of the classroom—the only place Mr. Bauer could impose strict discipline. The history instructor was thrilled to be able to give Spielberg a high mark based on his excellent answer.

While he watched the teacher conduct his grade calculation, Spielberg nervously pushed his wire-rimmed glasses—which had a tendency to slide down—back up toward the bridge of his nose, resisting the urge to run his hand through his wiry, black hair.

A moment later Mr. Bauer raised his head and announced, "Congratulations Mr. Spielberg, you have earned a '9' on today's exam. You may take your seat sir."

"Thank you sir," the thoroughly relieved student replied. As he sat down, he imagined how proud his parents would be once they received Mr. Bauer's email. Dinner at home tonight would be filled with happy conversation about Spielberg's future and his own ambition to become a sought-after filmmaker in Salvation Time, one whose films would tell the truth, unlike the ones produced by his ancestor long ago.

Mr. Bauer glanced at his watch, noting he had just about enough time left to test the final five students. He proceeded immediately to the next one.

"Mr. Chirac, sir, please stand up to take your exam," the teacher instructed a tall boy with a very high forehead and droopy, dimpled cheeks. As he stood at attention, the student looked stately, statuesque and dignified, his uniform neatly pressed, his thin lips forming a slight trace of a smile on his dark-skinned face. Yet he suffered from a chronic case of jock itch, which seemed to flare up when under extreme pressure as was the case at that very moment. Unable to resist the urge to scratch his balls, Chirac gave in, prompting the ire of his teacher.

"I am ready sir," he replied.

"Mr. Chirac, what have I told you about touching yourself inappropriately in front of the class?" the teacher sternly inquired.

"Ah oui, please forgive me sir but I just had to scratch my balls as the itching was driving me *craz-ee!*"

While the entire class erupted in uproarious laughter, Mr. Bauer resisted his own urge to laugh out loud, understanding the realities of life in a physical body for members of the male species. After silencing the class with a firm, no-nonsense look and a hand gesture he quickly decided to let the matter drop and move on to the questioning.

"Alright then Mr. Chirac, tell us about the prevailing attitude toward evil during the End Days versus Salvation Days."

"Ah *oui*, sir," Chirac began, "back in the End Days powerful people enabled evil for their own gain. These people clung to moral equivalence. They refused to call evil out because they didn't want to be labeled 'racist' or 'intolerant.' Yet during the End Days the evildoers who committed atrocities like the September 11 terrorist attacks always bragged about it. They loved to take credit for their actions because they were very proud to cause suffering and death in the name of Allah and their 72 virgins.

"But western civilization liked to appease evil. It refused to learn the lessons of history that appeasement of evil only breeds more evil. Neville Chamberlain was an appeaser of evil. He took Adolf Hitler at his word and declared 'peace in our time' in the year 1938. Chamberlain had stupidly signed a nonaggression pact with Germany where Hitler promised he'd never go to war with Britain again. But as history proves, Hitler was just lying and playing games with a man who was too naive to be a world leader.

"In Salvation Time, we do not appease evil and we do not enable it. It's all about doing the right thing even though it's not always easy. We have a council of volunteers called the Moral Branch. This Moral Branch keeps politicians in check. It works hard to make sure they do the right thing and that their power is very limited. In Salvation Time we only have politicians around to keep things running smoothly."

Here Chirac ended his oration, awaiting the second part of the test. Mr. Bauer nodded, then asked, "Mr. Chirac why are you here in Salvation Time to restore an ancestor's name to goodness?"

"Well sir," the student began, "my ancestor Jacques Chirac was also an enabler of evil back in the End Days. He was the French President when Muslims attacked the US on September 11 and instead of doing the right thing by supporting his ally, he spoke out against using force to protect western civilization. And in his country of France, Muslims who had moved there from their own countries to become French citizens were allowed to terrorize non-Muslims for Allah without punishment. Chirac's government didn't do anything when these Muslims refused to obey French laws—the laws of the new country they'd chosen to migrate to in the first place. And because native French citizens weren't reproducing much while the Muslims were having lots of babies, the whole French culture was in danger of disappearing.

"The French people began to understand what was happening to their land and they spoke out against it, but their corrupt leaders like President Jacques Chirac didn't care. These losers running France wouldn't listen to their own citizens, the same people who elected them to run their country. This was when the French people's attitudes toward everyday Americans started to change. Up until then they had looked down upon Americans even though tens of thousands of American soldiers had been buried in French graves all around the country after they fought and died to save them from the Nazis.

"But thanks to my ancestor the French people woke up and knew they had to stand together with the Americans against evil. Yet this was not new in French history. At different periods during the End Days, the French people had become aware of the evils of their political class. It was never the ordinary French citizen but his corrupt politicians who always aided and abetted evil. Like the Vichy Regime during World War II under the control of Marshal Philippe Pétain who collaborated with German occupying forces in exchange for an agreement not to divide France between the Axis Powers.

"There was also French political corruption in the 19th century with its monarchy. The French Crown controlled ordinary French people the same way the British Monarchy controlled its subjects."

Here Mr. Bauer stepped in as he'd done previously with other students. "Mr. Chirac, what are some of the positive contributions these everyday French citizens made to their society and the world, in spite of their corrupt leaders?"

"Well I first want to mention sir, when the French Revolution began in 1789 it inspired a movement toward democracy in Europe. That same year General George Washington was inaugurated as the first President of the United States after the American colonies defeated the British. Americans could not have won the right to self-govern if not for the French, including General Lafayette. He served as a major-general in the Continental Army under General Washington. So the French people played a huge role in the creation of the United States by helping its founders win the war against the world's greatest army at the time.

"Everything good that came out of France during the End Days came from its individual citizens—things like French wine, cheese, art, perfume and architecture. Everything bad that came out of France came from its ruling political class.

"My arrogant ancestor Jacques Chirac always had politician's attitude of superiority about Americans and he looked down on the American President George W. Bush as a war-mongering cowboy. Instead of working with him to present a united front against a common enemy—Islam—Chirac enabled evil. I am here to restore the name to honor and integrity."

From his seat in the classroom, George W. Bush looked on with some amusement. Chirac stole a glance in his direction, embarrassed by the admission even though his classmate didn't seem bothered by it in the least.

Mr. Bauer then congratulated Chirac on earning an '8' and advised him to sit down before the boy felt the urge to scratch himself again in front of his classmates. Chirac quickly took his seat, relieved it was finally over. Now it was time for Mr. Bauer to move on to his next student, a round-faced girl with chipmunk cheeks and shoulder-length hair that had obviously been straightened with a flat-iron. This student hated having to wear a skirt as part of her uniform because unlike most of the other girls in her class she had unattractive legs and as a result, much preferred pant-suits. But rules were rules so she had no choice but to obey while in school; once out in the working world, she swore she'd always wear pants and jackets.

"Ah Miss Hillary Rodham! We've come to your portion of the exam at last. Please stand up."

"Yes sir," the girl replied, jumping out of her chair in a fit of nerves.

"Tell us about the state of education in the final decades of the End Times compared with education in Salvation Time," the teacher requested.

"Sir in the End Days, especially in the United States, the public education system was controlled by powerful teachers' unions and a massive centralized government. This government had created an unconstitutional Department of Education under President Jimmy Carter."

"If I may Miss Rodham, why was the Department of Education unconstitutional?"

"Because sir, the Tenth Amendment in the US Constitution gave each state the right to manage their own business; education was part of that. The Founders never wanted the states to be centrally controlled by the federal government."

"I see, Miss Rodham. You may continue. Tell us what happened after President Carter established the Department of Education."

"Well sir, teachers unions took advantage of the government-controlled educational curriculum for their own self-serving ends. They used taxpayer money to fund gigantic pensions for bureaucrats, conduct social engineering experiments against the moral teachings of parents, and create generations of dependency on government. By teaching children revisionist history, like their country was founded by 'racist old white men,' government-run schools instilled deep shame and hostility for the United States. Really, American students should have been taught to respect their nation's founders. Sure they weren't perfect, but they did do something pretty amazing—they created a limited government system where individuals had control over their own destinies. They knew individual rights come from God and that for men and women to be truly free, government power had to be kept in check.

"Just like Hollywood public education spread propaganda to make students believe they needed a big government to tell them how to live and what to do. They did this on purpose to make kids believe that without *Big Brother* they were helpless. It was all just a lie to keep them dependent instead of self-reliant. In American public schools God was taken away and prayer was forbidden because the corrupt political class didn't want students to know that the foundation of America's Constitution came from Judeo-Christian principles.

"To professional politicians a country of informed, self-sufficient, self-reliant and self-motivated citizens who didn't need or want a big, meddling government was a serious threat to their power. That's why they taught students that they were 'victims' of an 'unjust' society created by America's Founders. This worked especially well with non-white students. They were easy targets for victimhood because of the United States' unfortunate period of slavery. That ended in 1865 after the Civil War.

"In the final centuries of the End Days, public schools used propaganda like the global warming hoax to pit kids against their parents. These public schools destroyed parental moral authority. They taught little kids about sex—including homosexuality and gay marriage—whether their parents liked it or not.

"And if an honest teacher felt it best to hold a student back because of poor grades and lack of knowledge, they were punished. The kid would be 'socially promoted' to the next grade even if repeating a grade was best for him because they didn't want to 'hurt' anyone's feelings. But public schools were not doing these kids any favors. Repeating a grade would have been good for them but those in power didn't care. It was all about the agenda. This was the same reason why so many politicians fought against school vouchers even though the voucher program had been very successful everywhere it had been used."

Mr. Bauer interrupted again. "And what were these vouchers, Miss Rodham?"

"Sir, vouchers made it possible for poor kids stuck in lousy schools to get a good education at higher quality schools. Yet the same politicians who pretended to care about the poor fought hard against them. And even though home-schooled children did so much better academically and personally than their public school peers, the government also tried to ban parents from home-schooling because they feared losing power over the people.

"That's also why a program called Common Core was forced upon parents and school children just before Armageddon. Major corporations and politicians joined together to mandate this terrible curriculum in the public schools, all for their own self-interest and profit. Most parents and teachers quickly saw through it and fought back against this attempt to indoctrinate and dumb-down their kids. The fierce resistance to Common Core was ongoing right up until the G20 terrorist attacks.

"In Salvation Days, all of this has changed. We educate children to become independent thinkers, financially secure adults and morally upstanding people who want to help others become the best that they can be. And we give them all the tools they need. We prepare them for the real world like when we take them to open up a bank account as soon as they turn 12 so they can learn how to manage and save money.

"These days it's all about the practical application of knowledge at school and at home. Kids don't just get an allowance from their parents—they have to earn it. They must do something useful for the money like mowing the lawn, doing the laundry and cleaning the house. We teach them the value of a good work ethic when they're little. During the End Days this work ethic had also been a huge part of raising kids. That is, until government-run schools set out to create a nation of dependents. The country had gone from Ralph Waldo Emerson's *Self-Reliance* philosophy to an entitlement mentality.

"In Salvation Time we also teach kids good money-management skills; by the time they turn 17, they're competing with each other over who has the most money in their bank accounts. This competition isn't driven by ego but respect. Students with higher account balances have earned their peers' respect because they have shown financial discipline and intelligence. They become role-models for other kids.

"Our schools also teach practical trades like auto maintenance and repair, electrical installation, plumbing, sewing, and cooking—everything they need to know to become independent and be of service to others in the 'real world.' And unlike the End Days, in Salvation Time it's not a 'right' for every kid to go to college. Instead, they discover their educational future when they become teenagers. That's when they must take the Life Purpose Class. The LPC helps them figure out why they want to do certain things with their lives.

"For kids who have the desire and skills to go into a profession where they need a higher degree like a medical doctor, we encourage them to work hard to achieve their goals—as long as they're motivated by a real interest in serving and not just making money."

Again Mr. Bauer stepped in. "Miss Rodham, how is it possible to determine their real motives?"

"Sir, the LPC confirms whether or not their motives are noble and pure. And once we know that for sure, we use a system like the one the Israelis used under Prime Minister Eyal Grad to help these students get the education they need to reach their goals—without going into thousands of dollars of debt.

"Let's say they want to go into medicine after they take the LPC. These kids are sponsored by their government when they turn 16 to go through military service with the goal of earning a medical degree. By the time they're 18 they join the army with two years of medical classes under their belt. Once they complete their military service, they finish their schooling and become accredited doctors with medical degrees. In return for the government paying for their education, they must spend five years in a government hospital, where they treat patients in their field of specialty.

"But they also get so much more. Once they are *practicing* medical doctors they get all kinds of special perks like discounts on food, restaurants, movies, theme parks, concerts, festivals and cultural events. To inspire them to always give their very best to their patients, colleagues and hospital each week on a Sunday afternoon a show called *The Good and Bad Hour* features a selected doctor in the prestigious *Best Doctor of the Week* segment. The doctors profiled are voted on by their patients and peers who use social media and email to cast their vote each week. That means that every doctor featured in this segment earned it. They're NOT there because they paid for the honor. In Salvation Time, that's considered a bribe and any doctor who tries it could lose their license. Besides, the truest measure of success is in the voting results; any doctor who wins a featured spotlight on the *Best Doctor of the Week* news segment is always in demand."

Here Hillary paused and waited for feedback, suppressing a strong urge to let out a loud, obnoxious cackle.

"Nicely done, Miss Rodham. Is there any other medical innovation you'd like to share with the class that we've not yet discussed? Perhaps something else pioneered by Israeli Prime Minister Eyal Grad just before Armageddon?"

"Oh yes, sir, thank you for reminding me," she answered, grateful for the not-so-subtle hint.

"In Salvation Time we also have *Robo-Docs*. These are electronic booths located in every neighborhood, usually in a shopping center or mall. So if you're dealing with a medical problem like insomnia or chronic migraines you can visit a Robo-Doc, sit in front of the computer screen and tell it your ailment. It will then ask you to place your hand on the screen so it can check your vital signs. This computer is connected to a huge network so it can make a diagnosis based on the person's unique make-up and medical history. If it figures out you need to go to a 24-hour clinic, it will advise you to do that. If it decides the problem can be solved with a certain therapy or medicine, it will tell you exactly what you need to do. These Robo-Docs cut down on the need for so many human doctors and makes medicine inexpensive and accessible for everyone."

"Excellent, Miss Rodham. Now please tell us about your ancestor's role in perpetuating the deeply flawed system of public education that existed during the End Days and what you are doing to restore her name in Salvation Time."

"Well sir, my ancestor Hillary Rodham Clinton promoted the myth of a benevolent big government. Her political campaigns took in lots of cash from taxpayer-funded teachers' unions that didn't care about quality education for children or the best interests of their teachers. Hillary Rodham Clinton's book, *It Takes a Village* was a tribute to government indoctrination, a propaganda tool to get citizens to buy into even more centralized control. Hillary was addicted to the power that came from elected office. She also loved the power and prestige that came with her appointment as Secretary of State by President Barack Hussein Obama—the famous *Food Stamps President*.

"Like her husband, she had an amazing talent for avoiding accountability for anything bad that happened under her watch."

"Can you give us an example of this, Miss Rodham?"

The student winced, knowing she had to be honest but dreading the answer she knew she had to give. She took a deep gulp of air and continued.

"Sir, the worst thing that happened under Hillary's watch was when she was Secretary of State. On September 11, 2012 four Americans were slaughtered after an eight-hours-long embassy attack in Benghazi. It took months after that for anyone in D.C. to even make her testify and when she finally did, all she could say was, *'What difference does it make?'* when some senators pressured her to give them a timeline of events leading to the murders. It's true that enough Americans pressured the White House to force her resignation a few weeks later and appoint former Alaskan Governor Sarah Palin. But even after she resigned, people began talking up Hillary Rodham Clinton's presidential run in 2016. Unbelievable!"

The student's tone was incredulous. She was utterly ashamed of her End Days ancestor and completely stunned by the Americans who kept supporting her no matter what she did.

"Anyway," she sighed, "I am working to restore the name of Hillary Rodham Clinton to goodness in part by writing my own book *It Takes an Individual to Help a Village*. It's all about the power of each individual to make positive, lasting contributions to others and society."

"Very impressive Miss Rodham," the teacher complimented. "I commend you for writing a book and I look forward to reading it when it's done."

"Thank you, sir," she replied, obviously pleased. While Mr. Bauer engaged in the task of grade calculation a nearby student snickered, his bulbous nose twitching. He felt an overwhelming desire to wag his finger at Hillary and chide her for being rigid, cold and unfeeling, though he'd hardly spent enough time around her to even know if that was the case.

Bill Clinton was far too busy chasing after the easy, pretty girls in the school much like his classmate Joseph Stalin, with whom he competed for the honor of screwing Eva Braun the most.

With his bedding of Eva the night before, Stalin had taken the lead. And despite her promise to her teacher this morning to start honoring and respecting her body, neither boy believed she was up to the task. Eva was much too susceptible to her own animal nature. There was no doubt in either one's mind that they'd each have a chance to spend some *quality time* with Eva Braun more than once during their trip around the world.

As he sat in his chair, Clinton also fantasized about having his way with at least one new girl in every country on their itinerary. Although forbidden to smoke in school he also had a penchant for imported Perdoma cigars, which he often indulged in during his free period on those occasions when he'd been able to sneak them in.

"Congratulations Miss Rodham, you have earned a '9' on today's exam," Mr. Bauer announced. You may take your seat."

"Thank you sir!" Hillary shot a smug look in Bill's direction, picking up on his thoughts telepathically. She knew if not for cheating off of her homework and class notes, there's no way he would've even made it past the second grade. God knew when it came to controlling his sexual impulses, the boy had zero restraint. One thing was certain: Hillary would *never, ever* become one of his conquests. Not that he would even bother.

Besides, she'd been harboring romantic feelings for fellow classmate Debbie Wasserman-Schultz for over a year now, feelings she hadn't yet found the nerve to act upon. Hopefully during their trip she would gather the courage to confess her love. Could Debbie possibly feel the same for her? Hillary wasn't yet sure, but she was determined to find out.

Noting their non-verbal interaction, Mr. Bauer quickly ascertained who his next "defendant" would be.

"Mr. Clinton, please stand sir and share your knowledge with us."

A six-foot, two-inch Bill Clinton arose from his chair with an aura of arrogance and conceit that did not go unnoticed.

"Yes sir," he replied.

"Please wipe the smirk off your face sir and tell us about the attitude toward sex in the End Days versus the attitude about sex in Salvation Days," Mr. Bauer requested.

"My apologies, sir," Bill Clinton began, using the most remorseful tone he could muster. "Ah sex in the End Days…let's see." His raspy voice trailed off as he considered the question.

"Well sir, I'd have to say that in the End Days sex was used as a weapon, a way to hold power over other people. You see during the End Days the animal urges of human beings had control over the soulful part of them. There were lots of humans who balanced their biology with their spirituality back then, but they were outnumbered by people who just couldn't. For them sex was like a drug. It was also abused by powerful people to control and influence others, and to make even more money.

"During the Sexual Revolution in the 1960s, people rejected traditional values. Called *Baby Boomers*, this selfish generation defied their parents who were known as *The Greatest Generation* because of their service and bravery during World War II.

"Baby Boomers were a spoiled bunch. Because their parents had lived through the horror of war they were way too permissive with their children. The Baby Boomers grew up to believe they had a right to do, say, and have whatever they wanted, whenever they wanted, no matter the consequences. They let their natural animal urges win out over the spiritual side of their humanity. Women in the 1960s started to believe that being 'liberated' meant being treated like a piece of meat. So they imitated immoral men who just had sex for its own sake, for their own selfish desires, with no commitment."

Mr. Bauer stopped the student to pose another question. "So Mr. Clinton, did this behavior have negative long-term consequences?"

"Ah yes sir, it sure did," he replied. "By the time the new millennium rolled around it had created a society of broken homes, divorced parents, sexually transmitted diseases and all kinds of emotional problems. Thanks to the *free love* movement—"

"What do you mean *free love* Mr. Clinton?" The teacher sternly looked around the room to put an end to the adolescent snickering over this salacious topic. It wasn't easy talking about sex with a roomful of   teenagers even if they were living in Salvation Time now.

"Well sir, it was called free love but it was really about casual sex. *Sex without commitment.* This attitude caused a lot of problems in the last few decades of the End Days because it killed the idea of working at a marriage for better or for worse, and keeping your marriage vows. Kids were being raised in single-parent homes, there were lots of dysfunctional people walking around, and anyone who valued traditional dating and the idea of avoiding sex until marriage was mocked by their peers and pop culture. Jacques Chirac talked about the French reproduction rate but it wasn't just a problem in France. All over western civilization, reproduction rates dropped. The term 'hook-up' was popular around this time too. It described casual sexual interactions that took place among strangers and even middle school students who were not emotionally ready to deal with the consequences.

"The victory of the animal nature of man over the spiritual nature of man caused serious problems. Instead of viewing every individual as made in the image and likeness of the One Creator—a soul having a human experience—society became very superficial. It became obsessed with youth, physical beauty and sex. Plastic surgery became a drug—and not just for rich people. Everyday working people who were afraid of growing old went under the knife too because everyone wanted to be young and *hot*.

"But who could blame them?" Clinton's gravelly voice asked hypothetically. "During the End Days, if you were a pretty woman with large breasts, a tiny waist, shapely legs and a tight butt, you were in demand. A healthy man would notice this kind of woman on the street, whether he was married or not. If the man was capable of controlling his normal sexual urges, at best he'd whistle or flirt with her and move on. But at worst, he'd approach her for sex, whether or not he was breaking his marriage vows. And most beautiful women were just as immoral as the men in those days. And if the man had money, forget about it! This kind of woman had no problem hitting the sheets with him, even if he'd already committed himself to another woman through marriage or engagement.

"This impossible goal of physical perfection drove men and women to spend millions on breast and penis implants, tummy tucks, liposuction, face-lifts and all sorts of surgical procedures. In the End Days most human beings forgot all about spirituality and their own soul's eternal nature because of a cultural obsession with physical looks.

"Hillary mentioned public schools. Well they were also guilty because they gave out condoms like candy and helped kids get abortions behind their parents' backs. A huge centralized government used taxpayers' money to pay for things like birth control and abortion, even if it went against their religious beliefs. For all of their crying about government 'staying out of the bedroom' feminists and politicians liked having the government *in the bedroom* to force taxpayers to fund private citizens' sexual activities. So uh, yeah, sex was definitely used as a weapon during the End Days.

"But in Salvation Time, human beings are much more soul-driven and in control of their animal nature. If a man sees a pretty woman on the street he doesn't stare, flirt or try to lure her into bed, and in return, he gets the satisfaction of knowing he's done the right thing. Parents and schools work together to teach kids about sex only when they are old enough. These lessons include respecting themselves and each other. Adults have conversations about sex with their kids teaching them that it's a sacred gift from the One Creator as an expression of love between two married people, and a way to keep the population growing. Personal responsibility is a big deal in Salvation Time so parents and teachers talk about why adults should pay for their own birth control. They also discuss how mature adults would cope with a pregnancy if that birth control fails, because nothing is 100 percent guaranteed—except abstinence. The belief here in Salvation Time is that if you are old enough to have sex, you are old enough to deal with the consequences.

"And as other students said, politicians in Salvation Time are clerical workers who don't have any of the End Days trappings of power and prestige, so sex isn't used anymore as a weapon for political favors. For single people who can't survive without sex, there's a place called 'Sin City' where they can screw a prostitute as much as they want without hurting anyone else.

"Sin Cities are in every community in Salvation Time because we understand that human beings are imperfect; there will always be people who just cannot control their sexual urges. These men and women need a place where they can get off in a safe, clean and private environment. That's why every Sin City is far away from family neighborhoods, yet easy to get to. To cut down on STDs, prostitutes who work in Sin City must see a doctor every week, use protection every time, and have good personal hygiene."

Here Clinton paused and turned to look at his classmate in the far-left corner of the room. "So Mao, you might want to keep that in mind if you ever want to get any," he informed him. With that, the whole class broke out in uncontrollable laughter while poor, mortified Mao's black face nearly turned beet-red.

"Mr. Clinton!" The teacher's stern tone signified he was clearly not amused. He ordered the student to apologize immediately and warned the class to get back to order at once.

"I am sorry Mao," Clinton offered sheepishly, struggling to catch his breath. Mao just continued to sit quietly at his desk with his eyes cast down. It had been an embarrassing day for him and he couldn't wait to go home now that he'd passed the exam.

"Mr. Clinton, please finish up your answer sir before I consider failing you for your rudeness toward your classmate." Realizing the threat was credible Clinton bit his lip before continuing.

"Yes, sir. The prostitutes in Salvation Time run their legal businesses independently—unlike in the End Days when they were controlled by ruthless pimps who would beat them up and murder them. Because we know now that as long as we're souls living in a body, we're going to experience the normal, natural urges that come with being a sexually healthy human being. In Salvation Time, we've made accommodations for that."

There was a noticeable enthusiasm in Clinton's voice as he spoke, notwithstanding Mr. Bauer's reprimand; everyone could easily tell that this was a topic he loved to opine about. The teacher however, understood that Bill Clinton's obvious love of carnal pleasure ran deep through countless generations of his family and as such, the boy couldn't help but be enthused and excited when discussing it. Sex was after all, a major motivating factor for the Clintons' arrival in Arusha after the Armageddon War.

"Ok Mr. Clinton for your bonus question, what did your ancestor have to do with using sex as a weapon during the End Days?"

"Sir, my ancestor William Jefferson Clinton was a famous womanizer, adulterer and rapist. He got away with his many crimes against women with the help of the media and the women's movement at the time, which was all about a big-government agenda, not truly the rights of women. Because he was a Democrat in the late-20th century, Bill Clinton was never made to pay for his sins and crimes. Instead of telling the truth the political class, media, and pop culture attacked Bill's victims as liars and denied them their day in court. Women like Paula Jones, Juanita Broaddrick and Gennifer Flowers never got justice.

"Then there's the cigar, the blue dress and the Oval Office in the White House. My ancestor had sex there with a woman young enough to be his daughter. He took advantage of Monica Lewinsky because she was no match for Clinton's charm and power. When the embarrassing details came out about how he put a cigar into Lewinsky's pussy—"

"Mr. Clinton!" Once again, Mr. Bauer expressed his disgust, this time over his student's use of the crude, popular End Days term for a woman's sexual organ. "What have I told you about showing proper respect?"

"Sorry sir," he apologized. "Uh, he put a cigar into her vagina and then back into his own mouth only to have a camera catch him spitting out some of her pubic hairs and—well, let's just say ol' Bill not only made a laughing stock of the United States Presidency, he also humiliated his wife and daughter.

"Even though Presidents before him like Ronald Reagan had so much reverence for the Oval Office that they wouldn't even take off their jackets in the room, Bill Clinton had no problem dropping his shorts, getting a blow job and finding creative sexual uses for Perdoma cigars with an underage intern when he should have been doing the people's business.

"While he was preoccupied with sex, his administration dropped the ball—so to speak—on the threat of Islamic terrorism after the first World Trade Center bombing in 1993. Instead of treating it as an act of war, Clinton let his Deputy Attorney General Jamie Gorelick build walls between law enforcement agencies like the CIA and FBI to forbid them from talking to each other about possible threats to the country. Under Clinton's eight-year administration, the United States kept appeasing evil in spite of even more attacks by radical Muslims—like the one on the USS Cole in the year 2000, which killed 17 American sailors and badly injured 39 others.

"Then less than a year later, in the first term of the next President George W. Bush, Islamists completed the worst attack on American soil on September 11, 2001. Unlike Pearl Harbor, this attack targeted innocent civilians in their workplaces and on passenger airplanes, and not just a military installation. They also slammed a passenger plane into the Pentagon because it was the symbol of American military power.

"Many blamed George W. Bush for the attack. He deserves *some* blame but as the banned ABC network documentary *The Path To 9/11* proved, my ancestor William Jefferson Clinton deserves most of it. Deep down, Clinton knew this too but because his ego was so big he forced ABC to edit the film and used his power to stop them from ever showing it again on television after its one and only airing in 2006. Clinton intimidated ABC into refusing to sell the film as a DVD so people could buy it. Sex and power were the two driving forces in my ancestor's shameful life, and in spite of his many sins, he became an obscenely wealthy man traveling the world and speaking to adoring crowds. The "D" for Democrat after his name insulated him from all responsibility.

"In short Mr. Bauer, I have much to atone for here in Salvation Time."

"You have done very well for yourself today," the teacher assured him as he began the process of grade calculation on his hand-held computer. Clinton's bulbous nose twitched with anxiety as he awaited Mr. Bauer's verdict.

"Congratulations Mr. Clinton, you have earned a '9' on today's exam. You may sit down, sir." The student George W. Bush, who'd watched the interaction with his usual amusement whenever his ancestor was named, gave Clinton a wink and gestured a hearty *thumbs-up*.

Bill's black cheeks turned a bit crimson as he offered a slight hand wave of acknowledgment in Bush's direction before sitting down. But before Mr. Bauer could move onto the next student, Clinton quickly stood up again.

"Uh Mr. Bauer sir?"

"*Yes* Mr. Clinton?"

"Uh sir, may I say something to George W. Bush? It's about the End Times and our ancestors."

"Make it prompt, sir." The teacher motioned at a surprised George W. Bush to stand up and face his classmate Bill Clinton.

"I uh, just wanted to apologize to you on behalf of the Clinton family for uh, well first for my ancestor Bill Clinton removing all the W's from the White House keyboards and stealing the china and silverware before your ancestor moved in on his Inauguration Day. That was…uh…well that was really lousy. But not nearly as awful as letting you take the brunt of the blame for 9/11. So we're really sorry, W," Clinton finished sheepishly.

"Ah, apology accepted!" George W. Bush replied excitedly in his thick Texas drawl. It felt good to be absolved on some level for the atrocities of the past. The two students smiled at each other from across the room.

"Was there anything else, Mr. Clinton?" Mr. Bauer asked in a slightly amused tone.

"Ah no sir, I'm done, thank you," the student replied, settling back into his chair.

"Very well then," the teacher continued, "we are down to our last two students." As he moved from his spot near the window toward the center-front of the classroom, portable computer in hand, the two remaining untested students watched him with trepidation. In the next moment, the teacher looked up and set his eyes upon a 17 year-old male with intense black eyes and bushy black hair. A slight trace of a developing goatee and mustache was evident on his young face.

"Mr. Manson, it is your turn to stand for your exam question," Mr. Bauer informed him. "Please get up so you can impress the class with your knowledge of the prison system during the End Times versus the prison system in Salvation Time."

Understanding his student's family history and his diligence in researching the topic, Mr. Bauer knew there was no one in his class more qualified to address this topic than Charles Manson. He eagerly awaited the student's answer to the question.

From his seat, Mahmoud Ahmadinejad watched with satisfaction as the only boy in the class as short as he got up and stood at attention. Manson propped up his diminutive, five-foot, two-inch frame as best he could, hands at his sides, deliberately holding his narrow shoulders back in an attempt to retain good posture throughout the test.

"Yes sir, Mr. Bauer," he responded. His voice was deep and gravelly with a slight trace of a *hillbilly* West Virginia accent that had also reincarnated through several generations. As he stared at his teacher, his wild eyes nearly threw the normally unflappable Mr. Bauer off of his game. Though a bit unsettled internally, the history instructor nevertheless presented an aura of calm confidence.

"Please tell us about the prison system in the End Days and compare it to the one we have now in Salvation Days."

"Yes sir!" the boy responded enthusiastically, "I am so ready for this question because I have spent many weeks studying and researching the subject. In fact, Mr. Bauer, I am absolutely sure now that I want to be a judge or a warden someday. I feel very inspired to redeem myself and my family!"

Mr. Bauer held back an urge to joyfully laugh out loud in response to Manson's exuberant announcement. He was thrilled for him but first wanted him to demonstrate his newfound knowledge to the class for the benefit of all.

"Well that is fantastic news, Mr. Manson. But before you embark upon your noble career, please answer the exam question." A slightly embarrassed Manson continued.

"Of course sir, my apologies!" he exclaimed, "I didn't mean to get ahead of myself. Uh anyway, back in the End Days, the prison system in just about all countries throughout the world was run by your corrupt, hell-on-earth, End Times governments. Even though the death penalty was enforced in some places, most convicted criminals enjoyed their long sentences within the confines of a prison."

"So you are telling us that these criminals actually *liked* being in prison, Mr. Manson?"

"Sir, I say 'enjoy' because even prisoners who'd committed evil crimes had privileges that much more deserving citizens didn't. Like soldiers who put their lives on the line defending freedom or law-abiding poor people who couldn't afford to feed their families even though they had jobs and worked hard.

"In the End Days prisoners were well-fed and got plenty of exercise. They also had lots of books and if they wanted it they could have a higher education. And these are just a *few* of the perks they got. So even if they'd been found guilty of murder and other violent, vicious crimes they could still eat, drink, exercise and earn a degree— all paid for by taxpayers' because corrupt governments controlled the prisons. And the revenue these governments collected from good working men and women were partly used to sustain the prison system.

"In Salvation Time though, we are in an *Age of Responsibility*. This means that when you're convicted of a crime and sent to prison, your punishment is just beginning. You're pulled out of society so you cannot harm anyone else but you get a choice of whether or not to work while you're there. Being a prisoner during Salvation Time means being productive—you are sentenced to live in a new kind of prison run by a smart, streamlined Salvation Time government. This prison is an independent city within *Sin City* that produces electricity, manages waste, provides utilities, manufactures products and grows food for its surrounding communities.

"In Salvation Time, convicted criminals are sent to prison not just to protect the innocent and punish them for their crimes, but also to help them become productive human beings and better people. Each prisoner has a choice of learning a new skill—landscaping, growing food, repairing electrical equipment, manufacturing useful products—whatever skills are needed. When they're paroled after serving their time these practical skills help them find a job in the 'real world'. If they can find a job, chances are they won't go back to a life of crime and end up in prison again. That happened a lot in the End Days. In Salvation Time, working prisoners get paid for the jobs they do, but at lower wages than in mainstream society. Every convict has his own bank account to pay back his victims and send money to his family back home. Criminals who work must open a bank account so they can make payments to their victims and take care of their families.

"Unlike in the End Days the Salvation Days prison system is designed to rehabilitate its prisoners, to help them positively change their lives. But if a prisoner wants to stay in jail even after his time is up, he can. He can create a life within the prison system. This is another big change from the way the prison system worked back in the End Days. For many criminals knowing they can stay if they want to is comforting because life on the outside is just too hard for them. So it's good for them and good for society.

"This new prison system has also destroyed the dysfunctional End Times bureaucracy, not just with government-run prisons but also government-run emergency agencies. So if a country or state has a natural disaster like a bad hurricane, the trained prisoners from a Salvation Days prison are the ones who get out and help with cleaning up and restoring power for their surrounding community. And the prisoners at every Sin City worldwide are the ones who provide city and municipal services like water treatment and infrastructure maintenance—at a much lower cost to residents than during the End Times.

"These Salvation Time prisons support themselves by growing and selling their own food on their large, for-profit farms. Because they are managed by a small, smart Salvation Time government and lifetime inmates, Salvation Time prisons are much better than End Times prisons.

"We got rid of the death penalty because we know that once out of a body a soul returns to heaven, which is a reward. Killing a convicted killer, pedophile, rapist or any other criminal is not a punishment at all. So instead we give them a choice: *Do you want to work or be lazy?* And as with all life choices each one has its rewards and consequences.

"Prisoners who choose to work while serving time have a good, if controlled, life. They're allowed basic cable with decent programming, limited access to the internet, physical recreation in a gym and some entertainment. But they're denied access to cable channels featuring explicit sex and violence, and access to pornography sites online.

"Working prisoners also receive decent housing, deluxe food and nice clothing. These folks can also use their bank account to help their families and pay back their victims. And they can get a higher education and enjoy good music and art. For their animal nature, employed prisoners can have sex once a month with a Sin City prostitute. So there are many incentives for prisoners to choose to work.

"But those prisoners who refuse to work don't get decent housing. They live on an outside tent on the prison grounds. They receive no money because they are choosing not to earn it. Because they're being lazy they don't get an education, good food, entertainment, and once a month sex. These prisoners are fed, but their food is bland and boring. Overall, it's very degrading to be a non-working prisoner. If you're a straight guy you're forced to wear pink, 'girlie' style uniforms. This is completely humiliating.

"And I should have mentioned before that those guilty of the most violent crimes like murder, rape and pedophilia cannot ever return to mainstream society but they too can learn a trade, work, and earn money during their entire stay in Salvation Time prison if they want. If you are a hardened criminal that means you stay there until your natural death."

Here Manson stopped, hoping his answer met the teacher's requirements. After a brief pause Mr. Bauer noted, "You are correct, Mr. Manson. Now for your bonus question, why was your family forced to move to Arusha?"

Ah, the question Manson dreaded, fully aware of his regrettable family history and the fact that his answer would help determine his exam grade. He took a deep breath and continued.

"Sir, my ancestor Charles Manson was a sociopath and a cult leader. He recruited naïve young women from unhappy homes into his so-called 'Manson Family' along with some male losers. By the time he planned and ordered the gruesome Tate-LaBianca murders in the year 1969, he'd already spent half of his life incarcerated for many different crimes like auto theft, armed robbery and fraud even though he was only 35 years-old.

"Manson didn't stab or shoot the seven innocent adults and one unborn child who were murdered that summer, but he did direct his blindly obedient followers to do it so he was just as responsible. And Manson ordered his family members to use the victims' own blood to spell out words like 'POLITICAL PIGGY', 'PIG' and 'HEALTER SKELTER' to make it look as if the *Black Panthers*—another violent, anti-social and racist organization—were the guilty ones.

"This all happened during the era of free love started by hippies. The hippies hated my ancestor Charles Manson because he was 'the guy who spoiled the party' just when ordinary Americans were starting to see hippies as 'cute.' But then the murdering Manson Family came along and that all changed. But really, the Haight-Ashbury in San Francisco had become a drug-infested, violent place long before the Manson Family went on their killing spree. If only the prison system back then had been willing to keep Manson locked up in Terminal Island—something he himself begged for—maybe none of these murders would have taken place."

Here he stopped and awaited Mr. Bauer's reaction.

"Mr. Manson, do you believe your ancestor Charles would have done much better under a Salvation Time prison system?" The teacher obviously knew the answer but wanted to draw it out of the student to assist him in his own understanding and development.

"Yes sir I do," Manson replied confidently. "Not only was my ancestor Charles unable to cope with normal life, he was also a vegetarian. Growing his own food on a Salvation Days prison would have been a productive way for him to spend his time. We know from his imprisonment on Terminal Island that he indulged his love of music. He wrote song lyrics, learned to play the guitar and studied Scientology. When his time there was up he begged the authorities to let him stay, knowing he wasn't capable of being a productive, non-violent citizen.

"But they wouldn't let him stay in the prison. They sent him back into society where he soon found the Haight-Ashbury in San Francisco and hallucinogenic drugs. There my ancestor Charles also found sexual freedom because at the Haight-Ashbury there were no restraints on sex at all. It was an 'anything goes' type of life. Once Charles Manson understood that illegal activity was no longer needed to satisfy his urges he began to organize the 'Manson Family.' He recruited its first member during his time at the Haight-Ashbury—her name was Mary Theresa Bruner—but she was only the first of many young girls Manson lured into his violent, drug-infested world."

Suddenly, the student realized he'd been intensely staring at his teacher during this entire monologue, a habit he'd inherited from his ancestor.

"Sir, I apologize," he said to Mr. Bauer. "I certainly did not mean to stare at you so harshly while giving my answer. It is a habit I am trying to break."

"Understood Mr. Manson," he replied sympathetically. "Is there anything else you would like to add before I calculate your grade?"

"Yes, I would like to say that as guilty as my ancestor Charles Manson was—and he was definitely *guilty*—I would also like to let the class know when I did my research, I felt sorry for the guy. He was born to a poor, unwed 16 year-old mother who became a prostitute and totally neglected him. For the first few weeks after he was born he didn't even have a real name. He was called 'No Name Maddox' before his mother finally called him Charles Milles

Maddox. She married a guy named William Manson, which is how Charles ended up with that last name. But the marriage didn't last.

"Manson's mother was a drunk. She even sold him once to a childless waitress for a pitcher of beer! His uncle had to go get him days later. Then Manson's mother spent five years in jail for burglarizing a West Virginia service station, so Charles was placed in the home of his aunt and uncle. When Manson's mom was finally paroled, she physically embraced him—an incident he would later describe as his *only* happy childhood memory.

"But after that, his mother made it very clear she didn't want anything to do with him. She even tried to put him in a foster home to get rid of him. When none was available, the court placed him in a boys' school in Indiana. He ran away from it 10 months later to go back to his mother, who rejected him *again*.

"I mean, can you imagine *your own mother* being so cruel?"

The student paused for a moment and looked around the room at the faces of his teacher and classmates, as if they were the jury and he a defense attorney for the late Manson centuries after his innumerable crimes and vicious, bloody murders.

"Because of his messed up home life and his small size, Charles Manson was also bullied by the other kids," the student continued while everyone continued to listen with genuine interest. Mr. Bauer was proud of him for articulating these painful truths about 20th century sociopath Charles Manson, hopeful that the other students would take his words to heart and understand the lesson.

"Anyway," Manson declared, "I just wanted to fill you all in on some of the personal history of my ancestor Charles because it is a lot more complicated than what they talked about at his murder trial. And even though we all know his soul chose that particular life for its own reasons, its own growth lessons—just as all of us in this room did—I figured it was worth a mention. I believe his horrible childhood helped turn him into an amoral sociopath."

"Thank you for sharing that with the class, Mr. Manson. Is there anything else you would like to add before we move on?" Mr. Bauer asked.

"Well sir, I'd like to thank you for not making me the last student called upon today," the student offered light-heartedly, attempting to dispel the somber mood.

"During his life of crime my ancestor Charles was always the last to be captured so I am thankful to be breaking that cycle with this morning's exam."

Mr. Bauer couldn't help but laugh. "You are quite welcome, Mr. Manson. Thank you for your intelligent, informative and courageous answers. It is evident that you prepared yourself well."

With that, the teacher consulted his hand-held computer for a grade while the short student eagerly awaited its result. A moment later, he announced, "Congratulations Mr. Manson, you have earned yourself a '9'. You may sit down, sir."

"Thank you sir," he replied happily, taking his seat.

"Alright students, we are winding down today's exam," Mr. Bauer declared while strolling down an aisle on the left side of the room. He stopped when he arrived at his destination—the desk of a 17 year-old girl wearing large, prescription eyeglasses; her wiry long hair was pulled neatly back into a low ponytail at the nape of her neck. Her full lips were tightly closed as she sat primly at her seat, hands folded on top of her desk.

"Miss Bader Ginsberg," he addressed her warmly, prompting a slow smile as the student raised her eyes to look at her teacher. "You have the distinction of being the last but certainly not the least to be called upon today. Please rise and share your knowledge with us."

"Yes sir," the girl softly replied, obediently standing at attention.

"What was the role of the justice system during the End Days versus its role in Salvation Days?"

Barely five-feet tall, the petite Bader Ginsberg looked as if she could be knocked over with a feather, yet her attitude in class was one of fierce academic competitiveness. That was one of the positive qualities that had incarnated through the centuries within the Bader Ginsberg family tree, which also had an unfortunate history of shame as with the other kids in Mr. Bauer's history class.

"During the End Days sir," she began with a subtle trace of a Brooklyn accent in her voice, which had also traveled through time and lingered in the family DNA, "the justice system was all about political correctness and power."

Then beating her teacher to the inevitable follow-up question, the student began her confession.

"My ancestor Ruth Bader Ginsberg was a perfect example. She had the honor of being the second female justice on the United States Supreme Court after Sandra Day O'Connor, and the first Jewish American female justice. But she was also way to the left of the political spectrum and the United States Constitution. Justices back then—at least in theory—were required to interpret the law according to the principles of the Constitution. They were not supposed to legislate from the bench. But during the End Days, many leftist justices like Ruth Bader Ginsberg abused their power for this very purpose.

"No surprise she'd been nominated by President Bill Clinton in the year 1993. Another justice had retired and it was Clinton's prerogative to nominate someone. His Attorney General Janet Reno suggested my ancestor. During Bader Ginsberg's mandatory confirmation hearing before the United States Senate Judiciary Committee, she refused to answer questions about her personal views on most issues. She wouldn't talk about how she would decide specific hypothetical situations as a Supreme Court Justice.

"Even though many Senators on the committee had been frustrated by her stonewalling, they still caved in and confirmed her in a 96-3 vote. She also refused to explain how she planned to make the change from being an advocate for left-wing causes as a former director in the ACLU—the American Civil Liberties Union—to exercising wise, constitutional judgment as a Supreme Court Justice but the senators didn't care. This 96-3 vote included a huge majority of Republicans, a party that pretended to care about the Constitution. During the End Days, most elected Republicans only cared about their own self-interest as members of the permanent political class in Washington D.C. They had no interest in doing the right thing because of a totally corrupt system.

"Throughout her career Ruth Bader Ginsberg advocated for using foreign laws to shape United States law in judicial opinions. One of her worst decisions was when she sided with big government over the people in a 2005 case called *Kelo vs. Connecticut*. Bader Ginsberg was one of five Supreme Court Justices who ruled that local governments could seize people's homes and businesses against their will for private development. This was a major defeat for some Connecticut residents. One of them had lived in her house since her birth in 1918. Another had just finished remodeling hers and had enjoyed the view of the water from her home. The decision also set a bad precedent for the future of private property rights—rights that were outlined clearly in the United States Constitution. But my ancestor didn't give a damn about an individual's right to their own property. To her, the Constitution meant nothing.

"These private homes in Connecticut were scheduled for destruction not for *public projects* like roads or schools, but for an *office complex.* This was a clear case of big government teaming up with private industry against ordinary citizens. *Maybe* if she'd made the ruling to fund projects for public use, it could have been justified; but Kelo was a terrible example of crony capitalism, which is in opposition to the positive capitalism we experience now in Salvation Days."

Here the student stopped to take a breath, waiting for a cue from her teacher. Mr. Bauer nodded at her before advising her to continue.

"Thankfully now, massive government bureaucracy does not exist. As many students already said, politicians no longer hold tremendous power and influence. They only exist to keep the system running efficiently. They don't have the prestige or wealth that their counterparts did during the End Days. Because they are just clerks who work in ordinary offices and live off of their *own* money—not *taxpayer* money—the justice system in Salvation Days has produced a truly compassionate society. As Charles Manson told us, our prison system is designed to help human beings become better people, instead of just punishing them for their crimes and removing them from mainstream society. We must all remember the mistakes of the End Times so that we might continue the much-improved system of justice we now have in Salvation Time."

"You are correct, Miss Bader Ginsberg," Mr. Bauer complimented. "Now, can you explain the role of judges and lawyers in Salvation Time specifically and how it differs from the End Times?"

Bader Ginsberg offered a confident smile to her history teacher, knowing she could definitely answer in the detail required for a good grade. She'd studied this aspect of the justice system very diligently and was thrilled to have a chance to prove it to her teacher and her peers.

"Yes sir, Mr. Bauer," she began. "During the End Days there was total corruption in the legal industry and justice system because of self-serving trial lawyers and dishonest judges. These people created a harmful, litigious society because of their own greed and materialism. But it is very different now. Lawyers here are just administrators who are forbidden to become judges. They exist for a specific purpose: to provide judges with the legal information they need to make fair decisions. In sharp contrast to the End Days, here in Salvation Days, lawyers are banned from advertising on television, radio or even on the internet.

"This is because there was so much 'ambulance chasing' during the End Days you couldn't turn on the TV without seeing ads from lawyers seeking to profit from other people's misery. There is no need for that anymore. That's because school curriculum includes legal classes where students learn about how the law works—everything from filing a complaint in small claims court to defending themselves—basically a complete rundown of all they need to know about the inner workings of the Salvation Time legal system. It has been purposely and deliberately simplified. No longer are everyday citizens forced to take on crushing debt just to retain a lawyer. That model has been shattered.

"Judges in Salvation Time must be at least 50 years old and private citizens with upstanding morals and ethics and proof of having run a successful business. Their terms as judges run for five years. They are held accountable by a volunteer committee made up of good community leaders; kind of like how the Moral Branch keeps our elected politicians in line. Each judge is assigned a lawyer to be their secretary and act as an administrator of the court. Things mostly run very smoothly here. What an improvement over the End Days' legal and justice systems!"

With that, Ruth Bader Ginsberg concluded her remarks as a visibly impressed Mr. Bauer complimented his student on a job well done while he calculated her grade. The student anxiously awaited his decision, lips tightly pursed together again, hands displayed at her sides. She felt fairly confident she'd aced the answer but didn't want to take anything for granted. Mr. Bauer was a demanding but fair teacher who never gave out perfect '10s' no matter what. But she was hoping to rate at the high end of the grading scale and a moment later, her wish was granted.

"Congratulations Miss Bader Ginsberg," Mr. Bauer announced, "you have earned a '9' today. You may take your seat."

Visibly excited, the jubilant student nearly jumped up and down as she exclaimed, "Oh thank you sir!" before settling back into her chair and resuming her dignified pose with hands folded on top of her desk. The teacher smiled as he turned to move back to the front of the classroom to finish out the day's lesson, now that all students had been properly tested and graded. He returned the hand-held computer to its electronic port and addressed the class.

"Congratulations to all of you for your excellent work today. Each one of you has successfully passed the Salvation Time oral exam and consequently, you will all graduate and go on the milestone trip around the world together. You should be very proud of your efforts.

"In the remaining minutes before this final history class adjourns, I wanted to offer my brief, parting thoughts. I hope it became clear to you while listening to the other students and reciting your own answers that although every circumstance and family history is unique, the underlying causes of the problems your ancestors helped perpetuate during the End Days are the same.

"Whether we are talking about an international banker, a monarch, a dictator, a sociopath, or a president of the United States, the driving forces and emotions at the center of their behavior are greed, selfishness, hatred, ignorance, egomania, jealousy, fear, self-loathing, fanaticism, evil and narcissism. Certainly the manifestations of these feelings were all distinctive to each individual and not all of them to the same extent or degree. But in every family history, you can distill the bad behavior down to these all too human weaknesses and frailties.

"And as Mr. Manson so eloquently reminded us, every individual soul chooses the circumstances of their human experience *before* they are born—that includes sex, parents, siblings, upbringing, financial status, sexual orientation, country, century—every aspect of a human being's life has been purposely selected by his or her own soul before inhabiting an earthly body. You of course already know that from your own past life regressions, but it is always good to be reminded of these truths.

"Our job here is to create to the best of our ability, a mirror of heaven on earth; to make the nations of this earth function as closely as they possibly can to the mores and standards of the afterlife. Thanks to inherent human weakness, it's impossible for us to fully recreate heaven on earth but what we've achieved in Salvation Time has attained the goal of close alignment with heaven. It's all about positive individualism. Now we create a win-win for each person because when society helps the individual, the individual in turn helps society.

"That is why I am such a strict, demanding teacher: if you don't understand the lessons of history, you are doomed to repeat them. By imparting knowledge and helping you to draw your own conclusions about the events and people that shaped the End Days, incited the Armageddon War, and ultimately ushered in Salvation Days on earth, I have helped to ensure that you will continue to improve upon what has already been accomplished.

"Now before we adjourn today's class, let's revisit that fateful day in October, 2012 at the G20 summit."

∞ Step Two ∞

Catalyst to Armageddon

On a cold, blustery October day, representatives from 20 countries arrived at the Willis Tower, ostensibly to confront and resolve the most pressing issues of the day including the distribution of energy and resources, and the elimination of poverty and starvation within the Third World. Though it was still October, in keeping with its nickname *The Windy City*, strong gusts of frigid air whipped through the skyscraper-lined streets of Chicago, briefly startling each G20 participant as they made their way out of their limos and into the main lobby of the tower. Once comfortably inside the walls of the heated building, they boarded the elevators that would transport them to the site of their high-altitude conference, engaged in the pleasant small talk that typically preceded such gatherings. As soon as the G20 was officially underway, serious dialogue and hostile debate would ensue.

Present within the ranks of these global leaders were Prime Minister Eyal Grad of Israel; Secretary of State Sarah Palin of the United States; Prime Minister Ibrahim Ahmed of Saudi Arabia; Prime Minister David Cameron of England; Premier of the State Council of the People's Republic of China, Dingbang Yu; Chancellor Arika Reinhardt of Germany; President Jacques Durand of France; President Muhammad Khatami of Iran; Prime Minister Shinzo Abe of Japan; Prime Minister Julia Gillard of Australia; President Dilma Vana Rousseff of Brazil; and President Vladimir Petrov of Russia. Eyal Grad's participation in the summit came as a shock to his colleagues as it had been widely assumed that in light of Grad's wildly unpopular policies—enacted in reaction to the isolation of Israel in the fight against Islamic terrorism—Israeli President Nissam Zabory would have taken his place.

However, Eyal Grad relished his status as a *villain* in the eyes of the rest of the world which now included former longtime ally the United States, although Secretary of State Sarah Palin remained quite sympathetic toward Grad and his tiny nation in spite of her country's betrayal. In fact, for the first time in her life she felt shame for her beloved country—or at least its current governing body—for its shocking treatment of Grad and its suicidal refusal to confront the evil of Islamic Jihad in spite of the attacks of September 11, 2001 and the even more recent Benghazi Embassy attacks of September 11, 2012. Most Americans shared her outrage. In the aftermath of the vicious murders of US Ambassador Christopher Stevens, information management officer Sean Smith, and two security officers who were former Navy SEALs, Tyrone Woods and Glen Doherty, they were even more enraged by their government's attempted cover-up. American citizens then demanded   the resignation of Hillary Clinton as Secretary of State and pressured the White House to appoint Sarah Palin to the position.

Notwithstanding her misgivings about the potential to be used by the thoroughly corrupt administration, Palin had accepted the position with the determination to do everything in her power to repair the relationship with Israel.

But Grad's promise to crack down on Muslim acts of barbarism hadn't been the only reason he'd been elected three years prior to the G20 Summit. A brilliant innovator, Grad had clearly explained his ideas for making life infinitely better for his countrymen through the procurement of inexpensive education, healthcare, energy, gold and food, and through the implementation of a new justice system. Excited Israelis took him at his word and enthusiastically voted for him in a landslide election. And just as he vowed, the new Prime Minister enacted policies that greatly improved the quality of life for every Israeli citizen while the country had been isolated from the rest of the world. Ironically, the rest of the world had no knowledge of Israel's excellent progress under Grad's leadership thanks to a corrupt media that refused to report it. So instead of being revered as a statesman and someone to emulate, Grad had been condemned by most as the second coming of Hitler. Sarah Palin of course, remained the exception to this rule even though she too was unaware of the success of Grad's domestic policies.

Although she despised these extravagant meetings for being a waste of time and taxpayer money, as the new US Secretary of State she saw this gathering as an opportunity to publicly support the Prime Minister of Israel in person—the White House be damned. She'd advise Grad privately of her support for Israel and apologize for the actions of her government. She'd also make a public declaration in direct opposition to the American President. It would be an unprecedented move but Palin was no ordinary, self-centered, power-obsessed American politician; she was an extraordinary, genuine leader who always stood up for what was right in spite of the consequences.

As they made their way to a 97th floor conference room framed by sparkling glass windows offering a panoramic view of the cosmopolitan Chicago skyline and a turbulent Lake Michigan, the world leaders knew they'd soon be absorbed in impassioned arguments as to how to implement the most efficient solutions to the world's most vexing problems. Some would be motivated by a genuine desire to initiate a positive, new direction; others out of nothing more than pure, unadulterated greed and self-interest, though they'd couch their words carefully to conceal their real agenda.

While the tension between all of them was palpable—almost electric—it was most evident in the interactions between Eyal Grad, Sarah Palin and Ibrahim Ahmed. The relationship between the United States and Israel had been rapidly deteriorating since 2008 but most dramatically over the previous six months thanks to the new Israeli Prime Minister's decision to forcefully crack down on Islamic terrorism. At the same time, the United States' traditionally cozy alliance with Saudi Arabia had become even friendlier, much to the delight of Ahmed and his Muslim accomplices.

Though he was a staunch conservative in a very liberal country, Grad had been swept into office by a large mandate. This was partly due to the fact that fed-up Israelis had expressed their revulsion at the latest outbreak of nonstop violence and bloodshed perpetrated by Muslim Shahids at the ballot box. They voted for a leader who'd promised to put an end to it once and for all.

These Shahids, self-described *God warriors*, had been unleashing their fury all over Israel bombing buses, malls, schools and outdoor marketplaces in their bloodthirsty quest to destroy *infidels*, impose a worldwide Muslim Caliphate and—for those who martyred themselves for the cause—attain their 72 virgins in the afterlife. Even worse, the Shahids' murderous rampages had actually been emboldened by some Israeli citizens, liberal Jews who'd treacherously snitched on the covert activities of their own Israeli Defense Forces and intelligence community to tyrannical Islamic regimes throughout the Middle East.

Eyal Grad had built his campaign platform on two fundamental pillars: taking a strong, definitive stand against Islamic violence and improving the lives of all Israelis by way of a new approach to vital industries and domestic policies. Once elected his first official act had been to hold a press conference on television where he boldly proclaimed Israel's new direction. In terms of Islamic terrorism, he vowed to end the death and destruction once and for all by unleashing the full fury of the Israeli Special Forces which would include killing the family and friends of suicide bombers–*along with the Imams who sponsored them to blow up mosques*–and *their* families.

A man of his word, Grad's proclamation was immediately followed by fearless action, sending shock waves through the Islamic world as the Israeli military fulfilled their Prime Minister's promise of brutal retaliation. As expected, this aggressive policy immediately destroyed the jihad movement in Israel, inciting the disapproval of the rest of the free world, most especially the United States and Europe which were still under the dangerous influence of *dhimmitude*—a fatal side effect of the cancer of political correctness.

And when Grad delivered an ultimatum to the United States to immediately stop selling weapons to Israel's enemies like Saudi Arabia, Egypt and Iran, diplomatic tensions reached their breaking point. The US and the rest of the free world completely abandoned Israel. Then came the Benghazi Embassy attacks and renewed hope that with the elevation of former Alaskan Governor Sarah Palin to Secretary of State the close relationship between the United States and Israel might be restored.

Notwithstanding Palin's unapologetic   championing of Grad's country—which put her at odds with her own government and even some left-leaning libertarian members of her own political party—the fact remained that the US remained under the leadership of a narcissistic President. A President who believed his lofty rhetoric and endless apologies to the Muslim world for his country's alleged crimes could somehow magically dissolve a centuries-old vendetta. Since his election in the year 2008, the United States had been treating Israel like a thorn in its side, rather than a trusted ally aligned in the common cause of freedom and peace. This was all very typical of the arrogance of the current US Administration when it came to the conflict in the Middle East and the reality of Global Jihad.

Indeed, an incident that occurred in the elevator on the morning of the G20 summit reflected this chilling reality when Grad and Palin found themselves riding to the 97th floor of the Willis Tower with none other than Ibrahim Ahmed. Ahmed taunted them that despite Palin's insistence on aligning herself with the *Little Satan* she was delusional if she believed the current United States administration would ever offer Grad any kind of meaningful support. He snidely reminded them that not only was the current United States President sympathetic to Muslims, he was himself a Muslim—and his ability to hoodwink American voters into electing him twice should serve as sufficient proof that this man would have his way when it came to *fundamentally transforming* both the US and the Middle East.

Hadn't it already begun with the so-called Arab Spring? To the horror of Palin and Grad, Ahmed erupted in evil laughter over the brutal slaughter of Coptic Christians as one of the horrific consequences of the US President's pro-Muslim agenda. By the time the elevator doors opened, the repulsed Israeli and American leaders couldn't get away from him fast enough.

Once they entered the massive ballroom, Palin took Grad aside and led him to an unoccupied table decorated with freshly starched white linens and a crystal centerpiece filled with autumn flowers in crimson, yellow and burgundy. Although the buffet tables lining the perimeter of the room featured sterling silver serving pieces brimming with typical American breakfast fare, Palin and Grad were content to huddle over a continental breakfast of strong, black coffee and freshly baked croissants. She planned to initiate a conversation in which she'd confirm her unfailing loyalty and her contempt for her own country's actions. She'd collaborate with Grad to counteract all of the madness and find a way to put an end to radical Islamic terrorism.

Deep in her heart she knew most of the American people shared her viewpoint which was evident in their passionate lobbying for her to become the next US Secretary of State. For his part, Grad genuinely appreciated her efforts and regarded her as one of a dying breed—that rare citizen-leader who rises out of humble circumstances to make her country and the world a better place. Yet Grad was also fully aware of the uphill battle she faced in what he perceived to be a futile effort. Besides, once forced to become their own innovators, Israelis had finally stopped looking outside for the solutions to their problems and instead, solved them among themselves. From the lottery system to the medical profession to energy production to education initiatives, Israel had surpassed the world in terms of its achievements. Isolation had definitely had its advantages.

And as Grad looked into the earnest, beautiful face of his American colleague his mind formulated a diplomatic response to her appeal.

But just as he was about to speak, something unexpected happened.

A thunderous, reverberating blast that penetrated the eardrum with enough primal viciousness to cause temporary deafness before it assaulted the human hearing mechanism with an intense, full-bodied and relentless ringing tone. A violent tremor that began slowly, then precipitously increased in intensity as it terrifyingly rocked the tower from side to side causing everyone in the room to collapse to the floor, the contents of their fine China breakfast dishes and elegant coffee cups tumbling furiously all over the patterned red and gold carpet in concert with the long buffet tables.

The scene was reminiscent of a Category 5 hurricane which in its fury transforms innocuous, ordinary things like patio umbrellas and chairs into hazardous flying missiles: crystal bowls brimming with fruit salad tumbled to the ground violently spewing liquid, shards of glass and chunks of melon, pineapple, and strawberries in every direction. Airborne pastries, bacon, sausage, scrambled eggs, Belgian waffles and silverware slammed ferociously into the walls and windows. Silver urns filled with scalding coffee and steaming water for tea regurgitated their liquid in volcanic-like eruptions. Windows shattered, sirens blared and screams of terror replaced the sounds of boisterous, frenzied debate, piercing the air with visceral desperation, panic and urgency. In that moment, policy differences were immediately forgotten, thoroughly eviscerated by the overwhelming fear of death and the inherent will to live.

Amid this gruesome scene of chaos, mayhem and fatality, a dazed Sarah Palin squeezed her eyes shut and held her hands tightly over her ears as she lay in a fetal position on the carpet, the force of the blast hurtling her to the ground. Her shoulder-length, golden-streaked brunette hair was soaked with blood, having suffered a devastating blow when the round table she'd been seated at slammed ferociously into her forehead. As Grad had futilely attempted to shield his American colleague, one of the massive bronze chandeliers was ripped from its mooring on the ceiling above, hurtling into his skull. Crashing in a heap to the floor with grey matter oozing from his brain, Grad also sustained severe damage to his right leg and foot as well as various internal organs when a projectile dining table landed oppressively on top of him.

Ghastly shrieks reverberated throughout the conference room for what felt like an eternity as attendees experienced the acute, devastating and immobilizing pain of severed flesh, fractured bones, skull contusions and the rupturing of internal organs. For many of them, it was a brief flash of spine-tingling physical, emotional and mental upheaval before the transition into a state of pure bliss.

For others, it was just the beginning of a revitalized journey, one that would eventually transform the world forever.

Eyal Grad blinked his eyes in an attempt to make sense out of his surroundings. Everywhere he looked, everything was dazzling white—from the doctors in white lab coats to the patients in white gowns to the white-carpeted hospital hallways. At least he *thought* he was in the hospital, though he wondered why he found himself standing in a line resembling similar ones he'd frequently experienced at the Tel Aviv airport. But why would he be in the hospital feeling as good as he did? Although he could see that his body was bloodied and bruised he felt inexplicably light and energetic—not at all like a typical hospital patient who'd suffered a trauma. In fact, he couldn't remember a time when he'd felt better than he did right at that very moment. Then he glanced downward and realized he was dressed in a white hospital gown.

"Why I am wearing this?" he asked incredulously, to no one in particular. Then he heard a familiar, friendly voice.

"Prime Minister, good to see you here!"

He turned to face Secretary of State Palin, noting that she also was dressed in white.

"*Here?* Where the hell is *here?*" he demanded.

"Looks like a hospital to me," she shrugged, summoning her typical American humor. "Thank God we survived that explosion!"

"Sarah, how is it possible you can even speak?" he cried out in disbelief, remembering how she'd collapsed to the floor following the blast. "As I recall, you should theoretically be dead by now!" At this point Grad still hadn't realized that he'd been speaking to her telepathically.

"I could say the same about you," she replied sweetly, remembering his close proximity to her when their conversation had been so violently interrupted. Given the horrific event they'd both endured Sarah Palin couldn't comprehend the fact that her colleague and friend was still alive and kicking, let alone speaking to her. But before she could utter another word, he interjected excitedly.

"Sarah, look! Some of our G20 companions are here too!"

Grad shifted his gaze outward as Palin followed his lead. Together they watched in silence as the leaders from Saudi Arabia, China, Iran, Germany, Japan, France, Russia, Brazil, Australia and England appeared to be engaged in similar conversation, all dressed in the same dazzling white. Staring intently at them, Grad and Palin realized they weren't moving their lips at all yet they were easily communicating with each other, which puzzled them even more. In that moment they had the exact same thought:

Where are we?

As the two continued to observe the other world leaders, they noticed a strange phenomenon: once their vision penetrated the pure veil of white covering each leader, it was evident that each of their bodies had been brutally mangled to varying degrees. Their earthly nemesis Prime Minister Ibrahim Ahmed had sustained four broken ribs, two broken legs and irreparable damage to several internal organs. And yet, he along with everyone else looked happy, content and peaceful.

How could this possibly be?

Grad then shifted his gaze back to Palin when something amazing happened. While on the surface she initially appeared as healthy as he, save for the dried blood on her forehead, once his eyes zoomed in and transcended the outer barriers of skin, he witnessed the more serious consequences of a badly fractured collarbone, severely punctured lung, several broken ribs, a crushed kneecap and a shattered left leg. As Palin zeroed in on Grad, she flinched at the gruesome nature of his physical injuries, from the oozing grey matter emanating from his fractured skull, to his crushed vertebrae, to his ruptured lungs and brutally mangled right leg and foot.

Then in the blink of an eye, Grad found himself standing alone in front of a large, imposing white desk. Seated behind it were three distinguished figures dressed in royal purple and white. The lines in their faces revealed a wisdom borne of experience; their flowing silver hair inspired reverence and awe. The lone female of the trio sat in the middle, her slender fingers holding a long scroll to which she frequently referred. Her luminous violet eyes and mesmerizing smile stood out among her feminine features. To her left and right, her fellow Council members met the gaze of Eyal Grad.

"You didn't finish your work Eyal," The Council calmly informed him. "We recommend that you finish it." The entities spoke as if they'd just seen him a second ago, prompting even more confusion in the mind of the Israeli leader.

"I am in a hospital," he thought to himself. *"What are these doctors talking about? This is not about work. I'm sick!"*

In the next instant an emboldened Eyal spoke up forcefully. "What kind of hospital is this? What are you talking about, go back to work? You need to get to work on fixing my broken body!"

"Shhh," they soothed him, to no avail.

"Why are you trying to shush me, *you're* the doctors, you're the ones who need to get to work on healing *me*! *I'm* the one who's suffered devastating injuries here!" he insisted in a tone of outrage.

"Eyal," they continued patiently, "we recommend that you to go *back* and finish your work."

Prompted by The Council's use of the word "back" he suddenly realized he'd crossed over to *The Other Side* where these highly advanced beings of light were reminding him that he still had a job to complete on the earthly plane. Instinctively remembering the rules of reincarnation, he then began to absorb as much information as possible in his mind—information he'd put to good use once back on earth—without them noticing. The last thing he wanted was to return to three-dimensional material existence having forgotten the lessons learned in the spiritual realm; souls were forbidden to impart this knowledge to a human being's mind once they resumed their life within a physical body. It had to be this way for the sake of each individual soul's growth and development while limited to the parameters of flesh, bone and blood.

"What kind of work?" he inquired.

But The Council remained silent.

Finally, Grad spoke up again. "Ok I'll go back but not like this. Look at me! If I go back like this I won't be able to finish my work, I'll *be* work for other people. I'll be brain-damaged, paralyzed and dependent on a wheelchair, not to mention the charity of others who will have to take care of me and pay my bills. If you insist on sending me back like that I'll take a gun, shoot myself in the head and be back here in two seconds!"

The Council slowly nodded in agreement.

"Alright then Eyal, we'll help you with your recovery. With our assistance you'll recover fast and you'll *almost* be normal."

Thus reassured he declared confidently, "As long as I'm 95 percent it's fine with me. I can finish the work. Because I *always* finish my work, no matter how long it takes." Then in the next breath he inquired, "What kind of *work*?"

"We have a special assignment for you this time. You are going to help usher in Salvation Days on earth."

"Salvation on earth! What do you mean, *Salvation on earth*?!" He wasn't sure if he should feel happy, overwhelmed, angry or depressed.

"Eyal, there's no need to fear this assignment. In fact you should feel very proud to have been selected for the noble purpose of facilitating Salvation Days. It will represent the victory of the spiritual over the material. It's when the world will function much more in alignment with heaven and in accordance with the principles of goodness, logic, common sense, love, charity, humility, simplicity, courage and integrity. You will help move the world away from greed, selfishness, brutality, oppression and tyranny and into a new era of enlightenment when it will operate as closely as possible to the principles of heaven. Of course, being on the earthly plane for the purpose of learning and growing, the human experience will never attain heavenly perfection. But we know that with leaders like you, it can mirror this spiritual existence much better than it does now."

Inspired by this vision and its exciting possibilities, Eyal Grad replied that the assignment was very appealing to him, that he would definitely like to play an important role in reshaping the world according to their instructions. Once he accepted their offer, he suddenly left The Council and found himself seated in what appeared to be a theater hall with his G20 colleagues flanking him—Sarah Palin to his right, Ibrahim Ahmed to his left. All around, he heard each of the leaders recounting their own experiences with their own unique Councils, which sounded very similar to his own, including the assignment to help usher in Salvation Time and the immediate transfer to the theater hall upon saying "yes."

"Prime Minister!" Sarah Palin greeted him enthusiastically, once aware of his presence.

"Ah Sarah, here we are again," he replied warmly. "Tell me, what happened with you?"

"Well I found myself before The Council, three incredible beings of purple and white light who informed me I still had work to finish on earth, that I was to be part of a team of world leaders who would help bring about Salvation Days. It was very strange at first."

"How so?"

"They said, 'Sarah we've been expecting you' as if we'd planned this get-together in advance. At first I thought they were doctors, so I scolded them that as much as I wanted to get back to work, they'd have to heal me first. I reminded them that I already *was* a workaholic, having a long record of accomplishment as a small business owner, city council member, mayor, oil and gas commissioner, governor, former VP candidate, Tea Party leader and US Secretary of State. Not to mention being a wife, mother of five and grandmother of two.

"They were very amused by my lack of understanding before they explained the concept of Salvation Time, and how I'd be one member of a distinguished team selected for the cause. Funny, as soon as I accepted the job with the agreement that my physical injuries would be mostly healed, it was like—*poof!*—suddenly I am seated in this theater hall talking to you."

"It was just like that for me too!" Grad exclaimed.

"Same here!" Ibrahim Ahmed interjected.

"Far from 72 virgins, I was confronted by the same type of Council that gave me my Salvation Time assignment," he further explained. "Like both of you, I initially thought I was in a hospital and was very agitated that these 'doctors' were talking to me about getting to work instead of tending to my injuries. The second I agreed to The Council's request, I found myself seated in this theater hall with you and the other selected G20 members."

Then, prompted by a humorous thought, Ibrahim Ahmed of Saudi Arabia erupted into joyful, musical laughter—the exact opposite of what he'd demonstrated in the elevator back in Chicago. Palin and Grad regarded him quizzically.

"Oh," he clarified, "I am just imagining my fellow Muslims back on earth and how surprised they'll be to discover just as I have, that they've been harboring a serious delusion about the nature of heaven and what awaits them after death. It's certainly not 72 virgins!"

The three leaders shared a good, hearty laugh, their previous earthly contentions forgotten.

Once they regained their composure, they surveyed their environment to discover that they were seated in the round, in a graduated amphitheater featuring a prominent stage in the middle, on top of which stood three ornate, high-backed and as yet unoccupied chairs. In the circular rows extending out beyond the stage and in front of the Salvation Twelve's designated places sat some very prominent souls. As the G20 members looked on, they attempted to identify them. Grad immediately recognized the Twelve Tribes of Israel, Abraham, Isaac, Jacob, Joshua, King David, King Solomon, and the prophets Samuel, Ezekiel, Isaiah and Elijah. Sarah Palin recognized Oliver Cromwell, US Founding Father Benjamin Franklin, former US Presidents Abraham Lincoln and Andrew Jackson, Maryam the Mother of Jesus, and the Gospel writers Matthew, Mark, Luke, John and Thomas. Ibrahim Ahmed noticed the presence of Genghis Khan, Napoleon, Alexander the Great, Martin Luther, Mother Teresa, Nikola Tesla and Mahatma Ghandi.

As Grad, Palin and Ahmed looked on Napoleon suddenly stood up and stomped away from the rest of the group of souls seemingly in a fit of French superiority, inciting gales of laughter from the G20 onlookers. "Wow even in the afterlife Napoleon has retained the short man's complex and ego!" Grad exclaimed humorously.

But in the next moment, they were consumed with sheer awe, reverence and excitement as the realization hit them that they were in the presence of some truly phenomenal world leaders. There they were, hanging out with some of the most Advanced Souls to ever incarnate on earth including the stately Abraham Lincoln who appeared to be engaged in serious conversation with Oliver Cromwell, while others like Benjamin Franklin spoke about charity with Mother Teresa and the Mother of Jesus. All were dressed in shining robes that subtly and repeatedly changed color from pure white to ivory to purple and back to white again in an iridescent rhapsody. Though surrounded by the *New Souls* in the room who pointed, giggled and chattered on like star-struck teenagers, these Advanced Souls did not acknowledge their presence though they chuckled among themselves at their juvenile behavior.

"Ah look at these newbies!" they remarked affectionately. "Now they're so enthusiastic, so fresh and energetic. They have no idea of what awaits them when they return to their bodies and earth. Guess we should let them enjoy themselves while they can!"

While the freshly arrived souls from the G20 summit were still watching in utter amazement, fully unaware of the reason for the presence of these Advanced Souls and former earthly leaders, a large, imposing figure appeared on the stage holding a staff in one hand. Tall, robust, muscular and masculine with kinky, shoulder-length dark hair, a square jaw, ruggedly handsome face and penetrating brown eyes, he took his place in front of the chair in the center. In the next instant two other figures appeared on the stage, taking their places in front of the chairs to his left and right.

The figure in the middle introduced himself with the simple greeting, "Hello, I'm Moses." An audible gasp filled the theater hall as the G20 members had a collective, simultaneous thought—*"Of course, it's Moses! We recognized him by the staff he carries!"*

Without missing a beat, Moses then introduced the gentleman to his right as Mohammad, prompting more astonishment from the crowd. Noticeably shorter than Moses, Mohammad appeared very skinny and frail, with dark, beady eyes, an olive complexion, and a long, black, scraggly beard and mustache. As he nodded in greeting to the crowd Grad, Palin and Ahmed were struck by his remarkable resemblance to one of the world's biggest evildoers, Osama bin Laden. But before they could comment, Moses then introduced the figure to his left as Jesus Christ, who upon hearing the introduction, raised his telltale hand in a welcoming gesture.

"Of course that's Jesus!" Sarah Palin exclaimed. "Look at the nail mark on his hand!"

Jesus was of average height but unlike Mohammad his physique was as strong, solid and robust as that of Moses. His long, wavy, dark hair fell just beyond his shoulders, complemented by a matching mustache and beard which enhanced an attractive, virile face.

In contrast to the other beings present in the amphitheater Moses, Mohammad and Jesus were all dressed in gleaming, kaleidoscopic robes that alternated color from dazzling white to bright purple to sparkling lavender, signifying their celestial status and credentials as Ascended Masters. Following the introductions, Moses continued.

"I am God's selected project manager, the Project Manager of Salvation Time. He has chosen me to help facilitate it and bring it to fruition. You may remember through your scriptural studies that I've had experience with this sort of thing before, although thankfully this time around I am managing from The Other Side and not in human form in a hot, dry desert. Let me tell you something, it wasn't exactly a walk in the park guiding a million and a half Jews for 40 long years through brutal, dry heat and sand with no air-conditioning, no showers and no plumbing. It was nag, nag, nag, 24/7—'*Moses, are you sure you know what you're doing!*', '*Moses, we're hot and tired!*', '*Moses we can't do this!*', '*Moses, you're a liar, God didn't send you to take us through this hellish desert!*', '*Moses, we're thirsty!*', '*Moses, we're hungry!*', '*Moses, we can't go on like this!*', '*Moses, we despise you!*'"

The G20 members giggled out loud, happily taken aback by the Biblical icon's spontaneous sense of humor.

"Sure," he noted wryly. "You all laugh now but that's because you weren't there. It would have been bad enough transporting any race of human beings under those unforgiving conditions but a million and a half *Jews*? Sheer torture!"

Jesus and Mohammad exchanged knowing glances as they laughed along with the crowd.

"So of course God sends me *again* to work as a project manager," he sighed in mock resignation. "Ready or not, here we go! Except this time we have to bring Salvation to the whole earth, not just to the Jewish people. It can't just work in one country; it has to work on every country on earth. *That* is why we're here. And that's why all of these Advanced Souls and previous world leaders throughout history are here also. From Alexander the Great to Mahatma Gandhi to the Biblical prophets and kings to the Gospel writers to the Twelve Tribes of Israel—all are here to help you prepare to make your earthly contribution to the implementation of Salvation Time.

"Before you return to your physical bodies and home countries, you will receive instruction and guidance from all souls gathered here. We want to help you in your assignment to usher the world into Salvation Days. You've got a very big and important project on your hands and you should be extremely happy and proud to have been selected because it proves you have the sterling character required for such a monumental task. If God chose you, he knows what he's doing. Therefore I don't want to hear any whining about how you're not up to it. You *are* up to it; otherwise God would not have selected you to participate. And I know I speak for Mohammad, Jesus and all of the Advanced Souls gathered in this hall when I tell you we are honored that you're here to usher the world into the next stage, and that you can count on our assistance as you work toward fulfilling God's most ambitious project to date."

Moses surveyed the room, gauging the reaction of the selected Salvation Twelve to his announcement. To his delight and satisfaction, all emitted an obvious willingness and enthusiasm to accept God's urgent request. He then continued.

"Before we go any further let's first define Salvation, shall we? Salvation arrives on earth when the spiritual triumphs over the material. It's when human beings finally put positive character traits like common sense, integrity, honesty and goodness in control on earth instead of greed, selfishness, and obsession with power, youth and money. Always with the understanding of course that human beings are sinners. Not because they are inherently evil but because by overcoming failings and weaknesses humans elevate their souls from one level to the next. Sin will still exist even in Salvation Days. It's just that in Salvation Days, sin is no big deal.

"Once you commit a crime, for example, you take your punishment, move to the next level and everything is forgotten. During Salvation Time, when you sin you are given the chance to make restitution for that sin by accepting and fulfilling an honest punishment before rejoining mainstream society. It's a system of *real* justice and honesty—not lying and cheating—where even if you did something harmful and wrong your punishment will fit your crime. Then when you've made complete restitution, you move to the next level. Once your sin is atoned for, you'll never commit that same sin again but you may succumb to temptation and commit another—and that's alright. You'll serve your punishment for this new sin before moving up to the next level in your soul advancement. The process is infinite. There's no limitation—no matter how many times you fall short, you'll still have a trillion more sins to commit and pay for because that is the only way a human being's soul can progress on its journey to a closer relationship with God. It is not something that can be learned in school but something that can only be accomplished and experienced by actually doing.

"Your job as the leaders of the 12 countries selected is to set up the system in each of your nations based on positive characteristics including but not limited to humility, justice, honesty, integrity, charity, generosity, industriousness, spirituality, honor, sincerity, helpfulness, intelligence and selflessness. Because the process of bringing Salvation Time to earth is such a huge undertaking, we've assembled previous world leaders—the Advanced Souls you see here—to answer your questions and prepare you in advance of your return to the physical plane. I advise you to listen carefully to what they have to say about the most pressing problems confronting all sovereign nations of earth. We'll start with one of the most important issues: financial freedom and money.

"How are all of you going to bring the world into a situation where people will have plenty of money to thrive and live comfortably, without fear of being unable to provide for themselves and their families? What must be done in order to prevent massive governments from extracting the hard-earned money of everyday citizens who are working diligently and living honest, decent lives?"

Moses fixed his dark eyes upon one particular member of the Salvation Twelve seated in the amphitheater. "Prime Minister Eyal Grad, I would like you to begin the discussion of this topic by explaining what you did in Israel with the Citizens Lottery System, or CLS."

A humbled Grad arose from his seat, eager to share the success of one of the systems he'd created in the aftermath of Israel's isolation.

"It would be an honor, Mr. Moses. Thank you for the opportunity," he began politely.

"First, I want to let everyone know that the Citizens Lottery System has exceeded our expectations by producing 30 millionaires per week in a country of about six million people. As per its intended purpose, money is constantly circulating in every local community in

Israel, to the benefit of reputable small business owners and individual citizens who demonstrate the positive characteristics you've already mentioned—things like integrity, honesty and a good work ethic. I want to stress also that this Citizens Lottery System—CLS—is separate and independent from the traditional, existing lottery system with which most of us are very familiar. It hasn't taken the place of the old lottery system, it's just offered as another completely voluntary option for anyone who wishes to participate. But unlike the existing lotto, the CLS has some very strict guidelines in place—rules that every interested citizen must fulfill and obey as a condition of eligibility."

Here he paused momentarily to gauge his audience's interest. Everyone's eyes were upon him, eager to learn as much as possible about this intriguing system of wealth accumulation and monetary circulation.

"Please continue Mr. Grad," Moses instructed. "Tell us about the technicalities of your system."

"With pleasure sir," he continued. "Let's say you're an Israeli citizen and you want to participate in the CLS. You first must call a designated phone number to the CLS office in Jerusalem to apply for approval. You will give them your name, your social security number and address so that they can initiate and complete the mandatory background check. The reason you must submit to a background check is because the CLS requires that each participating citizen prove that they are a person of strong moral character. Of course we understand that as human beings we all commit sins but as long as there is no record of criminality or violence in your application for a minimum of five consecutive years, you are free to join in the Citizens Lottery System. However, a minimum of five years crime-free is absolutely mandatory, with no exceptions.

"So as a hypothetical, let's say you were convicted of stealing four years ago and have since made restitution to your victims in a fair punishment. You just have to wait one more year before you'll be eligible to participate in the CLS—provided of course you refrain from committing any other crimes. Meanwhile, you can still buy lottery tickets in the traditional lottery system, which still exists and produces winners, though not nearly as many as the CLS. That's because the whole purpose of the CLS is to reward good behavior.

"How does it work?

"Well once you're approved and eligible you can purchase CLS tickets at just about every convenience store, supermarket and shopping mall throughout Israel. However, you may only purchase one ticket per week, valued at $50. If you decide to be clever and 'outsmart' the system by purchasing $150 worth of tickets...well, the government will be more than happy to accept the extra $100 as a gift because you will only be issued one $50 ticket for that week. You get one shot per week: no more, no less. Once purchased, you run your card through the scanner while the clerk punches numbers at random. Whatever comes up comes up in this fully computerized system, which assigns you six numbers. If at the time of the drawing no one wins, we then randomly select five numbers to see if that produces winners. If no winners come out of that, we drill down to four numbers, repeating the process as many times as it takes until one-hundred thousand people win. Because the CLS is executed from an electronic database we know who these one-thousand winners are. We then continue to randomly draw numbers until we extract 30 final winners.

"Congratulations, you've won the Citizens Lottery! What's next?

"Well you don't receive your money in a lump sum, but instead in the form of a debit card with a credit line in the amount of your winnings. You also receive a rule book, along with special log-in credentials to the CLS website where the rules and regulations of the lottery system are also accessible, along with lists of approved local vendors. These vendors include home-builders, plumbers, electricians, painters, manufacturers and landscapers as well as private schools, doctors and other services. If you don't already own a home you must buy one with your CLS money. For the duration of your life, this home will be yours but upon your death it's returned to the CLS.

"The whole purpose of requiring local patronage of small business owners and service providers is to get this money circulating immediately back into the community. It's designed to create wealth for people in their local areas. And with money, people can relax as life becomes easier. They can send their kids to private school, buy the home of their dreams, pay for their expenses and enjoy their lives.

"Meanwhile every single vendor on the CLS website has undergone extensive background checks and has been determined to provide consistent, high-quality service. Once you've employed a vendor through the CLS you must also submit a Quality Control or QC report so we can ensure that all vendors continue to live up to our high standards. And the better the service they provide, the better it is for them because it keeps them flush with new customers and projects, enabling their businesses to expand and hire more employees. In short, by an individual citizen winning the CLS Lottery everyone benefits—painters, plumbers, manufacturers, doctors, etc.— because the money circulates endlessly within the local communities."

Before Grad could utter another word, one of the Advanced Souls in the room literally beamed as he ascended from his chair.

"Nicely done Mr. Grad!" former US President Andrew Jackson glowed, inciting the Ascended Masters and the rest of the Advanced Souls to light up in the same show of appreciation. Before he could continue, Moses interrupted.

"Am I to assume you would like to add to this conversation Mr. Jackson?"

"If I may, Mr. Moses," he replied deferentially.

"You may have the floor sir," he confirmed while Grad and the Salvation Twelve looked on in awe.

"Mr. Grad, as you may already know during my time on earth I was known as the first working-class president," Jackson continued.

"As an orphaned young man who raised himself out of poverty after my experience as a POW during the American Revolution, the plight of the common man was always foremost on my mind. Oh yes, I did some things I'm not proud of during my time on earth, including killing thousands of native Americans at the Battle of Horseshoe Bend. While in human form, we're capable of exceptional acts of heroism and accomplishment, and regrettable acts of barbarism and cruelty. I was certainly no exception to this rule when I inhabited an earthly body known as Andrew Jackson, seventh President of the United States.

"After I defeated the British in the Battle of New Orleans, many Americans called me 'The Second George Washington' and 'The Hero.' It wasn't long before I heeded the call to run for the highest office in the land because it was my opportunity to take a stand against the centralized banking system. Centralized banks controlled the circulation and availability of money to the detriment of decent, everyday working people. As a relentless champion for common folks I was determined to put an end to this money monopoly.

"When I decided to run for President I knew I had to base my platform on revoking the charter of the Bank of the United States because it had too much power over the American economy through private bankers. We'd seen this throughout history with centralized banks like the Bank of England and the money traders of Biblical and Roman times. To a humble frontiersman like me, the Bank of the United States—with its board of directors tied to industry and manufacturing—was naturally biased in favor of the urban and industrial northern states. It was also unconstitutional and antithetical to the principles of individual liberty and equality.

"With my only concern the best interests of the American people, I couldn't wait to engage in this so-called 'Bank War,' which pitted me against Nicholas Biddle. People who shared my view of centralized bankers properly referred to Biddle as 'Czar Nicholas.' I vetoed the re-charter bill for the Bank of the United States during my first term as President. It then became the central issue of the 1832 election, when Biddle made life miserable for small business owners by raising interest rates and making the money supply scarce. Eventually I destroyed the Bank of the United States by pulling federal deposits out of it and into state banks. I also paid off the national debt in the proudest moment of my presidency. Sadly at this juncture in history, I remain the only United States President to ever have done so."

Jackson heard an audible sigh from the crowd and turned to look at the lone American political figure in modern life that even came close to his stellar record of achievement and tireless pursuit of liberty for all.

"You wish to comment Madam Secretary?" he asked.

"Ah Mr. President," Sarah Palin lamented, "you have no idea how out of control our debt is under our current corrupt and reckless administration—close to $18 trillion and skyrocketing daily! What I would give to have a leader like you who would work in earnest to eliminate our debt. You would remind them all of the origin of the term *Jacksonian Democrat*, from which today's Democrat Party has radically strayed in favor of big-government socialism. To be fair, the Republican Party could also learn a thing or two from you, judging by their eagerness to follow in the Democrats' footsteps with their diluted version of statism."

"How right you are Madam Secretary! If I went back to earth today there would be no place for me within the Democrat Party. And just like you, if I were to become a Republican, I'd be fighting the same battles that have made you so famous and revered among the common people. I want you to know, you have been exactly the kind of leader you describe," he genuinely complimented.

"Thank you sir," she humbly replied.

"With this new assignment you will play an important role in solving your country's fiscal problems and helping   ordinary citizens enjoy the fruits of their labor, thanks to a truly limited governmental system. And might I add, I most certainly do know of the dangerous debt the so-called leaders of the US have amassed. If I didn't know about God's plans for the Salvation Twelve, I'd be....well, I'd be gravely dispirited, so to speak!"

The Salvation Twelve laughed in unison with the Ascended Masters and the Advanced Souls at Jackson's joke. But in the next moment the mood sobered again as the former US President resumed his serious discussion.

"In spite of paying off the national debt and destroying the Bank of the United States, I was wrong about one very important monetary principle," he admitted. "I wanted to abolish paper money and put the United States on the gold standard, which in retrospect was a terrible idea. I want to call upon former United States President Abraham Lincoln to explain why a paper money system is superior to all others."

With that, he gestured to the man known in human life as *Honest Abe* and the *Emancipator of the Slaves* to join him in addressing the audience on the all-important topic of money and finance. Abraham Lincoln smiled and accepted the invitation.

"Thank you, Mr. Jackson," he acknowledged. Then turning to face the designated Salvation Twelve, he continued. "I must confess, although I am credited with freeing the slaves and ending a tragic period in United States history, in the beginning my main concern was the preservation of the Union. Centralized European bankers were still smarting over the fact that President Andrew Jackson had succeeded in destroying the Bank of the United States. Like America's Founders he understood the inherent hazards of fractional reserve banking, centralized banking, and monetizing debt based on what he'd seen with the Bank of England, and what he'd learned from studying the history of the money traders all the way back to the Roman Empire.

"Our Founders along with Mr. Jackson knew that if Congress had the authority to monetize debt via a central bank rather than operating the government exclusively on taxes and real borrowing, the amount of spending they could authorize would be unlimited. Which is why in Article 1, Section 8 of the United States Constitution it reads that Congress was granted only the right *'To coin Money, regulate the value thereof, and of foreign Coin, and fix the Standard of Weights and Measures.'*

"In the run-up to the American Civil War, the practice of fractional reserve banking—which permits a bank to lend out more money than it actually has available on deposit in cash—ran rampant within countless state-chartered banks. This created widespread instability throughout our young country. For lenders, a depression is a wonderful development. However, since war is a major cause of debt and dependency, wealthy European bankers were excited by the prospect of exploiting a civil war if they couldn't have their centralized bank with a license to print money indiscriminately. As then-Chancellor Otto von Bismarck of Germany stated, *'The division of the United States into federations of equal force was decided long before the Civil War by the high financial powers of Europe. These bankers were afraid that the US, if they remained as one block and as one nation, would attain economic and financial independence, which would upset their financial domination over the world.'*

"And on April 12, 1861 the Civil War began. Inevitably, I arrived at a point when I needed money to finance the war so I traveled to New York with my secretary of the treasury to apply for the necessary loans. Because the money traders were so invested in the dissolution of the Union, they offered me loans at 24-36 percent interest. I flatly refused because I did not want to plunge the American people into that kind of debilitating debt. So I turned to an old friend, Colonel Dick Taylor, to solve the problem of financing the war. His solution?

"'Just get Congress to pass a bill authorizing the printing of full legal tender treasury notes, and pay your soldiers with them and go ahead and win your war with them also.'

"When I expressed concern about the American people accepting these notes, he assured me, *'The people or anyone else will not have any choice in the matter, if you make them full legal tender. They will have the full sanction of the government and be just as good as any money; as Congress is given that express right by the Constitution.'*

"So on my trusted friend's counsel I agreed to this solution and printed 450 million dollars' worth of the new bills at no interest to the federal government, using green ink on the back to distinguish them from other notes. With them, I paid the soldiers and bought their supplies.

"At the time I stated, *'The government should create, issue and circulate all the currency and credit needed to satisfy the spending power of the government and the buying power of consumers. The privilege of creating and issuing money is not only the supreme prerogative of Government, but it is the Government's greatest creative opportunity. By the adoption of these principles, the long-felt want for a uniform medium will be satisfied. The taxpayers will be saved immense sums of interest, discounts and exchanges. The financing of all public enterprises, the maintenance of stable government and ordered progress, and the conduct of the Treasury will become matters of practical administration. The people can and will be furnished with a currency as safe as their own government. Money will cease to be the master and become the servant of humanity. Democracy will rise superior to the money power.'*

"My friends, this new system worked out so well I seriously considered adopting it as a permanent policy, which would have been to the benefit of all *except* the money traders. They responded by writing an editorial in The London Times which ironically made the case for paper money.

"To quote the European bankers,

'If this mischievous financial policy, which has its origin in North America, shall become endurated down to a fixture, then that Government will furnish its own money without cost. It will pay off debts and be without debt. It will have all the money necessary to carry on its commerce. It will become prosperous without precedent in the history of the world. The brains and wealth of all countries will go to North America. That country must be destroyed or it will destroy every monarchy on the globe.'"

Summoning his natural sense of humor, Lincoln paused dramatically for effect before using a modern-day phrase that caused the entire amphitheater to erupt in laughter. "Well *duh!*" he exclaimed. "Wasn't that the whole point of the American experiment to begin with, to cast aside controlling monarchies and inspire other nations to throw off oppressive governments?"

"One would think!" Andrew Jackson quipped. "But as you and I know from chilling experience, these European bankers would stop at nothing to hold onto power. They set out to destroy those who would return the privilege of printing money to representatives elected by and accountable to the people. More tellingly, it's also the reason why you and I both faced assassination, though in your case these banksters   succeeded in sending you back to heaven, disrupting the good work you'd done on earth permanently."

"Very true," Lincoln agreed. "Your would-be assassin Richard Lawrence misfired with both pistols and was later found not guilty by reason of insanity. Yet after his release he bragged to his friends that powerful people in Europe had hired him to do the deed and promised to protect him if he were caught. In my case, after winning re-election in 1864 I would have put an end to the national banks' money monopoly extracted from me during the war. As I'd written to a friend back in the day, *'The money power preys upon the nation in times of peace and conspires against it in times of adversity. It is more despotic than monarchy, more insolent than aristocracy, more selfish than bureaucracy.'*

"Just before I was murdered, my former secretary Salmon P. Chase lamented his role in helping secure the passage of the National Banking Act stating, *'My agency in promoting the passage of the National Banking Act was the greatest financial mistake in my life. It has built up a monopoly which affects every interest in the country.'*

"And on April 14, 1865 just 41 days after my second inauguration, and just five days after Lee surrendered to Grant, John Wilkes Booth shot me at Ford's Theater. My death was mourned by Otto von Bismarck, who believed it to be a disaster for Christendom. He complimented that *'there was no man in the United States great enough to wear my boots'* but most importantly he feared *'that the foreign bankers with their craftiness and tortuous tricks will entirely control the exorbitant riches of America, and use it systematically to corrupt modern civilization.'*

"Von Bismarck felt certain that these bankers '*will not hesitate to plunge the whole of Christendom into wars and chaos in order that the earth should become their inheritance.*' He well understood their diabolical plan. And 70 years after I died, allegations surfaced that these international bankers were indeed responsible for my demise at the gun of an assassin."

Lincoln stopped here as all of the souls gathered fell silent after listening with rapt attention. Moses allowed some time for the Salvation Twelve to absorb the information then instructed the two former Presidents to wrap up their portion of the program as it was necessary to move onto the next topic.

"As you wish Mr. Moses," they consented. Addressing the Salvation Twelve, Jackson then summarized the lesson.

"I hope our presentation has made it clear to all of you that during the End Times, the money traders and later the centralized bankers made life miserable for the good souls living as humans on earth who only desired to work and create a better life for themselves and their families. This unadulterated greed which dictates that the world's monetary resources remain under the control of a few privileged elites *cannot* and *will not* stand. You must work hard to turn it around. A good place to start is by implementing the same Citizens Lottery System that has created so much abundance in Prime Minister Eyal Grad's Israel. While you will have to customize it according to the needs of your individual countries, such a system will undoubtedly yield the same excellent results for each of your citizens as it has for Mr. Grad's."

Turning to Lincoln, Jackson inquired if he had anything to add.

"I concur with you, Mr. Jackson. I am also glad you have seen the errors of pushing for the gold standard and the superiority of a paper-backed monetary system," he further added in a slightly amused tone.

"Yes well, lucky for me I won't actually be implementing these monetary changes on earth," Jackson grinned. "I'll just be watching it unfold from here while enjoying the bounty of heaven."

Jackson, Lincoln and the rest of the Advanced Souls enjoyed a good laugh before Moses again interjected, eager to explain the next assignment to the Salvation Twelve on yet another crucial human life issue.

"Alright gentlemen," he scolded playfully, "thank you for your input. You may take your places again while I call upon Mr. Tesla to speak to us about energy." The two presidential souls nodded to the audience before disappearing and reappearing in their assigned theater seats. In the next moment, Nikola Tesla manifested on stage.

"Thank you, Mr. Moses," he said, his brown mustache and long angular face instantly recognizable to the New Souls in the audience. Of all the members of the Salvation Twelve however, it was Secretary of State Sarah Palin who took a special interest in this former electrical and mechanical engineer, inventor, physicist and futurist. Having been intricately involved in energy issues during her tenure as Governor of Alaska, she was eager to hear what he had to say. Reading her mind, Tesla looked directly at her and made a request.

"Madam Secretary, please rise and tell us about the biggest energy challenges you faced during your time on the physical plane. Your achievements have not gone unnoticed in the spiritual realm."

"Thank you Mr. Tesla," she replied humbly. "Honestly, the toughest challenge I faced wasn't a lack of natural resources but an abundance of negative character traits, thanks to the fallibility of human nature. I'm referring to the staggering arrogance and self-interest of greedy politicians and oil company executives who abused their power and cut deals with each other to line their own pockets at the expense of the people. And some of them were members of my own party—a party with a platform of fiscal responsibility, ethical behavior and adherence to the United States Constitution!

"It got so bad that at one point I even resigned from my job as Chairwoman of the Alaska Oil and Gas Conservation Commission in protest against a fellow commissioner and state Republican Party Chairman. I was extremely unhappy that this man had been conducting party business on state time and did not want to be associated with someone so obviously lacking in integrity. It didn't come as any great surprise that he was later fined $12,000 for violating state ethics laws.

"But the oil companies were also a problem. At any given time they had a number of projects under consideration based on various factors, most notably return on capital. These oil companies were investing in other projects around the world while Alaska's projects sat waiting, denying jobs to citizens and energy resources to my state and country's hungry markets. So as governor my interest in speeding up development of my state's resources was motivated by a desire to create good jobs and to help my country become energy independent.

"Probably my most famous fight with big oil was with Exxon Mobil. I attempted to revoke their license to the Point-Thomson oil-and-gas field, one of the largest undeveloped fields in the USA, because they'd been sitting on it for *26 years*! Since they'd failed to develop it quickly enough, we were losing jobs and energy. When Exxon Mobil announced soon after that it had brought in equipment and planned to drill the following winter, many credited me for the decision while others doubted I had anything to do with it. I didn't care either way; I just wanted them to move forward or else face the consequences. It's like my favorite modern president once said,

"'There is no limit to what a man can do or where he can go if he doesn't mind who gets the credit."

Palin paused, suddenly aware of a glaring absence.

"By the way, why isn't President Ronald Reagan here? And for that matter, where is Prime Minister Margaret Thatcher? Seems odd they wouldn't be part of a gathering like this when you consider their many accomplishments on earth, not the least of which being the defeat of communism without firing a single shot."

Tesla smiled as the 40th President of the United States of America and the former Prime Minister of England at once manifested on stage with him while an amused Moses, Jesus and Mohammad looked on. A stunned Palin lit up excitedly from within at the sight of her earthly role-models.

"President Reagan, Prime Minister Thatcher you're here!" she exclaimed.

"Oh don't you worry, we're definitely here, Sarah," Reagan and Thatcher communicated in unison. "We're watching the Salvation Twelve assignment unfold from our own special vantage point, confident that the Advanced Souls gathered in this theater hall will provide everything you need to usher in Salvation Days on earth. Thank you for thinking of us. We're very proud of you."

Sarah Palin beamed, unable to speak or shift her gaze anywhere else for what seemed like an eternity. She felt incredibly humbled and unworthy in their presence, a transmission of thought they immediately absorbed.

"Yes, you are most worthy Sarah or you would not have been selected for this mission, along with the rest of the Salvation Twelve team."

Reagan and Thatcher scanned the room, making eye contact with each of the New Souls tasked with initiating God's special project including Eyal Grad who watched in awe with the rest of his colleagues. "We are very proud of *all* of you," they clarified. "Listen well to these Advanced Souls because they will show you the way." Then with a nod to Moses, Jesus and Mohammad they vanished into another state of being.

"Happy?" Tesla teased. Palin nodded at him with a satisfied smile.

"Well, now that that little meeting is over, can we please get back to the issue at hand?" Moses sternly interjected. "We have much to cover and time is of the essence....at least on earth. Mr. Tesla, let's get to the point, shall we?"

"Yes sir," he replied respectfully, returning his gaze back to a slightly embarrassed Sarah Palin who apologized profusely to Moses, Jesus and Mohammad.

"It's ok Sarah!" Jesus consoled her. "Now just let Mr. Tesla finish what he has to say. I think you'll be pleasantly surprised." She nodded at him before returning her attention to Tesla.

"Now then," he continued, "while I am most impressed with your actions on earth, I must tell you there is a much better way to provide energy cheaply and abundantly for the citizens of all nations. And that is by tapping into the power of earth, which produces its own natural heat in endless abundance. By using thermal energy extracted from the earth's core to run electrical generators and turbines you'll produce energy cheaply—practically free. This will also transform the energy industry from a hydrocarbon base to an electrical base, eliminating the need for what many of you on earth still wrongly refer to as fossil fuels. This is completely bone-headed.

"The very term 'fossil fuel' is a big lie. It originated out of ignorance because 100 years ago when humans started using oil, they thought that petroleum fuel originated from the fossils of extinct dinosaurs. Today we know that hydrocarbon fuel does *not* come from fossils; it's not a byproduct of extinct dinosaurs but a natural result of an earthly process in which water from the sea flows into the core of the earth, breaking down and creating a new molecule of hydrocarbon between the hydrogen from the sea water and the carbon from the rocks. Anyway, I just needed to clarify that point because it drives me crazy that anyone on earth still buys into the *fossil fuel* bunk.

"But getting back to the matter at hand, when you make the transition to plentiful, electrical energy, you won't have to deal with the arrogance, pride, egomania and greed of oil industry executives or politicians."

"So we need to build more nuclear power plants?" Palin asked. "Because as you probably know that's been another bone of contention for decades, ever since the Three Mile Island incident in 1979."

"My dear," Tesla answered, "that's one thing that puzzles me the most about the so-called leaders inhabiting the earth these days. And what's wrong with some of these scientists? Don't they know there is absolutely no need to even build nuclear power plants in the first place? You are all sitting on an earth that produces its own natural heat; it's simply a matter of extracting it."

"And how do we do that Mr. Tesla?"

"By taking advantage of a natural phenomenon on earth you already know as the Ring of Fire, an area where a large number of earthquakes and volcanic eruptions occur in the basin of the Pacific Ocean. The Ring of Fire is a direct result of plate tectonics and the movement and collisions of lithospheric plates. Your colleague Eyal Grad has already tapped into this resource, perfecting the process of extraction so well that now all of his country's cars are powered by electrical energy. We'll pick his brain about it in a moment," Tesla promised. Grad illuminated over the prospect of sharing his success in this regard.

"That sounds good to me!" Palin laughed. "But how exactly will this work? Have you seen how dangerous these so-called 'smart cars' are? How will people get around? Are we eliminating private vehicles?"

"Oh heavens, *no!*" Tesla exclaimed. "We're all about empowering individuals in Salvation Time, not taking away their freedoms. The cars they'll have will be even stronger and safer than the popular ones in use now. The major difference is that these cars will operate purely on electricity. And interstates and highways will continue to exist but they will be equipped with 'charging lanes' much like the slower traffic right lanes you have now. Except the purpose of these right charging lanes will be to recharge cars that are running low on electricity.

"So if you're riding along in your car in a normal speed lane and notice that your electrical supply is running low, you simply pull over to the right charging lane which will be equipped with energy strips over which your tires will roll as you slow down to a speed of about 30-40 miles per hour. This will recharge your car as you drive. Best of all, it will cost pennies to recharge your car, as opposed to the high gasoline prices you're all dealing with now, thanks to existence of commodities created by the current system that raises prices and makes everybody miserable."

"Surely there will be some maintenance costs involved?"

"Of course, Sarah," Tesla continued. "There will certainly be some maintenance involved in keeping the lines working safely but since most of the work will be done by the jail system it will be very inexpensive. In the Salvation Time Prison System, cheap labor combined with cheap electricity means very low prices for the consumer. The prison in each city or municipal area will be responsible for transporting electricity to the communities they serve.

"As a result, energy prices will be dramatically reduced, thereby making life infinitely more comfortable for the everyday citizen. He'll no longer have to run to the gas station and cough up five dollars a gallon to fill his tank. And the environment will benefit too as this system eliminates greenhouse gases and hydrocarbon gases. When you extract heat from the ground, you don't burn anything. And though the cars will be even bigger and stronger than the ones you all drive now, they won't burn diesel or gasoline. They'll run on electricity making them faster for those of you who like to put the pedal to the metal."

Everyone in the room laughed—even Napoleon, who was still off in his own corner, pretending he wasn't listening to the program. Of course, having lived and died in a period that preceded the invention of the automobile, it wasn't as if he could claim such an experience while in human form on earth. When the laughter died down, Sarah Palin asked another question.

"Mr. Tesla, what about trucks and farm equipment? These vehicles are vital to the development and distribution of food. Will they also run on electrical power?"

"I am so glad you asked about that Sarah. Trucks and farm equipment will still run on hydrocarbon fuel but because the demand for it will be extremely reduced thanks to electric cars, gasoline will be very cheap. Thus vehicles that operate on hydrocarbon will be very inexpensive to run. This will also create a trickle-down effect on the cost of food, which will become blessedly inexpensive. The cost of food will be about 75 percent of what it is currently, so that a loaf of bread that now costs $3.00 will only cost 25 cents once this system is in place. By revolutionizing the energy industry, you will cause prices to drop everywhere. You'll improve the quality of life for all citizens who will live much more comfortably and easily. Isn't that correct Mr. Grad?"

Eyal Grad's ears perked up at the mention of his name. He'd been listening intently and nodding along with Tesla's suggestions because he knew from his own experience that they worked just as he described. Yet he was humble enough to wait for his turn to speak even after Tesla referenced him earlier in the conversation. For an Advanced Soul like Tesla to acknowledge Grad's role in implementing such a system in his own country in the aftermath of isolation filled the Prime Minister with a very real and welcome sense of satisfaction and accomplishment.

"Yes sir, that is correct," Grad responded. "In Israel we converted to geo-thermal and electrical energy using the tectonic plates found at the bottom of the Dead Sea and the Jordan River. The portion of the so-called 'Ring of Fire' in our area extends all the way from the Dead Sea to the Golan Heights to Northern Israel. I commissioned Israeli scientists and industrialists to invest in extracting the heat and converting it into electricity. We drill into the ground and use the earth's natural heat to supply our energy needs. It's really all about common sense.

"In these new electric cars, all you need is a motor and a transmission—no valves, no pistons, no fuel, no oil filters, no fuel filters. It's very simple because electric energy makes cars cheap, easy to maintain and much more efficient. Cars that run on petroleum only get about 20- to- 35 percent efficiency but cars that run on electricity get 80- to- 90 percent efficiency. Now there is a generator on the car that works on petroleum just to generate energy to the battery.

"But it's nothing like what these other countries are still using on earth at this point in time. In Israel, people now have plenty of money because they're not spending it on gasoline. Instead of filling up weekly, they only visit the gas station maybe once every three- to-four months. And without the need for fake fossil fuels, there's no carbon monoxide pollution.

"Just as you described, since we converted to this system in Israel we have solved our energy problems. People have their financial freedom and the freedom to drive their own cars anywhere they choose, using heat from the earth that came from God. Further, this system has vastly improved the travel experience because we have highly efficient bullet trains that also run on electricity, making it easy and cheap for everyday people to visit new places all around the world. Airplanes still exist and run on hydrocarbon fuel but again because the demand for it has been considerably reduced, the cost of a plane ticket is a fraction of what is used to be. Therefore, if people don't wish to travel by bullet train, airplanes are a viable option. And of course, they are also used for commercial purposes like transporting cargo and equipment worldwide. Given all of its benefits, this energy system must be implemented in every nation on earth immediately."

"Very impressive, Eyal!" Palin exclaimed. "We never did get around to discussing this at the G20 Summit, so I am so glad you were able to share it with all of us here."

As if to summarize this portion of the project assignment, Tesla loudly cleared his throat before scanning the room and looking into the eyes of each of the Salvation Twelve.

"Do you all agree to begin moving your respective countries from a petroleum-based energy system to an electrically based one?" he inquired very seriously, signifying the importance of his request. One by one, each of the Salvation Twelve souls emitted a brilliant light, signaling consent and excitement.

"Excellent!" he remarked happily. "I trust you will all look to Mr. Grad for advice and input since he's already led his country through this energy transition with stellar results.

"Nicely done, Mr. Tesla," Moses declared. "And thank you Madam Secretary and Mr. Grad for your thoughtful questions and commentary." Then his raised his staff as an alert that it was indeed time to move on to the next topic. Tesla vanished from the stage as quickly as he'd appeared, returning to his place among the Advanced Souls.

Just then a pure white sparkling orb descended from above. Centering itself directly above the stage, the vibrant celestial energy gradually transformed into the shape of a human being as it continued to emit brilliant, pulsating light. The New Souls were so dazzled by this spectacle they struggled keep their focus upon it.

In the next moment, this new presence shifted its attention to Eyal Grad, who stared back in awe and trepidation.

"Eyal, do not be afraid. I am so glad to finally have the chance to meet you," the figure addressed him warmly.

"W-who are you?" the Prime Minister asked in a barely audible whisper.

"I'm your grandfather, Eyal. We never did get to meet in earthly life, so—"

"Of course, it's *you* Saba!" Eyal exclaimed, suddenly overwhelmed by the realization. He'd heard much about his beloved grandfather from his parents but due to the evil actions of men on earth, had never had the chance to know him personally. Together at last in the afterlife, the two souls warmly embraced as an aura of alternating violet, blue and white surrounded them. Consumed with pure love, all souls gathered reveled in the feeling of unbridled joy elicited by the reunion.

After a few moments, Moses spoke up. "Alright gentlemen, we're all genuinely touched to witness your acknowledgement of eternal love. We rejoice with you. But I must remind you, Mendel Grad, that God requested your appearance here in this amphitheater for a higher purpose. It's not only to embrace Eyal but to cover a very important topic. Please, educate us sir."

"As you wish, Mr. Moses," he replied humbly, releasing Eyal who continued to stand on the stage with him.

He scanned the room as he began his instruction. "Thank you for indulging my grandson and me. While in human form, we never had the chance to know each other because I was taken away to Auschwitz just prior to Eyal's birth."

An audible, collective gasp reverberated throughout the room.

"Yes, it was absolute torture," Mendel admitted. "The pain and suffering inflicted upon innocent people by evil, militant men is almost indescribable. When they weren't murdering us in the ovens, they were gassing us in the showers. In between they severely beat us, tortured us, forced us to work like slaves and inflicted all sorts of indignities upon us. These egomaniacal bastards looked upon us as human waste, unfit to take up space on earth. And yet, God allowed this to take place for a very specific purpose."

"Saba, how could God approve something so diabolical and wicked?" Eyal asked incredulously. "As you yourself stated, these victims were innocent people. Why did God allow Hitler and his minions to commit massive genocide?"

"Well Eyal, from your perspective I can understand how it appears that way. And yes, what the Nazis perpetrated on earth was pure evil; there is no argument about that. However, you must also remember that before they were born into their earthly bodies, the souls of those the Nazis terrorized purposely selected this mission on earth. They saw their entire lifetime long before they ever took human form. We also have to keep in mind that God endows all human beings with free will. Hitler and his men used their free will to torture and murder millions; we the targets of his hatred, however, failed to exercise ours. Or more precisely, we failed to use our free will to do the *right* thing. We chose fear over courage; cowardice over rebellion. Instead of fighting, questioning or resisting, we got used to being the world's scapegoats and figured, 'It won't be so bad.' We could not have been more wrong.

"Instead of seizing the chance to confront evil as God wanted us to do, we simply went along with it. Even if the end result had been the same, the lesson we learned in that lifetime is that it's far nobler to go down *with* a fight than to become submissive sheep, easily led to slaughter.

"If only we had banded together and used common sense, we might have been able to save ourselves. By choosing to meekly obey the Nazis and forget that we are also children of the One Creator worthy of dignity, respect and life, we failed the test for that incarnation. God challenged us and we fell short."

The room fell silent as all souls pondered Mendel Grad's wise but sobering words.

Once satisfied that they'd absorbed the lesson, Moses spoke up. "Thank you, Mr. Grad for your testimony. Do any of the New Souls have a question for him?"

"Saba, have any of these souls who were once Nazis reincarnated since then?"

"Oh yes Eyal," he answered confidently. "Depending on where they were in their own development, some of these former Nazi souls came back in the next lifetime as sick, homeless Haitians to make up for what they'd done. Others opted to return as religious fanatics—suicide-bombing Islamists in one lifetime, rigid orthodox Rabbis in another. Remember, life is an eternal opportunity to learn, grow, repent and move closer to God. The cycle is endless."

Every soul in the room illuminated in response. Moses then advised them it was time to move on. That's when Mendel Grad asked for permission to speak. After Moses nodded his approval, he continued.

Looking into the eyes of his beloved grandson he complimented, "I am very proud of you, Eyal. Unlike me, you confronted evil on earth by taking a bold stand against Islamic fundamentalists. You made a promise to your people and once they elected you, you kept this promise. Instead of cowering in fear, you stood strong. Because of your courage you've saved countless lives on earth, enabling them to exercise their free will and fulfill their lifetime's purpose. I am spending my time here on The Other Side pondering your bravery and deciding what my new challenge will be when I reincarnate again."

Overwhelmed with emotion, Eyal could barely whisper, "Thank you, Saba" before his grandfather then addressed the soulful crowd.

"I urge all of you to follow Eyal's example," he firmly advised them. "Evil exists for a purpose. It's God's test for the upstanding citizens on earth. Will you choose fear or will you choose courage? Your decision has a ripple effect on the entire world, so choose wisely."

Then with a final embrace of his grandson, Mendel Grad dissolved into the atmosphere to return to another level of existence.

Eyal Grad remained humbled by his grandfather's words and consumed with gratitude for having been given the opportunity to finally meet him. He vowed to remember this interlude when he returned to his body.

Without missing a beat, God's project manager resumed his duties. "Mr. Cromwell," he addressed another Advanced Soul in attendance. "Please join us on stage that you might share your insights and instruction on how the justice system must operate in Salvation Time as opposed to how it has worked on earth thus far."

"Yes sir Mr. Moses," Cromwell respectfully replied, appearing before the Salvation Twelve on the raised platform. The New Souls gathered radiated with excitement at the sight of the man famed for his courageous championing of the rights of the common people during his lifetime in 17th century England, when the country was ruled by an oppressive monarchy.

Although Cromwell had incarnated nearly 400 years after the signing of the Magna Charta, recognized as the cornerstone of liberty and justice in western civilization, Cromwell's monarch King Charles I, had tyrannically ruled over his English subjects in accordance with the Divine Right of Kings. Righteously angered by the monarch's demands of complete obedience from his subjects as the king "appointed by God" to rule over them, Cromwell had dedicated his life to dethroning King Charles and establishing a representative governmental system in which the rights of individuals would be respected and upheld. Thus he'd earned a distinguished place in British history as the most powerful commoner to have ever lived because leading up to the End Days Cromwell had retained the distinction of being the only man to have given England its sole experiment in republican government. There was no more appropriate Advanced Soul to speak to the critical issue of a justice system than that of Oliver Cromwell.

"First," he began, "I would like to echo the sentiments of the Advanced Souls who've already taken the stage by reminding you how proud we are of all of you and how much faith we have in your abilities to help establish Salvation Time on earth. I know from experience how difficult a challenge it can be to reign in the powerful in order to secure the rights of everyday citizens but the world is at a point now where this is not only possible but necessary.

"And as Andrew Jackson said, while in human form we're capable of both heroism and savagery. If you studied anything about the history of England and Ireland, I'm sure you know I was also quite barbaric toward the Irish. For this I am very sorry.

"But let's tend to the matter at hand, shall we?

"In my time on earth I dealt with a power-hungry monarch who labored under the delusion that God had appointed him personally to micromanage every aspect of his subjects' lives. However, most of you today are dealing with a justice system corrupted by greedy lawyers who are also driven by self-interest. These losers, these selfish bastards, keep writing laws to benefit themselves and their cronies at the expense of the people so that the Divine Right of Kings has transformed into the self-proclaimed omnipotence of the legal profession.

"I've noticed this particularly in the United States, where most of your entrenched career politicians are also lawyers. Pity, the country whose constitution was based upon the glorious Magna Charta—which secured the rights of both noblemen and peasants and protected them from arbitrary actions against their persons or property by an overreaching sovereign—is now run by a permanent political class that brazenly defies the principles of its founding document and subverts the rights of its people."

Madam Secretary Sarah Palin shook her head sadly as she listened to Cromwell's sobering words—words that accurately described the current state of her country's governing elite and the plight of its over-taxed, over-regulated and overly imposed upon citizens. She listened carefully as he spoke, along with all of the New Souls in the theater hall.

"However," Cromwell continued, "the justice system needs a complete overhaul in every country, not just in the United States. Some of you may be thinking, 'Oliver how exactly do we do that?' Well ladies and gentlemen I am here to give you the blueprint for a fair justice system. And it begins by curtailing the power and influence of these loser lawyers who are screwing up the system worldwide!"

A collective laugh reverberated around the amphitheater as New Souls, Advanced Souls and Ascended Masters alike acknowledged the truth of Cromwell's hard-hitting speech.

"Now then," he continued. "You must change the legal profession from one of dominance and power to one that's the final refuge of scoundrels and idiots. The title of 'lawyer' must become a symbol of someone who cannot hold a job anywhere else—no longer a title held by those with a lust for power and an overriding selfishness that drives them to corrupt the entire system for their own ends.

"Thus in Salvation Time, lawyers will be only pencil-pushers and administrators. They will be forbidden to run for any kind of public office whether at the local, state or federal levels. Their entire function will be as consultants in the process of writing laws—that's it. If you choose to become a lawyer in Salvation Time, you forfeit your right to ever become a mayor, a city council member, a congressman, a senator or a politician of any sort. You may not advertise your services on television or on the radio but solely through word-of-mouth and the exchange of business cards. To sum it up, in Salvation Time   lawyers will be only administrators helping the system work efficiently."

Cromwell paused and scanned the room, gauging the reaction. Pleased to see all of the New Souls pulsating in agreement he continued.

"So now that the role of lawyers in Salvation Time has been clarified, let's talk about the requirements of running for political office. Do you all agree that a huge part of the problem today involves career politicians who've never even held a job in the private sector or more importantly, have never run so much as a lemonade stand?"

"That's it exactly Mr. Cromwell!" Palin blurted out. "Right now the US has a Community Organizer Chicago politician in charge, surrounded by nothing but career politicians. They are ruining a once great and prosperous nation!"

"And that's why Sarah—each and every one of you must change the requirements of political office in your respective countries," he explained. To eliminate career politicians you must mandate a minimum of five years' experience running your own business prior to running for office. Every individual who seeks to become a public servant must have had the experience of making a payroll, turning a profit, managing employees, satisfying customers and generally running a respectable, successful business both in terms of income generated and products and services created.

"This real-world, practical experience will help ensure that these folks make good decisions based on sound reasoning, fiscal responsibility and ethical considerations. When you successfully implement these requirements, there will be no way someone like a George W. Bush or a Barack Hussein Obama will ever get elected again. Last but certainly not least, you must also abolish so-called 'political dynasties.' Particularly during the 20th century of the End

Days, the United States fell captive to this nonsense, creating an entitlement mentality within politically connected families much like the Divine Right of Kings. Individuals born into families that included senators, congressional representatives and presidents presumed it was their right also to go to Washington D.C., which helped solidify a permanent political class of elites. I'm telling you there must never again be a Clinton, Bush, Kennedy or any other political dynasty ever again, on any country on earth," Cromwell ordered.

"Sounds good to me!' Palin and Grad simultaneously transmitted. For reasons unique to each of them, Cromwell's edict resonated clearly. Throughout her own political service, Palin had repeatedly confronted arrogant power-brokers from well-connected families who, threatened by her unmistakable connection to the common people, set out to destroy her and her family. And for both Palin and Grad, the current President of the United States was a chilling embodiment of rampant ignorance, narcissism, arrogance and dhimmitude.

"I think you'll both agree," Cromwell noted in response to their thoughts, "that the traits you despise in the current Leader of the Free World also apply to judges, which is why you must radically change their roles and requirements. Just as with existing politicians and would-be politicians, judges must have a proven track-record of success as business-owners for a minimum of five years before they even consider rising to a position of power in which they will determine just rulings for those on trial.

"Furthermore, they must be at least 50 years old with good morals and ethics, as determined by a special committee formed for the exclusive purpose of recommending eligible citizens for judicial appointments. Once nominated, these aspiring judges must undergo extensive psychological testing to ensure their sound mental health. Once they pass, they will then be placed into a training program where they'll sit with an existing judge on a daily basis so they can observe his or her decisions and the way they work in a court house.

"As per the job description, a judge has the discretion and ability to exact the right punishment for a criminal based on a multitude of factors including whether or not he or she is a first-time or a multiple offender. Judges must demonstrate their wisdom and understanding that human beings are not machines, but unique creatures endowed with their own gifts and characteristics from their

Creator. Therefore in dealing with them, judges must acknowledge that every situation is different, that there is no such thing as a 'one-size-fits-all' solution in terms of justice or penalty. Because they are variable, each human being must be judged on his or her own merit, record and crime. As a judge you must show humility and fairness in meting out punishment, always with the intention of helping the individual become a better person and a productive member of society. This effort also requires creativity and the recognition that in some cases, a punishment might not be appropriate. Perhaps instead the person would be better served by taking a course, doing community service or even being set free with a warning. The bottom line is that the rulings rendered by judges must be proclaimed for the benefit of all so that they create a win-win scenario.

"Which leads me to my final topics—Sin City and the Salvation Time Prison System. As you may know from your study of history, I was a devout Puritan during my time on earth. In fact, I was so moralistic that as Lord Protector I tried to legislate the morality of British citizens—a big mistake. Folks, God naturally endows human beings with certain needs and urges because it is only through human weakness that our souls can grow and learn while in a physical body. Therefore, in Salvation Time we must accommodate the needs of those who are incapable of balancing their animal nature with their spiritual nature while also respecting the dignity of all human beings, especially those raising families.

"So housed within the designated Prison System of each community, I recommend the building of a 'Sin City' where those who cannot control their sexual impulses can have them satisfied by prostitutes. Unlike the current system, in   Salvation Time prostitutes will be the owners of their sole enterprises—not *owned* by violent, immoral pimps. They will be required to visit a doctor regularly to ensure the absence of sexually transmitted diseases and their places of work must meet all sanitary requirements. And ALL prostitutes must operate their businesses from within Sin City—nowhere else. If they're caught on a street corner in the middle of a neighborhood they will be appropriately fined and possibly lose their license."

Cromwell again scanned the amphitheater for signs of approval or disapproval from his audience. He was pleased to note that all were lighting up again, communicating their agreement.

"Now then," he resumed, "as for the Salvation Time Prison System, it will exist both to punish criminals for the mandated time proclaimed by a judge and to house an individual for life, if that is his wish. Understanding that God sends about 10 percent of the population to earth for the sole purpose of screwing things up that the rest of us might learn from them, we must make accommodation for these people. A large majority of them are simply incapable of living in mainstream society without constantly committing crimes against innocent citizens. The Salvation Time Prison System will offer them the option of staying there for life if the idea of returning to civilization once they've completed their sentence is just too overwhelming.

"However, they will have a choice as to the type of living conditions they'll get. If they choose to work, they'll earn reduced wages for putting time in on projects like the for-profit farms, factories and power plants. If appropriate for the nature of their crime, they will use this money to make restitution to their victims and help support their own families back home. Since they've opted to work, they'll also have access to higher quality food and clothing, in addition to cable television and internet."

Here Cromwell paused and noted: "If only I'd been so lucky to have such technologically advanced tools at my disposal when I took on King Charles—what a pity!" He let out a deep, dramatic sigh prompting the theater hall to erupt in laughter. A moment later however, Moses chided the former Lord Protectorate to get on with the program as there was still much to cover.

"Indeed Mr. Moses," he respectfully acknowledged. "Well, we've discussed the prisoners and lifetime residents who choose to work so let's talk about those who wish to live there permanently as lazy bums instead of productive workers. These folks will reside in a tented area unprotected from natural elements. They'll still be given clothing but it will be very basic stuff, not nearly as nice as their counterparts who choose to work. They'll have no access to cable television or the internet. Whereas those who work will have the privilege of monthly connubial visits with a Sin City prostitute, those who refuse to work will forfeit this privilege. And of course, they will receive nourishment but their food will be bland and basic—even worse than English food!—not nearly as tasty as the morsels enjoyed by working prisoners.

"Overall the Salvation Time Prison System will exist to protect the innocent, house the guilty, and supply the energy and nutritional needs of the local community it serves. By putting this system in place, you will save taxpayers a tremendous amount of money, protect society as a whole, and preserve the dignity of those human beings God sends here to commit crimes and challenge law-abiding citizens. Much like judicial rulings rendered by thoughtful judges on a case-by-case basis, this is also a win-win scenario for everyone involved."

When Cromwell finished speaking Moses tapped his staff a few times on the stage then asked if the New Souls had any further questions. That's when Eyal Grad emitted rays of light.

"Yes, Mr. Grad?" Moses acknowledged.

"Mr. Moses, I just wanted to thank Mr. Cromwell for his input. When I was elected three years ago, one of the things I promised Israeli citizens was that I would overhaul our justice system. While we've made impressive progress in every other area, we're still working on improvements to justice. I can't wait to implement Mr. Cromwell's ideas."

"Very well, Mr. Grad," Moses answered. "The Ascended Masters and Advanced Souls will be watching from The Other Side. He then thanked Cromwell and advised him to retake his seat, signaling the end of this particular discussion.

"Now then," Moses continued, "it's time for a conversation about medicine. I call Mother Teresa and Benjamin Franklin to the stage." In an instant, the two Advanced Souls appeared before their audience.

"Thank you Mr. Moses," they humbly replied. "We would like to ask Eyal Grad to open up the dialogue by sharing with us the exceptional improvements he enacted in his own country with respect to healthcare and the medical profession. Mr. Grad?" The Prime Minister beamed. He was eager to inform his colleagues about Israel's successful health care system.

"Thank you Mother Teresa, Mr. Franklin," he began. "After my country's isolation I decided we could no longer depend on other nations for medical advancement and innovation. We had to find a way to make healthcare and medicine cheap and effective, with a doctor-patient ratio of 20 to one. So my administration determined that our immediate goal, our most pressing job, was to produce 3,000 doctors per year. And I am proud to say we achieved our objectives.

"How did we do it?

"By using common sense and logic; by setting the system up to win, not fail. We realized that our job was to help aspiring doctors pass medical tests and earn their degrees with the understanding that yes, you do need a certain amount of intelligence to become a doctor but that the most important thing in medicine is the physical body. Every human being's body does most of its own healing because the best doctor in the world is within. Every patient simply needs the right person in the form of a doctor to guide them on the path to healing and wellness. Someone accredited to advise them, 'Hey listen, you need to do this; you need to take that.' These doctors don't have to be super-geniuses because the body heals itself.

"Today in Israel there's a doctor living two-to-three houses or apartments away from every citizen. So if you have a medical question there's always a medical professional nearby to ask. Drugs are also very inexpensive, with pills costing pennies as opposed to dollars. That's because we've eliminated excessive and burdensome government regulations and fines that imposed millions of dollars on pharmaceutical companies before they could even bring a drug out of clinical trials and into the market.

Yes, testing must be done to ensure safety and effectiveness. Clinical trials must be rigid and strong. Therefore our solution was to create a volunteer committee of retired doctors to provide oversight and input into the research and development of drugs. And although these doctors declined any kind of monetary reward for their time and expertise, we decided we'd compensate them anyway, in addition to featuring them on prominent television programs to express our gratitude and give them the recognition they deserve. We also eliminated the oppressive fines on pharmaceutical companies that made their products so expensive for the average consumer."

"Wonderful, Mr. Grad!" Mother Teresa beamed. Then turning her attention to all of the New Souls, she reprimanded them, "I hope you are all listening carefully to Mr. Grad because he has laid the groundwork for a successful and humane medical system. All of you must do as he has done, especially with respect to the pharmaceutical industry. You demand that your governments get out of the pharmaceutical business and let them do what they need to do, which is to produce good drugs to help people heal. And stop with the greed!"

"Amen Mother Teresa!" Grad exclaimed. "In Israel today we have an abundance of excellent doctors and plentiful, affordable drugs. This means all citizens can get the medical attention they need at a much lower cost. Because Israelis have money in their pockets they can choose whatever they want. Their lives are easy now, not crazy and chaotic. So when you have a health issue that demands medical attention, you go the hospital where they'll give you cheap, but effective drugs and cheap but effective clinical treatment. Meanwhile, doctors still make money in a profession that remains lucrative and fulfilling.

"Money constantly circulates for the benefit of all. Problems occur when money is pent-up and becomes a commodity; money should *never* be a commodity! An abundant flow of money must circulate continuously and endlessly, with everyone's participation in the cycle, not just an elite few. These elites intentionally choke the entire system to create a money shortage. We no longer allow this in Israel. And whether you hire a doctor, a landscaper or a painter, payment is required upon completion of the service. If you don't like something, you can always follow up with legal action against the service provider but you must pay them immediately for services rendered. I recommend that all countries follow our example."

"If I may Mr. Grad," Benjamin Franklin began, "who runs your Israeli hospitals?"

"Sir, our hospitals are mostly government-managed. But keep in mind our Israeli government is much more streamlined than ever before. It's not an intrusive government seeking to control how much money everybody makes but a smart government that works from the bottom-up and administers from behind the scenes. Unlike what we've seen during most of the End Days, our politicians are nothing more than clerks that ensure everything is functioning properly. And as I mentioned, we reward the retired doctors who form our oversight committee with money and recognition simply because it's the right thing to do."

"My compliments sir," Franklin replied earnestly. "I just have one other question. You know when I was in human form I always said, 'An apple a day keeps the doctor away.' You've mentioned traditional medicine and pharmaceuticals but I'm wondering, do your

Israeli doctors also practice what's still frustratingly known on earth as 'alternative' therapies? By that I mean treatments that address the whole of a human being—physical, emotional, spiritual and psychological."

"Mr. Franklin I am so glad you brought that up," Grad enthused. "Yes, in Israel we very much promote and provide all sorts of healing modalities including hypnosis, past life regression, massage, acupuncture, Reiki, chiropractic, aromatherapy and just about all treatments not yet considered 'traditional' in most countries. We firmly believe in holistic healing because all of these therapies play a vital role in the overall wellness of human beings.

"And again because money is plentiful and constantly circulating, because the cost of necessities like food, fuel and education are greatly reduced, because we've established a workable medical system that satisfies everyone, individuals can easily pay for whatever treatment their doctor recommends. There's no longer any fear about obtaining the medical care you or your loved ones need because it's affordable and it works well. Our Israeli healthcare system is a huge success."

Mother Teresa and Benjamin Franklin lit up with pride. "Congratulations, Mr. Grad! You and your Israeli colleagues have done tremendous work in this very important area, thanks to your leadership and determination."

An excited Grad couldn't help but pulsate in response; after all the time spent revitalizing just about every industry in his nation, it was gratifying to receive such high praise from these two Advanced Souls. A moment later, Moses' now-familiar tapping interrupted the interlude.

"Mother Teresa, Mr. Franklin, your final thoughts before we move to the next item on our agenda?" he inquired.

"Yes, Mr. Moses. We just want to encourage all of the New Souls here to follow Mr. Grad's example and create a similar system in each of their countries. If they do, they will solve one of the world's most difficult problems and make life infinitely better for their citizens. We request that Mr. Grad act as a consultant if called upon since he's pioneered this new and superior method of bringing low-cost, high-quality healthcare to Israel. Mr. Grad, do you accept this responsibility?"

"It would be an honor," he assured them.

In the next moment, Mother Teresa spoke up again. "Mr. Moses, I would also like to address the issue of housing with Mr. Grad since during my time on earth, I worked with the poor and sick who had nowhere else to go. Mr. Grad, how are you dealing with the problem of homelessness?" she asked pointedly.

"Mother Teresa, I am happy to answer that," the Prime Minister replied. "Under my administration's leadership we created a mandate that every citizen must have their own place to live—a government-managed apartment. These apartment complexes are located in specific districts within local communities, and those who live in them must submit to random drug testing and keep their residences clean. To ensure that they comply, we hold weekly scheduled inspections during which government officials must be allowed into their private living space. If the person is found to be a neglectful housekeeper or taking illegal drugs, he temporarily loses the right to live there and is sent to the nearest prison for a prescribed period of time.

"But because these apartments are so well-constructed and comfortable, most people take good care of them. In fact, even those who are gainfully employed and earning a good living sometimes choose to relocate to these government-subsidized complexes, although they must pay rent. Those who live there because of unemployment and homelessness 'pay' for their apartments by keeping the neighborhood clean. They pick up trash, provide landscaping services and make home repairs for their neighbors, like plumbing and electricity. Of course, if they do not have training in these areas, we put them through the necessary classes as a requirement. So rather than this being just a hand-out, people are required to do something productive in exchange for a nice place to live. We believe this is the most humane way of solving the problem of homelessness."

Grad paused, awaiting her reaction. He was thrilled to see all souls in the room transmitting their approval, including Mother Teresa.

"I am very proud of you, Eyal," she beamed. Then turning her attention to the rest of the Salvation Twelve, she encouraged them to follow his example. With that, the two Advanced Souls dissolved into the ether and reappeared in their reserved seats in the amphitheater.

"Alright Mr. Grad," Moses continued. "Looks like you'll remain center stage again as we delve into the crucial matter of education. Please explain to all of us how you've resolved the issue of affordable education in your country."

"Thank you, Mr. Moses," he replied. "Again because of isolation, we were forced to become our own innovators in the area of education too. My government understood the urgent need for medical doctors, engineers, architects and other skilled professionals who would need access to a higher education before working in these fields. We became very determined to prove to the world that we could make life easy for our citizens in the wake of their rejection of us because of the way we handled Islam. Understanding that with more educated people around life is much better for everyone we set out to make access to education free—from kindergarten all the way through high school. So all you have to do is show up regularly, apply yourself in the classroom, study hard and earn good grades. And this in turn will give you a better shot at a fulfilling, happy life.

"However, our school curriculum isn't just about book-smarts. Our teachers impart practical knowledge to our students like how to open a bank account and how to save and manage money, in addition to hands-on study of various trades like plumbing, car repair and maintenance, painting, and home-building. Israeli students receive a superior education for the least amount of money.

"I can immediately sense that some of you are thinking, *'Eyal, this all sounds great but how is it possible that your country can provide free education from kindergarten through high school?'* Remember my friends that Israel now prints its own money, enabling our government to pay for the building and maintenance of school facilities, the salaries of our teachers, and all supplies necessary for a quality education. Our excellent educators make good money and because we've greatly reduced the cost of things like food, fuel, and electricity money goes much further than it did in the past. There's no need to impose tuition on parents. Parents can relax, knowing their children are learning all of the skills they need to function as productive, well-adjusted adults. And because there's an abundance of money for teachers' salaries, more citizens than ever before are entering the profession; we never have a shortage of teachers.

"So now you are thinking, *'That's great Eyal but how do your citizens obtain access to a higher education if they choose to become doctors, engineers or scientists?'* And that's a very good question, one we had to consider thoughtfully before implementing our current system. We looked around and we noticed that intrusive government interference in the school loan business had artificially inflated tuition costs for colleges and universities. That these institutions—knowing that students could get a loan funded by taxpayers in the guise of a government subsidy—could raise tuition on a whim, hurting everyday working people and students alike. After all, upon graduating they'd be faced with an enormous debt even before getting a good job.

"To change this, we came up with a system where if you would like to continue your education after high school, if you have the ability to pay some money toward your higher education you will be required to pay tuition. If on the other hand you want to attend college but don't have the money, we work on the honor system: you can still earn your degree with the understanding that you will fully reimburse the school once you're out and working. If you choose to fulfill your financial obligation to your college and demonstrate good character you'll qualify one day to become a judge. If you don't pay it back, you will ruin your reputation. And in Israel right now, reputation is everything, as it should also be in Salvation Time."

Every entity in the amphitheater emitted brilliant light. Then a voice in the audience transmitted a question.

"What role do parents play in the education of their children in Israel?" Secretary of State Palin asked.

"Ah Sarah, I am so glad you brought that up because parents play a vital role in producing good, honest, responsible, hardworking and respectful citizens. In my country we recognize that this all begins in the home which is why we're so proud of the way Israeli parents raise their kids. They only receive allowances in exchange for doing very specific tasks around the house—laundry, dishes, house-cleaning, taking out the trash, cooking, cutting the lawn, etcetera. Each job is assigned a value or pay grade. For example, mowing the lawn might be worth $20, doing the laundry $15—whatever the parents decide—and the kids are free to do as many chores as they possibly can in any given week.

"In fact, in most households kids compete with each other over who can complete the most tasks and therefore make the most money at the end of every pay period. Working mothers come home to a clean house and a hot meal after a long day on the job, which makes life much more enjoyable for them. Families can spend time together doing fun things when mom and dad get home, not household chores. Parents and children keep track of everything on an electronic worksheet and when the designated day rolls around, the father tallies up each one's payout according to the number of chores they've completed and the dollar amount assigned to each. By the time they turn sixteen, kids can pay for their own cars and insurance—whatever make and model they can afford. In Israel there are no more spoiled kids because by setting them up with responsibilities at a young age, we set them up for life."

"That's fantastic Eyal!" Palin beamed. "My husband and I have raised our own kids the same way. It's been tragic to witness the results of absentee parenting in our society as a result of cultural decay, stressful work schedules and financial challenges. I know if we get back to these time-tested basics, we can restore the United States just as you've restored Israel."

"I guarantee all of you that if you put a similar educational system in place in your countries and encourage parents to impose responsibility on their children you will reap the same benefits," Grad declared. "All you need is the will to do it."

"Excellent Mr. Grad," Moses praised him. "I must say I am very impressed with your accomplishments on earth. Do you have anything else to add before we move on?"

"Mr. Moses I first want to say that my work on earth as a life coach, assisting individuals to make similar improvements in their own lives has prepared me well to take on the broader challenge of making life better for my county as a whole. I am very thankful to God for enabling me to do my work through the gifts he's given me.

"If you don't mind, I would just like to make a few other points about money, which we didn't cover earlier."

"You may continue, Mr. Grad," Moses nodded.

"Thank you, sir. It occurred to me that some of you might be wondering about inflation," he addressed his Salvation Twelve colleagues. "After all, with the cost of things like food, medicine, fuel and education being so inexpensive now, how did my country avoid it? I didn't have a chance to mention before that I also pioneered a method of producing synthetic gold, which has also devalued the existing gold market as you all know it—at least in my country. This synthetic gold is identical to the gold that you all still consider a precious metal; no one can even tell the difference."

"Alright Eyal," Ibrahim Ahmed interjected, "I'll bite. How did Israel avoid inflation given all of these dramatic changes to the economy?"

"Mr. Ahmed, the structure as you all know it has been completely turned upside-down in Israel. Now instead of corrupt politicians, real estate tycoons and corporations sitting at the top of the pyramid and making life miserable for everyone, we have instead elevated society's creators–entrepreneurs, artists, musicians, school teachers, factory owners—individuals who create things that improve the quality of life for others. Anything useful or beautiful that human beings create is now expensive, whereas before medicine, education, food, fuel, energy and gold were the most expensive things, making life extremely hard for everyday people.

"In Israel today, land ownership is also limited to 50 acres per citizen, similar to a policy instituted by a Roman Emperor centuries ago in an effort to curb corruption. One restriction: when the landowner dies, his properties must be sold. His children, of course, may receive the money from the sale if that is his wish, but they may not stay in the same homes on the same properties. We implemented this policy to rid Israel of political dynasties once and for all. The only exception to this rule is if a child has a physical problem like autism, which would make it very difficult for him to adjust to a new environment.

"Lucky for me this is working well in my country and unlike that poor Roman Emperor, no one has tried to assassinate me, although they *did* try to blow me up recently!" Grad enjoyed a good laugh at his own joke while the other souls groaned. He then quickly composed himself.

"Anyway Mr. Moses, I recommend that all countries follow the Israeli example because I can tell you from experience it works."

"Indeed Mr. Grad. You have used your God-given talents and skills magnificently during your time on earth. And you will soon do it again." Then he addressed the New Souls. "Do you all pledge to reproduce Mr. Grad's educational and economic solutions in your own countries and to inspire parents to instill a good work ethic in their children from a young age?"

All souls lit up excitedly.

"Excellent!" Moses declared. "And now we've arrived at the final lesson and assignment before sending you back to your physical bodies and earthly homes. And that is the one from which all others flow—religion."

"It hasn't escaped our notice here on The Other Side that most of the hatred, violence and animosity on earth is perpetuated in the name of religion. This rancor between competing theologies would be amusing if it wasn't so destructive and deadly, not to mention completely absurd. Why is this fighting completely wrong and unnecessary? Because there is only *one* God.

"We're all here—Jesus, Mohammad and me—and we know it's the same God. So what's all the fighting about? The world cannot move into Salvation Time with all of this hostility, bitterness and war perpetrated in the name of organized, divergent religions."

Jesus and Mohammad nodded their heads in agreement as they remained seated in their designated chairs.

"So now that I've identified the most pressing problem on earth, what's the solution?" Moses continued. "First, we must unite all religions under one very basic, fundamental truth: there is ONE God for all. This God does not belong to any one religion: he just IS. He's not exclusive to Judaism, Christianity, Islam or any other organized religion. It's the same God for all souls, all living creatures—the I AM WHO I AM; the Alpha and the Omega. He has no beginning and no end.

"And for the Creator life on earth is all about becoming a better person, doing productive and uplifting things for your fellow humans, and making life better for everyone—not perpetuating an endless cycle of violence in his name. For that reason Jesus, Mohammad and I recommend that you shift the world into a One God Religion on earth, where you will help to unite people instead of separating them. In order to achieve this noble goal, you must incorporate the very best of every existing religion and integrate it into one major religion to create unity among people all around the world, rather than hatred, war, violence, poverty, death and destruction. It's unity over hate, love and connectivity over fear and loathing.

"Sounds great right?" he rhetorically posed with a slight trace of sarcasm. "But how exactly do we shift the faithful from all of these divergent religions into The One God Religion?"

"Mr. Moses, if I may interject," Mohammad spoke up, rising from his chair.

"Take it away," Moses instructed with a slight turn in the prophet's direction. He pointed his staff at Mohammad as confirmation it was indeed his turn to share his insights on this critical topic.

"I pledge to help all of the New Souls with this effort because I know what the problem is," he began. "First, I am very aware of the Islamic fanatics who are currently causing 99 percent of the violence, bloodshed and destruction on earth in the name of Allah. I just want to point out this is not because of me; I couldn't even read or write during my lifetime. Other people wrote the Koran. They enshrined violence and the mandate to kill all infidels into the book and there was nothing I could do about it. Thanks to these writers, the Koran also bred mental and physical poverty within the Muslim community, so that even when Muslims moved to a more prosperous country they brought their poverty of mind and body with them, perpetuating a cycle of misery. I am very sorry because this was never my intention. But remember, the whole world was violent at the time—*everybody* was violent. It was normal to use force as a means of achieving your objectives."

Then visually locating one of the Advanced Souls in the audience, Mohammad asked,

"Isn't that right Joshua?"

All of the souls gathered followed Mohammad's gaze to the Old Testament figure, whose soul lit up at the mention of his name.

"When Joshua got the command from God to take Israel, he used tremendous violence toward the other people who'd been living on that land," Mohammad continued.

"Why?

"Because first of all, the way we see it here on The Other Side there is no death; by killing somebody all you do is send them to heaven. So you don't really kill them, you just basically move them into another dimension—you send them back here. Joshua used this

166

tool because God knew that by clearing out this geographical area, the Israelites could then take it over. And that's exactly how *I* did it. I wasn't any more violent than Joshua, or King Solomon, or King David because we all did the same thing. Alexander the Great and all of these Advanced Souls—we all did the same thing because that's what we knew at the time. We were living in a hell situation in the End Times. But now we are shifting into a new era, bringing in Salvation Days on earth and the old ways must be discarded.

"Now I completely understand it's going to take a little time for people to get it. So I'm going to help you with these radical imams and leaders of Islam who will furiously resist the movement toward The One God Religion. How? I'm going to talk to them when they're dreaming. In case you didn't know, at night when you go to sleep your body rests but your soul travels to heaven. Therefore when the souls of the major Islamic leaders like Mahmoud Ahmadinejad, Abdullah Faaruuq and others are here on The Other Side I will talk to them and convince them that this is the right thing to do.

"Of course when their souls return to their bodies they're not going to be consciously aware of my instruction because they're not allowed to know what's going on over here. But slowly, slowly these dreams will start to affect them. And these dreams will be positive toward The One God Religion. Eventually most of them will get it—not all but most. Unfortunately Salvation Twelve, you will be left with no choice but to go to war with those radical leaders who refuse to understand and comply. You will *have* to kill them. But remember you don't really kill them, you just send them back here. And it's ok; don't you feel bad about that. Those people that you kill, they *need* to come to heaven because they're too stubborn; they're not ready to accept the change-up we are offering. That's perfectly fine. Since they refuse to accept The One God Religion, you just kill them and they will return to heaven. Don't worry; in the next cycle they'll incarnate again....everything is good."

As Mohammad finished his speech, Moses noticed one soul in particular pulsating in the audience. "Yes Mr. Khatami?" he acknowledged.

"Mr. Moses, may I have permission to speak?" the leader of Iran respectfully inquired.

"You may sir," Moses allowed.

During his time on earth prior to the G20 explosion, Khatami had displayed a tendency to be a little more flexible despite the fact that he descended from the Ayatollah, a radical Shi'a. Yet because Islam was crazy and fanatical, Khatami was still very much a jihadist at heart.

"You all recommend The One God Religion. And you know what? Having been sitting here with Mohammad, Jesus and you Mr. Moses, I finally understand that we're all from the same family. As I review my actions and attitude while inhabiting a physical body on earth I am disappointed in myself for allowing myself to be so narrow-minded and vicious. I am very sorry." Khatami's words were sincere and heartfelt.

"We forgive you," the Ascended Masters assured him. "You will atone for your previous sins by helping to move the world into The One God Religion and Salvation Time. Remember, you are among just twelve people chosen by God for this all-important mission. You should feel very proud."

"Thank you, Masters," Khatami responded. "Knowing how difficult it will be to shift the entrenched mindset of Islam's current leaders from hating and killing all infidels into encouraging Muslims to embrace unity with all people through The One God Religion, I am especially thankful for Mohammad's help."

"It is not only my pleasure but my sacred duty," Mohammad assured him. "After I died other people transformed the Koran into something I don't even recognize—a book filled with violence and atrocities against the innocent. I do not in any way condone what these writers commanded in Islam's holy book. It has caused nothing but pain, sorrow, suffering and death on earth. I want to play a role in changing all of that, knowing how challenging it will be for Islamic leaders especially to usher in Salvation by moving their people into a unified religion."

In reply to the prophet another voice in the audience chimed in. "I would also like to thank you, Mr. Mohammad," Ibrahim Ahmed declared. "I'm sure you know about all of the evil that's been perpetuated in Saudi Arabia all these years in the name of Islam. My barbaric country treats its female citizens like property, denying them very basic human rights—from simple things like the right to go out in public alone and drive a car, to much more serious things like the right to be respected and honored as a wife and to enjoy their sexuality. We force them to wear oppressive burqas in the name of 'dignity' but there's nothing dignified about controlling women because you believe they're nothing but whores instead of valuable creations of God worthy of respect. The same holds true for our treatment of non-Muslims. I joked earlier with Eyal Grad and Sarah Palin that my fellow Muslims have a rude awakening in store when they get to heaven and realize they won't be greeted by 72 virgins, but the task ahead of the Salvation Twelve on earth will be even more difficult for the leaders of Muslim countries."

"Hey wait just a minute Mr. Ahmed," Eyal Grad spoke up indignantly. "If you think you have your work cut out for *you*, what about *me*? How am I ever going to convince fanatical Jews that The One God Religion is the way to go?" Grad paused for a moment then pleaded his case to the group's leader.

"Mr. Moses, you of all people know how difficult those Jews can be! For crying out loud, it took you 40 years to get them through the freakin' desert! You have my utmost sympathy and respect for accomplishing the impossible but how am *I* going to deal with them?"

Moses replied by asking another question. "Ok, who here wants to answer Mr. Grad?" Another figure suddenly appeared on stage. "I'll do the honors, Mr. Moses," he replied.

"By all means Rabbi Schneerson," Moses instructed this new presence.

"I'm going to participate in Mohammad's excellent plan," Schneerson began. "When my religious people's souls come to heaven as their bodies slumber, I am going to talk to them. I'll tell them, '*Listen, you have shift to The One God Religion because it's good for you. You all have to unite because the world is heading for a big crisis and the purpose of Salvation Time is to prepare the earth for an all-out battle with other galaxies.*' You know, the earth is not the only planet in the universe, even though many of you still believe that. UFOs and space aliens *do* exist. The creation of the new world is coming up. And every nation on earth must be united before the world as you know it will be ready to take on this battle. The only way you'll survive on earth is if you're united with new technology, new ideas, and a new vision about life. But you must unite NOW. Within 300 years or so, this battle will come up because the world will then be ready for it.

"Why is God allowing this?

"Remember, the physical dimension is all about challenges. It's *not* heaven. Heaven is only when we die. So once you've successfully ushered in Salvation Time, the next challenge will come from outside of the earth."

"Wow, is that really the plan?" Grad blurted out.

"Yes Mr. Grad, but you won't be around for that portion of it," Schneerson answered. "Your job is to work with the Jews on earth now to move them into The One God Religion, an effort I will help you with from this side by talking to them in their dreams. And then when the Armageddon War erupts, eventually we'll knock all mosques out of Jerusalem, including the Dome of the Rock, which as you know was created in 691 at the order of Umayyad Caliph Abd al-Malik as a replacement for Mecca, which is why it's so ornate. At the time of Mohammad's death, Islam split into two—the Shi'a and the Sunni. He wanted to move its center to Jerusalem, thinking everyone would go to Jerusalem to pray in the real mosque but it didn't work out that way."

Mohammad nodded his head in agreement as the Rabbi spoke.

"The center stayed in Mecca for the Muslims but the mosque was still sitting there in Jerusalem. And inside was just a big rock—the same rock where Abraham took his son Isaac to slay him for God. This represents the old philosophy. In those days, people viewed God as a powerful entity that demanded complete obedience, even if it meant killing their own children as a sacrifice to him. When God's angel stopped Abraham from killing Isaac, it brought about a shift, a new way of thinking: God doesn't want you to sacrifice anyone's life for him!

"Anyway, once we create unity among people we'll finally knock this freaking mosque down and build a new temple: The Temple Mount of the One God Religion. Everybody can come and visit from all over the world. We'll still keep the rock as a tourist attraction and charge three dollars per person to see it. We'll make money and everybody wins. No more fighting, no more arguing, no more violence."

"Thank you Rabbi Schneerson," Moses stated, signaling the end of his soliloquy. He then turned to Jesus to ask for his input.

"Thank you Moses," he replied, eager to clarify some important things about his own ministry and the ensuing internal and external conflicts that characterized much of the history of Christianity.

Facing the Salvation Twelve Jesus began, "First, I want to acknowledge the sincere devotion so many of you have demonstrated toward me since I ascended back to heaven centuries ago in human terms. In spite of all the misguided teaching about my life and mission, most of you assembled here managed to keep my word and spread my good news for the betterment of the world.

"It's not your fault that those who wrote the Gospels 30 years after my death inflicted a lot of pain and suffering on Jews whom they blamed for my crucifixion. I never intended for my life and ministry to be the rationale behind the genocide of the Jewish people during the Spanish Inquisition and countless other evil events throughout human history. Nor did I intend for the church enacted at my command to become a corrupt hierarchy that imposed control over my faithful. You've heard my story of throwing the money traders out of the temple in anger. Let me tell you, I was just as angry about some of the disgusting practices committed in my name on earth. Totally corrupt things like the sale of indulgences designed to extort money from innocent people afraid of going to hell

"And I know that the messages we've imparted today, especially about reincarnation and the nature of heaven and hell—which we define as the time a soul dwells in a body on earth and *not* a fiery punishment—will not be easily accepted by most traditional Christians. That's perfectly alright because like Rabbi Schneerson, I too will work on Christian leaders while they are asleep. When their souls come back here, I will encourage them to embrace The One God Religion for the sake of peace and prosperity on earth. Just as with the others, it will take time for them to absorb and accept these changes. Some will stubbornly refuse no matter what. But that's ok because enough of the leaders will get it, and they will help you usher in Salvation Time. Just be patient with them. And know you have my unconditional love and support."

With that, Jesus ended his speech with a nod to Moses.

"Thank you, Jesus. And thank you to all of the Advanced Souls who participated in this meeting to prepare the Salvation Twelve for the task ahead. God is pleased with you. Now then, it is almost time to send all the New Souls back to their physical bodies but before we do that, there is one final matter to address."

With that, Moses rapped his staff forcefully several times on the stage as a billowing plume of smoke at once appeared and disappeared, leaving a suspended LCD TV screen in its wake. Behind it emanated pulsating rays of brilliant light, changing continuously into varying degrees of gold, yellow and white.

"Ladies and Gentlemen," Moses began. "Again I have the honor of conveying God's commands to his people. Except this time they apply to everyone, not just the Jews. And instead of ten, we now have twelve. Please pay very close attention and bring these new commands back to earth. Without further ado, I present God's Twelve Commandments."

THE TWELVE COMMANDMENTS

1. I am the One God of all creation; the God of Abraham, Isaac, Ishmael, Jacob, Moses, David, Solomon, Jesus and Mohammad. Do not commit to other gods because it will only bring lying, confusion and trouble.

2. Do not lie because when you lie, it comes back to you. When you lie, you lie to yourself.

3. Do not steal because when you steal, you steal from yourself.

4. Honor your father and mother, as long as they are respectful and positive. Remember, you have chosen your parents for a reason, to learn lessons while on earth. If they're bad people, do not follow their example. Instead, be a good person in spite of them.

5. Do not murder, especially in my name. You may kill animals for food, but you must not kill them indiscriminately.

6. Do not use violence against any creation of God. This includes humans, animals and trees.

7. Do not rape.

8. Do not be jealous of anyone. Jealousy is a poison that will kill your soul. God bestows every human being with his or her own talents and gifts, so there's no need for it. Instead, use your time on earth to discover who you really are. When you do that, jealousy disappears.

9. Do not let your physical body control your soul. Do not let your animal nature triumph over your spiritual nature. Let your God soul control your animal soul and your life will improve.

10. Be generous, good, humble, sensitive, understanding, loving, non-judgmental and open to everyone and everything around you. When you project positivity, positivity will come back to you tenfold.

11. Remember that you are undergoing a test. This life is a test. It may appear to be long but it's actually very short, so produce the very best actions from within. The more positive actions you take the more positive results you'll experience.

12. Use the power of God, which is positive imagination, to drive your life in a positive direction.

The sun rose brilliantly over the verdant hills of Jerusalem, which was just beginning to stir with the typical activity of a brand-new day. High atop a grassy mountain stood the Hadassah Medical Center, renowned in the region as one of the very best institutions for a myriad of medical ailments including severe trauma. There was no better place for Israeli Prime Minister Eyal Grad to be in the aftermath of the horrific G20 explosion. He, along with all of the surviving world leaders, had been airlifted back to his country and hospital to begin the arduous process of recovery immediately following the assault.

Although still blissfully isolated from the world and enjoying the benefits of their Prime Minister's innovations, in the eight weeks following the brutal attack by jihadists and anarchists, Israeli citizens feared the worst. Prime Minister Eyal Grad had remained in a persistent coma, and no one was certain if or when he'd ever awaken again, let alone return to his governmental duties. People had been flocking to their temples to pray for his recovery, sending supportive emails via the Israeli government website, and barraging the hospital with flowers and other tokens of their appreciation and concern. In spite of presenting a positive front in public interviews and press conferences, Grad's doctors remained privately skeptical that his severely broken body would ever heal, even if he did finally regain consciousness—which became less and less of a possibility the longer he stayed in a coma.

So on this particular Jerusalem morning, there was no reason for Grad's nurse to expect a miracle as she began her early shift and made her way past the assigned security guard, with whom she exchanged a brief greeting, and into the Prime Minister's private ICU suite to perform the routine task of checking his vitals. She nearly fainted at the sight awaiting her.

"When the hell am I getting out of here?!" an indignant Eyal Grad demanded. Amazingly, he was sitting up in bed, his dark, overgrown curly hair grazing his neck, his deep brown eyes pulsating with urgency and impatience.

"Prime Minister, you're awake!" was all she could say, still reeling from shock.

"Of course I'm awake! Get my doctors in here immediately; I must get back to work!" His tone was firm and unyielding.

"Yes of course, Prime Minister, right away!" With that, she ran out of the room in search of Grad's medical team but not before breathlessly alerting the guard to this unexpected development. "He's awake and he wants all of his people to get over here immediately! What should I do?" she inquired.

"Don't you worry about that, I'll take care of everything," the guard assured her before pulling out his smartphone to call Grad's trusted cabinet and advisors. Thus assured, the nurse quickly nodded at him before rushing off to find the doctors.

Thousands of miles away, in an Arctic land populated by majestic mountains, magnificent scenery and rugged terrain, the

Alaska Regional Hospital in Anchorage fielded endless phone calls and media inquiries over the condition of Secretary of State Sarah Palin. Like Grad, she'd been in a persistent, eight-week coma that showed no signs of letting up in spite of the excellent care, fervent prayers and thoughtful gifts she'd been receiving from medical professionals, family, friends and Americans from coast to coast.

Notwithstanding her capable doctors and nurses and the love of her spouse and children, it appeared nearly impossible that Palin would ever recover from the devastating injuries she'd sustained in the G20 explosion.

And yet, in the wee hours of the morning marking eight weeks after her arrival at Alaska Regional, Todd Palin felt his wife's fingers move ever so slightly in his hand. At first he thought he must be dreaming; he'd been sitting vigil by her bedside from the moment she'd been transported here, and she hadn't so much as twitched an eyelid. Sleepily he brushed it off as exhaustion as he rested his head back on the chair cushion, only to feel her fingers move again against his hand, this time with more deliberate force. He shot up in his seat, opened his eyes wide and noticed his wife's eyelids fluttering just before her big, brown eyes greeted him with love and recognition.

"Todd," she whispered as her lips formed a slow-moving smile across her still-beautiful though badly bruised face.

"You came back to us," he replied softly, overcome with gratitude and love as he slowly stroked her hair. "Thank God!"

"Oh yes, God definitely sent me back to you and the kids," she replied haltingly. "But boy do I have my work cut out for me."

"Here we go again!" he laughed. "She's barely awake after miraculously surviving an explosion and all she can think about is getting back to work. That's my Sarah!"

Then he lightly kissed her forehead before leaving the room to share the good news with her doctors.

Back in the Middle East, about eight-hundred miles away from Eyal Grad's hospital room, Ibrahim Ahmed slowly awakened from a long slumber as he lay in his bed at the Jeddah National Hospital in Saudi Arabia. His doctors had all but given up hope of his ever recovering and had prepared his family for the very real possibility that Ahmed might never regain consciousness. Yet as a new morning dawned over the arid peninsula eight weeks after the devastating terrorist attack, Ibrahim slowly opened his black eyes to notice a being in a long, white coat leaning over him. Startled, the figure recoiled slightly before addressing him.

"Do you know who you are?" the presence inquired.

"Of course I know who I am," Ahmed replied slowly but forcefully. "I am Prime Minister Ibrahim Ahmed of Saudi Arabia. Who the hell are you?"

"I am Dr. Zudhi Jassar. I've been one of several members of your medical team tending to your injuries. I am very pleased you have finally come out of your coma, Prime Minister. You gave us all quite a scare."

Ahmed relaxed a little as he gradually acclimated to three-dimensional life again. Then, remembering the blast, he urgently inquired, "What's been going on in the world while I've been away doctor?"

Dr. Jassar eyed his patient soberly. He was fully aware of the implications of stressing him out by sharing the truth, yet he also knew that the Prime Minister did not suffer fools gladly. Better to lay out the basic facts calmly; if necessary, he could always administer a sedative to soothe the agitation.

"I'm afraid Prime Minister that the world has finally arrived at the time predicted by all three major religions—Armageddon."

From a conference room in his Jerusalem office, Eyal Grad conducted an emergency staff meeting. Another two weeks had passed since he'd first emerged from his coma, during which the world had descended into even more chaos, destruction and bloodshed. Israel remained as isolated from the rest of the world as it had been prior to the G20 terrorist attack. The difference now was that the stakes were much higher because the country's former allies were arming Israel's enemies with weapons, military equipment and logistical support in preparation for major conflict. As promised by the Ascended Masters and Advanced Souls, each of the Salvation Twelve leaders had almost fully recovered from their injuries, though they retained some remnant of a handicap.

In Grad's case, a plate in his skull and pins in his right leg and ankle, along with grueling physical therapy, had made it possible for him to function in the material world. Although he retained a bit of a memory problem and was not quite as mentally sharp as he was prior to the explosion, for all intents and purposes, Grad was back to normal. And he was eager to strategize with his team on Israel's war effort. Seated at the long table were high-ranking members of the Israeli Defense Forces, along with Grad's most trusted advisors. All in attendance were truly amazed and grateful to have their revered Prime Minister back in action, and they listened attentively to his instructions.

"Thank you all for your prayers and support," he began. "I am thankful to be here to lead our country through this perilous but necessary war. I want to be very clear however, that this will not simply be a conventional war involving armies and weapons but also a psychological war on the hearts and minds of our enemies. And it all begins with a virus."

There was an audible gasp in the room as they attendees questioned their hearing abilities.

"I'm sorry Prime Minister, did you say *virus*?" the medical director of the IDF finally asked. His presence at the meeting had been requested personally by Grad, who'd sworn him to secrecy.

"Well to be precise, a *fake* virus," he clarified. "I need you and your medical team to create a fake virus that will cause a fake plague throughout the entire Middle East and force the United Nations to mandate DNA testing all across the region. In response to the crisis, the U.N. will have no choice but to set up different locations in each country where all citizens must go to provide a DNA sample. This will then enable doctors to match up the right antibodies of virus to overcome this harmless scourge."

"So let me get this straight," Grad's designated doctor interjected. "We're going to create a *fake* virus to cause a *fake* plague to trick the U.N. into setting up DNA clinics all around the Middle East to solve a crisis we *ourselves* manufactured?"

"That is correct Doctor," the Prime Minister replied. "But please understand, my motivation here is not to play games with other people's health or lives. The underlying goal is to prove to the Arabs and all citizens of the Middle East that they are descended from the same lineage as Jews. We must get them to understand that we all share the same DNA and thus we are all one. And the only way to do that is to create a fake plague."

"And how exactly do you propose we accomplish this?" the doctor pursued.

"Through a covert operation where we send members of the IDF into every Middle Eastern country. We have military members who are fluent in Arabic, Aramaic, Greek, Kurdish, Persian, Turkish and every language spoken throughout the region. Their job will be to interact with the locals, win their trust, and eventually contaminate the water supply with this fake, harmless virus so that all residents contract it. I'll be working closely with our military commanders to implement this operation immediately following this briefing."

Everyone in attendance understood quite well that Grad meant business. They'd experienced the same unyielding passion, resolve and determination during his run for office and after his subsequent landslide victory when he vowed to end the jihad in Israel once and for all. Grad promised and delivered back then; there was no reason to believe he would not do the same now.

"If there are no further questions about the DNA testing," he continued, "I would like to address the media strategy." When no hands went up, the Prime Minister began to describe the necessary psychological warfare.

"Alright then, the next order of business: I command that the IDF attack and destroy all radio stations, news bureaus and media outlets that perpetuate hatred, violence and jihad in the name of Allah and the Muslim religion. First and foremost on the list is Al-Jazeera, the most powerful peddler of Islamic propaganda in the region. I give the order for Israeli planes to blow it up but immediately following the destruction of Al-Jazeera, designated IDF soldiers in helicopters above the scene must lower new transmitters to the ground, where another team of soldiers will install them on the same frequency. These media-savvy soldiers will then begin broadcasting positive messages to the Al-Jazeera viewing audience.

"When the people in these countries turn on their television, they will think they're still watching Al-Jazeera but thanks to our Israeli team the previous messages of hate will be replaced by broadcasts about unity, love, positivity and The One God Religion. Instead of hearing the Al-Jazeera anchors and reporters rant on about 'evil, dirty Jews' who must be wiped from the face of the earth, they'll hear about the goodness of Israel, America and the west. They'll learn about Israel's uplifting innovations and how they've transformed daily living. They'll discover how Israel has made energy, education and medicine inexpensive while making money plentiful, which is why life is so good for them. Best of all, they'll learn that Israel wants to lead their countries in the implementation of similar policies which will dramatically improve the standard of living for all men and women throughout the Middle East.

"Meanwhile, people will be receptive to these bold new messages because DNA testing will have proven to them that they are all descended from Jewish DNA, that they themselves were Jews in the past. Therefore, the Jews are their brothers and sisters, not their enemies. And when they hear about The One God Religion they'll begin to understand that we are all made by the same Creator—and that this Creator demands an end to the fighting and bloodshed over religion.

"Finally, our Israeli broadcasters will end every program the same way—by looking earnestly into the camera as if they are personally speaking to each viewer and saying, '*You are all our brothers and sisters. We warmly invite you to join us in The One God Religion to promote peace, love, harmony and prosperity for all. Please stand with us in bringing Salvation Time to the Middle East. We love you and look forward to working with you to create positive, meaningful and lasting changes within our region.*'"

The Prime Minister further explained that by laying the groundwork with the DNA testing and the media transformation, the physical war would proceed much more smoothly and come to an end fairly quickly, though not without bloodshed and suffering.

And when the war finally began in earnest, Grad took advantage of a great opportunity to demolish the Dome of the Rock and quietly build the model for the new temple—The Temple Mount of The One God Religion—in the Judah desert on one of the military bases. He assembled a team of builders and directed them to construct the new building in a pre-fab format, with the intention of flying each section of the new temple by helicopter to the site of the demolition, where it would be methodically installed once the remnants of the old temple had been swept away.

Thus, the moment the world armies began advancing in the direction of Jerusalem, Grad gave the order to destroy the Dome of the Rock. And once this object of endless contention and conflict had been completely eviscerated, IDF soldiers cleared the rubble and paved the way for the installation of The Temple Mount of The One God Religion—the everlasting symbol of the dawn of Salvation Time.

While Christians and Muslims went to war with each other over who owned the rights to Jerusalem—completely excluding Israel from the conflict—designated members of the IDF busied themselves with the new temple construction. Thus the War of Gog and Magog raged in fulfillment of the prophecy of Ezekiel, with Muslims armies from Iraq, Iran, Turkey, Syria, Saudi Arabia and Jordan shooting missiles at the American, Italian, German, French and English armies. These targeted Christian nations returned fire with equal force and ferocity. In spite of the destruction and bloodshed, both sides managed to avoid civilian casualties, though thousands of their soldiers suffered gruesome fatalities and injuries.

These Muslim and Christian forces were so preoccupied with fighting each other for control of Jerusalem that they'd completely forgotten about Israel. Having already been pariahs for more than three years, Grad's country had no problem being left out of this particular conflict. While the violence raged on, Israel took solace in the construction of the new temple and its significance as a harbinger of much better times to come.

And in the ensuing weeks just as Grad had predicted, the preceding virus and media offensive began to create intolerable internal conflict for the leaders of the enemy Muslim armies including Syria, Jordan, Iraq and Iran—in spite of the fact that the typically hostile Shi'a and Sunni had united in their shared hatred for Israel. Though the Muslims had been wholly focused on defeating Christian infidels, their revulsion for the 'Little Satan' hadn't wavered. That is, until Grad's brilliant strategy started to produce its intended results. Only then did Israeli forces take up arms out of necessity because the Armageddon War could not come to an end without their facilitation and involvement.

Once the 'fake' virus had replicated in the sense that it created countless spies and informants in the embodiment of military officials, generals, captains and commanders from opposing countries, these once militant Muslim fanatics provided technical and tactical information to the IDF, enabling them with the knowledge of exactly when and where to attack, and which specific strategy to pursue for military success. Thanks to these informants, one major Israeli strike wiped out an entire army while also minimizing collateral damage for civilians. Formidable enemies like Turkey and Russia were easily defeated.

In every case of a defecting enemy combatant, the story was almost identical. Whether a high-ranking military officer from Iran, Iraq, Syria, Saudi Arabia or Jordan, the individual would offer the same testimony to the Israelis: "Hey, thanks to the DNA testing I know that I am also a Jew. I don't agree with what my country is doing; I don't want to be at war with Israel or any other nation. And I would like to help by giving you vital information on locations, attacks and strategies so you can determine the best way to defeat them."

Ultimately, Grad's approach to the Armageddon War worked as intended. The IDF struck such abject fear into the hearts of their enemies that their armies retreated back home with a plea to end the conflict and a promise that they no longer desired to perpetuate the cycle of violence that had plagued the Middle East throughout the End Days. In all of these nations, trained IDF Special Forces fluent in the local languages and customs had laid the foundation by dropping down in various communities and successfully interacting and communicating with the townspeople about Salvation Time for the purpose of winning over their hearts and minds.

Dressed as locals, these IDF forces shared the success of the Citizens Lottery System and government-printed paper money, along with the production of cheap fuel, energy, food, education and medical care. They promised that if each of their countries followed the Israeli model, they would thrive and prosper in the same way. Most importantly, these highly skilled IDF soldiers convinced everyday people all across the Middle East that there was but one God for everyone, and therefore no longer an imperative to promote violence in the name of Allah. The vast majority of residents in these once stridently Muslim nations had willingly agreed to transition peacefully into The One God Religion.

Simultaneously, as a result of Prime Minister Eyal Grad's well-reasoned and masterfully executed strategy the nation of Israel returned to its Biblical borders, encompassing Syria and Jordan. Under his leadership all citizens lived harmoniously with the knowledge and understanding that they all shared the same heritage, biological make-up and omnipotent Creator.

As for the magnificent Temple Mount of the One God Religion, it retained one remnant from its predecessor—the rock of Abraham—as a reminder that God condemns the barbaric ritual of human sacrifice, especially when committed in his name. As had been predicted on The Other Side when the New Souls received their instruction from the Ascended Masters and the Advanced Souls, the rock soon became a famous tourist attraction, generating even more prosperity and abundance for Israel.

But there was one more very important step to take to officially move the world into Salvation Time. And that was the sentencing at the Armageddon Commission after the war.

Once the cease-fire had officially been declared, Israel set up the Armageddon Commission. The descendants of the world's evildoers and useful idiots who made life unbearable during the End Days were rounded up all over the globe, arrested and taken to the trial in Megido to receive their punishment. These included families by the name of Hitler, Stalin, Tudor, Manson, Clinton, Bush, Chamberlain, Rothschild, Braun, Wasserman-Shultz, Bader Ginsberg, Spielberg, Tung, Castro, Soros, Mussolini, Medici and many more. While the fully-armed IDF lined the hearing room, individual descendants from these family lineages were given a brief opportunity to plead their case after listening to an explicit recitation of every evil act committed either by their ancestors or as was the case with Debbie Wasserman-Schultz and some others, they themselves.

However, they were expressly forbidden to justify their own actions or the actions of their relatives in any way. Since the Commission judged them by their deeds or their family's deeds exclusively, words served little purpose. History had provided all the evidence necessary to prove their guilt.

Thus the Commission unanimously proclaimed that these families were to be sent immediately to the walled neighborhood within Arusha City where they'd remain for a 400-year punishment. For the 400 families that resisted this sentencing, relocation was imposed by the barrel of a gun; for the remaining 100 who saw the light and willingly agreed to go, the transition was much more pleasant. Having planned ahead, the Commission had allocated the necessary resources to build a wall around the city, provide the requisite infrastructure and set these families up with the tools they'd need to begin the long process of atonement.

This isolation would continue until the Race Unity Regional High School Class of 2412 passed an exam demonstrating their knowledge and understanding of the End Times and the events and circumstances that finally—thankfully—led to Salvation Time.

∞Step Three∞

Salvation Time

The students of Mr. Bauer's history class rushed outside into the bright sunshine and balmy breezes. Having passed the *Steps to Salvation* exam, they were free to relax and enjoy the rest of the day. Some eagerly went home to begin packing for their long-awaited trip around the globe; others hung out in the large courtyard behind the Race Unity Regional High School, chatting excitedly about their upcoming graduation ceremony, the end of the Race Unity Experiment, and their global voyage.

As usual, Hitler lagged behind the rest of his classmates. This was because Mr. Bauer had agreed to test him privately, lest the strain of confessing the sins of his ancestor cause a mortifying accident in front of his peers. This decision deviated dramatically from the teacher's protocol. But after Hitler's parents and the school nurse pleaded the case for one-on-one testing, he'd agreed. With bullies like Joseph Stalin and smart-asses like Bill Clinton in the class it was the right thing to do.

And in typical fashion, moments after Mr. Bauer proclaimed he'd earned an '8' on the exam Hitler asked to be excused so he could relieve himself. The teacher had barely granted permission when the student disappeared in a flash out the door, his frantic footsteps reverberating down the hallway. Mr. Bauer couldn't help but laugh as he gathered his belongings and prepared to head home. He was also looking forward to having a few days off to unwind before the commencement ceremony, fully aware of the serious responsibilities and inevitable headaches he'd be dealing with as the Class of 2412's chaperone.

As Hitler made his way out of the bathroom and into the courtyard thoughts of Eva and Joseph overpowered him. Sure, he was thrilled to have passed the history test with a respectable grade. For most of his academic career but especially since completing the 11th grade, the menacing *Steps to Salvation* exam had hung over him like a dark, black cloud. He'd heard terrible things about it from other graduates of the Race Unity Regional High School—even the ones whose ancestors hadn't been nearly as evil as his. And for the past several months Hitler had been plagued by nightmares in which he'd pee all over the classroom floor as he struggled through his confession while Stalin, Braun and the rest of his classmates burst out into loud, sinister laughter.

But as he squinted and shielded his eyes with his hand upon entering the sunlit courtyard the only thing on Adolf Hitler's mind was the image of Joseph and Eva together in that bedroom. He felt thoroughly defeated as he wallowed in the embarrassment of Stalin bragging about being with the only girl Hitler ever loved. If not for his parents' insistence he'd probably skip the trip altogether, find a job and work as hard as he could to erase the memory of the previous night forever.

By this time Stalin, Clinton and Braun had long since left campus along with most of his classmates. Only Steven Spielberg remained, sitting on a bench in a relaxed pose with his elbows resting on the back support and his legs stretched out on the pavement.

"Hey man, where you been?" he greeted Hitler. "Everyone else is long gone."

"Well why are you still here?" he retorted.

"Ah, I just wanted to savor the moment, you know, drink it all in. The sights, the smells, the scenery—"

"Just like a real filmmaker," Hitler interrupted with a chuckle.

"You got it! I just remembered on the way out that this would be our last day as students in our uniforms at RURHS. Next time we're on campus it will be in caps and gowns. So I just wanted to imprint the memory of this amazing day."

"Well, good job on the test."

"Thanks, man. I really had to study hard because my parents were demanding a high grade. All I've been hearing my entire life is how much my family has to atone for, and how I was the designated member of this generation to finally make it right. Talk about pressure! So glad it's *finally* over," he sighed dramatically.

"I'm sure," Hitler replied sympathetically, taking a seat next to him on the bench.

Then, hit with a sudden realization Spielberg exclaimed, "Hey, I don't recall *you* taking the test today! What happened?"

Before he could respond, two junior boys approached them breathlessly. Judging from their disheveled appearance and flushed faces, it was obvious they'd been running fast across the broad lawn that connected the senior courtyard to the part of the building that housed the underclassmen.

"Hey, what's up?" Spielberg offered in greeting as Hitler nodded at them.

"How was it?!" they exclaimed in unison. Although he knew exactly what they were referencing, Spielberg thought he'd have a little fun.

"How was what?" he asked, feigning ignorance.

"Aw come on Spielberg, you know what we're talking about!" one of the boys cried impatiently. The future film director laughed hysterically.

"Alright, calm down *Il Duce*, I'll fill you in." Then leaning forward on the bench with his legs now tucked underneath, he looked them squarely in the eye. "I have to admit Mr. Bauer did a nice job making us feel comfortable. The best advice I can give you is to study hard, know and understand the material, and just be very honest about your ancestors' crimes. Remember, every kid in the class is ashamed of something so don't be embarrassed."

"Yeah, that's easy for you to say," the other boy remarked skeptically. "Your name isn't George Soros!"

"Or Benito Mussolini!" his friend chimed in.

"Please," young Soros continued. "Do you guys know *anything* about my horrible ancestor? He thought he was a god just because he made billions of dollars as a hedge-fund manager. Funny, he didn't even believe in the real God but he had a god-complex. He ruined entire economies of countries like France all because of his big, fat ego and his quest to mold the whole world into his left-wing vision. He used propaganda like the man-made global-warming hoax to control people.

"And he was such a sneak. Before the Armageddon War, he worked hard to ruin the United States because he hated freedom. So he used his billions to set up shadow groups to elect progressive, left-wing Democrats who shared his evil agenda. I hate everything about the guy, especially having to carry his stupid name!"

Spielberg chuckled. "Well, thank you for the history lesson. Look, Soros, it's not easy for any kid who lives in Arusha to deal with family atonement and this mandatory test. No matter the family tree, everyone who lives here has a history of shame. It's just the way it is. I'm sure your buddy Fidel Castro is dreading next year too, since his ancestor was another evil commie. But you can tell him to relax because Bauer does his best to help you get through it—as long as you can prove you've done your homework. Isn't that right, Hitler?"

"Hitler?" Spielberg repeated. The three students focused their attention on Eva Braun's would-be boyfriend who'd been staring forlornly into space. It wasn't until Spielberg snapped his fingers right in front of his eyes that Hitler returned to the present moment.

"What?" he asked in an irritated voice.

"I was just telling Mussolini and Soros they have nothing to worry about with next year's *Steps to Salvation* test as long as they study hard and know the material."

The kids then awaited his reaction.

"Y-yeah, that's true," he finally agreed.

"Geez Hitler, did you fail the test or something? You sound like you just came from your best friend's funeral!" Spielberg observed.

"*I* know why he's sad," Soros offered. Whether he wanted to admit it or not, the young Soros was just as devious as his ancestor; he loved to spread hurtful gossip around school. "I hear he walked in on Eva Braun and Joseph Stalin screwing at a party last night. There's a rumor going around that he peed on the carpet when he caught them!"

Soros and Mussolini broke into gales of laughter as the realization settled in Hitler's mind that he was probably the laughing stock of the entire school by now. He must've been blind and deaf to the smirks and whispers of obnoxious teenagers as he made his way to first period history class earlier that morning, completely lost in his own misery and preoccupied with having to pass the test.

News of the escapade hadn't yet made it to Spielberg, who in spite of his own sneaky nature, was overcome with momentary compassion for his humiliated classmate. Sitting next to him on the bench Hitler looked as if he'd burst out crying at any moment.

"Alright that's enough! Don't you guys have a class to get to? The bell's about to ring any second....go on, get out of here!" Spielberg admonished them as the two boys took off.

Then turning to his classmate he consoled, "Hey Adolf, I'm— I'm really sorry man. I had no idea. Don't pay any attention to those stupid kids."

Hitler continued to quietly stare into space.

An increasingly uncomfortable Spielberg tried to lighten the mood. "Ah women, can't live with 'em, can't shoot 'em, huh?"

Just then Hitler shot up from the bench and scrambled back into the building to use the men's room, leaving Spielberg alone to contemplate the plot and characters for his first full-length movie.

The sleek, contemporary bullet train gleamed in the bright East African sun as it awaited a very special group of passengers. It had arrived at the Arusha City Station hours before the confining walls of the Race Unity Region had finally been knocked down in an elaborate ceremony hosted by the Arusha City mayor and various city administrators. Jubilant residents on both sides of the wall had gathered in joyous expectation to experience this long-desired event. And when the mayor at last gave the order for demolition crews to "tear down these walls" the boisterous cheers of the hundreds of thousands in attendance echoed throughout the region. The mayor then pressed a button on a remote control causing the gigantic wrought iron doors of the previously sealed gate to slowly and steadily open up to a long, gold carpeted walkway.

As the Race Unity families held hands and stepped out through the newly opened portal, their hearts were filled with wonder, gratitude and exhilaration in spite of their nervousness. The graduating students were especially excited: not only were they about to finally lay eyes upon Arusha City and their neighbors, they were about to encounter new and interesting people and places all over the world. It felt like a dream as they took in the sight of the jubilant crowds and assembled media crews while their ears delighted in the sounds of an uplifting African drumbeat and accompanying music.

"Wow man, we're finally out!" they exclaimed happily.

The Race Unity dwellers were amazed to discover that everyone in Arusha City had dark black skin but unlike them, also bore distinctive African features. All were clapping, smiling and singing in an exuberant welcome to their fellow citizens. Many reached out to pat them on the back, shake hands and offer hugs as the procession continued all the way to the Arusha City Train Station.

Mr. Bauer studied his hand-held computer intently as he stood next to the entrance to the magnetic trans-global bullet train. Although moved by the joyful sounds in the distance, he'd opted to meet the group at the station, taking his role as chaperone very seriously. The momentous occasion 400 years in the making was finally here, and he was preparing to take attendance to ensure that every student from the 2412 graduating class arrived on time. Given the abundance of television crews, excited onlookers and euphoric families—and the noise and chaos they collectively inflicted, his simple task was about to become much more difficult. Though slow to anger, Helmut Bauer hoped he could remain patient; he understood the kids' justifiable excitement but he also knew they had a strict schedule to maintain. It was critical that they arrived at each destination on time to avoid having to forfeit a stop on the itinerary.

The history teacher was especially looking forward to traveling to Germany and visiting his geographically estranged family. As low-level Nazi sympathizers, they'd avoided mandatory relocation to Arusha after the Armageddon War. And as with so many others, he'd kept in virtual contact with them through weekly Skype calls. But even though technology had afforded the blessings of visual communication, there was still no substitute for an in-person visit. Mr. Bauer's plan was to sneak in a nice one during a designated "free time," when the students would be allowed to explore a place on their own until the mandatory curfew kicked in. That's when he'd take roll call to ensure everyone was present and accounted for before the next day's activities.

He was also eagerly looking forward to their visit to Jerusalem which would immediately follow their stopover in Cairo. Months earlier, he'd been delighted to receive word from Israeli Prime Minister Moshe Yalom that he'd secured lodging for the 2412 class at the luxurious King David Hotel—courtesy of the Israeli government and its citizens. Since the rest of the trip would entail staying at discount hotel chains in the interest of frugality, the teacher looked forward to indulging in a bit of opulence while in Israel.

But first he had the challenging task of locating and boarding the 21 students for whom he'd be held responsible throughout the duration of this incredible voyage. No easy feat since they were now scattered among the impressive crowd mingling with neighbors, reporters and city officials. Just as in the classroom, reining in immature teenaged behavior would be fraught with challenges. However, reprimanding these kids within the classroom walls was one thing; having to keep them in line while traveling the globe opened up new and potentially dangerous circumstances. Yet everyone knew Mr. Bauer was exactly the right person for the mission. Though they had understandable concerns about the trip, the moms and dads of the class of 2412 had the utmost confidence in him to safely return their kids to Arusha City. Most of their worries were overshadowed by the sheer exhilaration of this wondrous moment in time. They looked forward to hosting family from other countries and continents while their children were away.

A short distance from the train entrance an enthusiastic Steven Spielberg was carefully capturing video of the occasion with his smartphone while conducting spontaneous interviews with various classmates. Most everyone happily obliged—everyone that is, except Mao, whose hygiene still hadn't quite improved sufficiently enough to earn Mr. Bauer's approval. He nearly broke Steven's phone as he swatted it away after the aspiring filmmaker had pushed him to his breaking point. He didn't feel like saying a few words for the camera, he just wanted to be able to sit with the rest of the class on the train.

"Aw c'mon Mao, at least you're coming on the trip with us. Don't be a party pooper!" Spielberg scolded playfully as he watched his classmate stomp away.

Unfazed, he navigated through the crowd in search of others. By then, those who'd not yet indulged him were too busy chatting it up with the major news outlets to be bothered with his little project. That's when a determined Spielberg spotted the African conductor standing off in the distance at the front of the train, looking very professional in his pressed navy suit and crisp white shirt. As he moved in his direction, Steven made eye contact and waved—a gesture the friendly man returned in earnest. As soon as the student reached him, he smiled brightly and extended his hand in a warm shake.

"Welcome! You must be Steven Spielberg," he enthused.

"Yes sir, I am. How'd you know?"

"Your passion for filming important scenes gives you away—well that and the fact that Mr. Bauer has told me all about you. My name is Samuel."

"It's an honor to meet you, sir," the student offered sincerely. He was thoroughly impressed by the man's aura of competence and serenity.

"It's my honor to meet you and escort all of you around the world on this magnificent train," Samuel replied.

"Sir, would you be willing to say a few words about it while I film you?"

The conductor smiled and nodded his head. As the captivated student recorded it all in his smartphone, Samuel explained that the magnetic levitation train or *maglev* was the transportation of choice in Salvation Time due to its efficiency, comfort and practically seamless ride. That's because the train actually levitated, offering passengers the sensation of flying without having to be thousands of miles above the earth.

Running on land at 600 miles per hour, the trans-global bullet train had dramatically cut down on travel time, making world travel a commonplace event for everyday people.

But before Samuel could go any further, an amplified horn blast abruptly ended the interview.

"Ah Mr. Spielberg, I'm afraid that's my cue, the dark-skinned man announced. "It's time to get back to my checklist so we can get underway. But don't worry; you'll soon see all of the train's magnificent features for yourself. During the ride, feel free to ask me any questions you might have."

"Thank you, sir!" the thrilled teenager exclaimed.

"Thank you for your hard work," he responded before returning to his important duties. The student just stood there smiling until a second horn blast alerted him to get moving ASAP. Returning the phone to his pocket, he ran with all of his might to the designated check-in area where his classmates were already assembled.

The maglev sped across the African landscape at 600 miles per hour transporting its passengers over 2,000 miles in just over three hours to Cairo, Egypt. In spite of the international media commotion at the train station, Mr. Bauer had managed to account for all passengers and check them in with plenty of time to spare. It certainly helped to have an efficient conductor and crew that instinctively understood the perils of dealing with hyperactive teenagers about to enjoy their first real taste of freedom.

And as each recent graduate had boarded the contemporary transport they'd gasped in wonder. An engineering marvel, the bullet train's aerodynamic outward design was equally matched by its spacious, luxurious interior. Arranged in two's on either side of a long aisle, the plush seats perfectly supported the human body. Comprised of memory foam and upholstered with soft velour fabric, each ergonomically sound seat reclined back at graduating angles to satisfy the creature comforts of each unique passenger. Large LCD screens arranged at the front of each car offered another view of the passing scenery in addition to generous windows throughout each section.

"Welcome one and all!" their effervescent hostess had greeted them with a big smile as she directed them to their proper places. "My name is Naomi and I'm honored to be part of the team escorting you around the world."

Statuesque and graceful with long black curly hair, smooth mocha skin, raven-colored eyes and pearly white teeth, Naomi looked like a fashion model from the End Days. But that's where the similarities ended. Because her outward beauty was matched by her luminous soul, sharp intellect and caring disposition. Of course, as boys like Bill Clinton, Joseph Stalin and Jacques Chirac drank in the sight of her inner beauty was the last thing on their minds.

Like the other two female attendants who busied themselves with securing carry-on bags in the overhead compartments, Naomi was dressed in a pressed navy uniform featuring a knee-length pencil skirt and tailored, long-sleeved jacket. The lapels and collar of her starched white blouse provided a stunning color contrast, along with her chunky gold jewelry. Although not nearly as physically attractive, her two female crewmates shared the same professionalism and impeccable grooming.

They were assisted by three male members of the crew who were just as friendly and helpful. Easy to spot in their pressed navy trousers and matching blazers as they stood at various points in the aisle, the men oversaw the boarding process and directed the kids to their pre-assigned seats. In total, there were seven bullet train crew members including conductor Samuel who remained out of sight in the front compartment.

The instant the boarding process had begun under the watchful eye of Mr. Bauer the previously tranquil train filled with the sounds of unrestrained laughter, giddy conversation and eclectic music streaming from smartphones. Having forgotten all about the tension, drama and angst of the previous week leading up to their history exam, the graduates felt nothing but sweet euphoria. Here they were, about to finally experience the unknown—a world that had once been forbidden due to a karmic debt that demanded a 400-year punishment. Now that they'd finally atoned for the grievous sins of their ancestors, these young people could hardly wait to reach their first destination, The Great Pyramid of Giza in Egypt.

This last remaining Wonder of the Ancient World was of particular interest to Anwar Sadat. As he'd taken his window seat next to Henry Kissinger, he contemplated how he might feel once in the presence of this famous landmark. Would it stir something within on a deep and profound level? He eagerly awaited the answer while he stared out the window at the passing landscape. To Sadat's left, an introspective Kissinger pondered his own future. As he reclined back in his seat and removed his trademark black glasses, he was grateful for the cool air conditioning onboard given his propensity to sweat buckets—even when not under the stress of answering difficult history exam questions.

Meanwhile, the five female members of the class explored the rest of the maglev. A giddy Golda Meir, Ruth Bader Ginsberg, Debbie Wasserman-Schultz and Hillary Rodham rushed down the aisle in the direction of the private rooms, the dining car and the lounge car with Eva Braun in hot pursuit. Hillary had been elated to have been seated next to Debbie in the coach section.

Having no interest in her female peers, Eva's only purpose in tagging along was to scope out the private rooms. She wanted to find out if an empty one might be available for a possible rendezvous with Bill Clinton. It had been way too long since they'd spent any time together.

Once she caught up with the rest of them she was greeted with barely concealed contempt.

"What are you doing here Eva?" Ruth demanded while the rest of her clique formed a protective circle around her and glared at their mutually disliked classmate.

Even in her sweet sundress, Eva's assets were quite noticeable. She appeared as model-worthy as their hostess Naomi, who upon sensing the tension between the young girls, quickly walked over to diffuse the situation.

"Can I help you with something ladies?" she chirped brightly.

"Uh we just wanted to check out the dining car and other accommodations," Hillary piped up.

"Of course," the hostess smiled in response. "Please follow me and I'll give you a tour."

As she spoke she gracefully made her way around them until she was at the front of the assembly. Then she turned her back to them and situated her body directly under the sensors on the ceiling, a few inches away from a large, oval door. When the sensors picked up on her presence the door slid smoothly and silently to the right, speeding up quickly as it moved. In a flash, it offered full access to the next impressive section of the train.

The girls let out a collective gasp as they took in the sight of the dining car. On either side of a gleaming white aisle stood elegant yet functional round tables covered with starched white linens. For maximum enjoyment, the tables also featured the same type of ergonomically sound chairs found in the coach section. Toward the back a few crew members were busy with kosher lunch preparations, laboring behind a sparkling, stainless steel bar which curved around in an ample arc to allow for plenty of work space and necessary cooking equipment. A glass-front deli case was filled with assorted beverages from bottled water to iced tea to fruit juices. Next to it, curved shelves that nearly reached the ceiling featured healthy kosher snacks like protein bars and bags of assorted nuts and dried fruits.

The irresistible aroma of fresh fish infused the atmosphere as the chef busily sautéed perfectly seasoned filets in a wrought iron skillet over a hot stove in the far corner behind the bar. Esther, another female member of the crew, skillfully chopped fresh pepper, squash and broccoli at her designated station while a large bag of Basmati rice waited to be steamed nearby.

"Wow, something sure smells good!" Debbie giggled. I'm hungry already!"

"Me, too!" Golda chimed in.

"Good, because lunch will be ready soon," Naomi replied warmly. "Unlike your seating arrangements once we announce a mealtime you are free to sit wherever you'd like in the dining car. So I hope you will socialize with everyone in your class and *not* just your best friends," she added with a knowing glance.

Hillary, Golda, Debbie and Ruth just shrugged in response to the not-so-subtle hint once she'd resumed their tour. Eva smiled smugly because she knew the other girls' behavior was motivated by jealousy. She nearly laughed out loud when she realized none of the boys—not even the desperate Mao Tse Tung—would ever want to go near any of one of them.

At last the group arrived at the destination Eva was most eager to check out: the car with the private rooms. These spaces were created specifically for business travelers and others who wanted to work, read or conduct phone calls in confidence. Most were designed to hold one person at a time but there were a few that accommodated up to four, with a small conference table in the middle. Eva frowned as she followed the tour and peered at these compartments, realizing they might not be conducive for the activities she had in mind. But when Naomi led them into another car featuring private showers and washing areas, her ears perked up. Maybe some creativity was all she needed to bring her Clinton fantasies into reality.

"Wow Naomi, this train is amazing!" Ruth exclaimed.

"Well we aim to please here in Salvation Time, Miss Bader Ginsberg," she chuckled. "And just wait until we board the tube train for trans-oceanic travel—you'll really be blown away! But I don't want to ruin the surprise so we'll just wait until we leave London for New York. I'm positive you will all be quite comfortable throughout our journey.

"Hey Naomi, how many people do these trains carry at one time?" Hillary inquired.

"These bullet trains are designed to transport 1,000 to 2,000 passengers at a time. It's only for this special occasion that an exception has been made because we wanted to reward all of you for your hard work." Naomi smiled proudly.

Eva's heart leaped in her chest as she rethought the possibilities. Judging by the length of the train there were plenty of private spaces far enough away from coach to sneak in some time with Bill; she hoped he'd remembered to pack plenty of Perdomo cigars.

Picking up on her thoughts telepathically, Eva's peers glared at her. They could easily sense that sex was on her mind—not that anyone even needed mental telepathy to figure that out. And while none were fans of Adolf Hitler, they still couldn't get over how she could treat him so badly or how in spite of it all he still chased after her like a loyal puppy dog. Surely even a nerd like Hitler could do much better than a floozy like Braun?

However, as the group followed Naomi's lead back to the main coach section Eva wasn't the only one having amorous thoughts. Now that she'd seen the private rooms, Hillary felt certain she could set a romantic scene for Debbie even though she was still uncertain about the girl's sexual preferences. Had Debbie's soul also chosen to incarnate as a lesbian? If she could just figure that out, Hillary felt certain she could make Debbie fall in love with her.

Meanwhile, a sympathetic Ruth Bader Ginsberg couldn't help but feel some sympathy for Mao Tse Tung as they passed him sitting all alone in the back of coach accommodations. Meeting his melancholy gaze for a brief second, she offered a shy smile as the corners of her mouth tentatively turned up. Unsure of what he was seeing, Mao just looked back at her with the same frozen expression.

"This could be a very interesting trip for a lot of reasons," she thought to herself as she settled back into her assigned place next to Golda.

The train levitated swiftly and smoothly above an imperceptible track as it carried its passengers to Cairo Egypt and The Great Pyramid of Giza.

###

"Ew, what's that funny smell?" some of the kids cried out in unison as they stepped off of the train and onto the platform at the Cairo Train Station.

"Shh, you idiots! These smells are wonderful," a completely overwhelmed Anwar Sadat corrected them. He closed his eyes and took a deep, satisfying breath as he extended his arms outward and reveled in the moment. To the rest of his classmates it appeared as if Sadat was having a religious experience. Golda Meir and Mahmoud Ahmadinejad smiled; although not quite as demonstrative, they shared the same visceral reaction to Egypt. From the second the train crossed into the country they'd been totally consumed and uplifted by its distinctive simplicity including its dust, dirt and odors.

A mortified Mr. Bauer was about to warn all of them about their behavior when the atmosphere suddenly filled with the sounds of Arabic music and loud, enthusiastic cheering. As the group slowly made their way into the main terminal, they were greeted by thousands of onlookers and news crews who'd descended upon the scene, filled with curiosity about the Race Unity kids and their teacher.

They wondered if the change in skin pigmentation had altered their personalities. Adolf Hitler, Joseph Goebbels, Joseph Stalin and Jacques Chirac were of particular interest, especially to the intrusive news media. Prior to their arrival Mr. Bauer had given the teens strict orders not to speak with media personalities, no matter how pushy they were. "Just keep your mouth shut and follow the group," he'd instructed. Even now in Salvation Time media sensationalism was alive and well, igniting the teacher's protective instincts.

The overwhelmed teenagers nervously stuck together as they walked, watching with trepidation as the crowd ogled them rudely. At one point an obnoxious reporter shoved a microphone in Adolf Hitler's face but he just stared straight ahead and kept moving in spite of his racing heart.

There were old men playing backgammon who pointed and laughed; shopkeepers peddling trinkets in a seemingly endless line of kiosks; and little kids squealing with obvious delight at the unique physical features of the Arusha travelers.

"Man, this is like being in a fish bowl," an annoyed Rothschild remarked to Hitler and Goebbels.

"Tell me about it!" they replied in unison.

"Yeah, I thought this trip was going to be fun," George W. Bush chimed in. "Now I can't wait to just get out of here and get to The Great Pyramid of Giza."

"Don't worry Mr. Bush," the teacher's baritone interjected. "There's an electric bus waiting for us outside the main doors. We're headed there shortly. For now, just smile, wave and remember it's because of all of your hard work that we're even here. It's natural for the rest of the world to be curious."

The students nodded in agreement and did their best to let go of anxiety, although it wasn't until the bus was well on its way to the pyramids that they fully relaxed again.

Mahmoud Ahmadinejad gazed out the window at the passing scenery, completely mesmerized. He would've remained in this hypnotic state for the duration of the ride had it not been for Joseph Stalin, who rudely nudged him out of his reverie.

"Psst, Ahamdinejad, look what I got!" he whispered with delight as he pulled an Arabic knife out of his pocket.

"Oh my God, where did you get the money to buy that?"

"I didn't," Stalin shrugged.

"Tell me you didn't steal it!"

"Shh! Don't say it so loud! Yes, of course I stole it. How else was I supposed to get it? In all of the commotion, no one even noticed."

Ahmadinejad rolled his eyes. "You sure about that?"

"Positive," the school jock grinned.

"Yeah well, just remember what they say about karma," his classmate warned. "Even if Mr. Bauer or the store owner never find out, God still knows. Remember The Twelve Commandments? Don't be surprised if this comes back to haunt you." In spite of his warning however, Ahmadinejad couldn't help but feel a pang of jealousy.

"Could I get away with stealing something, too?" he wondered. His pulse quickened at the thought.

Meanwhile Stalin laughed off his friend's admonition and wondered how he could put the knife to good use as the bus transported them to the site of the Pyramids.

###

Anwar Sadat stood speechless as he gazed up into the bright blue Egyptian sky. In spite of his active imagination, none of his preconceived ideas could have ever prepared him for the moment he'd finally lay his eyes upon The Great Pyramid of Giza for real. This famous End Days landmark literally took his breath away as it loomed larger than life from an enormous and meticulously constructed foundation of stone. While he wordlessly drank in the sight, it occurred to him that those who built it did so without modern technology or machinery.

"Mind-blowing, isn't it?" he heard a familiar voice say. He turned to see his classmate Steven Spielberg taking footage with his smartphone.

"Yeah, it sure is," he replied.

"Too bad I don't have a proper camera," Spielberg sighed. "My parents ordered a special one for me as a graduation present but of course it didn't get to our house *before* we left on the trip."

"Well I'm sure you'll get some good footage," Sadat sympathized. "Honestly, looking at the Pyramids I can barely think straight. Can you believe 20,000 workers built them without the technology we have now? It must've been brutal. And yet, they are 6,000 years-old—incredible!"

Spielberg nodded in agreement as he moved in various directions to achieve the desired angles for his documentary. He and Sadat—for reasons unique to each of them—had easily beaten everyone else to the entrance, overwhelmed with anticipation. In the distance, their classmates slowly made their way toward them. Mr. Bauer had arranged a special tour and they couldn't wait to go inside. Once all were assembled their concerned Egyptian guide issued a stern warning that anyone who suffered from claustrophobia had best enjoy the Pyramid from the outside. He'd also inquired as to the health of Mr. Bauer's knees and heart, warning him that the steep, narrow climbs could challenge even the healthiest and most youthful in the group.

Bauer had laughed and assured him that in Salvation Time 90 was the new 50. Therefore, he was still experiencing perfect health thanks to a sensible diet, advanced food supplements, plenty of exercise and strict adherence to daily meditation. Last but definitely not least, he'd had surgical implants of new electronic eyes and new embedded hearing aids. The man could see extremely long distances and hear faraway sounds with a clarity and precision that rivaled every one of his young students—which was why they were afraid of him.

"As you wish, sir," the Egyptian had responded courteously. Although he remained skeptical he immediately inferred by Bauer's tone that he was not taking "no" for an answer. He was sympathetic to history's teacher's point of view; after all, this was his first trip outside of Arusha and quite possibly his only chance to experience The Great Pyramid. Besides, the streamlined Egyptian government had enacted a sensible policy long ago that mandated the presence of a medical crew on the grounds in case of an accident or physical episode. They would ensure that none of the Arusha travelers were harmed, partly out of consideration for their safety and partly out of concern for Egypt's reputation.

Before the tour could begin, Mr. Bauer took roll call again. As soon as he'd accounted for everyone, he soberly reminded them about the claustrophobia warning and gave them a chance to opt out by raising their hands. When none went up he nodded to their Egyptian escort to continue.

They followed him into the Robbers' Tunnel which led them 89 feet straight ahead before taking a sharp left turn toward the blocking stones in the Ascending Passage. Originally dug by workmen employed by Caliph Al Ma'mun, the tunnel had been used as a public entrance to The Great Pyramid for many centuries and even now in Salvation Time remained the only tourist access to its interior.

Sadat and Spielberg brought up the rear, giving them a chance to observe the actions of their fellow classmates as they drank in the mystical scene. All were genuinely moved as they carefully made their way through the narrow passage flanked on either side by hieroglyphic enhanced walls that seemed to stretch all the way to heaven. Even class clowns like Bill Clinton, Jacques Chirac and Joseph Stalin had been stunned into silence. As he followed his peers through the tight walkways, Stalin kept one hand over the pants pocket carefully concealing his stolen Arabic knife. Could Ahmadinejad's warning come true? He tried not to think about that while he focused on the Egyptian tour guide's narration of the history of The Great Pyramid.

###

"May we have some menus please?" Mr. Bauer inquired of the young, handsome waiter after he'd introduced himself as Ayman Taha. As promised, immediately following the Pyramid tour he had taken the hungry class to an authentic Egyptian restaurant to sample some of the country's finest kosher cuisine. In his mind these kids had insatiable appetites though he well remembered the fond days of his youth when he also experienced constant urges to eat seemingly every minute. He was grateful for the ample supply of snacks on the train.

The humble eatery was infused with the scent of burning incense while the now familiar Arabic music filled the air. Anwar Sadat, Mahmoud Ahmadinejad and Golda Meir inhaled deeply and savored the multi-sensory Middle Eastern experience while the other kids nervously wondered what the food would be like.

"I'm sorry sir, but we don't have menus. Let me tell you what we have tonight."

The Arusha travelers listened eagerly as Ayman described a main dish called hawawshi, pressed ground beef with tomatoes, onions and coriander. It was served with sides of pickled eggplant and rice along with classic baladi bread.

"Don't worry, the kids will love it," he assured Mr. Bauer.

"The way this group eats I hope you have plenty of it on hand!" the teacher joked. Ayman cracked up before disappearing into the kitchen. A few minutes later he returned with a large pot of steaming cinnamon and ginger tea. While they waited for their meal, Mr. Bauer poured the hot beverage into porcelain cups and passed them around the table. He thanked his class for their good behavior at the Pyramid and reminded them that he expected more of the same when they arrived in Jerusalem—a destination that was only 45 minutes from Cairo on the maglev. Once they checked in at the King David Hotel, he instructed them to go directly to their rooms for quality sleep because the next day's agenda would be full and busy.

Ignoring their hunger pangs, the teenagers nodded enthusiastically while they prayed Ayman would return with their dinner soon. A little while later just as predicted the students quickly cleaned their plates while their amused teacher exchanged smiles with the busy waiter who spent most of the night running back and forth to the kitchen for reinforcements. Yet Ayman never once complained; it had been his great honor to ensure that their taste of authentic Egypt would always be remembered.

"Good morning and welcome to Jerusalem, Race Unity Regional High School Class of 2412!" Israeli Prime Minister Moshe Yalom exclaimed enthusiastically. He was flanked by Jerusalem Mayor Hanan Aharon and various members of the Israeli government in the magnificent lobby of the King David Hotel where various camera crews and networks including Al-Jazeera had taken up residence, along with a huge crowd comprised of curious Israeli citizens. Many of them had descended upon the hotel at the crack of dawn, eager to witness this milestone event.

Dressed in their finest clothing as required, the students were especially well-groomed for their debut at the most upscale hotel they'd ever seen, located in the most significant city of their worldwide tour. Even Mao Tse Tung had taken special care with his personal grooming that morning. Per their teacher's instructions, all of the graduates were wearing clean, starched shirts embroidered with the symbol of The One God Religion. They'd been required to purchase them weeks before leaving Arusha City for this very special occasion.

It had been mandated for the girls that a solid white, black or navy knee-length linen skirt accompany their custom-fitted blouses. Hillary had at first resisted fiercely. But once Debbie had passed the *Steps to Salvation* test and earned the right to travel, she'd considered it a small price to pay for the chance to initiate a meaningful relationship with her.

With the exception of Eva Braun the young women had opted for navy, believing that to be the most demure and figure-flattering color. Since her toned, fit body could pull off any style and color stunningly, Eva had selected white. Standing among her peers in a pair of high-heeled strappy gold sandals, she commanded the attention of the hopelessly smitten Adolf Hitler along with Bill Clinton and Joseph Stalin, neither of whom had been able to find an opportunity to be with her again, much to their chagrin.

Mr. Bauer looked as stately as ever in his navy suit and matching pressed white shirt. Upon entering the palatial hotel lobby the Arusha teens were taken aback when the entire place erupted into loud, joyous applause. Slightly embarrassed, they dutifully followed their teacher toward their welcoming committee and smiled as he eagerly extended his hand in warm greeting to the Prime Minister, Mayor and various Israeli professionals. These included the latest honoree for *Doctor of the Week*, artists, entrepreneurs and authors. Each individual had been specifically selected to take part in the ceremony because of their strong moral character and notable contributions to Israeli society.

"Thank you very much, Prime Minister, we're delighted to be here!" Mr. Bauer enthused.

The kids tagged along behind him through a long receiving line, shaking hands, smiling and thanking their hosts for their generosity. He'd instructed them repeatedly to be on their best behavior during this stopover and felt a sense of pride and relief that they'd taken his words to heart. He silently hoped they'd remain this courteous and respectful over their two-night stay and spare him any kind of embarrassment.

Once the pleasantries were exchanged the Prime Minister approached a marble podium to formally address everyone in attendance while the news cameras jockeyed for position. From his mandated spot in line with his classmates, a frustrated Steven Spielberg focused his smartphone on the Prime Minister but the view was partially blocked due to a bad angle and the throngs of pushy reporters standing in his way.

"Hello again everyone, we are honored to welcome you to Jerusalem and the King David Hotel!" Moshe Yalom warmly declared. "You know, I am especially thrilled to be part of this upscale event even though I'm just a lowly politician. My workplace isn't nearly as beautiful as this magnificent hotel so it's certainly a treat to get out of my drab office for a change."

His tone was light-hearted and humorous, prompting an appreciative collective laugh in response.

"Thank you," he humbly acknowledged. "Back in the End Days this hotel used to boast that it had once played host to hundreds of Prime Ministers, Kings and US Presidents. Now it brags about playing host to innovative entrepreneurs, artists and producers— anyone whose contributions have made life better, easier and more satisfying in Salvation Time. And it just so happens, a few of Israel's best and brightest are with us today."

With that, he gestured with his hand to the line of people standing to his right. They all nodded, smiled and waved at the crowd as the Prime Minister continued.

"I want to thank the hotel staff and the people of Israel for making this possible. They voted overwhelmingly in favor of hosting the Race Unity Regional High School Class of 2412 here for two nights to give you a taste of luxury. It's our way of saying thank you for you and your families' hard work of atonement in the Race Unity Region. We know there's still much to be done, but you've all taken a huge step in the process."

As he listened Adolf Hitler's dark eyes met the gaze of the Israeli leader. For a moment the teenager could've sworn that the Prime Minister's words were meant for him alone but he quickly brushed it off as nervousness. And hadn't the karmic debt *already* been paid? Otherwise, why else would they be here? Hitler quickly brushed these questions aside; he was already fighting his overactive bladder which was begging to be relieved, but he knew there was no way Mr. Bauer would allow him to create a distraction while Moshe Yalom was speaking. The men's room would have to wait—as would his nagging questions.

Hitler averted his eyes to the left side of the line where Eva Braun was standing between Bill Clinton and Joseph Stalin. He noticed that she remained at attention with eyes affixed to the main event unfolding before them. Clinton and Stalin, however, were sizing up the most physically attractive women in the room including those on the welcoming committee. These smart, generous, capable and highly accomplished females included inventors, painters, doctors, engineers and writers. They stood among their male peers waiting for their turn at the podium.

The ceremony seemed to go on forever as each one addressed the audience and spoke of the country's latest innovations and their role in making life better for their fellow citizens. There was even a history lesson—as if the class needed another one—about Eyal Grad, Armageddon, and the arrival of Salvation Time, courtesy of the nation's most revered school teacher, Arnon Volfson.

Mr. Bauer was then called upon to accept a very special award—a key to the City of Jerusalem—as acknowledgement of his role in educating his students about the Steps to Salvation.

With a big grin on his face, the gracious teacher accepted the gift from the beaming Prime Minister as cameras flashed furiously and hands applauded heartily. In the next instant, a tuxedo-clad orchestra began to play traditional Hebrew music from a balcony directly above them.

For Mr. Bauer's students the scene was absolutely surreal. Never in their young lives had they been exposed to such pageantry. Sure, they'd had all of the modern conveniences of life while growing up behind the walls of the Race Unity Region. But they'd never experienced anything like the   incredible feast for the senses currently unfolding before them.

A few moments later as they were seated in an elegant dining room for a sumptuous lunch buffet many like Golda Meir, Nathan Rothschild, Anwar Sadat, Mahmoud Ahmadinejad, Charles Manson, David Duke and George W. Bush wondered aloud how the upcoming visit to the Temple Mount of The One God Religion could possibly outdo this amazing event.

Not Adolf Hitler.

He was way too preoccupied by the sight of Eva Braun shamelessly flirting with a cute waiter while discussing menu options. As he sulked in his chair, he wondered what the Prime Minister could've possibly meant when he talked about more work to be done. For the student it felt as if his karmic debt would never be paid. Wasn't it enough that he'd already chosen to come to earth in this incarnation as a sensitive artist type with a prematurely weak bladder? It seemed to Hitler he'd been atoning for the past every single day of this particular lifetime. Then there was the matter of his unrequited love for Eva Braun, who repeatedly rejected him. What more was there to do? As he pondered these insufferable questions, he hoped he'd find the answer at the temple.

###

The stunning Temple Mount of The One God Religion cast a mesmerizing spell upon its new visitors the moment their electric tour bus rounded the final turn and offered them a full, unobstructed view. Although visible throughout the entire city of Jerusalem—and therefore in plain sight of each of their hotel room windows—seeing it up close had a profound effect. Growing up as devout followers of The One God Religion they'd been fully versed in the history of this incredible structure and how under Prime Minister Eyal Grad's orders, a builder named Nir Sthainer had erected it during the Armageddon War while the Christian and Muslim armies fought each other.

Yet as they stepped off of their transport and onto the southern retaining wall even the normally stoic Mr. Bauer was consumed with powerful emotion. An observant Steven Spielberg, ever-vigilant with his smartphone, managed to capture footage of his teacher actually wiping away a lone tear that had escaped from one of his moist eyes and slowly trickled down his dark face.

Although deeply moved by the temple Spielberg managed to secretly scan the group and film each of his classmates' first impressions. Even flaky Eva Braun seemed genuinely dazzled as she stood staring at it.

In the next moment the rich baritone voice of their history teacher shook them out of their daze. "Alright everyone," he ordered. "Please get in line so our guide can lead us through the temple. I also want to remind you that I expect you all to be on your very best behavior throughout the tour. Please show the proper respect and reverence—no exceptions."

The students dutifully lined up in the pre-assigned order while their Israeli tour guide—a pleasant, middle-aged woman named Sarah—smiled in response to their deference to their chaperone. She felt honored to have been selected by her peers to lead them through the temple and she couldn't wait to witness their reaction to Abraham's Rock, the Ark of the Covenant, the walled inscription of The Twelve Commandments and the artistic depictions through sculpture and painting of The Twelve Holidays of The One God Religion.

"Thank you, Mr. Bauer," she said with a nod. Then turning back to face the students continued, "Alright kids, before we move through Robinson's Arch and into the Basilica, I first want to point out where we are right now. To the east, there's the Mount of Olives; to the south, the walls of the City of David."

They followed her hand gestures as she spoke, overwhelmed by a sense of pure sacredness as they drank in the scene of old Jerusalem. Sarah explained that the Mount of Olives, a mountain ridge east of and adjacent to Jerusalem's old city was named for the olive groves that had once covered its slopes. Back in the days of the three major religions, Christians had revered the Mount of Olives because of its association with Jesus and his mother, Maryam. Followers of Christ had also believed it to be the place where Jesus ascended into heaven.

The City of David was the oldest settled neighborhood of Jerusalem and the location of King David's palace. Here, King David had also established his capital. Located on a narrow ridge running south from the temple, it had also been a major archaeological site in the later years of the End Days even though it had mostly been inhabited by Muslims.

As they gazed at these breathtaking vistas the young tourists and their teacher took note of the tall, modern buildings that rose up in the distance. The scene was simultaneously a stunning contrast between ancient and contemporary, and a remarkable testament to the endless continuum between the End Days and Salvation Days. All were filled with wonder.

Spielberg was so enraptured by the scene he was filming he nearly jumped out of his skin when he heard his teacher call out to him for a third time in a very stern voice indicating it was time to move on to the tour—or stay behind on the electric bus.

"Coming Mr. Bauer!" he exclaimed. He scrambled to rejoin the group near Robinson's Arch, where they would begin a long climb up several sets of stairs and landings before entering the Basilica on the upper level.

Sarah led them through the steep ascent, keeping a watchful eye on Mr. Bauer yet mindful to avoid insulting him by inquiring about his physical condition. She quietly admired his endurance as she guided them to their destination. Notwithstanding the multitude of steps required to get there, he arrived with more energy and enthusiasm than the teenagers.

Sarah explained that the Temple Mount of The One God Religion had been modeled after the ancient King Herod Temple. She pointed out the rows of columns that seemed to stretch endlessly throughout the massive landing, and the doubled stoas—or covered walkways—around the outer walls that protected worshipers from the sun and rain. She shared the history of how back in the End Days the Cohen and Levi families—descendants of Moses—had enjoyed a higher status than the ordinary Jews who would come to praise God. Moses had put each of these families in charge and over the centuries of the End Days they'd become completely corrupted as they reveled in their elite status. But now in Salvation Time, Sarah explained that Cohen and Levi are honorary names reserved for ordinary people who've earned the right to them through their service and contributions to others.

As he walked along with his classmates Anwar Sadat was quiet and introspective. *"Maybe I could someday earn the name Anwar Sadat Cohen?"* he wondered to himself.

Deep within, he recognized that God was reminding him of his soul's choice to serve as a priest in this lifetime, which would give him the opportunity to touch many lives by preaching love, tolerance and acceptance for all humanity. Yet these meaningful experiences had only confirmed that the results of his Life Purpose Class had been right all along.

The temple also had a profound impact on Golda Meir, though for a very different reason. Listening to Sarah talk about the history of the temple—most notably the fact that it had been built on the site where Abraham had once planned to sacrifice his son for God—ignited a new understanding about her ancestor. Instead of her own child, Golda Meir had sacrificed the lives of other women's children. At least Abraham had been acting on what he believed to be God's will for *his own son* until God's angel mercifully intervened. Not Golda Meir. In the End Days, thanks to her sinister plotting with her Egyptian and American counterparts 1,200 Israeli soldiers had been needlessly killed.

Although the young Meir had studied her ancestor's life diligently in preparation for the exam, it wasn't until visiting Jerusalem and the temple that she truly understood the evil of her actions back in 1973. No wonder the Armageddon Commission had ordered the removal of all tributes to Golda Meir from the public square in Israel!

As young Golda quietly followed the tour alongside her classmates Ruth, Hillary and Debbie she wondered if Anwar Sadat and Henry Kissinger felt as shameful as she did.

In that moment, the young girl remembered the results of her Life Purpose Class years before which had indicated a career in teaching. She resolved right then to dedicate her life to working with very young children as a kindergarten instructor, with the goal of someday opening up several of her own schools. She would ensure a quality early education for each little one in her care to adequately prepare them for a successful elementary and high school experience.

Henry Kissinger strolled along with his friends Mahmoud Ahmadinejad, George W. Bush, Jacques Chirac and Nathan Rothschild. In typical fashion, he kept wiping an endless stream of moisture from his brow with a handkerchief. The challenging climb had exacerbated poor Kissinger's sweat problems but he was so caught up in the mysticism of the temple he didn't care. Like Golda, he thought back to the October War and his ancestor's cowardly actions. He felt overwhelmed with remorse and began to consider the ways he might make final restitution. *Perhaps he really should become an administrator of sanitation in Arusha as his Life Purpose Class results had already suggested?* It seemed fitting he should work at the Jimmy Carter Sanitation and Waste Facility back home. And if he ever wanted to move to another spot on the globe, he remembered Mr. Bauer telling them that these facilities in Jimmy Carter's name had been built in every country, major city and state. *Perfect!*

Mahmoud Ahmadinejad was deep in thought as he glanced over at Kissinger. Ever since Egypt, he'd been experiencing an intense stirring within his soul and he wondered if Kissinger had been undergoing a similar reaction to the Holy Land. Although these feelings were overpowering Mahmoud didn't feel as if he was being called to the priesthood of The One God Religion; it was more like God was urging him to remember his soul's purpose in this lifetime. He reflected back upon the sordid history of his End Days ancestor, a man who tortured and murdered innocents for Allah. But in spite of his family history of shame, Ahmadinejad also felt rejuvenated by the Middle East. He loved everything about it—the sights, the smells, the food, the warmth of its citizens. On the ride over on the electric bus as they'd passed through the marketplace he'd been drawn in by the beauty of the colorful Persian rugs for sale. He wondered if the people of Arusha would appreciate their exquisite craftsmanship and began to ponder the idea of becoming a Persian rug and antique dealer when he returned home. It would certainly be in line with his Life Purpose Class findings, which had led him in the direction of business.

Nathan Rothschild was also lost in thought as he caught sight of the two massive gold doors in the distance that would soon reveal the inside of the Basilica. While he moved along with the rest of the group he reflected back upon his study of the history of money and the story of an irate Jesus violently throwing the money traders out of God's house. As he looked around he tried visualize the scene in spite of the fact that this new temple had been built well over 2,000 years after Jesus' death. Although the Middle East didn't hold geographic significance in terms of his ruthless ancestor, he still felt the presence of the Creator reminding him of his soul's chosen path. He decided to make final restitution for the Nathan Rothschild of the 19th century by becoming a good, decent banker in Arusha where he'd dedicate his life to helping entrepreneurs secure the capital they needed to bring their great ideas into reality. And he also vowed to keep the banks in line so that they'd always put the consumer first. Since finance had been Rothschild's highest score in the LPC, it felt right that he'd receive final validation in the temple.

"Alright everyone, we've made it to the Basilica," Sarah announced. It's time for you to see the things you've all studied in school—Abraham's Rock, the Ark of the Covenant, The Twelve Commandments and The Twelve Holidays of The One God Religion. Are you ready?"

The students nodded enthusiastically. Most of their homes had replicas of these things, as did the Race Unity Neighborhood temple where they worshipped with their families. But to see the originals in detailed artwork and exquisitely chiseled stone and marble filled them with excitement. They were also eager to satisfy their curiosity about Abraham's Rock, which had been quite the draw for tourists all over the world ever since the Temple Mount had been built. The kids had often heard the story of how Prime Minister Eyal Grad had been inspired to turn it into a tourist attraction after the Armageddon War by making it a centerpiece of the temple. Since then Abraham's Rock had been producing significant revenue for Israel, even at a modest fee of three dollars per person. Of course, today's tourists had been exempted from that charge as part of the nation of Israel's welcome.

Sarah opened the golden doors to reveal a colossal enclosed area that sprawled out in every direction. Like the rest of the temple its vaulted ceilings were supported by soaring Greek columns. Spaced out at intervals along all four walls were vibrant, lavish tapestries celebrating each of the holidays of The One God Religion. In front of each tapestry, an elegant sculpture enhanced each one's material representation.

The Twelve Holidays of The One God Religion

Rosh Hashanah

Yom Kippur

Abraham's Rock

Simchat Torah

Thanksgiving

Shavu'ot

Hannukah

Christmas

Easter

Passover

Ramadan

Salvation Day

Eva Braun stared in awe at Abraham's Rock. After Sarah had given them the freedom to explore on their own she'd made a beeline to the middle of the expansive room to check it out up close. Most of her peers had joined her before quickly moving on to the magnificent golden Ark of the Covenant, the chiseled Twelve Commandments on the wall at the east end of the structure, and a walking tour through the artistic renderings of the Twelve Holidays. But Eva stood transfixed by this simple symbol of a radical shift in belief that took place thousands of years ago thanks to a devout man named Abraham.

"Kind of neat seeing it in person, isn't it?" Adolf Hitler asked. He'd been standing behind her, waiting for an opportunity to initiate a conversation.

"Oh hey Adolf, how's it going?" her tone was polite, if not overly enthusiastic.

214

"Enjoying the temple tour?"

"Yes, of course. Why wouldn't I?"

"Just making conversation," he snapped defensively. Hitler had no way of knowing she had other more important things on her mind, like fulfilling her soul's pre-selected career in show business. She dreamed of dancing on stage in sexy, glittery costumes while enthusiastic, adoring crowds cheered her on. The last thing she felt like doing was making small talk with Hitler so she turned her back to him to stare at the rock again.

"Fine, be that way!" he exclaimed as he strode away in a huff. Nearby Joseph Stalin, Bill Clinton and Jacques Chirac snickered as they witnessed the scene.

"What a jackass," Clinton observed in his raspy voice in between gales of laughter. Knowing Eva as he did it amused him endlessly that the inexperienced Hitler had such a juvenile crush on her. Would he even know what to do with her even if she did give him the time of day? Clinton highly doubted it but it sure was fun to watch him chase after her.

As he took footage of the various temple attractions, Spielberg's ears perked up in response the conversation taking place around him. Although they'd never really been good friends, part of him felt genuinely bad for Hitler. As he turned his attention back to the rendering of the Salvation Day Holiday he wondered what it would finally take for him to finally move on with his life and leave Eva Braun far behind.

The maglev sped on smoothly as it levitated above the tracks, bound for its next destination: Rome, Italy. Traversing the 1,434 miles between Jerusalem and Rome, it would deliver them to their destination in just two hours and 40 minutes. Before boarding the train again in the wee hours of the morning after just a few hours' rest, the kids and Mr. Bauer had enjoyed yet another lavish event in their honor—a lovely dinner dance in the main ballroom of the King David Hotel.

The succulent buffet had included authentic kosher Israeli fare including fresh hummus; vegetarian, chicken and meat shish kebabs; crisp, colorful salads; stuffed vine leaves; potato bourekas; eggplant salad; and an assortment of challah breads. All had hungrily pile their plates high and gone back for seconds and thirds—much to the delight of the wait and kitchen staff who'd prepared well to satisfy the appetites of ravenous teenagers.

Thoroughly spent now, most of the kids immediately settled into their seats to get a little more shut-eye before they got to Rome. In spite of their excitement about their impending visit with the Pope and tours of famous Roman attractions, they were simply too exhausted to stay awake—with the exception of Hillary Rodham. Energized by her amazing Israeli experience she was more determined than ever to finish her book *It Takes an Individual to Help a Village*. So she sat up straight in her seat, with her computer in her lap, typing away diligently. Beside her, the girl she loved slept soundly. Hillary had not yet found the courage to reveal her feelings to Debbie but hoped that being in a city like Rome, renowned for its romance throughout the End Days and well into Salvation Time, would inspire her to make a move.

A few rows down, a restless Eva Braun waited for sleep to overtake her. She wished their trip to the United States included a stopover in Las Vegas because she'd spent hours researching the famous city and had often imagined what it would be like to be a glamorous show girl on a Vegas stage. That's all she wanted out of this lifetime: glamour, glitz and endless partying. Her soul could come back and do something more meaningful in its next incarnation; this time around she was going to find a way to work and live in the original *Sin City*.

"Ah, Roma!" David Duke squealed with excitement as the train neared its next station stop. His eyes were glued to the window while his diminutive seatmate Charles Manson craned his neck to take in the view of the passing Italian metropolis. The golden sun was slowly rising above familiar landmarks like the Colosseum, Saint Peter's Basilica and the Vatican, bathing them in an intoxicating, otherworldly aura.

"Simply magnificent!" Duke sighed dramatically, waving his long fingers through his neatly styled Afro. "No wonder why Rome has always had a reputation for romance. I cannot wait to explore every inch of it!" While he didn't verbalize it to Manson, Duke was also hoping to connect with a handsome Italian guy during their brief stay.

"Yeah, it sure is pretty," Manson agreed.

"Pretty! Charles, Rome is magnificent, not pretty!"

"Well excuse me, it's *magnificent*!" he retorted sarcastically.

The two boys had beaten their teacher and the rest of their classmates back to the coach section after having been served a delicious kosher breakfast of fresh fruit, Greek yogurt, eggs, bacon and toast back in the dining car.

"Sorry Charles, I didn't mean to make fun of you; it's just that I've been looking forward to seeing Rome for so long and now that it's finally here I can hardly stand it!"

"It's alright," Manson assured him. "I understand why you feel that way. I'm just hoping Rome will be good for Mao and Stalin. Have you noticed the two of them hate each other more than ever?"

"I sure have," Duke replied. "Don't blame Mao one bit because I can't stand   sanctimonious Stalin either! You'd think he'd be a little more humble considering his family history. Poor Mao seems to be paying his karmic debt because he's always totally miserable."

"Yeah, I hear ya," Manson answered. "I'm ashamed of my ancestor too, but I know the best way I can make up for it now."

"Really? Do tell!" Duke encouraged him.

"Well, back at the temple I had a revelation. You know I told the class I wanted to become a judge ever since I started studying for the test. But I know I can't do that until I'm 50 and have a good track record running my own business. Then it hit me: I want to start a landscaping business. I may have to start out mowing lawns for money while I take classes and that's fine with me. I'm a simple man; I'm not very sophisticated. But I don't need be sophisticated to be a landscaper; I just need to provide good service. I don't need a high IQ to do it, either. And I love being outside. At least if I start out mowing lawns, I can work toward my goal of running my own business. Which was kinda what my LPC results were anyway. So I feel really good about it. I'm now sure this is what my soul agreed to do before coming back here."

"Good for you," Duke replied sincerely.

"What about you?" Manson asked. "Do you know what you're going to do with your life yet?"

The boy released a deep sigh.

"I don't know. When I took the LPC it said I should go into retail but I really wasn't feeling that. So when we were at the temple I was hoping I'd have some kind of revelation too—or at least some confirmation that the LPC was right," he admitted. "But I still don't know. I still can't see myself in retail so I'm hoping I'll find the answer somewhere along the way on this trip. I'm kinda jealous of the kids who confirmed their soul's purpose in the temple. Don't get me wrong. It got to me, too. It's just that being there really didn't help me figure out my soul's chosen plan for me in this lifetime."

"Well don't give up," Manson consoled. "We still have a long way to go. The answer could be waiting for you in Rome, Munich, or London—or maybe even Florida. Who knows?"

"Yep. In the meantime, I can't wait to get off of this train and get to the Vatican."

Protective of his privacy, Duke kept his goal of meeting and falling in love with an attractive Roman guy to himself.

Back in the dining car a drowsy Hillary Rodham gulped down another cup of hot, steaming coffee, hoping the caffeine would kick in well enough for her to completely enjoy their time in Rome. Although she'd typed over 1,000 words in her manuscript she was beginning to regret sacrificing sleep especially since Debbie was so energetic this morning. Watching her squeal with excitement as she caught sight of various Roman landmarks was truly endearing. Could this finally be the place to confess her love? As the train neared the station, Hillary pondered her next move.

Meanwhile, a contemplative Nathan Rothschild had mixed emotions about this visit. Staring out the window at the passing scene he could certainly understand why his classmates were eager to get off the train and explore the city. But he also realized that coming face to face with the beautiful artwork in and around the Vatican would be a reminder of the sordid history of money and the bitterness of the Protestant Reformation. Just staring out the window at Rome made him feel sad for ancient leaders like Julius Caesar, who'd been assassinated for doing right by his people. Rothschild was thankful they'd only be here for a day before boarding the train again to Germany—another destination he was dreading since it was the birthplace of his evil ancestor.

Of course, no one dreaded the stopover in Germany nearly as much as Adolf Hitler who fought to keep his eyes off of the especially lovely Eva Braun. She was seated diagonally across from him in the dining car looking ever so ladylike as she sipped her coffee and finished her breakfast. Wearing a floppy straw hat, a pink sundress and white espadrilles, she'd finally drifted off to sleep and awakened refreshed and ready to take on this impending leg of the tour with gusto now that she'd hatched a plan.

"Hey, can I give you a piece of advice?" a familiar voice with an annoying Texas twang asked. Hitler rolled his eyes before turning around to look at his classmate.

"What do *you* want, W?"

Bush just laughed and continued. "Uh Hitler, I know I'm not exactly a chick magnet but even I know that brooding over an unattainable girl is a complete waste of time."

"Really?" he responded in an agitated tone. Hitler's dark eyes glared at his classmate. In response, Bush's already black skin grew even darker due to his rising excitement.

"Look, I'm a pretty simple guy I *know*," he continued. "I like to stay in shape and keep healthy more than anything else. I cannot tell you how happy I am to finally be finished with school. If I never have to crack open another book, that'll be fine with me. Back in Jerusalem, I finally figured out my soul's plan for my life: I'm going to be a truck driver. It's simple, honest work for honest pay and that's all I want. The LPC had been right about me all along."

"Congratulations on your career choice Bush, but what does any of this have to do with me?"

"Look, all I'm sayin' is that sometimes you have to know when to give it up. And that girl over there," he noted as he pointed in Eva's direction, "is just not into you. So stop humiliating yourself, take a hint and try socializing with some new women. This is getting embarrassing, even for people who don't like you."

"Says the guy who still stutters like his stupid ancestor," Hitler shot back. In typical fashion, Bush just shrugged and laughed it off.

"Say what you will about him, at least he didn't chase after floozies. And once he found a good woman he stayed married to her his whole life."

Before Hitler could reply, he was preempted by another classmate who approached their table.

"Give it up W," Charles Tudor chuckled. "Hitler is hopelessly smitten."

"More like hopeless," Bush retorted, igniting howls of laughter from everyone within earshot. That's when Mr. Bauer once again rode to Hitler's rescue. Standing at the front of the dining car he announced in his booming voice that the train was about to reach its Roman station, and that all students were to report to the main coach section immediately.

As the class obeyed the teacher's orders, Hitler fought to control his weak bladder.

"Welcome to Rome, visitors and the Race Unity Regional High School Class of 2412!"

Pope Pius greeted the crowd warmly. As he stood behind a specially erected marble podium in Saint Peter's Square, he felt honored that they'd taken the time to visit with him. Standing among a small gathering of about 50 people including the Arusha contingent and 200 media members, he was both exhilarated and humbled by their presence. At first the students were surprised by the meager attendance, having intensely studied the papacies of the End Days. But Mr. Bauer discreetly reminded them that they were now living in Salvation Time where the Vatican's influence was greatly diminished. Popes were still revered by those who'd remained Catholic and others who respected the rights of human beings to worship as they pleased but they no longer enjoyed the trappings of immense power. And since the majority of people had freely chosen to join The One God Religion, popes in Salvation Days no longer attracted the huge and nearly unmanageable crowds of their predecessors.

A Caucasian version of Mr. Bauer, Pope Pius appeared to be around the same age, an affable man with a genuine interest in his fellow human souls and a sincere desire to maintain the peace and prosperity the world was now experiencing. In stark contrast to the popes of the past he was dressed in a simple black suit, crisp white shirt and black loafers. His neatly cut gray hair bore no semblance of a fancy mitre, just a plain, purple cap; his hands were free of anything resembling an ostentatious staff, allowing him to touch each visitor on the shoulder and shake their hand as he extended a personal greeting.

After delivering a few remarks he stepped down and began to mingle with his audience, working his way through the line accompanied by a lone security guard while the magnificence of Saint Peter's Square—with its exquisite columns, ornate statues and dancing water fountains—competed for his attention. Spielberg of course, had been busily filming this wondrous scene while the rest of his peers had stood awestruck as they contemplated the God-given talents of the human architects. For Anwar Sadat, Saint Peter's Square provided further proof of the righteousness of his decision to become a priest in The One God Religion; for Nathan Rothschild, an affirmation that something beautiful and timeless emerges out of even the worst of circumstances. This beloved Roman attraction might have come into existence because of rampant corruption but he couldn't deny it was also a tangible reminder of the talents with which God endows every individual. In spite of his earlier fears, Rothschild found himself renewed and inspired by the experience.

Once the Pope had acknowledged everyone else he turned his attention to the Arusha travelers. Extending his right hand to Mr. Bauer in a firm shake, he placed his left hand on his shoulder and thanked him for his excellence in teaching. Mr. Bauer graciously accepted the compliment before facilitating individual introductions of Pope Pius to each student. As they'd been instructed all of the teenagers displayed the proper etiquette as Pius inquired about their journey thus far and engaged them in conversation about their families back home. After he'd completed a meaningful one-on-one with all 21 students he announced his intention to escort them through the rest of the Vatican and encouraged them to ask as many questions as they'd like.

Many hours later, the group arrived at a lovely Italian bistro where they would enjoy one authentic, kosher meal before boarding the train and heading to their next destination. By now the sun was beginning to set, painting the sky in glorious hues of orange, pink, yellow and red. Between the stunning natural beauty of the heavens, the indelible impressions of the breathtaking frescoes and the quintessentially romantic ambiance of the restaurant, an amorous Hillary was nearing the point of no return.

As they took their places at small café tables for two outside, she maneuvered to get Debbie alone. Ruth Bader Ginsberg just glared at her as she rudely cut her off in line, desperate to dine with the girl she loved. She exchanged suspicious glances with Golda Meir as they watched a clueless Debbie smile up at her dining companion Hillary as she settled into her chair.

"I've been wondering about her and Debbie for a while now," Golda clucked as she sat down at the table now meant for her and Ruth.

"Me too!" Ruth exclaimed in a loud whisper. "Do you really think...?" Her voice trailed off, unable to complete the sentence.

"Do I think Hillary's a lesbian?" Golda posed bluntly.

"Shh, don't say it so loud!" Ruth warned her.

"Why? The truth is the truth and we're living in Salvation Time now anyway," Golda went on. "Hillary realized a long time ago that her soul chose homosexuality for this incarnation. Haven't you noticed she's always been sort of hostile toward the boys in the class? The thing is, I don't know about Debbie yet and I'd hate to see Hillary get hurt even if she does deserve someone a lot smarter."

They both snuck a furtive glance in the direction of their two classmates before a good-looking Italian waiter politely interrupted to take their drink order.

"Mmm, this tiramisu is heavenly!" Debbie gushed before popping another forkful of the creamy dessert in her mouth.

"It sure is," Hillary enthused before leaning over the table to gently wipe some lingering cream off of her face.

"Thanks," Debbie whispered in return, strangely aroused by the gesture. Sensing the moment had finally arrived Hillary took a deep breath and plunged in.

"You know, Debbie, we've been friends for a long time. And lately I've....I've...well, I've become aware of certain feelings I have for you. Very strong, intense, wonderful feelings."

Debbie just stared as she listened, still unsure of where all of this could be leading.

222

"I know the other kids make fun of you for being an airhead but I have always seen something sweet and genuine in you. And when no one else in the class believed you stood a chance of passing our history exam I always stood up for you. I knew you could do it. And then the day of the test you absolutely blew me away. I was so proud of you!"

"Thanks!" she giggled. "I think I surprised myself."

"But it's so much more than that. I absolutely love everything about you. I've been fighting this attraction to you forever and I just can't deny it anymore."

Realizing this was no joke, Debbie's face grew quite serious as she continued to listen. *Could this really be happening?*

"You make my heart sing in so many ways," Hillary admitted. "And I need to know if you feel the same way about me."

For a few moments silence hung between them as they stared into each other's eyes and absorbed the meaning of what had just been plainly stated. Hillary's heart began racing furiously in anticipation of a full rejection. But after what felt like an eternity, she noticed the corners of Debbie's mouth beginning to curve into a smile. Then, the unthinkable happened: she reached across the table and took Hillary's hand in hers.

"Oh my God Hillary, you have no idea how much I've wanted to hear you say that!" she confessed. "I figured out a long time ago that my soul had chosen to come here as a lesbian this time around. And I've been in awe of you forever. You're so smart, funny and beautiful. I know you don't like your legs but I love them. I was so afraid to tell you because I thought you'd laugh in my face. But I love you, Hillary. I really do."

"I love you too!" Hillary exclaimed before letting out her trademark cackle. As usual, it was loud enough to attract the attention of the rest of their group, prompting them all to turn around in curiosity. Abruptly brought back to reality, Hillary quickly covered.

"Oh Debbie was just telling me a funny joke," she explained. "Haven't you all heard a good joke before?"

Ruth rolled her eyes at Golda as they turned their attention back to dessert. Then Mr. Bauer took the opportunity to remind everyone to finish up soon because they'd be boarding the train in ten minutes. Once the rest of the kids were safely minding their own business, Hillary continued in a whisper.

"Being in this romantic city has made my feelings for you even more intense. I was so happy when Mr. Bauer assigned us together now that we've admitted our love I hope we can take it to the next level."

"Me too," she replied in a hoarse whisper that sent shivers up and down Hillary's spine. "I've been fantasizing about it for a very long time."

And an hour later as the maglev traversed the 574 miles to Munich Germany, Hillary and Debbie used the 45-minute ride to consummate their relationship in a private car.

###

In their Munich hotel room, a restless Adolf Hitler tossed and turned in his bed as he struggled to get comfortable. On the other side of the nightstand, an agitated Nathan Rothschild was growing impatient.

"Hitler, what the hell's the problem?" he finally cried out in exasperation. "Every two seconds you're either getting up to use the toilet or grumbling under your breath. In case you haven't noticed, I am trying to get some sleep here!"

"Sorry," he apologized as he climbed out of bed. He was glad Rothschild had finally reacted because he really needed to talk and had been trying to work up the nerve to initiate a conversation. In the next second, he picked up a remote and turned on the light in the tiny room.

"Aw geez Hitler, why'd you have to do that?" Nathan propped himself up against some pillows as he rubbed his tired eyes. Unmoved by his roommate's discomfort, Hitler pulled out a plastic bag from beneath the covers and proceeded to pull out several items including a wig, hat and sunglasses.

"What's all that?" Rothschild asked.

"A disguise to wear tomorrow. I know my soul chose to look like him but I'm sick of Germans staring at me! All they did was point and laugh at me when we walked through the train station. You should have seen the guy I bought this stuff from; he was totally obnoxious and wouldn't stop talking about how much I looked like

Adolf Hitler. I don't want people staring at me tomorrow when we go to Dachau!"

Rothschild couldn't help but laugh although he sympathized with his friend's plight. "Ah, so that's why you were late getting to the electric bus!"

"Don't laugh, Nathan. I'm really scared." Hitler's voice quivered as he spoke. Standing there in his boxer shorts and tank top, he looked more like a pathetic little kid afraid of the *Boogey Man* than a fully grown young adult.

"What are you so scared of?" Rothschild forced himself to be patient and kind in the hope that this conversation would end sooner rather than later.

"Dachau. I'm scared of facing Dachau." Brilliant and perceptive, Rothschild pondered his dilemma, needing no further explanation.

"Ah, I see," he began. "You and your family have spent years atoning for the crimes of your ancestor. *You*, especially, have carried the heaviest burden by choosing to go through life with his name and dealing with all of the pressure to pass the test with a good grade. So here you are, finally in the clear, and yet you still have one more thing to do—and that is visit one of the actual places where Adolf Hitler tortured and murdered innocent humans. And you're afraid of how it's going to affect you, being hit with the reality of it in person."

"Yes," the angst-ridden teenager replied. "I mean, I know what he did. I studied what he did. And I *hate* what he did. But haven't I been humiliated enough? Eva Braun won't even look at me and I'm a total laughing stock because I can't even control my stupid bladder—and before you say it, yes I know I chose all of it before I got here!"

Rothschild thought back upon the trials and tribulations of his pitiful classmate over the years. Walking in on Joseph and Eva had been the hardest cut of all for poor Hitler who was helplessly enamored with her in spite of her well-earned reputation as a party girl.

"I understand how you feel Adolf," he replied sympathetically. "But look at it this way: maybe confronting the history of Nazi Germany up close will finally complete the reconciliation. Just face it with courage, deal with it and move on. And remember, you also chose to come here with artistic talent, so the best is yet to come in this lifetime. You just have to get this one little thing out of the way."

"*Little* thing? You make it sound so easy."

"Ok, I'm sorry I didn't mean to make it sound trivial," he clarified. "I know it won't be *easy* for you. I'm not exactly thrilled to have to visit the birthplace of my evil ancestor either. But I figure once we get beyond Germany the rest of the trip will just be fun."

"I hope you're right, Nathan."

"If it makes you feel any better, Joseph Goebbels ought to be having a hard time with this, too. *His* ancestor isn't exactly innocent, you know."

"Yeah that's true," Hitler agreed.

"Have you talked to him about it?"

"No, guess I've been too caught up in my own stuff."

"Yeah, like Eva Braun," his roommate sighed. "Dude, she's a floozy. Just forget about her. I have a feeling her soul will need many more incarnations before she gets it. You need to focus on your own path. And after Dachau you're going to feel so much better."

"I hope you're right, Nathan."

"I'm *always* right. Just ask Mr. Bauer. Now for the love of God Hitler, turn off the light so we can get some sleep!"

Adolf Hitler stood speechless and paralyzed. In spite of Rothschild's well-meaning pep talk, nothing could have adequately prepared him for the moment he'd come into contact with the mind-blowing reality of his ancestor's evil actions. They'd just completed a guided tour of this grim facility where their knowledgeable host had shared the brutal history of the Dachau Concentration Camp. As he numbly walked along, Hitler heard her explain how the camp initially housed political prisoners when it was opened in 1933 but eventually evolved into a brutal death camp where thousands of Jews and others his ancestor deemed unfit for the "new" Germany suffered and died from malnutrition, disease and overwork. Many had simply been executed.

Staring at the horrendous images of bony humans with hollow eyes, broken limbs and irreparable psyches, Hitler thought that the executed prisoners had actually been the lucky ones. After a fleeting experience of intense pain at least their souls had been freed to return to heaven immediately; the others had endured endless savagery at the hands of wicked men—wicked men obedient to his wretched excuse of an ancestor. Even with the understanding that all souls choose their life's circumstances prior to birth—including Hitler's victims, it was still hard to take.

Reality slapped young Hitler viciously as he realized that the man whose name he bore had declared open season on Jews, artists, intellectuals, the physically and mentally handicapped, and homosexuals. For the student what had taken place in the 20th century was no longer a simple regurgitation of facts committed to memory for a history test; it was hardcore, solid evidence of the existence of pure evil. For the very first time, he understood why he'd chosen to incarnate with the challenges of an overactive bladder and a hypersensitive artist's disposition. After this horrendous experience young Hitler vowed he'd never again complain about these problems which paled in comparison to what these poor souls had willingly endured back in the 20th century.

Some distance away, Mr. Bauer observed his student. He was careful to remain out of view yet determined to keep watch to ensure Hitler's emotional, spiritual and physical safety. The wise teacher knew that this was something only Hitler could experience and resolve on his own. For that reason, he'd purposely sent the rest of the kids on to the German restaurant where they'd all enjoy a traditional kosher meal before indulging in some free time. Later that evening, Mr. Bauer planned to take an electric bus to his relatives' home while the teens went to a German beer festival in town.

Hitler sat on the bench staring quietly into space. It felt as if someone had just landed a devastating blow to his gut. He was vaguely aware that his classmates and teacher had all left him behind, much to his relief. The last thing he wanted was to put on a grueling emotional show for the amusement of obnoxious kids like Stalin, Clinton and Chirac who would most likely mock his pain and suffering. Besides, Mr. Bauer was only a text or phone call away. And until he felt ready to rejoin the group Hitler preferred to be alone while he processed his feelings.

###

"Where have *you* been?" Joseph Stalin asked smugly upon noticing Adolf Hitler's arrival. He'd just entered the private dining room of the German restaurant with Mr. Bauer and the jock wasted no time in giving him grief.

"Never mind, Mr. Stalin," the teacher intercepted before Hitler could respond. "Eat your dinner and behave yourself, sir."

The kids were seated at a long rectangular table boasting a kosher feast of sauerkraut, Bratwurst, asparagus, and pan-roasted potatoes. Judging by the ample pitchers of beer, their German hosts had no issue with serving alcohol to people 18 years old and younger, although most of the teens had opted for iced tea or water.

Mr. Bauer steered the new arrival to the end of the table where a place was available next to Nathan Rothschild across from Joseph Goebbels. Thankfully, Stalin and his cohorts Clinton and Chirac had settled at the opposite end where they were free to ogle the hot German waitresses wearing low-cut blouses and traditional dirndl dresses. Although he obeyed his teacher's orders, Stalin was suddenly aching for a fight with Hitler though he didn't quite know why. In the meantime he was content to eat, drink and stare at the beautiful female wait staff along with his buddies.

"Alright everyone," Mr. Bauer tapped a glass with a fork to get their attention. "Now that you're all here and accounted for, please pay attention. You are going to eat your dinner, which I've already paid for. Then you'll have a few hours of free time to explore the village. Go to the beer festival, shop, walk around—do whatever you'd like. Just make sure you're all back here in front of the restaurant by 11 p.m. where a bus will take us back to the hotel. I expect you all to be on time: no exceptions, no excuses. Do you understand?"

"Yes, Mr. Bauer," they replied in unison.

"Good. I am headed off to visit some relatives but you have my number if you need to reach me. As always, I'll have my smartphone on me."

As he turned to leave, the kids wished him well, thrilled to finally get some free time to explore without the limitations of guided tours and responsible chaperones.

"Want some Bratwurst?" Goebbels asked Hitler as the platter made its way down the table.

"Sure," he replied, handing him his plate. The process continued until Hitler, Rothschild and Goebbels each had a full, hot meal in front of them just waiting to be enjoyed.

"So Adolf," Joseph began after popping a mouthful of potatoes into his mouth, "what happened to you today? I mean, you disappeared for a long time."

Hitler took a deep breath. "Let's just say being at the concentration camp was wild," he responded carefully. "Yeah, I get it: everyone involved decided before they were born to be either victims or oppressors. That still didn't make it easy to walk through the concentration camp. And you know, for me especially, it was tough. I'm part of his family and I have his name."

"Yes, I understand," Goebbels remarked. "I walked off to get some air and spend some time alone for a while, too. But I was ok after that so I found Mr. Bauer and got back on the electric bus with the rest of the kids."

"So you felt something being there, too?" Rothschild pursued.

Goebbels sighed. Although the entire experience had a profound effect on him, he was much more guarded about his emotions.

"Yeah, it was kind of rough. I mean it is one thing to study what your ancestor did but it's something else to have to face it up close. It was hard. I am very ashamed of Joseph Goebbels."

"Did you get anything else out of it?" Hitler asked.

"Yes. I finally decided my career path," he replied. "I am going to become an ad man. I'm going to open my own advertising agency where I can use propaganda to promote good products and services. During the 15 minutes of promos in between each uninterrupted program I'll direct viewers' minds toward quality products and services. It's not a total surprise since I scored the highest in marketing, writing and communications way back when we all took the LPC."

"That's great!" Rothschild enthused.

"Good for you!" Hitler added.

"Hey Hitler, with your artistic skills, maybe you could be a graphic designer at my firm. Do you want to go into business together? Might be fun and profitable for both of us."

"Sounds like something to seriously consider," he agreed, feeling better by the minute.

While they chatted happily at one end of the table, Joseph Stalin downed a few pitchers of beer and became an agitated drunk at the other. With Clinton and Chirac egging him on, he vowed to take care of that "punk" Adolf Hitler now that his protector Mr. Bauer had finally given him the opportunity. He secretly patted the Arabic knife in his pocket, wondering if it could assist him in the effort.

"Aw man, I can't wait to see that," a buzzed Clinton enthused, his bulbous nose twitching. Having been unable to locate a willing female for some fun times with Perdoma cigars, he was feeling especially restless. Watching Stalin beat the crap out of Hitler wasn't quite as satisfying as screwing a hot babe but the night was still young. There was still plenty of time for both things to happen.

Adolf and Joseph hung out together, enjoying the German folk music emanating loudly from one of the open bars where a live band was playing. The cool evening breeze was perfect for savoring the outdoors, giving them a reprieve from smoky, confined spaces. Hitler had been in a constant state of contentment ever since his breakthrough at Dachau. Even his body felt completely different and relaxed. Not once since using the men's room before they left the restaurant had he even felt the urge the relieve himself.

As they took in the sights and sounds, they talked excitedly about their future plans to work together once Goebbels had secured the necessary capital for his ad agency.

Unfortunately the joy of the moment came to an abrupt end with the unwelcome intrusion of Hitler's nemesis, Stalin. Now a *raging* drunk, he was accompanied by his partners-in-crime Clinton and Chirac while several other classmates including Bush, Tudor, Manson, Kissinger, Sadat, Ahmadinejad and Rothschild followed close behind.

"*Hitler!*" he roared. In response to the bloodcurdling sound a shockwave ripped through Adolf's body.

"Joseph, just go away and leave us alone!" Goebbels yelled.

"Oh, I don't think so!" he bellowed. "Hitler and I have a score to settle here!"

230

"What *score*, Stalin?" Feeling suddenly emboldened, Hitler stood tall and ready for battle.

By this time the rest of the students had caught up to the unfolding scene. The young filmmaker of the group immediately whipped out his smartphone and began taking footage.

"What *score*? Your evil ancestor for one! Didn't you see all of the poor victims he tortured at Dachau today? You should be utterly ashamed of yourself!" Stalin slurred his words as he raved, making him seem more pitiful than scary.

"Yes Joseph, I did," Hitler declared calmly. "And I came to terms with it. I've atoned for it."

"Aha, you've *atoned* for it! Well tell that to the millions your ancestor murdered!"

"You know what, Stalin? Since we're talking about millions of murders, let's not forget *your* ancestor killed 45 million—many more than Adolf Hitler. What did he call them? Oh that's right: statistics!"

Having been served a heaping dose of reality, Stalin reacted in typical bullying fashion by throwing a punch at the truth-teller. Hitler ducked before returning his own fist as hard as he could into Stalin's jaw, initiating a counter-attack and full-blown fight while the entire graduating class looked on. Most were frightened and horrified with the exception of Clinton and Chirac who heartily cheered their buddy on.

"Oh my God, we have to do something!" Hillary shrieked. She looked around desperately for help; that's when Rothschild took action. Holding his half-empty bottle of beer, he waited for an opening as fists flew furiously. A few seconds later he made his move when Joseph inadvertently gave him clear shot at his forehead.

Stalin howled as the sharp glass bit ferociously into his skin, slicing open his forehead and igniting a gusher of blood. The stunned bully fell to the ground as he pressed his hands against the ugly wound, cursing Hitler as he did so. That's when the Arabic knife flew out of his pocket, to the astonishment of everyone except Ahmadinejad.

"Oh my God, somebody call Mr. Bauer!" Debbie screamed while a satisfied Rothschild pondered his brutal but necessary act of violence. Adolf slowly stood up, stumbled over to the bench and sat down, his chest convulsing as he fought to steady his breath.

"Super glue! Does anyone have *super glue*?" Hillary shrieked as she briskly paced through the assembly with her phone pressed to her ear. "Mr. Bauer says we need to close the wound with super glue!"

Wordlessly, Mao Tse Tung walked over to where she was standing and proceeded to pull a tube of the item in question out of his pocket while an impressed Ruth Bader Ginsberg looked on.

"Mao, you are really prepared!" she gushed.

"It's nothing," he shrugged. "My parents made me take it just in case someone needed it. Never thought it would be Joseph Stalin but oh well. I guess it makes sense."

With that, Mao got down on his knees next to his enemy's forehead and carefully applied the healing agent to the wound. At first Stalin resisted but quickly relented after Mao reminded him that he had two choices: accept his help or risk being disfigured for life.

By the time a concerned Mr. Bauer arrived on the scene, Stalin's wound had been thoroughly dressed and on its way to a full recovery.

"Glad to see our patient is on the mend," the teacher noted after joining Stalin on the bench and inspecting Mao's handiwork. "Looks like we won't have to waste any time since Mr. Stalin can get a good night's rest back at the hotel before we board the bullet train again in the morning." With that, he handed him two pain pills and a bottle of water. The grateful jock wordlessly accepted them.

Mr. Bauer then looked up at the crowd of students gathered around. A nervous Nathan and Adolf stood as far away as possible without drawing attention to their distance.

"Does anyone care to tell me what happened here?"

"I do!" Ruth Bader Ginsberg piped up, "Mao Tse Tung is a hero!" She glanced over at her crush whose black cheeks began to turn crimson with embarrassment. He was thankful the night sky gave him cover, though he liked the way he felt. *Could someone like Ruth actually have feelings for a guy like him?* The thought made his heart beat faster.

"Mr. Tung, it sounds as if you saved the day. Congratulations, sir!" the teacher complimented.

"Oh it was nothing Mr. Bauer," he replied modestly.

"Well, I beg to differ, Mr. Tung, even though I do appreciate your humility. As for you, Mr. Stalin, I hope this little incident has inspired you to change your bullying ways?"

Joseph Stalin nodded silently at his teacher as he patiently waited for the painkillers to kick in.

"By the way, Mr. Stalin," the teacher continued. "Care to explain where you go this?" he asked, holding up the Arabic knife.

The expression on the boy's face said it all.

"Don't look so surprised. This is Salvation Time where reputation is everything and all sins are atoned for. It's not important how I found out about you stealing this; the important thing is that you make restitution to the Egyptian shop owner. You and I will call him first thing in the morning to figure out the best way to do that. I think you've created enough drama for one evening."

Stalin's classmates laughed out loud as the class jock just sat there silently, his pride and his forehead smarting fiercely.

"Sin City, here we come!" Bill Clinton exclaimed joyfully as he clapped his friend Jacques Chirac on the shoulder. They were seated together on an electric bus bound for a remote area of the French metropolis. After having spent the day touring typical Parisian attractions like the Eiffel Tower, The Louvre and The Arc de Triomphe with the class the hormonal adolescents couldn't wait to be liberated to finally enjoy some quality time with France's best prostitutes.

Despite his chronic problems with jock itch, Jacques Chirac was also looking forward to a few hours of unrestrained pleasure with a sophisticated European female. Thanks to Stalin, he and Bill had been denied an opportunity to get it on with one of the many gorgeous German girls they'd seen at the beer festival. His little stunt had resulted in the return of their teacher and an early curfew, which was why they'd ditched him back at their downtown Paris hotel.

"Are you ready for some hot sex, son?" Clinton impersonated their teacher, causing both of them to double over in laughter.

"Yes sir, Mr. Clinton. Let's go!"

The two boys stepped off of the bus and practically sprinted toward the massive Sin City Paris gate—their portal to the   pleasures of the flesh.

Back in downtown Paris, Ruth Bader Ginsberg wandered into a lovely bath and body shop infused with the delightful fragrance of lavender. Ever since Mao had stepped up in Germany, her feelings for him had intensified, although his standard of hygiene still hadn't quite improved enough for her liking. She figured if she could buy him a gift of expensive French soap and cologne it would inspire him to shower more often.

"Bonsoir, Mademoiselle!" a friendly young woman greeted her as she made her way into the boutique.

"Bonsoir!" Ruth replied politely.

"May I help you?"

"Ah oui, do you sell men's products?"

"But of course, Mademoiselle! Please, come with me."

Bader Ginsberg followed her hostess through the endless displays of scented candles, bath salts, shower gels and assorted shampoos and conditioners into the men's section where she breathed in the manly smells of almond, amber wood, musk and citrus. She stared in awe at the shelves of hand-milled soaps and organic shaving gel and cologne. There was even a rack of plush terry cloth robes with matching slippers lining the back wall.

"Wow, this is amazing!" she remarked with astonishment. "We have some of this stuff in Arusha but I've never seen so many bath products in my life!"

"Well, you are in France now," the young clerk reminded her sweetly. "Did you have a special someone in mind?"

"I sure do," she replied.

"So tell me about him. Perhaps I can help you select the perfect gift."

"See that's the thing—" she started to reply before the boisterous conversation of familiar voices interrupted her. Ruth watched in dismay as Hillary, Debbie and Golda burst through the front door giddy with excitement. Their relationship out in the open, Debbie and Hillary held hands as they strolled through the boutique.

"See, I told you she'd be here!" Golda exclaimed. "I've had a feeling ever since he pulled out that super glue she had a crush on him!"

234

Bader Ginsberg's black cheeks turned red as she watched them approach, realizing her flimsy excuse about needing some time alone hadn't deterred suspicious minds. The French sales girl observed the scene with amusement.

"May I help you, ladies?" she asked innocently.

"Oh we're just here to look around," Hillary answered.

"You mean spy on me, don't you?" Ruth shot back angrily.

"Oh come on, Ruth, lighten up!" Golda encouraged her. "We're all friends here. And if Hillary and Debbie are brave enough to go public with their love you should be, too. Besides, we all know you have it bad for Mao—even if he does stink something fierce."

"Stop it!" Ruth defended him. "He's been working hard on his hygiene and he smells much better."

"Is that why you're here?" Debbie quizzed. "To help him along?" With that, the trio dissolved into giggles.

"Ladies, if you cannot behave I will have to ask you to leave," the sales clerk warned partly out of sympathy for Ruth and partly because she wanted to close a good sale tonight.

"We're sorry," Hillary finally managed to blurt out. Ruth just stood there with her hands on her hips, more agitated than ever as she glared at them.

"You know, the two of you ought to have a little more sympathy," she chided the lesbians. "Even now in Salvation Days knowing it's a soul's choice, it's still hard for some to accept homosexuality. And I never once made fun of you when you decided to announce your relationship on the train last night. So the least you could do is show *me* some respect."

"Oh my God, you're right," Hillary conceded sincerely as she absorbed the meaning of her words. "We're sorry," she added, "we had no right to make fun of you for falling in love, no matter who it is." She eyed Golda and Debbie knowingly.

"Yes, we're really sorry Ruth," they chimed in.

"I'll accept your apology on one condition," Bader Ginsberg replied. "Please help me pick out some nice gifts for Mao."

"With pleasure!" they cried in unison.

The relieved clerk happily resumed her sales presentation. And an hour later she beamed with pride as Ruth Bader Ginsberg left the boutique with several neatly wrapped packages including one large box containing a red terry robe and matching slippers. Now that her shopping mission was accomplished, she simply had to find the right time to present these exquisite French items to the boy she loved.

###

"Welcome to the Buckingham Palace Museum!" a courteous tour guide named Arthur greeted the Arusha contingent as they made their way to the grand entrance. A pleasant, slightly rotund man of about 50, Arthur had been looking forward to their visit. He smiled as he observed the wonder on the teenaged faces upon laying eyes on their latest tourist attraction.

"Quite impressive, isn't it?" he let out a jolly laugh as Mr. Bauer approached him to shake his hand and thank him in advance for his services.

"Oh you're quite welcome!" he replied, giving the teacher's hand a hearty shake. "I love showing off England's most famous landmark and it's certainly my honor to offer all of you a private tour."

After they exchanged pleasantries, Arthur motioned for them to follow him through the impressive, wrought iron gates.

As they walked into the courtyard, George Chamberlain and Charles Tudor stared in awe at the massive ornate building that had once housed English royalty in style and opulence during the End Days.

"Wow, it's hard to believe people actually lived here," Chamberlain noted. "It's so, so…"

"Ostentatious?" Tudor asked.

"Yeah, that's the word I was looking for," he confirmed. "Hard to believe that ordinary working people back then had no problem with kings and queens. I mean, what did they actually *do* to earn this kind of luxury lifestyle? Sheesh!"

Their amused tour guide overheard them and responded. "Well boys I know for a fact that Mr. Bauer here taught you all about the *Divine Right of Kings*. I know it's hard to believe it now but people really did buy into the notion that God personally appointed monarchs to rule over them. Thank God those days are over!" He let out another jolly chuckle.

"Yeah, no kidding," Tudor remarked, remembering the history of his own ancestor and his battle with Oliver Cromwell.

Chamberlain thought back to the LPC which had guided him toward a lowly career in city administration when he was a young teen. Turned off as he was by all of this pretentiousness, he realized the Life Purpose Class had been right on. He resolved to embark upon a career as a pencil-pusher in the Jimmy Carter Sanitation and Waste Facility back in Arusha.

As the tour continued, the kids were overwhelmed by the pure decadence of the former palace while Arthur led them from one expansive room to another. Even with their knowledge of history it was still mind-blowing that monarchs had actually lived so luxuriously while their hardworking subjects resided in meager homes, cooked their own simple meals and struggled to keep their families properly educated, clothed and fed.

Stalin observed the scene soberly. Ever since his fight with Hitler and subsequent first-aid administration by Mao he'd become very introspective. He had to admit that Hitler had been right to remind him about the 45 million people murdered under his ancestor's watch. It hadn't escaped his notice he was now walking through the very place where the English monarchy had recruited Charles Darwin to write his stupid book—the book that 20th century Joseph Stalin would later use as justification for genocide. He shook his head in disgust.

"Hey Stalin, how's the forehead?" Joseph turned to look at a sincere Mao Tse Tung.

"It's doing pretty well thanks to you," he genuinely replied. "I don't think I'll even have a scar you did such a great job. I still have some pain but I guess that's to be expected."

"Well, I'm glad you're ok," Mao answered humbly.

"Hey Mao—thank you, again. Really."

"You're welcome."

Ruth Bader Ginsberg beamed with pride as she watched their interaction while Steven Spielberg captured the moment with his smartphone.

###

"Good morning, everyone! Are you ready for the coolest part of the bullet train ride?" Naomi asked as the kids boarded in London. "We're headed for the ocean on our way to New York!"

They shivered with excitement, eager to experience something they'd only learned about in school up until now. Overflowing with curiosity they bombarded Naomi with questions as they pulled out of the London Station.

"One at a time!" she laughed.

While Big Ben, Westminster Abbey and Parliament disappeared in the distance, Naomi explained that both the land train and trans-oceanic train ran on pure electricity and magnetism. Even when traveling under the sea, the trans-oceanic train moved just as smoothly as its counterpart on land—at a much faster speed of 2000 miles per hour. Thus, it would carry them to New York City in less than two hours, due to the vacuum inside the tubing. Unlike its counterpart on land, it also moved through four massive, concentric carbon fiber tubes held up by cables anchored securely to the ocean floor. In between each massive tube was ample space for protection, with the train moving within the innermost tube. While Naomi expected that most of their trip would be underwater, the tubes could also be elevated above the surface, creating an illusion of riding on a cruise ship—without the turbulence created by waves. And to offer passengers spectacular views of sea life, the trans-oceanic maglev featured panoramic LCD screens throughout its interior walls, thanks to cameras on the outer tubes.

As they approached the coastal town of Newquay, Naomi encouraged the kids to settle in and enjoy the magnificence. They quickly took her advice and gathered excitedly on the plush, ergonomic couches in the lounge car, waving to the villagers outside as the train sped toward the water.

Hillary and Debbie sat huddled together, giggling like little girls. Ruth shyly took a seat next to Mao Tse Tung, still waiting for the right moment to surprise him with her gift. Golda sat next to George Chamberlain, for whom she'd started to feel something more than friendship since they'd bonded over their family histories during the Buckingham Palace Museum tour. Sadat, Ahmadinejad, Bush,

Manson, Kissinger, Rothschild and the rest of the boys spread out over several seats while Spielberg jockeyed for the best spot from which to film their descent into the sea.

The train raced through the tubing on its way to the ocean floor while the gigantic LCD screens showcased a vibrant, colorful subterranean world featuring endless varieties of fish, crabs, sharks and coral reefs. It was like being inside a gigantic aquarium yet there was no sensation of movement thanks to the solid construction of the carbon fiber tubing, which was stronger than steel. It was also cheap and easy to produce, making it the preferred material for train and vehicle construction. Even Mr. Bauer gazed in wonder at the display. He'd dreamed of this moment for years and was delighted that in next semester's class he'd have the benefit of an actual experience of the train to enhance his classroom lectures.

Suddenly noticing a glaring absence among his classmates, Charles Tudor silently wondered why Jacques Chirac still hadn't returned from the toilet. It hadn't escaped his notice that his seatmate had been acting kind of strange ever since Buckingham Palace when he couldn't stop scratching his balls. Tudor had simply assumed it was a bad flare-up of the guy's chronic jock itch but ever since they'd boarded the train in London, Chirac had been uncharacteristically reserved and serious. While everyone was mesmerized by the underwater world, Tudor decided to investigate. As he passed by the private rooms, he caught sight of something out of the corner of his eye. He turned to see Chirac writhing in pain in one of the conference spaces as he leaned back in his seat, his hands frantically rubbing his groin. Upon catching Tudor's eye, the troubled teen clicked the remote to let him in.

"Jacques! What's wrong?"

"Ugh, I cannot stop itching! And the burn—*Mon Dieu!*"

"Don't you have your jock itch spray with you?"

"Of course I do, you idiot! It's not helping!" Then in the next breath, "I'm sorry Charles but I am itching so bad I can't stand it!"

"I'm gonna get Mr. Bauer," Tudor announced.

"No! No...please. Get Bill Clinton, not Mr. Bauer."

"Bill Clinton?" he repeated skeptically. "Why him?"

"Just do it, Charles!"

With that, Tudor ran back through the compartments to retrieve the only other person who could possibly solve the mystery of

Chirac's urgent medical condition. A slightly annoyed Clinton reluctantly left his place next to their hostess, with whom he'd been shamelessly flirting, and followed Charles to the back of the train. He nearly doubled over with laughter when he saw poor Jacques Chirac, who had pulled down his pants and was now scratching bare skin beneath his underwear.

"What on earth is going on with you, son?" Clinton inquired in his *Mr. Bauer* voice.

"Oh knock it off Clinton, and close the door!"

"Ok if Tudor stays?"

"Yes, yes I don't care," Chirac replied impatiently.

"He says it's not jock itch," Charles offered. "What else could it be?"

"Clinton, how come you're not having the same symptoms? We both went to Sin City together!"

Charles' ears perked up.

"You went to *Sin City*?"

"Damn right we did," Clinton responded smugly. "Chirac and I really needed some so we figured we'd each have ourselves a French éclair, if you know what I mean. During our free time in Paris we snuck out to Sin City. Oh man...did that girl ever appreciate my Perdomas. I hope I can find some hot American chicks in New York and Florida just like that babe. Woo! I get hard just thinking about it."

Charles listened with fascination, visibly impressed. He was about to ask another question when Chirac preempted him.

"Never mind the whore, Clinton! I need to know if you're having the same problem. Look! My skin is even turning bluish-gray.....eww!"

Bill took a peak under Chirac's jockey shorts and nearly got sick.

"My friend, I do believe you have crabs...and not the kind that swim in the ocean."

"Crabs? What the hell are crabs? And why don't you have them?" he demanded.

"Guess your prostitute wasn't living up to Sin City standards," he shrugged. "Mine was obviously clean 'cause I'm not having a problem."

Poor Chirac's itching and irritation was getting worse by the minute as he rubbed the area harder and howled in discomfort.

240

"What are we going to do for him?" Charles urgently asked Bill.

"Well, it just so happens I brought a little something along in case of an emergency," he replied with a sly smile. Then looking up at Chirac he encouraged him, "Hang in there dude, I've got just the thing to help."

As Clinton emerged from the private room, Steven Spielberg ducked into an open compartment to avoid being seen. He smiled mischievously to himself as he hit the stop button on his smartphone.

The soaring Freedom Tower reached 1,776 feet into the clear, blue Manhattan sky, its contemporary glass panels glistening in the brilliant sunlight. The students and their teacher stood on the pavement with necks tilted upward as they stared in amazement at this modern marvel. Built by American architect David Childs in defiance of the Muslim terrorist attacks of September 11, 2001 the structure had a long and sordid history thanks to rampant greed, corruption and political correctness. These negative human characteristics had combined to nearly sideline the entire project which nevertheless was finally completed in the summer of the year 2014—almost a full 13 years after the incident.

"Hey Mr. Bauer," Spielberg began, "we're going up to the observation deck aren't we?"

"Yes Mr. Spielberg, we'll be heading up to the 100th floor a little later. From what I understand the windows are quite large so you should be able to capture some breathtaking views. How's the film coming along, anyway?"

"Ah better than I could've imagined, sir," he replied with a grin. Little did his teacher know but international landmarks were actually the least interesting scenes Spielberg had captured for posterity. And yet he couldn't help but feel a twinge of guilt as he sensed the pride Mr. Bauer obviously felt for him.

"Alright class, now that you've had your chance to gaze at this incredible structure we're going to visit the National September 11 Memorial and Museum. Please stay together." As he spoke he motioned for them to follow him just one block south of One World Trade Center—the legal name for the Freedom Tower—where they'd tour the tribute to the victims of September 11 and their rescuers built by American architect Michael Arad.

A forest of trees with two square pools in the center where the twin towers once stood, the memorial and museum had a profound effect on both George W. Bush and Bill Clinton. Looking around at this heartbreakingly beautiful scene, Bush thought of his long-ago ancestor standing amid the rubble surrounded by fire fighters a few days after the attack. With a bullhorn in his hand he'd cried out with fierce resolve, "I can hear you, the rest of the world hears you and the people who knocked down these buildings will hear all of us soon!"

That was before he fell captive to political castration, of course.

Meanwhile, as Bill Clinton wandered around he reflected back upon his study of American President William Jefferson Clinton and his refusal to recognize and confront evil. He realized that while many Americans automatically blamed everything on George W. Bush and Republicans, his sorry excuse for an ancestor had enabled September 11 by appeasing fanatical Muslims and treating every act of terrorism that happened under his watch as a law enforcement matter. Later to cover his own butt he coerced the network ABC not to sell DVDs of their truthful film, *The Path to 9/11*.

The teenaged Clinton soon spotted George W. Bush sitting on a nearby bench and approached him.

"Geez W, I didn't expect it to be so hard being here," he observed. Shaken out of his deep thoughts, a surprised Bush turned his head to look at his classmate.

"Where are all the others?" he asked.

"Ah, they went inside the museum."

"Not sure I have the stomach for that," Bush replied honestly. "You're right, Clinton. Being here where so many innocent people were murdered is tough. I was just thinking about how my ancestor W was strong at first but then caved in to propaganda and pressure. How pathetic!" The student's complexion took on a darker shade of black to match his agitation.

"Hey cheer up; he wasn't nearly as bad as mine. He let everyone heap most of the blame on Bush while he got a free pass," Clinton sympathized.

"Yeah, I guess you're right," he agreed.

They sat there for a few moments in somber silence until Clinton decided to abruptly change the subject to his favorite thing in life.

"So, have you bumped into any hot chicks along the trip? I gotta tell you, this French girl I hung out with in Sin City Paris—to die for!"

"Really," Bush replied, his black eyes growing wide with wonder.

"Uh-huh. But don't worry I'm sure there are some pretty girls working in Sin City New York. Want to come with me tonight during our free time?"

"Sure! But wouldn't you rather take Chirac along? I know you two are tight."

"Aw trust me Chirac won't be indulging in the pleasures of the flesh anytime soon!"

George looked at him quizzically, prompting Bill to burst out into laughter. Sometimes Bush's ignorance could be so endearing.

"Don't worry W, Chirac has crabs but he'll be ok. Here's a little piece of advice: when we get there tonight, make sure you ask your girl if she's up to Sin City hygiene and medical standards. Demand to see her business certificate. And don't forget the condoms just in case!"

With that he whipped out several packets of the latex items from his pocket, much to the delight of his newfound buddy.

"Wow Clinton, you think of everything!"

"Hey, I always travel prepared for every event and emergency," he bragged. "And don't forget I've got a box of Perdoma cigars back in the hotel room, too. It's time you learned from the master. Believe me, by the time you're done in Sin City your stuttering problem will be a thing of the past!"

"I'm looking forward to that!" Bush exclaimed, his Texas twang deepening with salacious anticipation.

###

"Wow, this is so beautiful!" Ruth Bader Ginsberg gushed. She was seated with Mao Tse Tung, Golda Meir and George Chamberlain in a lovely carriage, pulled by a magnificent white horse through New York's famous Central Park. Earlier that day, the boys had surprised both girls with an invitation to experience one of the city's most famous attractions during their free time. When the foursome had arrived at Central Park South between 5th and 6th avenues, Ruth and Golda squealed with delight at all of the gorgeous horses just waiting to offer tourists an unforgettable ride through Central Park and Manhattan.

Their friendly carriage driver Marty—a tall, handsome guy with sparkling blue eyes and a warm smile—welcomed them to the city and offered them a hand into the elegant, old-fashioned transport.

"Welcome to New York City! I'm honored to be the one taking you on this tour of Central Park. This here's Liberty," he explained with a nod to the horse. Then as they settled into the black cushioned seat he asked, "So, are you all enjoying your stay so far?"

"Yeah, it's great! I've never seen so many skyscrapers, museums and stores in one place!" Golda exclaimed. "But I think *this* is going to be my favorite part of New York."

The sun was beginning to set, filtering golden rays of light through the trees and casting an orange glow on the tall buildings in the distance.

"Mine too," George agreed, placing an arm about her and giving her an affectionate squeeze.

As Marty led the horse out of the line-up and onto the tour route he explained how this longstanding New York City tradition had nearly been destroyed by a corrupt, collectivist mayor named Bill De Blasio.

"Wait! I thought the carriage rides made a lot of money for the city," Tung challenged. "Why would a mayor want to outlaw them? Wouldn't people like you lose their jobs if that happened?"

"Absolutely! But Mayor De Blasio didn't care about any of that. He was in cahoots with his greedy real estate crony Steve Nislick. I know for a fact you guys studied collectivism in your history class. De Blasio was nothing more than a modern-day communist who used propaganda very effectively. He claimed he wanted to outlaw horse and carriage rides because of animal cruelty. But as with all commies, the reality did not match the rhetoric. In truth, he and Nislick wanted to seize the 64,000 acres the horse stables stood on so that they could develop hotels and make even more money for themselves—the little people be damned!"

"Wow that is unbelievable!" Ruth exclaimed.

"Well, it was the *End Days*," Mao reminded her. "It's bad but not surprising."

"Yeah, it kind of reminds me of my ancestor's horrible Kelo decision to seize private property," she sighed. "Except this was about taking good jobs away from good people and ruining other people's fun."

"So what happened, Marty?" Golda asked. "I mean, obviously they didn't get their way or we wouldn't be here right now."

"No ma'am, they did not, thanks as always to ordinary people who fought back. It was a tough go for a while but common sense prevailed. That's one reason why in Salvation Time no one person is allowed to own more than 50 farming acres and they cannot own more than three private residences. Commercial real estate is limited to either five shopping centers or 25 stores, whichever is greater. And when a homeowner dies, they cannot leave their home to their children unless there's a physical or mental handicap that would create a hardship by moving them. Otherwise, they must sell the home. Of course, they keep the money from the sale but the house must transfer ownership to someone else, a non-relative. Many people complained about that at first but it's to prevent the out-of-control corruption we had in the End Days when a single person could own unlimited real estate and use it to control and manipulate others."

The teens listened attentively before a thoughtful Chamberlain had another question.

"Marty, can I ask you something?"

"Sure!"

"You seem like a really intelligent guy. I'm not putting down your line of work but something tells me you haven't always been a carriage driver."

He burst out laughing while Golda gave her beau a sharp nudge, believing it to be a rude question.

"Thanks for the compliment, George," he answered. "You're right I haven't always done this for a living. After I had a great career in finance and made plenty of money helping entrepreneurs achieve their dreams I decided I wanted to do something less stressful with my life. So here I am."

"Good for you!" Ruth enthused.

"Shall we continue?" Marty asked, his azure eyes twinkling. The foursome gave him a hearty "yes" in unison. Then clearing his throat he announced his official transition from friendly political junkie to formal tour guide as he began to share factual information about passing landmarks.

"When are you going to give Mao his gift?" Golda inquired. She and Ruth were sitting on their hotel room beds, having returned in plenty of time for "lights out" even though they were too wide awake to sleep.

"Oh I don't know!" the girl exclaimed with noticeable exasperation. "I'm really not good at this and I can't seem to find the right moment."

"Well yeah but now that we've all broken the ice, it should be much easier. Look at me; I never in a million years thought I'd take a romantic carriage ride with George Chamberlain. I guess our conversation at Buckingham Palace really helped move things along."

"Yes, but how am I supposed to give Mao expensive French bath products without insulting him?"

"Well, look at it this way," Golda offered, "his soul chose to come back with these problems. But obviously it also chose to hang out with you; otherwise you and he wouldn't have been classmates all this time. And your soul chose to be a part of Mao's lifetime, too. Maybe part of that purpose is for you to help him overcome his hygiene problem."

"Yeah, that makes sense," she agreed. "I just don't want to insult the poor guy when he's been through enough already. I just hope he takes it the right way, that's all."

"He will. Just be very discreet and make sure you're both alone. You went to a lot of trouble and expense to buy those gifts. I think he'll be surprised and thankful."

"Do you really think so?"

"Yes, I do." Golda's voice exuded confidence. As if right on cue, a knock at the door interrupted their conversation.

"Wow, who could that be? It can't be Mr. Bauer unless something's wrong; we already checked in with him for the night," Ruth remarked as she got up to answer. Still buzzing from their wonderful evening, the girls had not yet changed into their pajamas.

Ruth nearly fell over when she saw Mao standing before her.

"Hi, I'm sorry it's so late," he began sheepishly. "I noticed your light was on so I figured it was ok to knock. Can you talk for a minute?"

"She sure can!" Golda enthused before her roommate could respond. "I was just going to talk a walk down to the lobby anyway since I'm way too jazzed to sleep. You two take all the time you need." Then with a wink at Ruth, she rushed out the door and headed to the elevators.

"Hello everyone, my name is Piper Palin and I'll be your tour guide for the White House Museum today," a lovely young woman of about 25 years announced with a smile. She had long, shiny, chestnut-colored hair, hazel eyes and a genuine disposition as she greeted the Arusha travelers outside of the building that once housed US

Presidents and their families during the End Days. Although it was a hot, humid Washington D.C. morning Piper's crisp, neat appearance was completely unaffected. Kissinger looked at her in amazement as he wiped his sweaty brow with his handkerchief and felt the moisture beginning to saturate his shirt. He couldn't wait to get inside the air-conditioned building.

"Hey if you think this is bad, just wait until we get to Florida," Sadat remarked, patting him on the shoulder.

"Thanks…thanks a lot," Kissinger retorted.

Holding hands, the newly coupled teenagers barely noticed the discomfort of the heat as they followed Piper into the building. Hillary and Debbie, Mao and Ruth, and George and Golda walked along contentedly, while the convalescing Jacques Chirac and Joseph Stalin stuck together. Their shared misery had afforded them a chance to bond back in New York, where they'd had many long conversations about life.

Stalin confided that ever since his altercation with Hitler in Germany he'd experienced a visceral feeling of relief, as if the incident had finally freed him to move on from the past. In the aftermath, he was becoming much calmer and much more stable. It was during this quiet time with Chirac that he'd realized he really wanted to become a soccer coach and help kids develop their talents on the field, which would also give him a chance to help them discover and develop their positive inner qualities. He felt a genuine desire now to become a responsible Arusha citizen and role-model—a decision that reflected the wisdom of his Life Purpose Class results when he was a much younger teen.

Chirac also had a breakthrough. After his traumatic experience with the nasty crabs STD he'd also calmed down. During his recovery, he'd had plenty of time to reflect upon his soul's chosen purpose and felt a strong desire to go into business as a boutique owner peddling designer clothing, lingerie and underwear for men and women. It came as such a relief to finally align himself with his spiritual nature, thus enabling this significant breakthrough. He also thanked God for Bill Clinton and his travel bag of STD remedies. He used to have fun joking about it, never imagining he'd be the beneficiary of Clinton's sexual preparedness. But if not for that healing spray, Chirac knew he might've scratched off every inch of skin in his groin area. *"God bless Bill Clinton,"* he thought with a smile.

Although his Life Purpose Class results had indicated such a career, Chirac hadn't been very confident about the results until now. He had to admit, God certainly did have a sense of humor.

Once inside the cool building Piper led them through the Oval Office, various parlors and eventually the Rose Garden, pointing out the historical significance of each attraction. Large framed photos of US Presidents from George Washington to Sarah Palin still graced the walls but Piper had been quick to point out that her great-great grandmother was the last one to have had the honor—and only because of intense pressure from everyday citizens who were thrilled to have elected her the first female President of the United States. Palin's administration had initiated the 400-year tradition of presidents and their cabinets living in their own humble homes, working in modest offices and driving their own cars to and from work.

"Wow, she's even more beautiful than her internet pictures," Hillary gasped as she and Debbie stood staring at the painting. "Beauty, brains and accomplishment—no wonder so many people liked her!"

"Yes, and what a great leader too," Debbie agreed. "When the rest of the world had abandoned Israel, she stood by Eyal Grad. I can see why she was one of the Salvation Twelve."

Nearby, George W. Bush took in the sight of his ancestor's portrait with utter amazement. He couldn't believe he looked exactly like the 43rd President of the United States—except for his dark black skin, of course. Even though he'd seen pictures of G.W. Bush on the internet, the larger-than-life portrait showcased their shared facial features with shocking clarity. For the longest time all he could do was stare at it.

Standing in the Oval Office, young Bill Clinton thought back to the Monica Lewinsky scandal that had nearly ruined his ancestor's presidency. Although he felt shame for President William Jefferson Clinton's lack of decorum and judgment in luring a much younger woman into the people's house for sex, he was thankful to have chosen the same kind of family libido for this incarnation. As he strolled around the room it occurred to him that perhaps he could become a filmmaker like Spielberg—except he would produce pornography films for Sin City in Arusha. Maybe someday he could even become an owner of a porno production company, too. This would be a safe way for him to satisfy his sexual urges without hurting anyone else and it would certainly be in line with his Life Purpose Class results which had pointed him toward a career in the arts. Bill smiled as he visualized his success.

"Enjoying your visit Mr. Clinton?" Mr. Bauer's baritone voice interrupted.

"Ah yes sir, I am," the student enthused. "I've just remembered my soul's purpose for this lifetime and I can't wait to get back to Arusha!"

"Not so fast, sir," the teacher laughed. "We still have to visit what Americans like to call The Sunshine State."

###

The maglev sped southward toward the tropical climes of Florida bound for Fort Lauderdale. Due to its exceptional capabilities, the once endless commute between D.C. and South Florida on an old-fashioned End Days train now only required three hours and 45 minutes of travel time on the bullet train. After enjoying a complimentary kosher breakfast at the local Days Inn, the Arusha travelers and their crew settled in for the ride.

Ruth Bader Ginsberg watched the passing scenery waiting for the presence of palm trees to indicate their entry into South Carolina. It had been a while since she'd seen tropical foliage and she was beginning to feel a little homesick. As she sat quietly in her seat, she smiled as she though back to the wonderful evening she'd shared with Mao in New York City. Golda had been absolutely right: far from being insulted, Mao had been extremely touched by her gesture, remarking that no one had ever given him such a thoughtful gift.

And she remembered fondly the following morning when she'd greeted him at breakfast and noticed the pleasant scent of musk. It had been well worth her entire savings to buy him the expensive French body products, though she was bummed out that she had no more money left to spend on herself and her family back home. She suddenly felt an overwhelming desire to steal something on their

Florida stopover. It was her last chance to bring something back to Arusha from their travels and unlike Stalin she'd make sure no one caught her. No way would she subject herself to having to call a store owner and apologize for shoplifting in front of her peers and teacher. She'd almost felt sorry for Stalin when Mr. Bauer forced him to make restitution, which included mailing back the knife to Egypt. She'd steal with a lot more finesse than the class jock. Ruth beamed as she suddenly caught sight of passing palm trees. Florida would be a grand adventure in more ways than one.

Alone in a private room, David Duke sat upright with his MacBook propped open on the table. He'd taken care to lock the door to prevent any unwelcome intrusions even though the rest of the kids were hanging out in the coach or lounge cars. His seatmate Charles Manson had announced his intention join Charles Tudor, Nathan Rothschild, Mahmoud Ahmadinejad and Henry Kissinger for snacks in the lounge so Duke felt confident he could surf the net in privacy.

He typed in his search criteria and hit enter. Elated by the numerous search result links, he clicked on the first one that caught his attention. His pulse quickened and his eyes grew wide when the landing page for a local Fort Lauderdale establishment filled the computer screen.

Staring back at Duke was the most handsome young man he'd ever seen. Standing in a beefcake pose showing off his alluring body, the bare-chested model had one hand on his hip and the other on the zipper of his open fly—as if teasing the viewer. Duke nearly salivated as his mind began to wander. How he longed to find this guy in Florida and make passionate love with him after dancing the night away!

After staring at the image for a while, he clicked on some of the other links to determine the location of this gay bar and restaurant called *Boardwalk*. He was thrilled to discover it was geographically close to some of the places they'd be visiting with Mr. Bauer and figured it would be easy enough to sneak out to during their free time. The only problem was their stupid 11 p.m. curfew. Maybe he could find a way to break it without getting into trouble; after all, that hot guy would be well worth the effort—and any potential punishment. His mind raced at the possibilities.

"So Charles, are you psyched to visit the Sin City Prison in Fort Lauderdale?" Tudor asked genuinely back in the lounge car.

Knowing how strongly his classmate felt about his ancestor and the End Days justice system, he was happy he'd have a chance to see it up close.

"Yeah, I sure am!" Manson replied enthusiastically. "I'm hoping I can get some ideas for my landscaping business from the way they take care of the land in the prison compound."

"Cool," Tudor enthused. "I'm really excited for you. Me, I want to make up for the lousy English food of the End Days. So I can't wait to see how they raise chickens, cows and turkeys because I want to be a high-end butcher and open up a nice deli when we get back to Arusha. I'm curious to see how they humanely slaughter the animals and prepare them for market."

Charles Manson shuddered.

"Ha!" Kissinger exclaimed. "Poor Manson still freaks out when he hears the word 'slaughter'."

"Can you blame me with *my* family history?" he asked pointedly. "But then I think about how my murdering ancestor and so many End Days evildoers like Adolf Hitler were vegetarians. Maybe if they'd eaten some meat and poultry, they would've been better people," he laughed.

Then he clarified, "Yes, yes I know it was their soul's choice before they got here; just making a joke."

"Relax, Manson. We're not in class anymore," Tudor chuckled.

"Thank God for that!"

The three teenagers cracked up and dug into yet another bag of dried fruit and nuts as the maglev moved ever closer to Florida.

###

"Welcome to Sin City and the Fort Lauderdale Prison System!" their tour guide Alan Danver greeted them as they stepped off of the electric bus and onto the pavement.

A cheerful guy of about 60, he was tall and slim with a receding salt-and-pepper hairline and dimpled smile. Purposely selected by his peers to escort the Arusha visitors around the compound, he felt honored to accept the responsibility and looked forward to sharing all of the wonderful Salvation Time advancements that had originated in his home state of Florida.

Once all were assembled in front of the large imposing metal gate that would lead them into the complex, Alan explained that Florida had pioneered several of the Salvation Time improvements in the United States including the justice system and the Florida Citizens Lottery System—modeled after Israel's highly successful example. He informed them that the Sin City Fort Lauderdale Prison System encompassed over 500 acres of land including the for-profit farm where prisoners grew fresh vegetables and raised cows, chickens and turkeys for human consumption. In the northeast corner of the compound, Sin City had its own shopping mall where customers could purchase adult items like sexy lingerie, oils, and sex toys as well as watch porno films in a 20-theater Adults-Only Metroplex. There were also plenty of gay and straight bars to cater to every sexual preference and musical taste from jazz to classic rock to country. Numerous bistros welcomed visitors to savor everything from typical American fare like cheeseburgers to more upscale dining options featuring Cuban, French, Asian, Middle Eastern and Italian cuisine—all kosher of course.

Bill Clinton's bulbous nose twitched at the mention of pornographic films. He hoped he could sneak away to watch a few while they were here since the plan called for free time once Alan Danver had completed the tour. David Duke noted the presence of gay bars in the area but couldn't get his mind off of the handsome guy on the *Boardwalk* website. He pulled out his smartphone to figure out the distance from their current location, determined to get there no matter what. He'd figure out some clever excuse to ditch his travel companions and make the acquaintance of the new object of his desire.

Alan opened the gate and led them to a long, canopied electric tram car that would provide easy access to the grounds while keeping them as cool as possible on this cloudless summer day. Their driver nodded and smiled as they boarded while Alan connected to the wireless speakers embedded in the car. Once all were safely seated, the tram rolled out to their first destination, the for-profit farm. Alan explained that the Sin City prisoners raised all of the produce and animals under the watchful eye of designated prison managers. These working prisoners had opted to be productive; therefore they were all compensated for their labor but at a much lower rate than their counterparts on farms outside of the prison system. Many used this money to make restitution to their victims and provide for their families back home. Because they'd chosen to work, they also had the benefit of a monthly conjugal visit with a Sin City prostitute, internet and satellite television access, high-quality food and well-made clothing. Most importantly, they also enjoyed shelter within the air-conditioned building where they were provided the basics of a comfortable bed and private shower, sink and toilet. While far from extravagant, these accommodations were clean and even included a kitchenette, plain chest of drawers, nightstand, chair and small closet.

However, prisoners who were lazy and refused to work were relegated to a special tented area outside where a common bathroom provided them with stalled toilets and a common shower area. While their nutritional needs were met with food and water, their cuisine was simple and bland. These prisoners were forbidden any contact with Sin City prostitutes and denied access to the internet and satellite television. If at any time during their incarceration a non-working prisoner had a change of heart, there would be a one-week minimum probation period to ensure their work ethic was up to standard before they'd receive the same benefits as productive prisoners.

Charles Manson listened with interest, reflecting back upon his ancestor. He remembered Mr. Bauer asking him during the test if he believed the 20th century Manson would've benefited by imprisonment in the Salvation Time justice system rather than the antiquated one of his day. Gazing out at the endless rows of vibrant vegetables cared for by diligent prisoners, Charles felt more certain than ever that his ancestor—as well as his poor victims—would have definitely been better off. Staring at the colorful lettuce, squash, cauliflower, peppers, carrots, tomatoes and corn stretched out over several acres, he was amazed not only by the quality of the produce but also the disposition of the workers. Completely focused on the task at hand, none of them seemed bothered by the intense heat generated by the summer sun. In fact, they appeared to be quite content as they went about their business. Some even looked up at waved at the passing tram car with genuine smiles on their faces.

Alan enthusiastically spoke of how food was so much cheaper for everyday Floridians because of the Salvation Time Prison System. Since it was produced by prisoners earning much less than the going wage, the benefit to the consumer was higher quality food at a much lower cost. Although these food items were sold exclusively at government-run supermarkets, all citizens could shop there. Not surprisingly, government employees preferred them over privately owned grocery stores and supermarket chains.

For the prisoners, this system gave them an opportunity to make real restitution and become better people in the process. Instead of simply being a just punishment for a crime committed, the sentence was also a practical way to prepare them for life on the outside. For those who opted to return to civilized society after completing their sentence the task of finding a good job in the *real world* was simple and easy—preventing the majority of   prisoners from backsliding into a life of crime. For innocent, law-abiding citizens it was also a welcome relief. For many employers, hiring a former inmate of the Sin City Prison System meant adding a good worker to the payroll.

Before Alan could continue, Charles Manson raised his hand.

"Yes, sir?" the tour guide acknowledged.

"Is it *really* true that prisoners can choose to stay for the rest of their lives if they feel like they can't handle life outside?"

"Absolutely," he replied. "We've learned from the failures of the End Days. We understand that no matter how advanced things become on earth there will still be human beings who cannot handle life in polite society. They've chosen to be that way with God's blessing. Remember the 10 percent he sends to earth to screw things up? We've made accommodations for them. They can stay here until natural death."

"That's great!" Manson exclaimed.

"Yes, sir. And if they choose stay after their original sentence is fulfilled, the same rules still apply. They can choose to work or not, but each choice has its own consequences as I've explained."

"Wait!" Manson challenged. "What if someone commits murder? They still get to return to society?"

"Oh, I should have clarified that," Alan apologized. "For prisoners who are here because they murdered one or more humans, or violated someone else's sanctity through rape there is no return to polite society. They must stay in our prison system forever. Back in the End Days pedophiles were permitted to live in family neighborhoods even though they were incapable of rehabilitation. No more. If you are convicted of murder, rape or pedophilia you can look forward to living out the rest of your life in the Sin City Fort Lauderdale Prison. The same rules apply in terms of choosing to work or choosing to be a lazy bum."

"Alan, are non-working prisoners really made to wear girlie pink uniforms?" Manson queried skeptically.

"Why don't you all see for yourselves," he replied, gesturing to his right as the tram made its way through the tented area. The kids burst out laughing when they caught sight of big, burly men wearing frilly pink uniforms trimmed with white eyelet. Unlike the working prisoners, these guys looked angry and mean as they made their way back and forth from the tents to the common bathhouses and back again.

"Geez, it's so hot I can't imagine choosing to be lazy," Hillary whispered to Debbie who was wide-eyed with wonder.

"I know," she nodded. "God forbid if I was a prisoner I'd definitely work so I could at least spend my free time in air conditioning."

Poor sweaty Henry Kissinger overheard her comment and silently agreed. Just being on this stupid tram car was enough to turn him into a puddle; he couldn't wait to be freed up to explore indoor places on his own.

Mr. Bauer suddenly raised his hand to ask their tour guide a question.

"Yes, sir?"

"Alan, has the Florida Citizens Lottery System cut down on crime in the state?"

"What a great question!" he answered. "I was just about to bring that up, Mr. Bauer because it's directly connected to the success of the prison system."

Then addressing the entire group as he stood at the front of the tram car he continued, "I know all of you studied in history class Prime Minister Eyal Grad and his Citizens Lottery System, the one he created in Israel just before the Armageddon War. Well a few years after the Armageddon Commission sentencing and the Race Unity Experiment, a local Florida congressman named Bill Posey decided to implement a similar system within our state. He was inspired by the fact that Israel's new lottery was turning out about 30 millionaires a week and believed if Florida could model their system it would cut down on crime dramatically. He believed so strongly in the concept he spent his own money traveling to Israel with his wife Katie to meet Grad in person and consult with him about it. Crime had become a serious problem in Florida because people were hurting for money. Bill Posey figured that by setting up a Florida Citizens Lottery System he could cut down on crime, protect innocent people, reduce the prison population and help local business owners and law-abiding citizens. And he was right. Once it started in the year 2020, the FCLS immediately produced 30 – 35 millionaires per week, generated income for local communities and reduced crime by nearly 70 percent."

Nathan Rothschild raised his hand.

"So it works the same way as Israel's with the debit card and the mandate to buy from local vendors?"

"Yes, sir! Just as you've studied in class Florida residents with a clean record for at least five consecutive years can participate. They're allowed to purchase one ticket per week at $50 once Tallahassee has approved their application and issued their FCLS participation card. When purchasing their ticket they must present both photo ID and this special card. Every week numbers are drawn at random and if necessary, the system drills down until eventually we extract 30 winners weekly. Each receives a special debit card to access their money.

"Those who don't already own a home are required to purchase one with some of their winnings. Everything purchased with FCLS money must come from local Florida vendors. If these vendors don't provide the products or services desired, lottery winners may use any vendor in the United States but they may not spend this lottery money on anything produced by foreign vendors or companies. The idea here is to keep the FCLS money circulating locally if possible; but if not locally then at least within the state and country.

"Is it true that winners must give up their jobs to work for their local municipality?" Rothschild followed up.

"Yes and no," Alan replied. "If an FCLS winner is under 60 and not currently working they must get a job with their local city or municipality if possible at a much lower salary than a regular employee. For example, if there's a Director of City Planning job available and it normally offers a salary of $100,000 per year a qualified FCLS lottery winner seeking employment can take the job for a much lower salary of $30,000. Over time as this process has played out it has saved taxpayers millions of dollars.

"If you're a FCLS winner and you already have a good job or own your own business you can keep it. In fact, if you're under 60 you must work. If you're an FCLS winner and you're older than 60 you don't have to have a job unless you want to but it doesn't need to be full time. In our state there are many FCLS winners over 60 happily working part-time just to get out of the house and interact with people. It's especially great for retirees if they want to get away from a nagging spouse."

Everyone laughed.

"Are there any restrictions on vendors?" Rothschild pursued.

"Yes. The FCLS goes to a lot of trouble to investigate all vendor applications before they're approved. We look for things like quality, efficiency, employee reviews and customer satisfaction. Once given our seal of approval vendors are listed on our website so winners can easily access the information before hiring anybody. It's a win-win for small businesses, customers and taxpayers."

"Sure sounds like it," Mr. Bauer commented, visibly impressed by Florida's Salvation Time advancements.

"Just wait until you see our power plant," Alan smiled. Then with a look to the side announced, "We're coming up on it in just a few moments."

The open transport gracefully moved through the complex, bound for the energy-producing area populated by numerous warehouses and a gigantic power plant spread out over several acres. The students looked on in awe as Alan began to explain the significance of this particular part of the prison.

"So here we are at the energy compound. This is where working prisoners who've been specially trained produce energy for the surrounding community. Just like food, electricity is much cheaper now for ordinary citizens. That's because we've learned how to effectively extract thermal energy from the earth's core *and* because working prisoners manage the process. Since we live in Florida and it's now hurricane season, locals can breathe a little easier. These guys and gals are fully prepared to help with clean-up and restoration should Mother Nature inflict serious damage upon us."

The students and Mr. Bauer took in the scene with wonder and admiration. Seeing a working Sin City prison was beyond their expectations even after spending so much time studying them. But as they'd learned along their journey, there was no substitute for the real thing.

A few minutes later the tram finally arrived in the Sin City retail shopping area, much to the delight of Bill Clinton who'd been dreaming of prostitutes and porno films ever since they'd arrived. This area of the prison resembled an upscale section of any modern city, with trendy bars and restaurants, a sprawling indoor shopping mall and appealing decor including a dancing water fountain and tropical courtyard. It was hard to believe that something so stylish could exist within a prison compound but as they stepped off of the tram car the dazzled teenagers couldn't wait to explore every inch of the place.

"Alright students, you may now indulge in your free time," Mr. Bauer instructed. "But remember, everyone must be back here by 11 p.m. tonight to board the bus back to the hotel. If you're not on time, you'll have the pleasure of spending the night in the tented area of the prison....and I'm pretty sure none of you want to do that."

He then reminded them of their plans to visit Fort Lauderdale High School the next morning to meet some of their peers and learn about the transformation of the English language from someone whose ancestor pioneered the process. The teens' eyes glazed over at the thought; the last thing any of them wanted to do was visit a high school. But they respectfully nodded at their teacher and wisely refrained from any expression of disappointment.

Once left to their own devices, they scattered away in search of new adventure.

###

Bill Clinton threw back another beer as he sat at the bar with George W. Bush. Night had finally fallen and the boys had wandered in and out of the many watering holes on-site until finally settling on an upscale gentleman's club. While gorgeous topless girls strutted to the pulsating music and suggestively slithered around poles on a long runway, appreciative men cheered them on and tucked hundred-dollar bills into their neon G-strings. A mesmerized Clinton and Bush watched the spectacle with carnal delight. W was still reeling from his visit to Sin City New York which had exceeded all of his expectations. He didn't think life could possibly get any better until he followed Clinton into this amazing place.

"Ready for another round, son?" Clinton teased.

"You betcha!" his new buddy enthused, raising his empty glass to the bartender. As they waited for their refills, they took note of some familiar looking faces sitting nearby.

"Clinton, look! Isn't that—"

"I do believe it's the descendant of Jesse Jackson. He looks just like the 20th century shakedown artist—except for his lily white skin of course."

"And isn't that Al Sharpton with him?"

"Sure looks like him," Clinton agreed. "C'mon, let's go talk to them."

They picked up their newly filled pilsner glasses and headed over to introduce themselves.

Although polite at first, Jackson and Sharpton were annoyed by the interruption, having been deep in conversation over how to manipulate the media and public opinion into believing that racism was still a huge problem in the United States—all in an effort to make easy money and preserve the memory and relevance of their crooked ancestors.

"Now that we've introduced ourselves would you mind leaving us alone?" Sharpton asked rudely. "We're in the middle of important business!"

"Hey is that any way to treat tourists from another country and continent?" Clinton playfully teased. He was truly interested in getting to know these two characters even though the feeling was definitely not mutual.

"Oh get lost, you uppity nigger!" Jackson exclaimed. "Maybe in your little corner of the globe racism no longer exists but some of us are still dealing with it!"

"Racism?!" W was completely perplexed by the notion. "Are you guys serious?" Since they'd left Arusha and embarked on their worldwide tour, every person they'd come into meaningful contact with had been nothing but courteous, kind and sincere—not to mention mostly Caucasian. Sure, the gawking crowds and rude reporters had been a little hard to take but for the most part people had been very nice.

The Arusha teens could only conclude that for some souls the temptation to incarnate and repeat the same destructive patterns of their End Days family members was too hard to resist. For Sharpton and Jackson, the process of enlightenment and atonement might take many more lifetimes. Could it be that even now there was money to be made by race-hustling? It seemed impossible to believe.

"Yes, we're very serious, you idiot!" Sharpton roared.

"Uh, you two do realize we're living in Salvation Time now, right? And have either one of you looked in the mirror lately?" Clinton asked. "You're as white as rice yet you're still playing the *race-baiting game*? Seems to me neither one of you has learned your history lessons very well."

"And what would you know about that?" Jackson snapped.

"I know that you haven't learned a damn thing from your family members," he retorted. "What a cryin' shame. C'mon W, we've got much better things to do than hang out with these two clowns!"

With that, the two boys left Jackson and Sharpton to their ingrained ignorance. They figured only God himself knew just how many more incarnations it would take before anyone would make full reparations for Al Sharpton and Jesse Jackson. In this lifetime, Bush and Clinton had certainly done their part on behalf of their own heritage. They had no interest in trying to persuade those who refused to leave old, worn-out thought patterns behind. Besides, the sexy Sin City prostitutes were waiting for them and they only had a few more hours left until curfew.

David Duke was thoroughly dazzled as he entered *Boardwalk*. Never before in his life had he seen so many hot guys in one place and he was immediately grateful for having found the right opportunity to escape. He just hoped he'd be able to find the cute one from the website.

"Good evening!" a friendly voice greeted him. Duke looked up to see an impeccably dressed young man holding a stack of menus. "Is this your first visit to Boardwalk?"

"How did you know?"

"Ah, you just have that look about you. But don't worry Wilton Manors and Boardwalk are like Las Vegas: what happens here stays here."

"Wilton Manors?" Duke asked, confused.

"Ah, it's just the name for this section of Fort Lauderdale where everyone respects everyone else's right to be who they are and express their love any way they choose."

"Sounds good," Duke replied, suddenly feeling nervous and shy.

"My name's Harry Reid, nice to meet you." As he spoke he extended his hand to Duke who quickly responded with a tentative shake as he returned the sentiment.

"Can I ask you something?" Harry continued quizzically. "Have you actually come out yet? Because you seem a little nervous."

"Y-yeah, I guess you read me right," Duke confessed.

"C'mon," his new friend encouraged him as he placed an arm around his shoulder. "I'm about due for a break and I'd love to hear your story."

He led him to a private office in the back of the club where the two sat down on a plush, oversized sofa and engaged in meaningful conversation.

David and Harry passed the hours talking about their souls' chosen sexual preferences, the crimes of Duke's ancestors, the Race Unity Experiment, the trans-global journey spanning several continents and countries, and their dreams for the future.

Harry explained that his family had also spent time atoning for the sins of their 20th century ancestor even though they hadn't been sent to Arusha. Over many generations they'd educated their children about the shameful greed, corruption and dishonesty of Senator Harry Reid during the End Days, especially his involvement with shady real estate deals that enriched his bank accounts at the expense of ordinary citizens. At one time, this despicable family member had even put US soldiers in grave danger by publicly declaring the Iraq War lost while they were still fighting evil overseas. Yep, Senator Harry Reid had ensured that future generations would have much to atone for.

As David stared into Harry's sparkling blue eyes and noticed his cleft chin, physically fit body and thick, golden hair he couldn't help but feel something more than friendship. Harry's honest confession certainly added to his allure and provided a bonding experience since Duke could completely relate. He might have set out to meet the hot model on the Boardwalk website but he was quickly realizing God had something even better in store for him. Harry was not only good-looking he was also kind, loving and compassionate. Duke's family history hadn't fazed him in the least because he too had a shameful past. Both young men were mutually impressed by each other's heartfelt honesty.

After a while Harry carefully moved closer to David on the couch in an attempt to initiate a kiss. He sensed his nervousness and didn't want to frighten him yet he couldn't ignore the longing in his heart. For a while they just gazed into each other's eyes before Harry finally sensed the moment was right.

Duke's heart raced wildly as he savored the sensation of soft lips and a moist tongue. What began rather tentatively soon transformed into an entrée for something even more intimate as Harry whispered into David's ear his desire to make love to him right there in the office. He assured him that no one would intrude upon their privacy once he lit up the *Do Not Disturb* sign on the office door.

"Let me be your first, David," he whispered.

"First and last?" he asked softly.

"Yes, yes. Your first and last. I've been waiting for the right one forever and tonight I know I've finally found him."

David Duke's heart leapt for joy in his chest as he grinned at his new boyfriend and nodded his assent. He couldn't think of anything he'd rather do than give in to the intense desire he was now experiencing. Harry promptly picked up a remote control and pressed a button, illuminating the privacy sign. Then he took Duke in his arms and initiated an evening neither one would soon forget.

###

"Oh my God, it's almost 10:30!" David shrieked. "I'm going to miss curfew!" He shot up on the couch, abruptly awakening a contented Harry who'd been relishing the feel of his body against his.

"Harry, Harry, please you've got to help me!" he pleaded. "I read online about those electric car call centers stationed along all of the roads. I'll need to call one to give me a lift back to Sin City."

"Relax my love, I've got a car. I'll drive you back in plenty of time."

The young men dressed quickly and headed out to the parking lot where Harry's sporty electric car awaited them. He opened the door for his boyfriend who slid into the comfortable leather bucket seat and prayed they'd make it on time.

Harry hopped in behind the steering wheel and hit the accelerator as he navigated the car onto the street.

"Don't worry," he promised Duke. "Sin City is just a couple of miles down I-95. I'll get you there." He squeezed his hand as he spoke, sending shivers of excitement up and down David's spine. Even under the stress of meeting curfew he was still tingling from their beautiful evening together. He just prayed their relationship could survive long distance until they could figure out a way to be together; their train was headed back to Arusha immediately following their visit to Fort Lauderdale High School in the morning.

"Damn!" Harry exclaimed as the car sped onto the on ramp.

"What?! What's the matter?"

"I'm almost out of charge. I gotta do 40 miles an hour in the charging lane so we don't sputter out. I'm sorry David. It's just a few miles. We'll get there on time."

Duke watched as Harry carefully lined up the car tires onto the electrically charged strips on the southbound highway's right lane. Although he was incredibly impressed by this modern-day advancement he was more concerned about making curfew. How he wished they could be in one of the cars speeding by in the other three lanes; the thought of spending this hot, humid night in an outside tent on the prison grounds was completely repugnant. Duke wondered if Mr. Bauer had been joking just to scare them into obedience but he wasn't willing to take a chance.

"Ah, here's our exit!" Harry finally announced. "Sin City is just another two miles west and we still have five minutes. We'll make it, I promise!"

And with no time to spare, he discreetly dropped David off a few blocks away from the designated meeting place where his classmates were already gathered. A wave of sorrow washed over him as he opened the car door and looked longingly at his beloved new boyfriend.

"Don't worry, we'll find a way to be together," Harry promised, reading his mind. "I'll wait for you. And in the meantime we've got Skype."

Duke leaned over and gave him a quick, warm kiss.

"I love you, Harry. And we *will* be together. You can count on it."

"I love you too, David. And I can't wait!"

Thus assured, David Duke shot out of the car and ran in the direction of his travel companions, reeling with excitement about the future. But just as he was about to reach the designated meeting place, he was stopped in his tracks by Mr. Bauer.

"You're late Mr. Duke," he declared.

"I know, sir and I'm sorry. I thought a few minutes wouldn't make a big difference," he softly replied.

"Ah but it does Mr. Duke, especially to the one who's responsible for 21 teenagers."

"You're right, sir. I apologize again."

"May I ask what detained you?"

For a few minutes he stammered and stuttered, his black cheeks burning.

"Mr. Duke, don't worry everyone else is safely inside the bus already with strict orders not to move. No one will hear us." The teacher instinctively knew what the student was about to confess but wanted him to own up to it in his own words.

"Uh, Mr. Bauer I met someone and fell in love tonight," he finally blurted out.

"You mean the young man in the sports car who dropped you off?"

"Yes, sir. His name is Harry Reid and he manages a bar and restaurant called Boardwalk in Wilton Manors. I found it on an internet search and decided to check it out. I never intended to break curfew like that or—"

"Please tell me you were very careful, Mr. Duke?"

"Oh yes sir, we were. We used protection," the student assured him quietly.

"Excellent," the teacher continued. "Look Mr. Duke, we all understand now in Salvation Time that homosexuality is a choice. It's a lifestyle some souls choose before coming to earth to provide the mental challenges needed to advance to the next level. Your soul made a decision to be a gay man this time around, and I respect that.

"However, our physical bodies were not made for this type of sexual activity so I want you to promise me that you'll always be very careful."

A relieved Duke thanked his teacher and assured him he'd always be mindful of this sage advice. Besides, he was fairly certain he'd just met the man he'd spend the rest of his life with in a monogamous relationship.

"Well congratulations and best of luck to both of you," Mr. Bauer enthused, placing an arm about the student as the both walked toward the bus. "Just remember it is *never* ok to break curfew, no matter how wonderful the reason or how handsome the guy."

Duke deeply appreciated his teacher's understanding and guidance. He was about to speak up again when the bus driver approached them on the sidewalk with a serious expression.

"I'm afraid the bus has broken down," he announced. "I asked the class to stay onboard while I came out to tell you."

"Well, can it be fixed?" Mr. Bauer asked. "We can wait while you call a mechanic. I know it's kind of late for that but—"

"Sir, didn't anyone tell you about our electric car call centers?"

The teacher shook his head.

"Oh Mr. Bauer, they're really cool!" Duke chimed in. "All of the main and secondary roads have them. You just go into the automated call center, tell it what you need and the cars come right to you."

"Is this true?" he inquired of the driver.

"Yes sir, the boy is correct. And there's one right here in Sin City just a few blocks down. You just type in your location on the computer and the driverless automated cars come to you. When you get in, you just type in your destination address and the car drives you there."

"Sounds fascinating. I'm looking forward to the experience and I'm sure my students will enjoy it, too."

"Excellent, sir," the driver said. "After everyone's off the bus I'll show you the way."

"Mr. Duke, please tell your classmates to get out now," Mr. Bauer ordered. Within a few minutes he had them lined up again on the sidewalk for roll call.

Their excitement about the electric car call center was soon marred by the teacher's realization that one of his students was missing.

"Has anyone seen Eva Braun?" he asked in a tone that meant business. The kids were startled into silence; this was the first time anyone had gone missing during a roll call.

"Mr. Clinton! What about you?"

"Ah no sir, I haven't seen her since W and I went to the titty bar," he replied in his raspy voice. The teacher bristled at his vulgar term but nevertheless scrolled through his phone contacts and fired off a text to Eva.

"Alright," he announced. "While we wait to hear from our missing student, we'll walk down to the call center and place our order."

His tone indicated he was in no mood for any more shenanigans. The students quietly followed behind him musing to themselves about the possible fate of their flaky classmate. In spite of her shortcomings, everyone hoped she was safe and had just lost track of time.

Several minutes later, the driverless electric minivans drove up to the curb as promised.

"Wow, that is so cool!" Spielberg gushed as he filmed the spectacle. All of the kids were amazed by yet another technological advancement designed to accommodate life's little inconveniences. By this time, many were also exhausted and looking forward to getting some sleep back at the hotel.

As Mr. Bauer prepared to load the last of the passengers into the fourth car, his phone began buzzing to alert him to a text message. He stepped off to the side to read it in privacy:

"Mr. Bauer, forgive me but I'm about to board a plane for Las Vegas. Please don't stop me. All I want from this lifetime is to be a

show girl. I'll call my parents when I get there. Thanks for everything. Eva."

"Well, I can't say I'm surprised," he muttered to himself. He'd had many visions of Eva making this choice, though he'd hoped she'd exercise her free will to move in another direction. Apparently, this soul was going to need many more incarnations before jumping a few levels ahead in its spiritual growth. With that understanding he returned his phone to his pocket and slipped into the fourth minivan before the caravan led them back to their Florida hotel.

###

"Students, while we're here alone Mr. Hitler would like to say a few words," Mr. Bauer announced. He'd just taken roll call at the Fort Lauderdale Station and settled everyone into the coach section of the bullet train. They'd soon be bound for New York, where they'd pick up the trans-oceanic train back to London before connecting with the land train that would return them to Arusha City.

"Thank you, Mr. Bauer," the teenager responded as he stood up and took his place next to him at the front of the aisle. The conductor and crew were busy with final preparations in the engine room and dining car, giving Hitler the perfect opportunity to address his peers in private.

The kids sat in stunned silence as they waited for him to speak.

"Yeah I know, shocking, right?" he joked. "Who'd have ever thought I'd willingly get up to give a speech?" The ensuing laughter thrilled his heart because he recognized that they were finally laughing *with* him, not *at* him.

"Uh, anyway," he went on. "I'm sure you all wondered why I didn't take my oral history exam in the classroom just like all of you did. I want to thank Mr. Bauer for letting me be tested alone with just him, knowing how tough it would be for me. And yes, I studied hard and got an '8,' in case anyone was wondering," he chuckled.

Once again, his audience cracked up.

"But," he continued, "visiting Dachau in Germany really opened my eyes. "Facing my ancestor's evil actions was even tougher

268

than I imagined. It hit me really hard. That's why I spent so much time there alone. I had to work through the pain, shame and guilt before catching up with you guys at the restaurant. And once again, Mr. Bauer understood."

He looked at his beaming teacher with love, admiration and appreciation.

"Which reminds me," Hitler added. "We all owe Mr. Bauer a round of applause for being the very best teacher and friend anyone could have."

With that he clapped his hands together enthusiastically until the rest of the students followed his example. Soon, the entire car was filled with the sounds of boisterous applause and cheering. The appreciative yet slightly embarrassed teacher felt his cheeks turn red as he smiled and nodded at the kids.

"Thank you all for being eager students," he stated humbly. "It's been my honor to guide and direct you. Now kindly finish your remarks Mr. Hitler."

"Yes, sir. I just wanted everyone to know I am very sorry for the crimes of my ancestor Adolf Hitler. I plan to live the exact opposite kind of life. I'm going to use my talents to uplift people, not hurt them. I just wanted all of you to know that. Thanks."

Everyone began clapping loudly again. That's when Joseph Stalin stood up and motioned for his peers to do the same. In a matter of seconds they were all on their feet, giving their classmate a standing ovation.

Hitler's soul was consumed with exhilaration. When the applause died down, Stalin was granted permission to speak.

"I just wanted to say how proud I am of you, Adolf….and how sorry I am for the way I've treated you all this time. You were right to remind me about my own ancestor's history of shame when we fought at the beer festival.

"The 20th century Joseph Stalin was also evil and an example of what happens when centralized government controls people. All of the innocent peasants he killed because he couldn't stand the fact that they were self-sufficient, growing and selling their own food in the market. What he did to them was absolutely horrendous—stealing their food and farm equipment and turning them into cannibals. What a savage!"

As he spoke, Stalin looked directly into Hitler's eyes. Both students' hearts filled with understanding.

"Anyway, like you Hitler, I plan to make my life the exact opposite of Joseph Stalin's. I'm going to use my athletic gifts to coach kids on the soccer field and in life. I will teach them to stay in touch with their spiritual side and to always treat other people with respect and kindness."

With that, he extended his hand to Hitler, who immediately shook it in return before pulling his former nemesis into a bear hug, prompting astonishment from the rest of their peers while Mr. Bauer wiped away tears of joy.

###

The maglev sped through the carbon fiber tubing as it carried its passengers back to Arusha. Many of them reflected upon their trip with fondness while looking to the future with optimism and excitement; others simply took the opportunity to catch up on much-needed rest.

David Duke reclined back in his seat, closed his eyes and dreamed of how wonderful his life was about to become with Harry by his side. That entire experience had not only resulted in lifelong companionship, it had also confirmed the results of the Life Purpose Class he'd taken many years before. He also appreciated Mr. Bauer's kind words of encouragement even after he'd broken curfew; it touched him deeply that the teacher truly cared about his safety and happiness.

Duke was absolutely ecstatic by the prospect of Harry relocating to Arusha and opening up a gay bar and restaurant with him. They'd been Skyping back and forth almost constantly since the night they met and fell in love. Immediately, Harry had indicated his desire to leave South Florida behind and join his boyfriend in this new African adventure.

"Could this really be happening?" David sighed with joy as he drifted off into a peaceful sleep.

Ruth Bader Ginsberg and Mao Tse Tung sat holding hands as they watched the passing sea life on the LCD screens. She breathed in the tantalizing smell of French musk and smiled. Not only had her boyfriend fully embraced the expensive gifts she'd purchased but she'd managed to steal some souvenirs from South Florida without anyone noticing. They were just little trinkets like magnets, key chains and paper weights decorated with flamingos and palm trees but at least she'd have some gifts to give her family when she got home.

Ruth relived the thrills that went up and down her spine when she shoplifted the items. It gave her a sort of natural high to get away with the crime and she rationalized that the combined value of the stolen items was negligible. It's wasn't as if she'd embezzled thousands of dollars from the Citizens Lottery or anything. Funny, just the thought of getting away with something that big sent massive tingles through her body.

"What are you thinking?" Mao asked, noticing the sly smile spread across her face.

"Me? I've been thinking that you are going to be the best chicken farmer Arusha has ever seen!"

"You really think so?" he asked hopefully.

"I know so, Mao. You're going to have a wonderful life," she gushed, planting a kiss on his forehead.

"Correction," he said, "*we're* going to have a wonderful life."

Ruth nodded before exchanging a quick kiss on the lips and leaning her head on his shoulder.

Across the aisle, Debbie Wasserman-Schultz was busy reading next to her girlfriend who remained deep in thought with her eyes staring straight ahead.

"Oh my gosh Hillary, this is *really* great!" an impressed Debbie exclaimed. She was reading the completed PDF version of *It Takes an Individual to Help a Village*. In spite of their hectic travel schedule and blossoming relationship, Hillary had managed to find the time to complete it.

"You truly think so?" she asked.

"Yes, I really do! You're amazing, you know that?" Debbie leaned over to plant a kiss on her cheek. "Has Mr. Bauer seen this yet?"

"As a matter of fact I have," the familiar baritone voice confirmed. "Miss Rodham, I must say you've outdone yourself. Congratulations!" Their teacher stood tall in the aisle, smiling down on the two young girls.

Hillary radiated pure joy. Between the excitement of the trip, her new love with Debbie and her plans for the future she could hardly contain herself.

"Thank you, sir!"

"You've earned the praise, Miss Rodham. I am looking forward to your book creating even more positive changes in the world once it's distributed globally."

"Yes sir, me too!" she agreed. "I know my purpose in this life is to use this book as a foundation for my consulting business. I plan to teach entrepreneurs how to be that individual who makes positive contributions to the village. I'm going to create a series of workbooks and a class curriculum. I can't tell you how excited I am about being a small business consultant to help keep Arusha thriving."

Her teacher beamed with pride. "I certainly hope you'll be willing to come speak to the students at RURHS to help guide them in their careers when the time comes," he added.

"I would love that, sir!" she exclaimed.

"Miss Wasserman-Schultz, what are your plans?"

"Oh sir, like my LPC said, my purpose in this lifetime is to work as a short-order cook. I love making breakfast food—eggs, omelets, pancakes, waffles, muffins, bagels. Before we left, I talked to the owners of Arusha Bagels and I start working there next week. I'm so excited….Hillary can come in for breakfast every morning on her way to the office!" The girl's exuberant giggles punctuated her words.

"Well congratulations to you both," he repeated with a nod before resuming his walk down the aisle.

"You know, he really is a fabulous teacher," Hillary noted. "We couldn't have asked for anyone better."

"Well, we kinda did, remember? Debbie teased.

"Oh right!" she laughed.

"Speaking of fabulous, wasn't it cool meeting the descendant of George Washington at Fort Lauderdale High School?"

"It sure was. And I guess it makes sense that someone from that family would've been the one to finally change the spelling of English words to match their sound—you know, when you think about the American Revolution and everything. Can't imagine what it was like before 2012 trying to make sense of English, especially for a foreigner."

"Seriously," Debbie agreed. "I don't get why they ever included letters that didn't make a sound into the spelling of words in the first place. Spelling the word 'nife' as k-n-i-f-e when the 'k' is silent? Or the word 'psychology' with a 'p' when it starts with an 's' sound? Makes no sense!"

"Well, it was the *End Days*," Hillary reminded her as she slipped an arm around her shoulder. "But I, for one, am looking ahead to our new life in Arusha. I can't wait to move in together!" she cackled.

"Me too!" Debbie sighed, resting her head in the crook of her girlfriend's arm. The two sat in contented silence as the bullet train sped through the tubes.

Mr. Bauer grinned as he progressed down the aisle and laid eyes upon slumbering students Adolf Hitler, Golda Meir, George Chamberlain, Anwar Sadat, Henry Kissinger, Joseph Goebbels, Nathan Rothschild, Bill Clinton, George W. Bush, Charles Manson, Mahmoud Ahmadinejad and Charles Tudor. They were spread throughout the coach section reclining in their seats with legs stretched out in front and arms draped over the chair rests. All had a look of total contentment as they breathed slowly in and out in the cadence of deep, restful slumber.

"They're finally spent," he noted happily as he moved into the lounge car where he found a fully recovered Jacques Chirac and Joseph Stalin engaged in conversation about their career plans.

"Hello there, gentlemen. Glad to see you are both looking well."

"Thank you, Mr. Bauer!" they replied in unison.

"Hey Mr. Bauer," Stalin spoke up. "I just want to thank you for guiding me to do the right thing. I'm glad I returned the knife to its rightful owner and I promise I'll never do something like that again. I feel so much better about everything after this trip, including my lifetime's purpose."

"You're very welcome, Mr. Stalin. Thank you for owning up to your crime and being willing to make restitution. I'm looking forward to watching your success as a soccer coach." The teacher smiled warmly at his student.

"Thank you, sir."

"Have either of you seen Mr. Spielberg?"

"I thought I saw him head back toward the private rooms a while ago," Chirac answered. "He seemed a kinda quiet, not his usual annoying self."

The trio chuckled knowingly; *quiet* definitely wasn't a word that typically described their unique classmate and student. After a moment, a contemplative Mr. Bauer became a bit concerned so he thanked Chirac and Stalin and left in search of the teenager in question.

Spielberg sat alone in a private space holding his smartphone in his hands as his tortured mind debated his dilemma. He knew he could start his career off with a bang if willing to humiliate some of his classmates in the process. After all, he'd captured some pretty titillating footage—like Jacques Chirac writhing in pain. It was so tempting to give into the urge to join forces with Bill Clinton and find success in the porno industry using his clueless classmates' human weaknesses against them. Poof! Easy money, instant success.

On the other hand, he could take the lessons of his ancestor Steven Spielberg to heart and finish making reparations by creating uplifting films that inspired human beings to do the right thing, no matter how difficult. Hadn't he passed the exam with an excellent grade in part by extolling the virtues of positive character traits celebrated in Salvation Time cinema?

Such was his moral quandary when he heard a knock on the compartment door followed by a familiar voice.

"Mr. Spielberg? May I speak with you for a moment?"

The student quickly hid his phone in his pocket, picked up the remote and opened the sliding panel.

"Hey Mr. Bauer."

"I heard you were back here; I hope you don't mind my stopping by. May I come in?"

"Yes, sir," he replied, his pulse quickening a bit. What on earth could Mr. Bauer know about the forbidden footage in his phone? He'd been so careful not to get caught and was pretty sure he'd stayed under the radar...at least until now.

Once safely inside, the teacher inquired about Spielberg's state of mind, giving him the opportunity to come clean. In response to his silence, the elder continued.

"You know, Mr. Spielberg I've been very proud of the way you've handled yourself in class this year, especially with your family history and all of the pressure of having to earn a high grade on the exam. And even with the disappointment of not receiving your well-deserved modern camera on time, you improvised by filming the trip with your smartphone. Instead of whining you took lemons and made lemonade, if I may use a popular phrase from the End Days. So I just want to encourage you to remain the optimistic, hardworking and ethical person you've been throughout your schooling. That will take you far in Salvation Time."

Before Spielberg could reply, Mr. Bauer patted him on the shoulder then pressed his hand against the consul to let himself out. The young filmmaker gazed out at the ocean and wondered what to do next.

A cheering crowd greeted the bullet train as it glided in to the Arusha City Station. From the windows, the ebullient travelers waved joyfully at their parents, siblings, friends, fellow citizens and news crews assembled outside. It was hard to believe that in the blink of any eye their long anticipated global journey was over but everyone looked forward to experiencing life in Arusha City, having been freed from the constraints of the Race Unity Region. They recalled how thrilling it had been to watch the confining concrete walls crumble as they walked through the gates on the way to the Arusha station just a week before.

And as the kids reunited with their loved ones they enthusiastically talked about their global experiences and exciting personal news. Many dutifully agreed to interviews with eager reporters in spite of their understandable desire to go home and relax.

But they'd soon find yet another surprise awaiting them: while they'd been living behind the imposing walls of the Race Unity Neighborhood, Arusha City had kept up with the times; therefore all of the commonsense advancements and modern marvels that had delighted them all around the world also existed in their home city— from an Arusha Citizens Lottery System to an Arusha Sin City Prison System. Far from being over, their journey of discovery was just beginning. And they'd learn as the years went by that Salvation Time had even more surprises in store.

Epilogue

Arusha City, Africa 2420

"Just look at them, Moses!" Jesus exclaimed as he, Moses and Mohammad witnessed the glamorous Arusha City premier of Steven Spielberg's breakthrough film, *Voyage through Salvation*. "They're so blissful, productive and good to one another!"

"Yes indeed Jesus," he agreed. "I have to admit I was a bit concerned about Spielberg there for a while. He wavered about his decision more than I would have liked."

"True," Mohammad interjected. "But in the end he used his free will for good and took the high road. One Bill Clinton per graduating class is more than enough!"

The three Advanced Souls shared a hearty laugh.

"Well at least Clinton is productive and enjoying his status as the porno king of Sin City, far away from innocent families. The system is working out just as we'd planned," Moses commented. "Don't you think so Mr. Grad?"

The former Israeli Prime Minister lit up at the mention of his name. "Oh yes indeed, Mr. Moses. I am very thankful."

"Well God is very pleased with you sir, as are the three of us," he remarked.

"Isn't Mao's devotion to his wife Ruth sweet?" Mohammad asked after a few moments. "Even after she was caught committing fraud and embezzling from the Arusha government and sent into the Sin City Prison System, he never wavered in his love and commitment. I enjoy watching their regular visitations. And I must say, she's doing an incredible job running the women's jail and overseeing the chicken houses, fish farms and vegetable gardens."

"Yes, both of their souls are living out their pre-selected choices rather well," Moses agreed.

For a while the Advanced Souls were quiet as they watched the Arusha Race Unity Regional High School 2412 graduates—now responsible young adults—congratulating their former classmate on his achievement while a multitude of news cameras flashed all around the red carpet.

"Look at George and Golda, so excited to be expecting their first baby!" Mohammad gushed.

"How are the soul preparations going for that child?" Jesus inquired.

"Everything is working out as planned. The Chamberlain baby's soul has been undergoing extensive interviews with God in preparation for incarnation in six months and I can't wait to see how he handles his assignment," Moses answered.

"Excellent!" The Advanced Souls sparkled as they continued to watch the gala unfolding on earth. Spielberg positively beamed as he greeted one well-wisher after another in front of the downtown Arusha City cinema. Then he took a microphone and proceeded to personally acknowledge the talent and skills of every member of the film crew before calling Nathan Rothschild to the podium where he publicly thanked him for providing the necessary financing for his first film.

"It was my honor Steven," Nathan responded sincerely as the crowd broke out into loud, enthusiastic applause.

"Ah, it really does my heart good to see this!" Grad enthused. "They're all so blissful and at peace."

"Yes, well keep in mind Mr. Grad that God has future challenges in store for their descendants," Moses reminded him soberly.

"Yes, I know. Galactic battles await their grandchildren and great-grandchildren in the future. I just hope they prepare them well. Hey by the way, did God's new rule about no more than four children per family officially take effect?"

"Yes it did," Moses confirmed. "God will be managing conception and soul incarnation as always but he's decreed that no matter what, there will only be as many as four conceptions permitted per family. It's his will."

The Advanced Souls contemplated this new reality as they continued to watch Spielberg's film debut.

"This is great but I'm especially looking forward to the young filmmaker's upcoming project," Eyal remarked. "Remaking Schindler's List in color to reflect the reality of Nazi atrocities in the 20th century will help ensure people never forget to acknowledge and confront evil in Salvation Time. I heard him talking in a meeting with the production crew about using blood and graphic images to make his point. Seems young Spielberg is on a mission to make final restitution for his dishonest ancestor. Good for him!"

All souls illuminated as their iridescent robes shimmered.

"After he completes this necessary remake, will he be inspired to create what he thinks is simply a fantasy film about intergalactic wars?" Mohammed asked.

"That's the plan," Moses replied. "Poor guy is already starting to see alien signals although he still can't quite figure out what's going on. He thinks his imagination is playing tricks on him, especially since he's been putting in such long hours. He has no idea that his concept for the new film is actually a foreshadowing of what's to come on earth but that's what makes our job interesting."

The Advanced Souls shared another laugh before disappearing into another dimension, leaving the newly minted Arusha City filmmaker and his friends to bask in the glow of achievement and the exhilaration of Salvation Time before the earth faced the next divinely approved challenge.

∞ Cast of Characters ∞

Debbie Wasserman

Hillary Clinton

Joseph Goebbels

Adolf Hitler

Anwar Sadat

Henry Kissinger

Charles Manson

Golda Meir

Charles Tudor

George W. Bush

Bill Clinton

Benito Mussolini

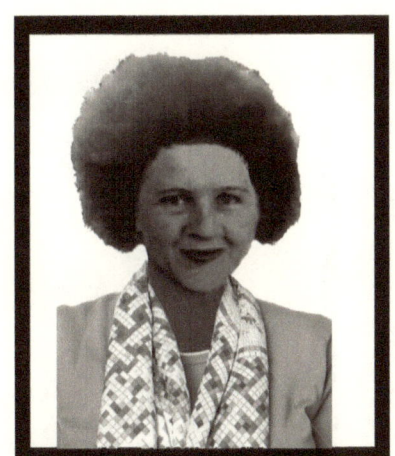

Eva Braun

Fidel Castro

Steven Spielberg

Joseph Stalin

Nathan Rothschild

Ruth Ginsburg

Mao Zedong

Mahmoud Ahmadinejad

Al Sharpton

Jesse Jackson

George Soros

Neville Chamberlain

Resources

1. Hitler's Henchmen - Bureaucrat of Murder - Adolf Eichmann
http://www.youtube.com/watch?v=3KylkPvI3lQ

2. Hitler's Henchmen - The Marshall - Hermann Goering
http://www.youtube.com/watch?v=XBjfyfA2I0g

3. The Cromwell Association
http://www.olivercromwell.org/

4. Mao's Bloody Revolution
http://www.youtube.com/watch?v=Wd0aW-4mV68

5. Andrew Jackson -- Good, Evil and the Presidency - PBS Documentary
http://www.youtube.com/watch?v=EGfxyeuy8u8

6. Mail Online/Daily Mail UK
http://www.dailymail.co.uk/news/article-2242258/Revealed-Henry-Kissinger-discussed-overthrowing-West-German-government-secret-spy-network-old-Nazis-aristocrats.html

7. The History Learning Site UK - The Yom Kippur War of 1973
http://www.historylearningsite.co.uk/yom_kippur_war_of_1973.htm

8. The Guardian UK - How Bush's grandfather helped Hitler's rise to power
http://www.guardian.co.uk/world/2004/sep/25/usa.secondworldwar

9. Jewish Virtual Library.org - The Inquisition
http://www.jewishvirtuallibrary.org/jsource/History/Inquisition.html

10. Spartacus Educational - The Divine Right of Kings
http://www.spartacus.schoolnet.co.uk/STUdivine.htm

11. Shraga Elam - The Yom Kippur War and the Kissinger Plot
http://shraga-elam.blogspot.com/2012/10/the-yom-kippur-war-and-kissinger-plot.html

12. Dr. Kent's Blog
http://drkentshow.com/wordpress/?tag=the-bureaucrat-in-charge-of-operation-paperclip-bringing-the-german-scientists-over-here-during-the-close-of-world-war-ii

13. Conspiracy Archive
http://www.conspiracyarkhive.com/NWO/project_paperclip.htm

14. Mail Online - Daily Mail UK - Why were Saudi royals with links to 9/11 allowed to leave the U.S. without being quizzed by the FBI?
http://www.dailymail.co.uk/news/article-2115127/Why-Saudi-royals-links-9-11-allowed-leave-U-S-quizzed-FBI.html

15. American Politics -- The Political Spectrum: Freedom versus Enslavement
http://thepoliticalspectrum.net/
16. The Bloody History of Communism
http://www.youtube.com/watch?v=3pzMHD0F4yQ

17. Library.ThinkQuest.org - The Holocaust
http://library.thinkquest.org/CR0215466/the_holocaust.htm

18. History Today - Coming to Terms with Fascism in Italy
http://www.historytoday.com/richard-bosworth/coming-terms-fascism-italy

19. The Other Reason for the American Revolution
http://georgewashington2.blogspot.com/2009/06/other-reason-for-american-revolution.html

20. Wikipedia - Nathan Meyer Rothschild
http://en.wikipedia.org/wiki/Nathan_Mayer_Rothschild

21. Judaica 101 - Yarmulke
http://www.ajudaica.com/judaica101/religious-articles/yarmulke-kippah/

22. History.com - The Medici Family
http://www.history.com/topics/medici-family

23. PBS - The Birth of a Dynasty (Medici Family)
http://www.youtube.com/watch?v=9FFDJK8jmms

24. Michelle Malkin - Dumb and Dangerous: America's Fast-Pass for Saudi Arabia
http://michellemalkin.com/2013/03/22/dumb-and-dangerous-americas-fast-pass-for-saudi-arabia/

25. National Review - Joel Mowbray - Perverse Incentives
http://old.nationalreview.com/mowbray/mowbray102202.asp

26. HistoryWorld.net - The Borgias
http://www.historyworld.net/wrldhis/PlainTextHistories.asp?historyid=208

27. HistoryWorld.net - The History of Christianity
http://www.historyworld.net/wrldhis/PlainTextHistories.asp?gtrack=pthc&ParagraphID=hmt#hmt

28. Wikipedia - Ruth Bader Ginsburg
http://en.wikipedia.org/wiki/Ruth_Bader_Ginsburg

29. The Washington Post - Judges Affirm Property Seizure
http://www.washingtonpost.com/wp-dyn/content/article/2005/06/23/AR2005062300783_pf.html

30. Cato Institute - Top Ten Myths of American Healthcare: A Citizen's Guide
http://www.cato.org/publications/commentary/top-ten-myths-american-health-care-citizens-guide

31. David J. Shestokas - Primer on Economic Systems and Societal Organization
http://www.shestokas.com/guest-commentary-reflections/primer-on-economic-systems-and-societal-organization/

32. Pamela Geller - Atlas Shrugs Blog - Texas Public School Students Made To Wear Burqas
http://atlasshrugs2000.typepad.com/atlas_shrugs/2013/02/texas-public-school-students-made-to-wear-burqas.html

33. The Daily Capitalist - How Mao Killed 45 Million People
http://dailycapitalist.com/2011/08/11/how-mao-killed-45-million-people/

34. Wikipedia - Nikola Tesla
http://en.wikipedia.org/wiki/Nikola_Tesla

35. Wikipedia - Menachem Mendel Schneerson
https://en.wikipedia.org/wiki/Menachem_Mendel_Schneerson

36. Wikipedia - Dome of the Rock
http://en.wikipedia.org/wiki/Dome_of_the_Rock

37. The History of Money - Abraham Lincoln's Green Back Dollar
http://www.xat.org/xat/usury.html

38. The Banking Swindle - Historical Perspective: The Banking Monopoly
http://criminalbankingmonopoly.wordpress.com/tag/abraham-lincoln/

39. Stop Printing Money .com - History of Money and Banking
http://www.stopprintingmoney.com/Learning/History_of_Moneyand_Banking/

40. Investopedia - Fractional Reserve Banking
http://www.investopedia.com/terms/f/fractionalreservebanking.asp

41. Conservatives 4 Palin.com - Governor Palin's Executive Accomplishments
http://conservatives4palin.com/2012/06/governor-palins-executive-accomplishments.html

42. Wall Street Journal - Palin Has Long Experience Dealing with Big Oil in Home State
http://online.wsj.com/article/SB122005404357685123.html

43. Baronial Order of the Magna Charta
http://www.magnacharta.com/

44. Wikipedia - Mohammad Khatami
http://en.wikipedia.org/wiki/Mohammad_Khatami

45. Wikipedia - Hagia Sophia
http://en.wikipedia.org/wiki/Hagia_Sophia

46. The Money Masters
http://www.themoneymasters.com/

47. The Other McCain
http://www.theothermccain.com

48. The Right Planet
http://rightplanet.com

49. The Human Family Tree: Scientific Adam and Eve –
http://channel.nationalgeographic.com/channel/a-night-of-exploration/videos/scientific-adam-and-eve/

50. Blocking The Path To 9/11
http://www.blockingthepathto911.com/

51. Original Photos purchased from Custom Portraits of Beijing, China

www.ingramcontent.com/pod-product-compliance
Lightning Source LLC
Chambersburg PA
CBHW031205020726
47499CB00002B/486